the
lemonade
year

the lemonade year

A NOVEL

Amy Willoughby-Burle

SHADOW
MOUNTAIN

For my husband and my children.
For my parents and my siblings.
For my family and my friends.
I thank God for you all.

Visit us at ShadowMountain.com

Library of Congress Cataloging-in-Publication Data
Names: Willoughby-Burle, Amy, 1972– author.
Title: The lemonade year / Amy Willoughby-Burle.
Description: Salt Lake City, Utah : Shadow Mountain, [2018]
Identifiers: LCCN 2017040905 | ISBN 9781629724119 (paperbound)
Subjects: | LCGFT: Domestic fiction.
Classification: LCC PS3623.I57767 L46 2018 | DDC 813/.6—dc23
LC record available at https://lccn.loc.gov/2017040905

Printed in the United States of America
PubLitho, Draper, UT

10 9 8 7 6 5 4 3 2 1

1

When someone buys two dozen lemons, a box of tissues, and a whole carrot cake at midnight, you have to figure something is wrong. The cake is for the minute I walk in my condo. The tissues are for my father's funeral. The lemons mean I'm losing my job.

I'm Nina Griffin, food stylist and photographer. One of those people who artistically arranges food and then takes pictures of it. The pictures that make almond-crusted salmon look like the best almond-crusted salmon with blanched, baby asparagus that ever was. The pictures that are meant to inspire you to cook, despite the knowledge that you'll never be able to recreate the dish the way it appears in the book. Yeah, that's what I do.

I make it all seem possible.

It's just a ruse.

Right now my publishing house has me working on *32 Ways to Make Lemonade*. Seriously? Are there really thirty-two ways to make lemonade? This is why I think my job may be in jeopardy.

But I don't have time to worry about that. It's past midnight, and I'm driving home from the grocery store with a carrot cake strapped down by the seat belt on the passenger's side and there's a white owl standing in the middle of the road. I get closer and closer but all the bird does is swivel its head around like that kid in the *Exorcist* and stare at me. I start slowing down, sure that at any moment the bird will lift off like it's capable of doing. But it doesn't. It just stands there, eyeing me, daring me. I fishtail to a halt, reaching my right hand out to catch the cake if it comes loose from the seat belt, while I watch as the front end of the car passes over the owl until he's out of sight.

I grip the wheel. Alone on the highway, forty years old, my marriage over, my teenage daughter sleeping at my sister's house to prove a point, my long-fought-over career slipping through my fingers, and my father's funeral two days away. But here I am, terrified by the possibility that there may be a dead owl on the grill of my car. So far—*so far*—I've been holding it together. But something about a dead bird with its hollow, little bird bones broken against the front of my car is the last straw. There has to be one, right?

I push open the car door in a panic, like maybe I can get there in time to give the little thing mouth-to-beak and he'll be ok—he'll be ok. It's all my fault. I should have just kept driving and perhaps the car would have just passed over him as he stood in the middle of the road, but, no, I slammed on the brakes and that made the front end go lower—like I was aiming for him, for crying out loud.

Geez, woman, I hear him say to me. *Can't a bird stand in the street anymore? What's the world coming to?*

I get out, slam my door, and slip around to the front of the car. It's late at night and I'm on a back road, but still a car screams past me in the other lane and I shudder. My headlights are blazing, and I expect to find the owl crushed against the grill, wings spread—trying to take off at the last second—to no avail. But there's nothing.

I should be thrilled, but panic digs deeper. Where did he go? Is he under a tire? Is there still time? Can I save him? I kneel down on the pavement to look under the car. Then *whoosh*—up from beneath the bumper and grazing my head, the owl rises and zigzags off—its wings clipping the hood on the way up and off into the black sky, a fluttering white speck headed for the safety of the trees.

I sit down in the wash of my own headlights and cry.

On the day my father died, the lady sitting next to me at the café across the street from my office had two bites of a bacon, lettuce, and tomato sandwich left on her plate. One of the bites had no bacon. The tomatoes were too ripe, and the lettuce was the pale green color of giving up.

When the charge nurse called, I excused myself from lunch with coworkers, saying I needed to get back to the office—that something was wrong with the layout and they need to speak to me.

"Who?" the nosy junior copy editor, whose name I couldn't recall, questioned. "I thought you were working on the lemonade thing. That's miles from press."

I'm not a very good liar on the spot.

"No," I said, standing up, trying my best to get out of there. "The other one."

There is no other one. They haven't acquired anything new in a while. All we're doing is catching up on commitments. In my department, this lemonade thing is the bottom of the barrel. I should have freelanced, but I took the staff position because of the security.

There is no security. The news in my ear that my father had passed was proof of that.

I'm not ready for this. I'm not ready. Not ready.

The words flooded my brain in a useless mantra. Who is ever ready? Even through long illness and inevitable demise, the heart still hopes, like a child who still believes in magic.

Addled, I left without paying my bill at the bacon, lettuce, and overripe tomato café. I texted an apology to Suzanne for leaving her with the nosy copy editor and my check. She wrote back to ask if I was ok. I tried to reply, but the whole process of written telephone communication via a handheld device capable of technological tasks beyond imagination seemed suddenly ridiculous to me. Everything seemed ridiculous. As if all the effort to create plasma-TV screens, 3-D everything, cars that could parallel park themselves, and phones that could video chat while surfing the net and washing your dog was just a distraction from the fact that none of it can make you immortal. It's all smoke and mirrors to hide the knowledge that your heart can still break, your eyes can still cry, and the people you love will leave you.

After the owl incident, the rest of the drive home takes on that surreal quality that things get after something weird has happened. Especially after something weird has happened in the midst of some life-altering milestone like the death of a parent.

A possum traipses out across the street as possums are known to do. I see it in enough time to slow down and let it pass, but it looks at me on its way across the blacktop like it has some knowledge of the owl incident of five minutes before.

Watch it, lady, the possum says to me, its voice the sarcastic rasp of a two-pack-a-day comedian. *We're supposed to be out here. You're supposed to be at home. So take your carrot cake and your lemons and get yourself back inside your empty condo with the horrible lighting in the bathroom and the portfolio you hide under the couch but pull out and dream over when everyone else is asleep. By the way, Nina, you're isolating yourself again—bad move.*

I'm amazed at the level of insight for a possum.

I make it home without turning anything into roadkill and park in my usual spot in the bowels of the parking garage below my condo building. Jack, my newly ex-husband after a matter of several expensive months, used to park next to me in sort of a building-wide "you park there, I park here, and these are our spots" arrangement. Jack's spot is still empty. I'm sure there's much discussion over who will get his place, but so far no one wants to be the first to park there. They all know that parking there means my marriage is over, and they don't want to be part of the fallout.

As promised, as soon as I get inside the condo I head for a knife and fork. As I'm slicing a piece of the cake and shoving off ideas of how I could have photographed it, my cell phone rings and a picture of my mother in a gaudy Christmas sweater lights the screen.

Mom is calling me after midnight. This isn't good.

"I'm that woman again, Nina," Mom says after perfunctory small talk, none of which addresses the time of night. "You know what I mean?"

"Not really," I say and take my plate of false security onto the balcony.

I love the view from my balcony—downtown lit up in the near distance, Appalachian Mountains drawing a wavy line across the North Carolina sky. Tonight though, the mountainscape looks like the heartbeat on a hospital monitor.

"Back when you kids were little," Mom says. "I was just so lonely."

I go back inside to get the rest of the cake. I'm wrecked from months of visiting my father at the nursing home, from fighting with Jack, from reassuring our overly perceptive teenage daughter that everything will be fine. Wrecked from lack of sleep and tears in the middle of the day. Wrecked.

"Was Lola not awake?" I ask, back on the balcony again, looking out over the view that I'm going to have to give up now that I'm single and soon-to-be out of job—another reason for my daughter, Cassie, to hate me. Not that she cares about my job, but this building has a pool and teenage boys who live here and if we have to go live with Grandma then she's *just going to die, Mother. Do you hear me—die.* Apparently this, all of this, is all my fault.

"I guess she's asleep," Mom says in confirmation that she'd rather be pouring out her sadness to her other daughter—the younger one, the more important one—but that I'll have to do. "Back then," Mom continues, "I was the only one of my friends to have kids. Everyone else was pursuing their career, and I was home changing diapers. I had dreams, too, you know."

"Really?" I ask, actually interested. "Of doing what?"

"Exactly," she says. "No one will ever know. Not even me."

I sigh more heavily than I should.

"I'd see the women in their fancy business suits and high heels buying exotic foods at the grocery," Mom continues, oblivious to me as usual. "They'd be carrying around that little basket that says 'I don't need to know what I'm eating next Tuesday because that's Ashley's bday and we're all going downtown to celebrate.'"

"Who's Ashley?" I ask.

"They're all Ashley," Mother spits into the phone and then puts on an old-school, Valley Girl voice. "Hi, I'm Ashley, I don't think I invited you. Oh, and by the way, you have baby vomit on your shoulder."

She does a fair job of sounding authentic, and I almost laugh. But I don't laugh, even though it was funny. She needs to tell someone all these things, and secretly I'm glad that Lola missed her call. I'll take being second choice right now just to be included.

"I used to be one of them, and they knew it," Mom says, recalling a time before I can remember. "But I became a woman with a child, with spit-up on her shoulder, with a grocery cart piled for two weeks, because, let's face it, who knew when I'd get it together enough to go out into the world again to shop for the necessities of life, never mind going downtown to celebrate someone's 'bday.' Remember when you used to go to a party just to go to a party—it didn't even matter if you knew whose it was?"

"Not really."

I picture Mom in her kitchen. She's animated, waving her arms as much as the constraints of having to hold the phone to her ear will allow. This is how she talks to Lola. When I come into the room, her body stiffens, her voice goes formal. I don't know her, and she doesn't know me.

"Is it so wrong?" Mom asks. "That when the three of you were finally asleep for the night, I'd make myself a drink? Maybe a Cosmo, or a martini, or a margarita—and pretend that I had something to celebrate too?"

It's then that I hear the tinkle of ice in a glass from the other side of the phone line. I think about my photography portfolio under the couch and my sister Lola's artwork hanging in the gallery downtown, and I think my mother and I are more alike than either of us want to admit—except for the drinking.

"Mom," I say, but am unable to follow it up with any sort of chastising comment that isn't really my place to make.

I can't ask her to be careful. I can't preach to her about self-medication with alcohol. I know she knows that she shouldn't open that door again, but Dad is dead. Thursday is the funeral.

I lift another bite of cake to my mouth, but I've suddenly lost the desire for cream cheese icing and fluffy, sweetened flour.

"Who knows," Mom says, and I feel the end of the conversation coming. "Maybe in this day and age, I wouldn't have felt so out of touch. People have their texting and tweeting—whatever that is—and their Spacebook to let the whole world know that they just did a thousand sit-ups or that their cat just ate a crayon or that little Emily has a fever of a hundred and one."

"Facebook," I say.

"What?" she says but keeps talking.

I hear her voice, but my attention wanders. She might be right. Maybe if she had had some connection to the multitude of people she once knew and all the people they once knew, then perhaps she could have posted on her wall *My youngest child, Lola, was just in a horrible accident, and if she lives, she may never walk again. And btw, she has some kind of brain damage that the doctor called the "Swiss Cheese Effect" and I could just punch him in the face.*

And people could reply *Oh, Cecilia, how awful.*

Hang in there.

We love you.

Or perhaps people could "like" her statement, thus validating her outrage and letting her know that they had at least taken the time out of their beautiful life to read her message to the cosmos and click on the little thumb before hopping to a YouTube video of a dog barking "The Star-Spangled Banner."

I think about posting *My father has died.* I don't know what symbols you would put in to create the appropriate little face—there must be one. Something worse than the little frown. The little face that would say *I've seen it happen to other people, and in theory I knew it would happen to me, but I didn't really believe it until now.* There is no series of punctuation marks to make up such a face.

Mom is still talking, and I realize I'm several sentences behind.

"Sorry, Mom, you were saying?" I ask.

"That woman," Mom says. "Back then, I was that young woman who other young women felt sorry for because I'd lost my sense of feminine power and had to stay home with the kids. Now I'm that woman that all those women fear again."

"What woman is that?"

"A widow," she says and more ice tinkles. "The poor woman

who put everything into her family and now she's all alone. And they're afraid to look me in the eye, because in the end, they all did it too, and now they see me as a trailblazer. But I'm burning down the brush of somewhere they don't want to go."

Mom is very dramatic.

I want to say something, but I'm not Lola, and I won't come up with the perfect thing that Mom needs to hear the way that Lola can. So I listen to the ice clinking in Mom's glass and know she's thinking of calling Lola again.

"I didn't think that, by the way," Mom says, startling me.

"Think what?"

"That I lost my sense of feminine power by having children," she says. "I actually felt sorry for the women who thought they should feel sorry for me. I think they were jealous. You always want the thing you don't have."

Yes, you do. I wanted a marriage and then I got one. I wanted a career and then we had a child. I wanted a child and then I got lonely. I got everything I wanted and then I was unhappy.

"I just meant that I loved having kids," Mom says, her voice pulling me out of my own head. "I just lost myself. I didn't start drinking because you guys made life tough. You made it wonderful. I just wasn't very good at it sometimes, and when things got hard, I fell down."

That's a confession she can't say to Lola. Mom is talking to me now, referencing an inside joke that isn't funny. Lola doesn't know our mother used to drink—she doesn't remember. Just Dad, my brother, Ray, and I remember the mother that Mom used to be.

"Is Cassie still at Lola's house?" Mom asks to change the subject, although it doesn't, not really.

"Yeah," I say. "This week she's picking Jack. Getting used to living away from me."

"She's going to live with Jack?"

"Of course not," I say, unsure. "That's why she went to Lola's house."

"I don't follow," Mom says.

I change the subject for real and ask Mom about the dreaded details of Dad's funeral. Mom talks for a few minutes about florists and caterers and aunts and uncles I don't really recall. If I didn't know better, she could be talking about a wedding or perhaps a baby shower.

"See you Thursday, Mom," I say like Thursday isn't Dad's funeral.

"Good night, sweetie," Mom says, like it is.

2

In the morning, I pick up my cell phone to check on Cassie, but Lola has already left me a message that Cassie decided to go to school today and that she'll see me at home later. Even though Cassie and I being in the house together creates a fog of tension so thick you can see it, I'd rather have her home than somewhere else.

I think about calling her father, but I have more pressing issues to attend to. The thought of going to the nursing home after work today to sign the final papers is so terribly depressing I'm not sure I can do it. The thought of finishing the conversation Jack and I were having about sorting out the custody arrangements when last we spoke is even more so.

I shake off the owl wings from last night and go into the bathroom to get dressed. That possum was right. The lighting in here is horrible. Not inadequate, mind you, just unflattering. No one should see themselves this clearly. I argh at myself as I get dressed.

I haven't told everyone at work about Dad. Just those people who know me well enough to see through my "everything is fine" façade. I took off Thursday and Friday for family business, but didn't say what the business was. Things are touchy at best, and I don't want to be that emotional, expendable employee when the cuts come—if I can help it. I may not be getting more photography work, but if I can prove myself to be an asset in other ways, perhaps they can keep me on for as long as possible. There will still be paperwork and follow-ups and other tasks I can do. It's not what I want to do, but it's something. Maybe everything won't fall apart. Maybe. I'm not good at the "glass is half full" thing. Maybe I just need a smaller glass.

My phone vibrates, and the screen lights up with a picture of Lola making a sarcastic fish face. My heart skips a bit whenever Lola calls. I slip out of the meeting I'm in, grateful that the lights are off for a presentation, but I feel my boss's eyes on me. She and I have known each other since we were kids, but that will only help me for so long.

I step into the hallway and answer the call. "Lola," I start, but she cuts me off.

"I need help," she says, and her voice is hushed but panicked.

"What's going on?" I ask even as I'm rushing to my office for my purse, set to ditch the meeting and get to my sister at any cost.

This has happened before. She'll be out at the grocery and forget how to get home. Or at a gallery showing and she'll lose sense of the people around her and who she's spoken to about what, or one of a dozen other scenarios that spell confusion and possible disaster.

I grab my bag and mime to someone else's assistant that I have to leave.

"I can't believe this," Lola is saying in a loud whisper.

I'm running down five flights of steps—no time to wait for the elevator.

"Stay on the line," I shout over the clang of my shoes on the metal steps. I get to the front door and whirl out onto the downtown street, trying to remember where I parked.

"Where are you?" I ask, spotting my car and sprinting for it.

"In the living room," she says.

I stop short and someone bumps into me from behind.

"At your house?" I ask.

"Yes," she says, dumbfounded by my question.

I exhale hard, embarrassed at my overreaction, but relieved that she's not calling from three states over having forgotten where she was going or why she was going there. I want to laugh and then strangle her for having that edge in her voice that made me think she was lost in the wilderness or being held at gunpoint.

"I'll be right there," I say to her nonetheless.

◆ ◆ ◆

Lola lives in a bungalow in the artist district a handful of blocks from where I work. Though my office is the business of art, her house is art itself. When I visit her, I feel like I'm walking into possibility, striding alongside what could be. I don't have a clue what to do with it though.

She answers the door before I knock and puts her finger to her lips to tell me to be quiet. She motions me past a stack of canvases resting on the floor in the tiny foyer and into the living room where she picks up the remote. Her house smells like paint and coffee and flowers. She presses a button and a commercial that she's TiVoed comes on. The volume is low, but I know it well. Everyone does. A cute, but goofy man wearing taped-up, science-geek glasses and pants that look like a raccoon ate holes in the knees, scratches under his arms and sings while he ambles up the perfectly manicured, neighborhood street toward the scene of a fender bender.

Your house is trashed, you've got a rash. Your car is broke, and it's no joke. Call on us so there's no fuss . . .

I make a face at her. She punches me in the arm and clicks off the television.

"You knew about this?" she asks.

"He makes you happy," I say.

My sister is dating a very famous commercial spokesman for a very well-known insurance company. Everyone knows this—except her.

She waves her hands at me to keep me quiet and presses her finger to her lips again.

"He's here?" I whisper. "Cassie didn't mention anything when we talked the other day."

Cassie rarely mentions anything when we talk.

"She mostly stayed in the guest room," Lola says. "She barely knew *I* was here. Don't take it personally."

I tilt my head at Lola, and she makes an *I'm sorry, I know that was dumb* face. Then she waves away the discussion of Cassie.

"Two months I've been seeing the guy," she whispers to me. "No idea who he was and now he's in my kitchen."

She points to the kitchen with panic in her face. I glance across the warmly lit living room and into the small, colorful kitchen. I remember helping her pick the colors: avocado, perfect plum, mango, and melon. My condo walls are white. Just White—that's the actual name of the color.

"It's not like he broke in," I look back to her and whisper. "You're dating him."

"But I didn't know who he was!" Lola says. She looks terrified.

I take her by the arm and walk her out the front door.

"Ok," I say, smoothing down her pitch-black hair with my hands. "Let's take stock. He's not a stranger. He's Chris. You've been dating for two months. You know him. He makes you really happy."

"He's the goofy guy from an annoying insurance commercial," Lola says, her beautiful face twisted up.

"No," I say. "That's a character from TV."

She breathes in and out very deliberately, nodding her head slowly. I mimic her actions until we're both calmer.

"Does everyone know about this?" she asks.

"That he's the guy from TV?"

She nods.

"Yes, sweetie," I say. "Everyone knows."

"Does he know that I don't know?" she asks, her face so pitiful.

"I don't know," I say. "But I do know he's crazy about you. And he's absolutely beautiful—no taped-up glasses, no rashes, no car crashes. Now let's go back inside."

I ease the door open like I'm sneaking up on a bear.

"There you are," Chris says, standing in the living room with two full coffee mugs in his hand. "You ok?"

"She's fine," I say. I take one of the mugs and hand it to her. "Hi, Chris."

He gives me that pressed-lip smile you give people when you know something bad is happening in their world and you know you can't really do anything about it. Looking at him standing in her living room, I can see how Lola hadn't recognized him, memory gaps aside.

In character, his sandy-brown hair is forced down with shiny, styling grease into a Poindexter that is the opposite of the loose waves and out-of-place curls he has this morning. With his faded jeans—albeit with a similar hole in one knee—a Ramones T-shirt and no glasses to obscure his thickly lashed blue eyes, anyone would be hard pressed to put two and two together. But it's there in his voice and in the lopsided smile, and some synapse must have fired just so in Lola's brain and bam—there the recognition rests.

"Good morning, Nina," he says. "Let me pour you a cup. You're staying for a bit, yes? Cream and sugar?"

I know Lola needs me to hang around for a while until the shock wears off.

"Yes," I say. "Thank you."

He turns back toward the kitchen. Lola is holding her mug with both hands, looking down at the liquid like she doesn't know what it is.

"Is this how I like my coffee?" she asks me, not looking up. "I can see there's cream. Is there sugar? Did I tell him this? Why can he remember how I like my coffee and I can't remember who he is? Why didn't I recognize him?"

She inhales sharply at a new idea that seems worse.

"Or is this not the first time that I'm figuring all this out?" she asks, desperate panic rising up in her voice again. "Have I had this conversation with myself before?"

She finally looks at me, and I notice she has blue paint in her hair.

"Have we talked about this before?" she asks, looking lost.

"No, honey, we haven't talked about this before," I say and touch her face. "And yes, you like cream in your coffee. Relax. Stressing out makes the holes widen."

"Stressing out makes the holes widen." She repeats her own mantra that I have just said to her, and then says it once more. "Stressing out makes the holes widen."

She sits down on the couch, and I take a spot in the armchair. She's gotten used to forgetting little things. Like the fact that she keeps buying the same tea with the really cool picture on the box only to rediscover that she doesn't like it once she's home and made a cup and hates it and then can't bear to waste it so she puts it in the "stuff for guests" drawer where there are already four boxes. But finding out that she's been dating a known persona—and a goofy-insurance-commercial one at that, no matter how cute he is—is a bit much to take in before noon.

She sips her coffee. "It's good," she says. "I do like it." She smiles and relaxes.

Chris comes back into the room and hands me a cup of coffee. Lola purses her lips and wrinkles her brow. Chris sits down on the couch beside her and sets his mug on the coffee table. "Sweetie," he says, "why is your face all turned up like that?"

"Thinking," she answers and looks at me.

"About your dad?" he says and nods.

I nod too.

"Sure," Lola says.

She can do this. She's been at it for years now. There are events that occur in your life from which you can never return, and you see what was as if looking through a foggy window. Everything is familiar, but inaccessible. Your previous life becomes a series of memorable events best forgotten. All you can do is move forward.

It's not like she's completely unable to function as a regular human being. She just has gaps and some are bigger than others, but she's got her systems—her checks and balances—and they work most of the time.

After a while Lola winks at me, and I know she's gotten her wits about her.

"Are you still going down to Elm Village today?" she asks me.

"Yeah," I say. "I guess I'll go ahead and get that over with since I ditched work already. I want to get home before Cassie gets out of school. Did she say anything?"

"Sorry," Lola says and looks like she really is. "I tried to bait her, but she was on to me. She's just confused. It's all really bad timing."

The divorce, the funeral, the conversation about possibly moving in with Grandma. Aren't all tragedies really bad timing?

"She'll be ok," Lola says. "We'll all be ok."

Chris puts his hand over Lola's, and the protective nature of such a small gesture seems to illuminate too many layers of loss.

"Are you ok if I go?" I ask.

"I've got her," Chris says and takes her hand fully.

He thinks we're talking about Dad, and I've got to give him major points for taking such good care of my little sister. I wish I could tell him that she'd figured him out—just to warn him.

"Go," Lola says. "I'm just being silly. You're right. See you at Mom's tomorrow."

Lola nods her head toward Chris and winks again.

◆　◆　◆

There's so much to do before a funeral that you can get caught up in the tasks and details and forget why you're doing it. Like going to a movie with so many previews that for a moment you forget what you're there to see. You can't even remember if it's something that will make you laugh or cry. I think it's a purposeful misdirection, a stalling technique employed by the world at large to help you deal with loss one piece at a time.

It's too cruel for the widow to have to go to the nursing home to collect the small number of things that once seemed so important and place them into the provided cardboard boxes that will likely never be unpacked. Lola and our brother, Ray, are spared by emotion and absence, in that order. But me, I am the appropriate blend of available, stable, and responsible.

At the nursing home, no one says the word "dead" to me. They all say "We're so sorry for your loss," like perhaps Dad has just been misplaced and will turn up underneath a couch cushion. It's not their fault. There is nothing good to say and saying nothing would be worse.

A young nursing aide named Oliver helps me load Dad's belongings onto a cart and take them out to my car. We don't say anything to each other as we walk out into the sunlight and unpack the boxes into my trunk. I suppose he's done this before, but

I haven't, and it feels like the asphalt is melting under my feet—a quicksand that only I am sinking into.

I thank him for helping me and extend my hand to shake. He takes it and presses my palm between both of his.

"Nate was an awesome guy," Oliver says, referring to my father in a familiar way that makes me jealous. "I miss him already. I hate this part."

I forget my own sorrow for a moment in the face of such honest emotion. What a weird job he has, caring for people he can't possibly make well.

"Thank you," I say, and I mean to press my other hand around his but instead I step closer to him and we embrace.

After the usual "hug time" expires, I feel Oliver attempt to step away, but I can't let go. I'm clinging to him in some pathetic effort to stop time. If I move, the funeral will take place. Jack will finish moving out. Cassie might go with him. Someone else will park in Jack's space, and I'll be stuck photographing lemonade forever.

Oliver steps back in to the hug. The side of his neck and the shag of his blond hair are a hideaway, and I have no idea what's come over me. I breathe in deep to get my wits back. I pull away from him enough to be face to face with him, and to my own amazement, I kiss him.

Right on the mouth.

Oh, my! What has come over me?

"I'm so sorry," I say, gasping at the horror of this thing I have just done. I cover my offending lips with my hands, my face hot with the inappropriateness of my actions.

Guys—I just kissed my dead father's ex-health care worker, who BTW is completely gorgeous and way too young for me!

This of course will get numerous *likes* and comments of *You go, girl!* and *Living vicariously, more details please.* But inevitably someone will respond with a *Your father died? I'm so sorry*, bringing it back full circle.

I shake my head and hands as if I can brush away the incident itself.

"Don't worry about it," Oliver says. He touches his fingers to his lips and furrows his brow slightly, but then quickly, he offers a comforting smile and says, "You're sad. We're sad, too."

I feel like I should explain myself to Oliver, about my marriage, its demise, how desperately I need companionship, how much I fear losing my job, how awkward I feel around my mother, and how losing Dad feels like I've been orphaned. How worried I am that my brother won't come to the funeral. How embarrassed I am that I just kissed a stranger.

I don't say any of it.

"Thank you," I manage, looking away from tranquil, soft green of Oliver's eyes and then back up again. "Do they train you guys on the right things to say? I'd like to compliment you to your supervisor."

"No," he says with a smile on his face. "I just know how you feel. Sort of."

I sense a story there, but it's not one that this relative stranger and I have time to share, even if I did just kiss him. He has work, and I have everything that comes after this moment.

◆ ◆ ◆

When I get home, Jack is at the condo, clearing out the rest of his stuff.

"Is Cassie home?" I ask, looking at the clock over the microwave and realizing I'm later than I wanted to be.

"She's in her room," Jack says without making eye contact.

I want to peek in and make sure she isn't packing too, but I don't want to seem overbearing. There's no good place for me to be, so I wander around like someone looking the place over, trying to decide if they want to buy it.

I stop by Cassie's door, listening in case I can hear her. Kids used to be noisy—music up too loud, yelling into the phone, video game music on high. Now no one actually speaks to each other; music is piped in through earbuds, childhood has gone silent. I decide she must be in there even if there isn't much evidence of her presence and slink off to the kitchen.

It wouldn't show by looking at it, but it's been over a year since Jack actually lived here. But now all the papers are processed and the jig is up. The marriage is officially over. I give Jack his space as he boxes and bags the things he cares about enough to haul away with him. I watch him decide for and against, holding things up, weighing their significance. I realize that I had come to think of Jack as rather unassuming, but today he's coming off pretty sexy in his dress shirt, unbuttoned enough to release his tie, and his sleeves rolled up at the cuff. His chestnut-colored and usually clean-cut hair is disheveled, and I know he's been running his hands through it in that anxious way that he does.

This particular part of a relationship's demise is like a terribly unfunny joke. You've done the yelling, the crying, the bargaining, the giving up. You've hired the lawyers and paid the fees, but now you have to hole up in the kitchen and chop vegetables for a dinner you're not really going to eat so that your disappearing other half can pack the last of his things in a cardboard box. Funny the way we try to put life in a box.

This stage of it all happens in some other twisted celestial plane where things take much longer than they should and you feel like a royal jerk for slicing carrots through the whole mess, but it would be rude to offer to help.

Let's speed this up now. Toss this in, too; my potatoes are on boil. If you hurry it up, you can be out of here before the biscuits are done.

"I think that's it," Jack says, coming into the kitchen and sitting at the barstool like he used to do on those rare occasions when he was home in time to catch me cooking as opposed to our usual routine of Cassie and me eating alone and then nuking the remains for him when he got home.

"Ok, then," I say.

There is nothing to be said about this process. Nothing that makes it any better, that is. It's surreal to divvy everything up like children portioning out candy and counting the pieces to make sure each gets their fair share.

You take the couch, and I'll take the love seat and recliner. You take the bigger of the saucepans, and I'll take those two little ones that you don't like anyway. We each get two plates, two coffee mugs, two glasses, and two sets of silverware.

"Are you going with me to the thing?" I ask, feeling silly at my inability to say the word *funeral* out loud.

"I don't think so." Jack swivels around, putting his back to me. "I don't feel like being the royal horse's behind all day."

"Don't you think not showing up will have the same effect?"

"Two totally different scenarios." Jack swivels back around on the barstool to face me. "One—I don't go, and your Aunt Rose asks you in that tone of hers why I'm not there, even though she knows good and well that we're divorced. You make some excuse for me, or you don't, and she tsk-tsks at you and goes on her merry way. People talk amongst themselves for a minute, but out of sight, out of mind, and I'm soon forgotten."

"And scenario two?"

"Two," he says, holding up two fingers for effect. "I go, and everyone leers at me all day because they know we've split and that I don't belong there anymore and if I look at my phone or yawn or get up to get a drink, it will be an indication of my lack of sincerity and they'll talk about me behind their hands and roll their eyes like I can't see them."

I want to come back at him with some pithy something, but he's right. Of course, scenario two makes things difficult for him whereas scenario one makes it hard on me. I could fire at him for that, but were the tables turned, I can't honestly say I would do any different. There's no sense to torture him. Despite the end of our time together and the events that led to it, I do love him. It's almost never a lack of love that ends things. There's always another side to the story.

Jack stands up, and I know he wants to get the heck out of here, so I don't press the issue. I walk around the counter to meet him, and we stand in front of each other in that awkward good-bye moment that you can only have with someone with whom you've shared the highest highs and the lowest lows. Someone you care about despite it all.

"Nina," Jack says and brushes my hair back from my shoulder. "I'm really sorry about Nate. If you want me to go, I will. If Cassie wants me to go, I'm there. All that other talk was just me blowing smoke—you know that, right?"

"I know," I say, meeting his gaze and quickly looking away. "You're right, though. It'll all go down just like you said, and there's no need to suffer it when you don't have to. People get too personal at funerals anyway. It's just an opportunity for them to nose into your private life."

"Then I should go," he says and nods. "You shouldn't have to bear the brunt of Aunt Rose's questions alone. And, hey, I can act like a jerk and no one will think anything of it. They'll expect it of me. It might be fun. Go out with a bang."

"You're not going out," I say. I notice that his sideburns are almost completely gray. Despite how I feel about everything that has passed between us, I have to admit it looks good on him. "Cassie still needs you around. *You* know that, right?"

Jack twists his mouth in a self-deprecating way. It's usually followed by a slow fade into his endearing smile, but today the smile doesn't come.

"Does she?" he asks. "I can't tell. This isn't really what I meant to do."

He's talking about losing Cassie, not me. I don't take it personally anymore.

"I didn't either," I say. "It is what it is."

Whatever it is.

This is another one of those weird circumstances of breaking up. Your guard is finally down now that the relationship is broken beyond all repair and you feel a strange comfort in saying all the things that you never said to the one person who would have understood you the best. You're finally the real you and he's the real him, but it's too late.

"So?" Jack asks. "The funeral?"

"I'll be ok," I say.

"Are you sure?" he asks. "Because you know Rose is going to ask about me just to get your goat. She'll pretend like she forgot about the divorce, and once you start explaining and backpedaling, she'll have you right where she wants you and she'll be as happy as a lark. She's an 'I told you so' looking for a person to scold."

What she "told me so" about was having another child. I married Jack when I was twenty-five, and he wasn't much older. We both wanted a pile of kids, and when we had Cassie right away, it seemed like the plan was going to work. But it didn't. When my thirtieth birthday loomed and nothing more had happened, I started to worry. I hadn't thought of it as infertility at the time, but when two, four, six more years went by and all the best laid plans of mice and men hadn't brought us another child, I became obsessed.

I got so focused on getting pregnant again that sex turned into a science experiment. The bedroom was a laboratory where I was in a white coat instead of a black negligee. Each month that didn't work out, I got angrier and angrier. I saw a therapist, and she told me I had to stop trying so hard to reach an unattainable goal. She said that was false hope. I said that was the definition of hope—the wish for something good, even in the face of its unlikelihood. But then we did it, we got pregnant just before I turned thirty-eight. It was like a miracle.

I miscarried at nineteen weeks.

So, now here I am at the door to my condo saying good-bye to my marriage. I want to tell Jack that I love him, and I know he wants to say it, too, but it's the sort of "I love you" that the word *bittersweet* was invented for and we let it go with a nod and a brief hug.

Later, I stand outside Cassie's room with my ear pressed to the door. I hear shuffling and her pencil scraping across her drawing pad. She draws these little anime characters that sort of look like her. She draws other figures, too, and I imagine they are characters from a story I don't know. Sometimes I wonder if she's drawing the brother she didn't get to have. She knew we were having a boy. We had even started a list of names. She had been so happy. I wonder if she's lonely. Another epic fail on my part. I wonder if I did anything right at all as a mother. I wonder if other mothers feel the same.

3

Funeral day, and I'm thinking about the sound a dental drill makes and that sickly sweet smell of the dentist's office. When I was little kid, I used to dread going to the dentist. What a freakish job—everybody hates you, and you have to stick your hands in other people's mouths. What makes someone want to do that? I remember the sickening feeling I'd get when I'd wake up on the day of my appointment, knowing that no matter what I did, there was no way out of it. The anxiety was brutal.

This is far worse.

I keep looking out the window to see if the rest of the world is still there. Everything feels surreal. I'm in a fog so thick I think I can see it in my closet. My heart is so heavy I can feel it in my arms and legs. My clothes are heavy, weighing on my shoulders like a coat too big for me. Maybe I've shrunk, grown younger. Perhaps when I look at myself in the mirror, I will see a ten-year-old girl.

I used to think that going off to college would make me an adult. Then I thought getting a job, getting married, having a child would prove to be the turning point. But no, I see now that it all starts today—the day I say good-bye to my dad.

I already see how it will play out. The parts that will hurt the most, the huge chunks of time where there will be nothing to do but endure. The unbearable hugs and people taking my hand—pressing it hard into their own. The polite, but contrived conversations that I'll be forced to engage in when I really just want to scream at everyone to get out and leave me alone.

Stop touching me, I will want to say as I yank free from their awful grip, *and thanks for the casserole.*

I think of Oliver, the nurse's aide, and the comforting way he put his hands around mine, making me feel for just a moment that I wasn't alone in my grief. When he pressed my hand between his own, it was different. I don't think about kissing him. Much.

"Cassie," I call against the closed bedroom door. "You about ready?"

Nothing. I knock.

"Cass?"

The door opens, and she's dressed in the same dark blue dress she wore to her piano recital last month.

"Is this going to be one of those open casket things where you have to go gawk at the dead body?" she asks, hiding her fear behind her sarcasm.

"No," I say.

I reach out to touch her arm, but she nudges past me and out into the living room before I can take hold.

"Where's Dad's chair?" she asks, standing in the empty spot that used to hold Jack's leather club chair. She circles around like it's there, but she just can't see it.

"It's with Dad," I say, picturing a space with nothing in it but a leather club chair.

I know Jack has found another place to stay, but I haven't been there. We haven't gotten that far yet—the switching off weekends and holidays, the arguing about child support paid and time spent. I'm not ready for that.

"There won't be anything to gawk at," I say, changing the

subject back to the funeral. "It's just out of respect anyway. People want to say good-bye."

"It's creepy," Cassie says and stomps the floor where Jack's chair should be. "Grandpa's dead. It's a little late for good-bye. And what's respectful about staring at a dead person—looking to see if they have nose hair?"

She's right.

"Grandpa was cremated," I say, realizing she didn't know that. "There will just be the urn."

"Oh," she says, her body going limp. "That's even worse."

Cassie's world has seen too many changes these last several months. She goes into the kitchen and pours the last of the dark roast into her "First Coffee, Then Your Inane Blather" mug. She's fifteen, sipping java and wearing a wrap dress that dares you not to notice she has hips and that she's morphing into that scary something between adult and child. She's right in front of me, and she's already gone. I don't even know when it happened. How I lost her.

She was there just a little while ago, clinging to my leg, pulling on my shirttail, showing me her drawings, telling me a joke so funny she could barely speak around her own laughter, and then . . . then some years passed and maybe I was busy working or answering e-mail, talking on the phone, doing housework—I don't know—but she grew up while I was looking the other way, and now she's gone. It's selfish of me, but I'm not ready to be un-important to her. I'm not ready for her to go, but there's nothing I can do to stop it.

I'm not ready for this. For any of this.

I want her back. I want my father back. I want it all back—safety and hope and time. But there is no way back. There is only picking up the car keys, opening the door, and passing through into whatever comes after this.

When we get to parking deck, Jack's spot is still empty. Cassie glances at the space where his car used to be, but doesn't ask about it. She doesn't tromp around it looking for a secret passageway back to better times. Instead she jabs her earbuds in and aims her face at her iPhone. I want to say something, have some meaningful conversation about loss and love and everything in between, but I don't know how.

We emerge from the darkness of the garage into a day too bright and blue. My cell rings as I'm waiting at a stop sign. Lola doing fish face. I'm not afraid of this call. This is her coping mechanism call. She's not lost in the jungle. She's just sad. Same difference I guess.

"Hello," I answer, knowing she's called to ask me something that seems off subject, trivial. She does that when she's about to fall apart.

"Hey, Sissy," she says, and the use of that long-ago nickname makes the road blur.

"Are you with Mom?" I ask, keeping my eyes on the passing cars and the tears out of my voice.

I had busied myself so much with the tasks of losing someone that I hadn't faced the task of saying good-bye. And especially not to Dad. I'm not sure I can do it.

"I'm in the driveway," she says. "Do you remember that time I got locked in the bathroom at a gas station on the way to Disney World?"

"Sure."

I don't understand the diversion so far, but it means she's not handling this well. I ease into traffic and turn toward our childhood home.

"I can remember how I got locked in, but how did I get out?" she asks.

"Ray knocked the door in," I say, one hand gripping the phone, the other tight on the wheel—hurrying to Lola like we all do whenever she needs us.

Breaking that door was one of Ray's first acts of reckless destruction after Lola's accident.

"I remember Mom saying all these silly, fake curse words from outside the door," Lola says. "Why did she do that?"

After Lola's accident and Mom's reawakening into a better, albeit unreal, version of herself, Mom tried not to say "undesirable words." So she said things like "Well, fruity Froot Loops," and "Tangle my angle." I'm not sure what that replaced for her, but when she said it, we knew she was upset.

I remember how nervous Ray had gotten when the door wouldn't open and even the station attendant couldn't help. Dad was on the pay phone trying to reach a locksmith when Ray decided to take matters into his own hands. He banged on the door and told Lola to move back and then he rammed himself into the door three or four times until it opened. He reached into the bathroom and yanked Lola out like he was pulling her from a burning building.

"We should have stayed at home," he had said. "She's not ready."

"We can't stay locked up in the house forever, Ray," Mom had said, fussing over Lola and checking the braces she wore on her ankles to keep herself steady.

Lola kept them covered up most of the time, but they were still there. They made her seem fragile and people wanted to take care of her. When she got the ankle braces off a few years later, eventually no one even remembered they had been there.

I still see the memory of them glinting on her legs, even now, sometimes.

"Why does Mom do anything that she does?" I ask, perhaps with more sarcasm in my voice than necessary.

Across the virtual phone line, Lola chuckles in agreement. "Is Cassie with you?"

"Yes," I say.

"Tell her I'm fine," Lola says, always more concerned about everyone else. "You know what I found under Dad's bed?"

"Why were you under Dad's bed?"

"That album cover," she says. "I wanted to play the record, but it's gone."

"The one with the monster face?"

"Do you remember the way he used to try to scare us?" she asks, her voice light and airy.

It was Dad's record—some has-been band that I had never heard of then or since. He used to play this game where he'd sneak into our room and make zombie noises, holding the album cover in front of his face to scare us. We'd scream and hide under the covers, our little hearts pounding, fear squealing out of us even though we knew it was all make-believe.

I look over at Cassie and wonder where make-believe has gone. So much is possible these days that nothing is magic anymore.

"I remember," I say to Lola, and then try to change the subject. "Where's Chris?"

Cassie looks over at me, clearly listening.

"He's inside talking to Mom," Lola says. "She knows, doesn't she? That he's from TV?"

"Mom's ecstatic," I say. "She loves those commercials."

"You told her?" Cassie asks sharply, figuring out what has happened. "Good. I hate keeping secrets."

I glance at Cassie, who has already turned back to her iPhone. "Are you far away?" Lola asks.

She needs me. And right now, even though I know it's selfish, I need Lola to need me. To make me feel like I have a purpose. Like there is some tangible thing that I can do for someone and that what I do means something.

◆ ◆ ◆

At Mom's house, I find it difficult to get out of the car. For a moment, Cassie doesn't notice that we have stopped, and it buys me some time. I can't help but see Mom's yard like one of Lola's paintings. Late April, grass painted Day-Glo green. Pink and white lopsided tulips, long buried in wait, have pried their blooms through the ground, and daffodils reach their golden buckets toward the sky. There are no leaves on the trees yet, except for the pink cherry blossoms and slightly off-white dogwoods—their short-lived color too anxious to wait for the rest of nature to catch up.

In this fictional painting, Lola will have captured the very precise spacing of the flowers edging the walk to the front door. Mom has a knack for that sort of control over things that spring from the ground. I envy that level of mastery over the world around her. Truth be told, it's all a cover-up. Pretty though, all the pink and white. I hope that Mom finds enjoyment in it. I hope it isn't all whitewash over an old fence.

But that's what we do. We make things into what we want them to be. We spin the world around us to match the thoughts in our head. If this was one of Lola's paintings, the neighbor's house in the background would be on fire and Chris would be standing in the yard aiming a water hose made of Christmas garland at the roof. There would be little girl sitting in the front yard, eating a pink tulip, and everyone who looked at the painting would think it was the story of their own life.

Inside, Mom and Lola are in the kitchen prepping Lola for the day. They don't notice us come in.

"Ok," Mom says and holds up an index card with a photo and a name on it. "Aunt Rose will be the one in the blue, polyester suit. It's her funeral suit. She wears it every time. Do you remember that?"

"No," Lola says. "But I do remember Aunt Rose. I'm not that messed up."

Cassie looks at me sharply, anxiously. I put my hand on her shoulder, whisper that it's ok. These games worry Cassie. I nod toward the other room, giving her leeway to leave. I feel guilty for enjoying the small moment of being needed, being her safety net.

"Now that's a shame," I say once Cassie is in the other room. "All those holes and Aunt Rose couldn't have dropped into one?"

Lola and Mom both turn toward me.

"You hush," Mom says, but there's a hint of a smile on her face. "We have company in the living room, so be nice. Where's Cassie?"

"She's already come and gone, Mother," Lola says. "She hates your card game."

Lola had noticed us after all.

"Don't you think you should warn Chris about Aunt Rose?" I say, opening a cabinet, searching for a coffee mug. "It's only fair. Without Jack to pester, Chris is a prime target."

"Oh," Lola says and groans. "Rose will have a field day with Chris. Do you think she's seen the commercials?"

Everyone has seen them.

"Nina," Mom shouts at me so suddenly that I jump, banging the coffee mug hard against the counter. "Why did you tell her?"

"I didn't tell her anything," I say, pulling out the coffee carafe to discover only the dregs.

"Both of you hush," Lola says, pressing her hands down against thin air in that *keep it down* motion that looks like a baby bird learning to fly. "He'll hear you."

"He doesn't know that you know?" Mom asks.

I put the coffee carafe and the now-chipped mug into the sink.

"This is crazy," I say and take the stack of cards out of Mom's hand.

This is Mom's family-gathering preparatory package. It's index cards of family photos of infrequently seen people mixed in with those more frequently seen, but annoying, and then peppered with people encountering some drama that Mom feels Lola should know about. I told Mom she should market it as a family game of some sort. She said that was rude. I thought it was an interesting way for people to keep up with family gossip and the like.

"Do you want to do this?" I ask Lola, holding out the note cards. "Or do you just want to wing it?"

Lola "wings" a lot of things.

"Maybe I'll just get plastered," Lola says. "I'll use being drunk as an excuse for any slipups."

Mom glances at me, and I look away. The drinking was before the accident. We're not sure how much Lola remembers prior to it. Mom's "problem" seems to have fallen into one of Lola's holes. Her memory is selective. It's not like she forgets how to walk or use a fork—although during the early years of her recovery both of those things happened—she just misplaces information. It's all in there; the recall function just doesn't work like it should. So she has to use visual aids sometimes. Hence her house being polka-dotted with Post-it Notes.

What day the trash is picked up.

Her neighbor's first name.

When the rent is due.

Which gallery is showing her art.

Lola is an amazing artist. That came after the accident too, although the talent for it was surely already there. It's just that since her brain wasn't working like it should, Mom and Dad didn't press the issue of good grades. They were just happy she remembered everyone when she came down to the breakfast table. She was allowed the freedom to be creative. She was good at it, and her success made us all feel better.

Sometimes, I think her brain works just like it was meant to and perhaps the accident was a way for us to let her be who she was meant to be.

After the accident, it seemed as though Lola would never come home from the hospital, that she would live forever at the rehabilitation hospital. I had a room to myself—something I had wanted, but once I got it, it was like living with a ghost. When Lola got out of the hospital, Dad threw a party for her. Dad and I decorated at home while Mom signed the papers at the hospital and put Lola in the car to bring her to us. Our older brother, Ray, stayed in his room.

It was a coming-out party for Mom as well. While Lola had been recovering, Mom had too. She'd started attending AA meetings and stopped drinking. This party was supposed to be a celebration of our new, reinvented life.

Dad hummed and joked and tousled my hair. Every so often he would call out for Ray to come downstairs, but Ray didn't. While Mom set up cake and brought out presents, Dad went up the stairs. I followed him and hid around the corner. Dad knocked on Ray's door.

"You sister is home," he said to the closed door, even though Ray had not answered. "She's asking for you."

Ray must have been standing just on the other side of the threshold because the door creaked open almost immediately.

"What about Mom?" Ray asked, avoiding eye contact the way a teenager will do even when they don't need to.

"Your mother is back too," Dad said and sighed. "This is a chance for us all to make a new start. Let's try, please. Even if we don't feel up to it."

Ray slithered out of the small space he afforded between our world and his. He had a present in his hand. Although it was wrapped in Christmas paper, Dad nodded his approval and clapped his hand on Ray's shoulder. Ray jerked away. Dad sighed again and let Ray walk down the steps alone.

"It's a start," Dad said to no one in particular. Then he looked back down the hall. "Let's go, Nina."

I snuck out of hiding, thinking I was in trouble for eaves-dropping. Instead, Dad took my hand and walked downstairs with me. In the living room, Lola was propped up on the couch, looking like any little girl sitting on a couch, except for the metal braces attached like bear traps on her ankles.

Ray thrust his gift toward her, but didn't step close enough for her to reach it. Dad took it from Ray and placed it on Lola's lap. I thought Ray would slink away to the recliner on the other side of the room, but he lowered himself softly onto the couch beside Lola, careful not to jostle her.

Ray watched as she opened his gift. No one said anything.

It was an elaborate paint set. Real paint. Not kid paint. Real brushes and mixers and things that I didn't recognize. It was expensive, and it explained all the lawn mowing he had done around town.

"It will give you something to do," Ray said, speaking quickly the way a person does when they feel they're talking out of turn.

"I'll paint a picture for you," Lola said.

She was ten. In the hospital, she had to be told who each of us were. But she seemed to recognize Ray. She looked at him like she had known him in a far-off dream. Later, she wouldn't stop painting pictures of him. It was like she knew him from before. Like she was trying not to forget. Like, even then, she was trying to make him remember who he was and show him who he didn't have to be.

◆　◆　◆

"I don't think winging it is a good idea," Mom says and holds out her hand for the cards.

"I'll look at the cards," Lola says and takes them from me. "Thank you, Mom."

"I'm just trying to help," Mom says, fidgeting.

"I know." Lola puts her hand over Mom's. "This isn't the time for you to worry over me, though. We should be fussing over you."

"It gives me something to do." Mom pulls her hand out from under Lola's only to put it on top like that old childhood game. "It's always time for a mother to fuss over her daughter. You can't take that job away. I won't let you."

Mom says it with a smile, like she's making a joke, but I know she means it. I know she's holding on tight. I am too.

Lola puts the cards on the countertop and walks out of the room. I watch Mom flitter around the kitchen, and I know she has slipped again and had couple of cocktails but followed them up with a pot of black coffee this morning—which is why I found nothing but the dregs. I guess if slips are going to happen, today would be the day. Still, it frightens me. Has enough time passed that she is really able to handle it—or are we on the doorstep of what used to be? I used to think that her drinking was a weakness, and I was ashamed for her. But now I'm more ashamed for myself. I was a child and I saw the world like a child sees it—full of rainbows and unicorns. I realize now that fairy tales are for those with weak stomachs.

I can't bear the kitchen anymore so I wander through the house, looking for Cassie. I find her watching television in the living room with Chris.

"Aren't you afraid your ad is going to come on?" she says and bites her lip—ribbing him.

He tosses a pillow at her and holds up the remote. "I'm at the ready," he says.

It's a playful moment that makes me both insanely jealous and sad.

"Have you seen your aunt?" I ask Cassie, wishing I had some funny something to say to wedge into the conversation—to belong.

Cassie nods her head toward the hallway, not looking at me directly.

"Be kind to your mother, kiddo," I hear Chris say to her as I walk away. "It's a rough day. It's not easy to say good-bye to your dad."

"I know," Cassie says quietly.

I feel my gut wrench. I know she's talking about Jack, and it makes me suddenly nauseated. I should go back and say something, but I can't image what that something is, so I keep walking away.

I find Lola in the sunroom. She is always looking for light. She sees my distress all over my face and hugs me.

"Thanks," I say. "I don't think I'm up for this today."

"No one ever is," she says. "How about we make a signal like on TV. If people are bugging you about Jack and all things relevant to that, you pull on your ear and I'll come to your rescue."

"Can the signal be that I punch someone in the face and you come to my rescue?"

"Absolutely," she says and then punches me lightly on the arm. "You should have told me about Chris."

I try to suppress a smile but fail.

"You just seemed to like him so much." I try to coax her hands off her hips. "It seemed cruel to burst your bubble."

"There you two are," Mom says as she comes into the room. "What's wrong with Chris?"

Lola and I both start to sing. "Your house is trashed, you've got a rash, your car is broke . . ."

"I love those commercials," Mom says, looking above our heads in a dreamy way. "The one where he's trying to pedal that car with his feet like the Flintstones cracks me up every time."

Mom laughs to herself and leaves the room.

Lola wrinkles her nose, her delicate features accentuated today by dark circles under her winter-sky, blue eyes. Her face looks like an approaching storm—snow and hail and hardship. She's beautiful nonetheless.

"Come upstairs with me," she says. "I have to show you something."

Upstairs in our old room, she reaches under her bed and pulls out an old record album.

"Look," she says and holds it up. "Here it is!"

I know she's thinking what I'm thinking—that he had it under the bed, ready to sneak it out and scare us with his favorite game even all these years later.

I still don't know who the band is, but I hold the record cover in front of me and make ridiculous growls and noises that are not at all scary. Lola laughs, which is what I was hoping for.

Mom yells up at us from the bottom of the stairs. "You girls get ready to go."

I suddenly feel like I'm ten years old and it's time to go to school and Lola bursts into the tears I want so badly to shed.

At the bottom of the stairs, Mom takes Lola from me. She puts her hands on Lola's cheeks and kisses her nose.

"I know that doesn't make it all better anymore," Mom says.

Watching them, I feel the bitter absence of Dad's embrace and my new inability to connect with a daughter I have known all her life.

After Lola's accident, more than twenty years ago now, Dad was the only reminder of the way things had been. Even though it hadn't always been good, at least it had been real. Mom had flipped a switch after the accident. First, she went crashing downhill, drinking more than ever, making us fear that the family was being picked off one at a time by some demon of tragedy.

Then Lola woke up, and Mom started over. She seized the opportunity to begin again. Lola didn't seem to remember anything or anyone and life was a blank slate. To Mom, it was like moving to a new town and creating a whole new sense of self. To us, it was like being put in the witness protection program—unable to tell anyone anything about life as we used to know it.

Chris comes to take his place beside Lola, and Mom beams at him. I fear she's going to ask for an autograph or, worse, for him to act out one of her favorite scenes. *Do the one where you have on the Superman costume and pretend to fly around the city.*

Lola moves away from Mom and wraps herself around Chris. He covers her over with his cape and flies them out to car.

Mom touches my shoulder and follows them outside.

"Cass," I call into the living room. "It's time to go, honey."

I listen for the sound of her getting up out of the chair, but there is nothing.

"Cass?"

Silence.

I step into the living room, expecting to find her ears plugged with music and her eyes stuck to the iPhone screen. Instead, she's standing by the window looking into the backyard. I walk over to her, knowing I will get this wrong no matter what I say. Wishing it could be the one time I had my superhero cape on as well.

"We need to go," I say, wanting to touch her, but fearing that little pull away that she does.

"Is Dad coming?"

"I don't think so. Maybe. Do you want him to?"

She shrugs.

"Are you going to be ok?" She looks at me so directly that my throat burns.

"Yes," I say, my voice cracking across the huge, one syllable word. "Are you?"

She shrugs again, and my heart breaks. Tears glaze over her eyes, and her lip trembles. There are too many layers of fear and sadness in her face. I know she can't bear for me to hug her just now, so I smooth my hands down her hair, holding the ends of it between my fingers like the finest fabric.

She lowers her head and walks toward the front door.

Out in the driveway, we all stand around the Buick, trying to come up with an excuse not to get in. Mom finds one.

"I forgot the photo boards," she says, looking relieved. Whether it was relief at having not driven away without them or at having found a way to stall a moment more, I'm not sure.

"Let me help you," Chris says and follows Mom back inside.

Cassie gets in the backseat and closes the door.

We had Dad cremated. So since there's no body for people to gawk at, Mom made these collages of when our family was perfect for people to view. Photos of vacations, holidays, graduations.

She's left off my wedding that is now defunct and any picture of Lola wearing braces on her legs. The only pictures of Ray are those little school pictures where he could be some kid with a bright future and no police record.

"Do you feel like we're in a movie?" Lola asks.

"Yeah," I say and wrap my arms around myself. "Not a good one, but yeah."

"What do you think happens next?" she asks.

A slight breeze lifts the bitter scent of daffodils to my nose. The air is both cool departing and warmth approaching, and the sunny yellow of the flowers are a jaunty juxtaposition to our stern black skirts and heels.

"We go the stereotypical funeral," I say, and Lola clutches my hand. "Our childhood pastor will give the eulogy. Everyone will be in black, except for Sue, who still wants to show off her new breasts, so she'll be in something low cut and loud. There will be some woman who no one really knows, but who seems terribly upset, and we'll spend the rest of the afternoon trying to decide if she was Aunt Millie's half-sister's daughter or that lady from Dad's work who came to your show that time and tried to make out with Jack."

Lola laughs. This is how we have always gotten through the tough times—by playing out our movie life.

"What then?" she says, and her face becomes like stone. "Will Ray come?"

Dad and Ray had never been able to sort out the details of a regular father-and-son arrangement. Ever since the night of Lola's accident, Ray and Dad were at odds. Warring in a battle neither one of them seemed to know the rules to.

"Of course Ray's there," I say, although I can't picture it. "And afterwards, we all come back home and eat too much green bean and fried onion chips casserole. We'll avoid Aunt Rose like the plague. We'll listen to people tell us the story of our lives as they know it. We'll cry a few times and laugh a lot—you can't talk about Dad and not laugh—and then we'll fall asleep in the twin beds upstairs in our room because we won't want to go home and start the rest of our lives just yet."

A room that mom hasn't changed since we left for college.

"Where will Ray sleep?" Lola asks.

Ray's room had been turned into a mini-storage facility—medical equipment and furniture from our parents' bedroom that took up too much space once they bought the hospital bed for Dad to have at the house.

Mom had kept Dad at home for as long as she could after the first stroke, but after a couple of scares and trips in the ambulance, her nerves were shot. For a while, she had someone come over to the house, but insurance wouldn't pay for round-the-clock, in-home care, and Mom worried the most at night. She couldn't let herself fall asleep for fear that something would happen and she would wake to find Dad sprawled on the floor with his head cracked open.

Dad seemed to dip into dementia not long after the stroke, and we never really got him back. Once, he woke in the night and went out into the yard. Mom found him the next morning sleeping by the mailbox. After a few close calls, it seemed there was nothing to do but place him in a facility that could care for him and watch him all the time.

There's a sadness that takes over in a place like that, and you start to forget the person you once knew and see them instead as this less-able replacement of themselves. A weird copy of the person you love—except they can't walk or speak clearly, and you wonder why someone would make a copy of your father and mess him up like that.

Ray never went to the nursing home. He kept saying he would. But now Dad is gone and it's too late.

"Ray will have to sleep in the bathtub," I say and Lola smiles.

We stand there for a moment. The world around us beams beautiful and oblivious.

"You're right." Lola sighs. "That is the way the movie goes." She turns her head away.

For a second, just a small one, we're out in the front yard, just like this, but I'm kneeling down in front of her, arranging a pair of rainbow-striped leg warmers over her ankles, covering the braces the best I can because it's the first day of school and Paul Brooks is new in town and all summer he hasn't seen the braces, all summer he's been entranced with Lola and her leg warmers in the heat and her coal-black hair. He's never seen her do anything "strange" and the most important thing to me is to help everything seem normal.

Mom and Chris come outside with the photo boards. They load the happy memories into the trunk, and Chris makes a goofy face at Lola. Her eyes widen, and I know she's seeing the commercial character in his expression. She smiles at him and winks at me.

"Let's go, girls," Mom says. "Sit up here with me, Lola."

Lola gets in the front, and I ride in back with Chris and Cassie. Mom moves her hand to turn on the radio, but seems to think better of it and doesn't. We ride in silence for a bit, turning down familiar lanes as though we could be going to the mall, the first day of school, over to Grandma's.

"Oh, look," Mom says, pointing out her window and slowing down. "The Mackelvoy place is for sale. Open house. I've always wanted to see the redo on their kitchen. Should we go in?"

"Mom?" Lola looks over at her and then turns around to look at me. She looks terrified.

"We're sort of busy today, Mom," I say.

"Of course," Mom says and chuckles. "Maybe some other time."

I look at Chris and wonder what he must be thinking, but he's looking at Lola. I look at Cassie, but she's staring out the window.

Mom speeds back up, and we continue the short distance to the funeral home. Although I've been down this path before, I take notice, now, of the houses slung back from the road, their fenced yards and clean cars a wishful dream of peace and tranquility. I see the new blooms around the mailboxes like a deeply planted shield, a useless attempt at warding off the deadly and devastating. There is no protection from the wiles of the world.

4

I hang back in the parking lot of the funeral home and let everyone else go in without me. I'm looking for Ray. I expect to see his face poking out from behind a bush, like in some stupid movie, but instead, I see him in his old Chevy Nova. I'm the only one who knows he's in town.

He found me at work the day after I called and told him Dad had died. He asked me not to tell anyone he was here. I asked if that was because he might not stay. He said yes.

"I should know better than to leave the doors unlocked," Ray says when I open the passenger side and get in.

"Look," I say, and I'm suddenly angry with him. "No one actually thinks that you're going to show up for this part. But you better be at that church. Don't you dare let this day go by and Mom doesn't see you and Lola doesn't see you and you finally manage to accomplish what you set out to do years ago."

"What's that?" He turns his garden-snake green eyes toward me.

"To break everyone's heart," I say.

He looks away.

"That's not what I meant to do," Ray says.

Most of the family still think he's in jail. They think maybe he'll get some sort of temporary release and come to the funeral

46

in an orange jumpsuit with his hands in cuffs and his feet bound up in chains.

I look at Ray's hands. He is gripping the gearshift like he's ready to speed off. I shouldn't have spoken to him that way.

I reach over and put my hand on his. He doesn't move his hand to reciprocate, but he doesn't move it away either.

"I'm just going to screw up no matter what I do," Ray says. "I shouldn't have come. I'll just make things worse."

"Showing up is the right thing to do," I say. "We want you here. You're part of this family."

An unexpected memory surfaces of summer vacation at the beach, long before things changed. Ray, baby Lola, and Mom were somewhere in the pier house getting ice cream and souvenirs. Mom wasn't drunk yet, and we were all trying to make the most of the day while we still could. Dad and I walked out onto the pier. I must have been only four or five, but I remember. I was hand in hand with Dad, and he was so much taller than I was that all I could see were his legs, his long stride down the creaking wood, and his hands—one holding mine and the other pointing out across the ocean at a shrimp boat in the distance.

Seagulls hovered and squawked over the boat like a loud, gray cloud.

"This is how they go fishing," Dad said of the birds.

I remember seeing a bird with a fish in its mouth jut up and away. Then I was lifted up onto Dad's shoulders. The sunlight sparked just in time for his face to white out of sight and then the light softened and from the top of his shoulders I could see everything that moments ago had been unknown to me.

Sometimes Ray seems like a person from a memory or a movie actor I can't quite place. Looking him hard in the face, I think—yes, I remember—he's that guy from back when we were kids, and we used to hang out all the time. He looks a little older now, but that's definitely him. We had this secret club that met in the linen closet. Then something terrible happened and everything changed.

"I can't go in there," Ray says. "It's too close in there."

I nod.

"I'll come to the service," he says. "I promise."

◆ ◆ ◆

Back at Mom's house, after the church service, I watch the men pass around photos and talk about their families. One story leads into another, like a thin rope made of strong sinew, a wisp of something deeper than bone. I forget how hard a man can love. How desperate and irrational the heart can be. I look around for Jack, feeling guilty for things that I can't do anything about now. Too many screaming matches between there and here.

My father, though, had been that quiet type of man whose offer of sincere emotion was a surprise. He was a jokester, a kid at heart, showing us his affection through play. Words often failed him. I had known that he loved us, of course, but hearing the stories told by other fathers around the mourning room brought the truth home to me. How much had my father wanted to reach beyond the restraints of his own malfunctioning body that was stuck in the nursing home to tell me himself? I tried to recall the small handful of times he had found words while he was there.

I see Ray with his close-cut, dark hair and three-day stubble, sitting in a folding chair in the corner by the back door. His ill-fitting, dark gray suit and starched white shirt hang on him like a costume. This is the suit he wore to court to look respectable and repentant, and to cover the tattoo sleeves on his arms. The suit—then and now—makes him look like a book stuck on the wrong shelf.

What if all the restraint he'd had has been exhausted? What

if, this time, jail and the pain of a tattoo needle and his general helping of self-loathing and beer can't keep him from splitting down the middle?

He sees me and presses his lips together. I tilt my head at him, thankful that he's here. During the funeral, he sat on the back row with some of the people I recognized from the nursing home. He lifted a hand to me, but when I waved him up, he shook his head.

I see Aunt Rose sauntering over to him, and I try to push my way through the crowd. She's talking loud enough to be heard halfway across the room and I know that she knows this.

"Well, Ray," Aunt Rose says, her hands on her hips. "I almost didn't recognize you. What did you think of the service, or were you there?"

I step over some kids coloring, all their little hues spread out around them.

"I sat in the back," I hear Ray say.

Someone stops me to talk about something, but I'm listening to Ray. I'm so close, but stalled just feet away from him.

"I suppose you're happy your mother had him cremated," Rose says.

"Why would that make me happy?" Ray asks, and I can almost see what he wants to say forming in a cartoon thought-bubble over his head. *Kiss off. I loved my father.*

You don't have to get along with someone to love them. Love or the lack of it was never the issue between Ray and Dad. Love is easy. Like is more difficult.

"I guess you would have preferred to see him off in a pine box," Rose says. "I wanted your mother to get one of the nice caskets. The kind with the stylish interior. But she decided to have him burned up like a pile of old leaves that you want off your yard before they kill the grass."

This is why no one likes Aunt Rose.

"Coffins are tacky," Ray says and looks beyond Rose to where I'm standing. "They look like my sixth-grade saxophone case."

I think about the bright blue, plush lining where the instrument fits in—a perfect cutout to keep it snug in place for safe travel.

"How awfully rude," Aunt Rose says to Ray. "Typical."

"Kiss off, Rose," Ray finally says, not even offering her the formality of her family title.

She gasps and huffs away.

I sense an opening in the one-sided conversation I'm trapped in and make my escape. I sit down beside Ray in an empty folding chair. This would have been Jack's spot, if he were here. It's like the time-out chair and Ray happens to have been the bad little boy today.

"I'm not in the mood for another lecture, Nina," Ray says.

"I came to congratulate you for annoying Aunt Rose," I say in an attempt to lighten the mood.

"What is it you want?" Ray asks, not ready to be lightened up.

"Just checking on you," I say. "I was a little harsh in the car and I'm sorry."

He looks at me with a mock expression of shock, and I think, *There it is, right there, my Ray. There you are.* I want to reach out to him like I'm grabbing onto someone who has fallen off a boat. *Don't go under, Ray, please don't go under.*

"Is that a white flag?" he asks.

"Truce," I say. "For starters."

He nods and loosens his tie. "This thing is a noose. This sucks."

I know he doesn't mean the shirt and tie.

"Yeah," I say. "It does."

We watch the tide of black dresses and dark sports jackets ebb and flow through the room. Faces become solemn and then less so in a strange rhythm of solidarity and stoicism.

After a while, Ray jams his hand in the breast pocket of his suit and pulls out a palm-sized photo. He hands it to me and shakes his head.

"Who's this?" I ask, looking at a head-and-shoulder shot of a brown-haired boy in a sweater that I'm sure he doesn't usually wear.

"My son," Ray says.

I scan the room instinctively for my Cassie. She tried so hard not to cry at the funeral. Why do we do that—put on a brave face? Hold it back, keep it in—until it rips its way through you like that beast in *Alien*. I see Cassie sitting on the floor with the little kids—cousins twice removed and random toddlers of indiscernible family relation. A little red-haired boy has crawled up in Cassie's lap. That was all I wanted. That was what I sacrificed everything for and didn't get.

"How old is he?" I finally say and turn the picture face down in my lap.

"Five," Ray says and takes the picture from me. "No one knows, and you can't tell Lola. I don't know what to do yet, and she'll make a big deal out of it."

Ray looks at the photo and tucks it back in his pocket.

"Like it's a reason for you to stay this time?" I ask with a discernible scoff in my voice.

I wince. I don't want to talk to him like this. I want us to be what we might have been if it had all happened like it should have. I know he wants that too. He's gruff and rebellious, but I know he loves us. I know he's ripping himself to pieces over all the things he should have done and didn't, or did and shouldn't have. That's what Ray does. He tears himself to shreds.

He picks up a coffee mug filled with clear liquid. I raise an eyebrow at him as he sips. He shoots me a dirty look when he swallows.

"I'm going to make you some coffee," I say and stand up from the metal folding chair.

"I'm fine with this." Ray lifts his cup to me.

I take the cup from his hand. "I'll be back."

"Always full of threats," Ray says, but he doesn't try to take the cup back.

Lola is in the kitchen, and she grabs my hand hard when I round the corner, almost making me spill Ray's contraband. I set the cup down on the counter.

"I can actually picture Ray sleeping in the bathtub," Lola says. "It makes me smile."

I've caught Ray looking at Lola from time to time, and I know he wants to talk to her but isn't sure what to say. He's been gone a long time.

"Don't rush him," I warn. "He's pretty Ray right now."

We both look at him from around the kitchen corner. I feel flighty and nervous, watching him. It's like sneaking up on a bird I know I'll never be able to catch. No matter how slow I go or how close I get, it will wing away from me. I think about that owl in the road. If Ray were a bird, he'd be that owl.

"You ok in here, sweetie?" Chris asks, startling the both of us.

Lola jumps and looks him in the eyes. "I didn't know who you were," she says, shaking her head, the truth suddenly spilling over. "I didn't know."

Chris looks at me, and I grimace.

"I didn't tell her," I say, holding out my hands in front of me like a surrender of truth.

"Now what?" Chris asks. His face tightens into a squint and his shoulders tense.

"Now what, what?" Lola asks, looking around as if some other revelation is just around the corner.

"I should have told you," he says, looking like he's just leveled her with a deep dark secret. "It was stupid not to. It's just a job. But I was sort of embarrassed."

"Why?" she asks.

"Have you seen them?" Chris says, wincing. "I was classically trained. I thought I was meant for something else, you know. But nothing else came. That character has taken over my life, and it was just nice to get it back for a while. It's stupid."

"No, it isn't," Lola says and takes his hand. "Besides, I'm likely to forget by next week."

Chris laughs and then catches himself, biting his lip. Lola punches him in the shoulder.

"I should have told you," he says. "You've been up-front with me about everything, and knowing the issues you struggle with, it was sort of mean for me to keep something hidden from you. Especially something that everyone else knew about."

He has no idea how close to home his words hit. There is too much that we hide from Lola.

"I'd love to keep my 'issues' to myself," she says, "but I have no choice. Otherwise you'd think I was crazy. Especially once I invited you to my house."

All Lola's cabinets have a basic description of what's in them. Some have words, painted in beautiful script: *cereal, mixing bowls, yummy snacks.* Others are painted with pictures of coffee cups and plates, wine glasses and pie tins. The drawers are the same—forks and spoons, measuring cups. And one that says *lovely random junk.*

"Your kitchen is a guest's dream," Chris says and touches her hair. "I've never once had to search for anything. I feel like I've been there forever."

What a lovely spin. I peek back at Ray. He's completely taken off his tie and is twisting it around his wrist. I look at the circle of little kids, but Cassie is gone. I open the cabinet and take out a coffee mug.

"What about you, Chris?" I ask him, turning back toward the kitchen. "Are you doing ok here? I see people trying to figure out where they know you."

"I'm not where they expect me to be right now—you know, inside the television. I'm just waiting for the jingle," he says, shaking his head. "Someone will put two and two together soon enough." He puts his arm around Lola's waist, and she sinks into him.

"It would lighten things up," I say. "You want me to sing it?"

"No," they both say at the same time.

They leave the kitchen together. I take a bag of coffee from the counter and pour too much into the basket of the coffee maker.

"Making enough for two?" Mom asks from behind me, and I jump.

I push Ray's cup farther back on the countertop, hoping she doesn't see it, figuring she can probably smell it. I should have dumped it out. I'm not used to spending one-on-one time with Mom so even something as simple as standing in the kitchen making coffee with her seems strange.

All those years ago, I got lost in the Lola shuffle. Mom got so caught up in her that the rest of us disappeared. I was the only girl I knew whose father took her shopping for her first bra and helped her decide which type of sanitary pad to buy when the time came. That had been a shopping trip for the books. I had been mortified, but as Dad and I stood in the feminine care aisle comparing one package to the next, trying to decipher the pleasantly worded absorption ratings, things got silly and suddenly less dramatic. Dad had a way of taking the edge off life in general.

We were finally assisted by a passerby—a young woman who looked at Dad with googly eyes the way women will look at a guy playing with a puppy in the park. For just a second, I wondered what life would be like, just me and Dad on our own in the world. Just for a second.

Afterwards, Dad and I sat in the car in the parking lot, laughing hysterically, too doubled over to drive home.

In my more bitter moments, I tell myself that Mom forgot me altogether, but I know that's impossible. She was only one person with four others to care for, and I'm sure that's hard to juggle in the best of times, to say nothing for the extenuating circumstances. But those are revelations that don't come to you as a child. Those are the definition of hindsight.

I wasn't sure who the day was harder on, me or Mom. But she'd been Dad's longer, so I'd have to give the day to her. The choice to love someone seems so doomed from the get-go. Even as you walk down the aisle toward him, every intention to stay together forever, you know there is no such thing. But no one thinks about that on their wedding day. Perhaps that's the reason for all the intricacies, the four-tiered cake with alternating yellow and chocolate layers, the little plastic bride and groom atop the thick frosting, the days of indecision that result in just the right shade of pink roses in the bouquet, the back and forth over the typeset on the invitations, the bridesmaids' dresses, chicken or steak, sit-down or buffet, what to use for the toast, and where everyone should sit.

It's all pomp and circumstance to distract you from the inevitable truth. That one day, one of you will agonize over the details again—urn or casket, blue lining or tan, silk or suede, which flowers at the front of the church, which stone for the gravesite, what to wear for this occasion now that you made it to *death do you part.*

I can be pretty pessimistic. Mom pats my hand and leaves me alone again. I wait for the coffee to brew and pour Ray a cup.

Through the pass-through in the kitchen, I see Jack outside in the front yard. I stop short. He's standing on the front lawn, looking nervous. I pick up Ray's cup from the counter and head back into the living room.

Don't go out there, I tell myself.

I go out there.

"What are you doing here?" I ask in a loud whisper, even though no one is around but the two of us.

"Cassie called me," Jack says and steps in to offer that estranged, significant-other, obligatory cheek kiss required on occasions that supersede the awkwardness at hand.

I jerk back from him.

"When did she call you?" I ask. "Is everything ok? Where is she?"

I look around suddenly and slosh some the contents of the coffee cup onto the grass, realizing that I hadn't grabbed the cup with the coffee.

"Vodka?" Jack asks, sniffing deeply.

"Ray," I answer.

Jack nods and touches a tulip with the edge of his shoe.

I stand there, nerves getting the best of me. I bring the coffee mug up to my lips and then remember that it isn't mine and that it isn't coffee. Jack smiles a little.

"Cassie wants to stay with me tonight," Jack says, getting us back on track. "Didn't she tell you she was calling? She told me she told you."

"Do I look like she told me?" I ask, squelching any good humor that might have been forming.

"She's had a rough time," Jack says, donning his Concerned Dad face. "Lay off her."

Suddenly, I want to throw the coffee mug, vodka and all, at Jack's head.

"You don't think I'm aware of that?" I ask. "You don't get to do this, you know."

"Do what?" Jack asks, and I believe he actually doesn't know what I'm talking about, which ticks me off even more.

"Be the good guy," I say. "You don't get to swoop in and save the rough day. You don't get to put out the fire that I've already exhausted myself fighting and call yourself the hero."

Jack scoffs and looks towards the house. I turn as well, watching to see if Cassie is coming out.

"Settle down," he says.

I throw the coffee mug, vodka and all, at his head.

He ducks past the ceramic, but the potent liquid sloshes across his shirt. He doesn't say anything; he just lifts his hands in protest. I hear the front door open and shut, and Cassie sighs when she sees me. She walks over to Jack.

"Hey, Pooh," he says and kisses her forehead.

I want to pick up the mug and throw it at him again.

"What happened to your shirt?" she asks, looking at me.

"I spilled a drink on myself," Jack says. "Wasn't paying attention to what I was doing."

Cassie rolls her eyes and snickers at him, and he pushes her playfully. I want this for her. Even if it hurts me.

"You could have told me you wanted to go, sweetie," I say. "I understand."

Cassie gives me the textbook, teenager head tilt and scoff, eye roll, and hands to hip all in one fluid motion.

"You wouldn't have let me call Dad," she says, so certain.

"Of course I would have," I say, feeling something like

heartbreak at her certainty that I don't care about her. "Do you have your key? Stop by home and get your things."

Not all of your things, I want to say. I notice that there are way too many cars in the drive and lining the street. Mom's neighbor's cat is sitting on the hood of someone's Lincoln Navigator.

"So, you don't care if I stay with Dad for a couple of days?" she asks sheepishly.

A couple of days? I look at Jack to see if he knew this part as well and if it's ok. He shrugs that, no, he didn't know that she wanted to stay a couple of days, but then nods that it's ok with him.

"No, honey, I don't mind," I say, although that isn't true. "I know this is a hard day and you probably want out. That's ok. I understand."

She rolls her eyes again. I think she'd rather I didn't understand her sometimes. Maybe I don't.

"Go ahead to the car," Jack says.

She runs to Jack's car as if I might change my mind. I want to yell at her to "Come back and give your heartbroken mother a hug," but no good will come of that. Jack and I face off, and I know I should apologize for the vodka bath, but I don't.

"Where are you staying, by the way?" I ask.

"Sarah and Bruce's house," Jack says. "They're in Europe for several months. It's free. Still have to pay our mortgage, you know."

"I didn't do this, Jack." I cross my arms in front of me. "I didn't make you leave."

"No?"

"Are you kidding me?" I ask, unfolding my arms and stepping back like I'm assuming some fighting stance with a less-than-threatening name like *wildcat-caught-in-trap* or *backed-in-a-corner-bear.* "Today is not the day for this."

"I didn't start it, Nina." Jack steps closer to me despite my hostile stance. He reaches for my hand, grabbing hold of my forearm instead. "I don't want this," he says and tightens his grip, his face firm and demanding.

I try to yank free of him, but as my arm slips through his grip, he catches hold of my hand. His eyes find my wedding rings still on my finger. He looks at me and I look away. The papers are signed and stamped, filed and final, and I'm still wearing my rings.

"Don't make it mean something," I say.

He runs his fingers softly over the rings.

"Shouldn't it?" he asks, his voice a whisper. "Doesn't it?"

I pull my hand free when I see Cassie walking back toward us.

"What are you guys doing?" she asks, looking back and forth between us. "Dad?"

"Nothing, Pooh," he says and lets go of my hand with a thick sigh. "Let's go."

Cassie looks at me, imploringly. I nod to her to go on and go.

"It's ok," I say. "Everything will be ok."

Because that's what you say to your child. How can you not? I want Jack to look back at me when he walks away, but he doesn't. He doesn't pause to look at me over the top of the car. He just gets in and leaves.

I pick the mug up off the lawn and go back inside the house. In the kitchen, I rinse out the vodka and retrieve Ray's slightly cool cup of coffee. When I finally make it back to the living room, Ray is gone. It's getting late in the afternoon, and most people are saying their good-byes. I have to stop a few times to hug and nod and tell whomever how much I appreciate their being here. A couple of people look at me imploringly—eyebrow lifting, sympathy exuding.

I inch my way through the crowd and out the back door, where I find Ray on the porch. He's sitting in one of Mom's lounge chairs, his legs straddled on either side. He's taken off his suit coat and rolled up the sleeves of his shirt. I hand him the coffee, sit in a lounge chair beside him, and stretch out my legs. We sit for a long few minutes and say nothing. I cut my eyes at him to see what he's thinking. I can't see anything.

"He's five?" I ask, trying to get Ray to talk to me again.

"Yeah," Ray says, and his tone holds no animosity.

I don't really know which question to ask first. It dawns on me whose child it is.

"Why didn't Nicole tell you?"

"She did," Ray says. He takes a solid drink from the mug, unfazed by the tepid temperature. The late afternoon air shifts back toward cool, and I fold my arms over my chest. Ray looks at me and I unfold.

"Oh," I say. "When?"

"She told me she was pregnant when she came to visit me at the prison, right after I went in," Ray says and downs the last of the coffee. "You know, through the glass and all that. She seemed pretty angry at me."

There's nothing I can say that will come out right so I don't say anything. I just watch the sun set behind Mom's dogwood trees and listen to the sounds of cars driving away, of people returning to the safety of their normal lives.

"I guess I didn't handle it well," Ray says, shifting in his chair and biting his lip. "She didn't come back or call."

I have to ask. "What did you say when she told you?"

"I said, 'That's nice.' I told her if she was lucky it wouldn't turn out to be mine."

"What did she say?"

"She said, 'Let's pretend it isn't.' So that's what I did."

I sit up and swing my legs off the lounge chair so I can turn toward him. "That may be the stupidest thing you've ever done, Ray. And you've done some stupid things."

"Thanks for this amazing level of support," he says.

"You're welcome. You deserve every word of it," I say, forgetting that I was trying to play nice.

Ray lifts the cup to his lips and then, realizing it's empty, tosses it into the yard. He rubs his hands over his face. Tattoos flow out from underneath his shirtsleeves.

"We're going to have to buy Mom some new mugs," I say. "I threw one at Jack earlier. Got your vodka all over him."

Ray peeks at me through his hands. His mouth is covered, but I know he's smiling.

I stretch back out on the chair and put my feet up again.

"I called her when I got out," Ray says. "I wanted to see her and the kid too."

"And?"

"She said it wasn't mine," Ray says. "I knew she was lying. Maybe it was a test; maybe it was an out. I don't know."

"What did you do?" I ask.

"Wished her luck and went on with my life," Ray says.

"How do you feel about that?"

"Is this a therapy session?" Ray asks, but doesn't look at me. "I felt like a jerk. I always feel like a jerk."

"What's his name?" I ask.

"Michael." Ray makes a strange little noise like a sigh and snort combined. "I guess she didn't hate me too much."

Michael is Ray's middle name, and Michael's mother, Nicole, is the woman Ray left behind when he went to prison for a few years for repeated stupidity, some minor drug dealing, and grand theft auto. The woman he didn't go back to once he was out. When you add jail to his self-inflicted exile, Ray's been gone for the better part of six years.

"So where did you get the picture?" I ask.

"She gave it to me yesterday," Ray says. "She found me over at the Thirsty Monk, said she heard Dad died. Wanted to see how I was doing."

"I miss her. She was nice," I say.

Ray smirks at me.

"Then she gave me the photo," Ray says, pulling it out from his pocket again. "Said I could call her."

"That's a good thing, right?" I ask.

"No." He shakes his head. "I think she needs money. Not that I won't give it to her. My lawyer says we can have the test done to find out if he's really my kid, but one look at him will tell you that." Ray flips the photo around for me to see again.

He's right.

"Do you want to be more than just the money?" I ask, suspicious of the weight this seems to be laying on him.

"I don't think I deserve to be," he says, and when I open my mouth to speak, he holds up a hand to stop me. "That's what I was telling her back then—through the glass. Nothing's changed about me."

"No?"

"Well, if it has, it's too little, too late," Ray says.

I reach over and take Ray's hand in mine. I fear he'll jerk it away, but he doesn't. Not at first. Our hands seem to grow hot around each other like a transfer of guilt and sadness, and when it seems Ray can bear it no more, he gently pulls his hand from mine.

He sighs and looks at the photo with such longing that my throat tightens. "Do you think I could just send the kid over here and let *him* tell Mom?" Ray asks. He looks hopeful and pitiful.

"I think that's a great idea," I say, feigning support, aware that we're almost joking with each other. "We can lose both of our parents to a stroke."

I know why he chose me though. Telling Lola would make him accountable. She would demand that he stay and would make him choose between his love for everyone else and his hatred for himself.

While he was in prison, Lola painted nothing but him. Ray as a child, Ray as a devil, Ray inside Ray. The art gallery that shows her work sold nearly every painting. I imagine all the living rooms and studies with little art lights illuminating some unknown young man whose sorrow won't let them sleep. At dinner parties, people will wander into the study, bourbon in hand, and ponder aloud to each other, "What could life have done to him to turn his eyes so dark? Have you tried the pâté? It's simply divine."

"He does look just like you," I say. "Poor kid."

Ray laughs. The sound of it seems to scratch its way out of his throat, like it's a sound as hard to make as it is to hear. He punches me in the arm and that old playfulness that we haven't shared since before Lola was hurt catches in my throat. This is how it all could have been.

I think sometimes that the ability to see what might have been is a cruel prank and I don't understand it.

5

Later, after the mourning party is over and Mom's sleeping pills have kicked in, Lola and I sneak up to our childhood bedroom. It's pink and frilly and rife with memory. We open our suitcases and pull on pajamas. We sit cross-legged, like old times, on my bed; she at the foot and me at the head, our knees touching. We both claim to be spending the night with Mom because we don't want her to be alone. While that's true, I think we're both trying to turn back the clock—even just a bit.

"Are you ok with Cassie staying with Jack for a while?" Lola asks, arranging and rearranging herself to get comfortable as if the braces on her legs have surfaced again.

"No," I say, looking at my phone where I've positioned it beside me on the bed. "But I'm going to have to be. It's part of the deal now, I guess."

Jack has already called to tell me that they stopped by the condo, got her things, and that if Cassie needs anything he will be sure to let me know.

I open up my messenger to confirm that Cassie has not replied to my third text about whether or not she needs me to bring her something, or did she want to tell Grandma good night, or did she remember to take her homework because she'll need to go back to school on Monday and does she think she will be at her dad's house until then?

What all of it really means, of course, is *Don't leave me, I'm not ready for this. I'm not ready.*

"Did Chris make it to his plane on time?" I ask, changing the subject. "I'm sorry he had to leave sooner than planned."

"I got a message a few hours ago that he was boarding," Lola says. "He should land soon. They're doing a new spot. I guess that's showbiz—even goofy commercials." She makes the same sighing snort that Ray did. "What exactly did I think caused him to have to go back and forth to LA?" She shakes her head and pulls at a loose thread on the old bedspread.

"I think this is the first time he's gone since you started seeing him. He's been on an extended visit for months now."

"I think you're right," she says, wrinkling her brow. "Where did I think he lived? Was he staying in a hotel all this time?"

She wiggles off my bed and scoots over to her own.

"I don't know," I say. "If I was known as the goofy insurance commercial guy and I met a beautiful woman who didn't recognize me, I wouldn't spill the beans either."

She nods and fiddles with the clock on her bedside table.

"Did Jack come inside?" she says, changing the subject yet again. "I didn't see him."

"No," I say. "He just stole Cassie from the front yard and left."

I make a face at her so she knows I'm exaggerating, but I'm sure she knows that already. Jack's not a bad guy. He was just a bad husband. I think. It's hard to see where you're going when you're lost. You feel shook up, and nothing looks like it would if you knew the way to get to where you were meant to be. Streets don't seem to connect like they should. Tree branches hang too far over the road, and mailboxes seem to leap off their posts and roll underneath your car.

"Probably for the best," Lola says. "How did it go? Him showing up?"

"I threw a coffee mug full of vodka at him," I say.

She snickers. "Welcome to your life, post-divorce."

"You make it sound like a disease," I say. A sickness I didn't see coming and one for which there is no easy remedy.

"Sorry," she says, seeing that I'm not playing into the joke. "I know there was a time when you wanted this to work out."

"Maybe," I say. "More like a time when I was naïve enough to think it would."

Correction—naïve enough to think that it would be easy.

"Did you think it would last?" she asks. "Going in."

"Of course," I say. "Everyone thinks that."

"Was Jack cheating back then? At the start of it?"

I don't mind when she asks me questions like that. Sometimes it's nice to have an opening to talk about things that most people hope you don't bring up because it's awkward for them to listen to.

"I don't know," I say, doubting that he was in the beginning. "He says he wasn't."

"Of course he says that," Lola says. "But he admits to cheating now, right. Like it was a one-time thing or something. Did he tell you how it didn't mean anything?" She rolls her eyes and makes a scoffing sound at the back of her throat.

"He says he never cheated at all," I say. "I saw him though, talking to that girl who worked in his office—that secretary. Body language says it all."

"I thought you said he owned up to it?" Lola said in confusion.

"He says he was 'seeing' someone." I make sarcastic air quotes. "But that he didn't sleep with her."

"Whatever," Lola says. "He's playing semantics."

"It might have been just as much my fault."

Every month that I didn't get pregnant, I built the wall between us higher. After a while, sex stopped being fun and became a basic scientific function. *A man and a woman have sex for the purpose of reproduction. Male and female sexual organs perform mandated tasks to achieve completion of the sexual act in which the male ejaculates sperm into the female. The sperm then makes its way to the egg and begins the process of new life.*

I can almost hear the monotone voice-over from those science films in high school. Except this voice-over goes on to say, *Except in some sad cases in which the poor male toils and labors and sends his fruitless sperm inside the inhospitable female for naught. It will be a useless journey and a battle lost, as the weak sperm peck at the steel egg until their energy is spent and they die.*

Not very sexy.

Then I did get pregnant and everything was great, I think. Then I lost the baby nineteen weeks in and everything broke apart like a plate dropped to the floor. It shattered into pieces that can never go back together, because shards so fine yet so important are lost—too small to see, yet big enough to make it unfixable.

"Maybe if I hadn't taken all the fun out, we'd still be together," I say.

"Doesn't give him the right to go elsewhere," Lola says, ever on my side.

"No, but it makes it understandable."

"It does?"

"This has been hard on Jack, too," I say to Lola. "I wish everyone didn't hate him. I don't hate him."

I want to, but I don't.

"I'm your sister. I can't help but get my hackles up. It just seemed like it didn't faze him and you were going through it alone. I don't understand that."

She's wrong about that, it did faze him, but I don't want to talk about it.

"Hackles?" I question, and she laughs.

"Darn tootin'," she says and throws her pillow at me.

I throw it back at her, and she holds up her finger. She reaches under her bed and pulls out the album cover. She puts it over her face like Dad used to do, and I want to burst into tears and laughter at the same time.

This is Lola's gift. To take what hurts and make it better.

"I love you," I say.

"I know," she says and puts the album cover under my pillow.

Lola goes back to her side of the room and fidgets for a while, looking lost. She gets under her covers and tosses back and forth. I know she's uncomfortable here without her lists. If a hole opens up in her head, she has nothing to close it with. At home, she has everything mapped out. An amnesiac's guide to her ever-changing universe.

I wonder what would happen if her system fell away beneath her. I see her like one of the fireworks from the night everything changed—launched into the sky on its way to nowhere but up. No course of action but to exploded into a million bits of color and fizzle out. I can still hear the boom of those fireworks. When I close my eyes, I see their light etched on the back of my lids. My mouth gets dry from the heat, and my heart races.

I look over to Lola, all these years later. There is nothing I can do about what has already been done.

Without Lola, there may very well be nothing. She might be one of a handful of people who holds the world together. She's one of those people without whom it doesn't really make any sense for God to have gone to so much trouble.

I'm grateful for Chris and hope that he and my sister will fare better than Jack and I did. I wonder about fate and the way people meet. How God must work it all out, just so. Who else could get past that stupid jingle except for the girl who can't remember ever having heard it? Who else could put up with Swiss-cheese brain but the guy who wishes everyone would forget who he is?

Well played, God. Well played.

But about all this other business, I say to Him, *I'm not so sure you're on the right track.*

"Ray came, you know," Lola says from under her covers, breaking my thoughts.

"Yeah," I say, not really listening as I check Facebook, Twitter, and everything else I can think of, looking for Cassie. "It's nice that he's here."

"That's not what I mean," she says and sits up in bed. "He came to the hospital, that first time. When Dad first got sick."

"Really?" I say, letting my grip loosen on the phone, my attention turn to the past. "I didn't see him. Nobody said anything."

"Nobody knew," Lola says. "I saw him in the parking lot. Remember when I went to get some sodas and you complained about how long it took me to get back?"

"I remember," I say, my voice giving away the disappointment of being left out.

"I saw him through the window," she says. "I ran outside. I was yelling out to him, afraid that he'd get back in his car before I got there."

I place the phone down and scoot to the edge of the bed.

"What happened?" I ask.

"He smiled," Lola says, and her face lights at the memory of him. "I hadn't seen him since he left the night of the gallery showing a few weeks after he got out of jail."

She's lost for a second in a secret part of a memory that doesn't include me. I'm jealous of Ray. He gets a part of Lola that I sometimes think he doesn't deserve, but that, nonetheless, I know is what keeps him alive.

"Did he come in?" I ask.

"No," she says. "He had been in North Dakota. Drove all the way. Did you know that's where he was?"

"No."

I rarely knew anything about Ray. When Dad died, it took a lot of message passing from one old friend to the next to find Ray. Knowing about Michael now stands out as even more odd.

"I tried to get him to come see Dad," Lola says. "But he said he couldn't go in. He said he'd seen me and that was all he really came for."

I'm jealous of Lola, too. She gets a part of Ray that no one else does.

"I wish he had come in," I say.

"Me too," Lola says. "I think he wishes it now."

I'm not ready to try to understand his reasons. "Well, he'll just have to live with that."

"Don't be mad at Ray," Lola says. "He came. It's hard for him."

"Poor Ray," I say. "It's hard for the rest of us, too."

I'm sorry Lola is taking the brunt of my sudden anger. I get up from the bed and wander the room aimlessly. I need to move before I shatter.

"I'm sorry, Nina. I know what this means for you. I'm sorry I brought it up."

I know she is. She knows how close Dad and I were.

"Don't be sorry," I say and feel guilty that I'm making her feel responsible for my grief. "It is important that Ray came. I told him as much today. Although not as kindly as I could have."

"You spoke to him," she says, trying to smooth it over. "That means more to him than I'm sure he let on."

There she goes again, weaving it together. Her cell phone

lights up and plays the insurance jingle. I tilt my head at her in a question.

"Just to remind me." She smiles hugely at her own cleverness. "It was on a ringtone app on my phone."

While Lola talks to Chris, I pull the album cover out from under my pillow and look longingly at the photo. I pick up my phone, but set it down without checking anything.

The process of grieving is exhausting. I feel it in my arms like I've been carrying around an anvil, looking for somewhere to set it down and not even understanding how it was that I came to be holding it. Besides, if I set it down now, my body would be so light I might float to the ceiling and what would everyone think? I can hear Mom now—*For Pete's sake, Nina, this really isn't the time to be floating around on the ceiling.*

I should consider myself lucky. I won't drift away into the gray-blue sky and be a dot in a black dress lifting higher and higher until no one can see me as anything other than a balloon jerked away by the wind. I'm heavy enough with grief to stay firmly on the ground.

I think about calling Jack, but I need to learn to face this new life. It seems strange that our time together is through. Things were bad for a long time, but the actual end seemed so sudden, like when you're a teenager in love and don't know that the other half of your union is already calling Sarah Whitmore asking to meet after school on Wednesday because you'll be in piano lessons and unaware that while you're playing your heart out, thinking of him, he'll kiss her for the first time under the bleachers where he first kissed you. You'll be thinking that when the lesson is done, you'll meet him at Dairy Queen like you always do, but he's not coming and you will sit there long into the afternoon, wondering what happened and why you are sitting at this cement circle with the hole in the middle, all by yourself.

Losing Dad came on sudden as well. Even after all that time in the nursing home, him drifting farther and farther away, the call that he was gone still came as a shock. Dad breathed out, and just never breathed in again. Like perhaps he just forgot he was breathing and would remember in a bit and we'd all laugh and say he was trying to trump Lola at forgetting the craziest thing and he'd say *I win.*

That day the stroke happened, I thought he was kidding. We were at Barley's Pizza and he was telling a joke and, mid-sentence, he started slurring his words and cutting out every other one and then he just slipped off his chair and was gone. He never got to the punch line. It hangs out there in front of me like a speech bubble in a comic, but I will never be able to turn the page and see what he would have said next.

Those years in the nursing home were like purgatory, though I don't know if it was his or mine. All of it is so precise and sur-real at the same time. The urine stink and medicine cups, the indignity of hospital gowns when he got too difficult to dress, and Dad's roommate, God bless him, talking about little men in sombreros sitting on top of the television.

When I visited, I would manage to smile all the way out of the building, nodding to the head nurse when she waved at me, and thanking the activities coordinator when she told me how much Dad enjoyed the banjo player who'd been there the other day, or the movie in the great room, or the whatever-the-heck-it-was that they rolled him to that he couldn't have given two licks about. I could even hold it together until I made the turn out of the parking lot. But once I was on the road and headed home, I'd always break down into sobs—those snotty ones that takes several hours to recover from completely.

Lola says her good-byes to Chris, and I try to snap out of my funk.

"Is it better that he knows you know?" I ask when she's off the phone.

"Yeah," she says. "He said that at first he thought it was nice that I didn't seem to care about the commercials. Then he realized that I didn't know about them. But once he figured out why, he felt terrible for letting it go on like that. He said it was just so nice to have the anonymity."

"So are you going to give it go?" I ask. "He seems to really like you."

"Yeah," she says, nodding pointedly. "He's says they'll start shooting the new spot next week. Mom will love it. He wants me to come out there and visit."

"Do you get to be on set?" I say excitedly, glad for this diversion in the conversation. "Can I come?"

"Sure," she says. "But you can't laugh when he sings the jingle."

"I don't know if I can agree to that," I say, unable to keep a smile off my face.

She throws her pillow at me again and bites her lip—just like Ray, so much like Ray.

She sighs heavily. "I doubt I'll go. It's all the way across the country. I don't know if I'm up for that. I'm a chicken, huh?"

"You're the bravest person I know," I say and hand her back her pillow. "Good night, little sister."

"I love you, too," she says to me.

In a short time, Lola is asleep. I see us years ago, before the accident even, before she forgot who she was, before her ankles were bound by metal braces and her life bent beyond recognition. Before we knew there were things we would never understand.

I lay back and close my eyes, wanting black, dark, nothing. But I see too much. I see Dad's nurses, my doctor with his solemn face confirming no heartbeat, Mom's neighbors bringing food, my neighbors asking about Jack's parking space. I see white tulips in the front yard, and I know that before long, they will open too far, bend back, and do their best to look like some other kind of flower, unrecognizable as what they used to be.

Once I'm sure that Lola is asleep, I slip my funeral clothes back on—less because they're the closest and more because they fit my mood—and I sneak out to the car. I never once snuck out of the house when I was younger and doing so now makes me think I can turn back time, get grounded, make us miss the fireworks that fateful night, make it all like it was before.

I ease out of the house and close the front door quietly behind me. Ray startles me out on the front porch. He's still wearing his suit. He's plastered.

"Dad's dead," Ray says. "Did you know that?"

I sit down beside him on the top step.

"I waited him out," Ray says, his words a thick slur. "And what did I prove, except that I am, in fact, the awful son people think I am?"

Ray is drinking straight from Mom's vodka bottle.

"What do you think Nicole has told him?" Ray asks, and I know he means Michael. "That I'm in jail? Or dead. I'm dead, just like Dad," Ray says with finality.

"No," I say, finally finding words. "You're not. You're drunk."

"Same difference," Ray says, taking a swig with one hand and holding the little picture of Michael in the other.

"He's talking to me." Ray holds the picture so it's face-to-face with him. "You hear him?" He tilts his ear like he's listening closely, then fakes a little kid voice.

"'Man up, mister,'" he makes the little boy in the photo say. "'Cut the crap and do what's right for once in your pathetic, wasted life.'"

Ray looks at me and shakes his head. "I want to tell that little face to watch his mouth," he says, faking a stern face and voice.

"But I got it coming. I want to say my name's not 'mister.' But so far as he knows, it is."

He's a little face in a photo and Ray's an awkward question, a subject best changed.

"Ray," I say, but I don't know how to finish the sentence.

He sets the now-empty bottle on the porch and tucks the photo into his wallet. He shucks off his coat and tie. He undoes the button at his collar and takes a deep breath.

"Are men supposed to be able to breathe in a suit?" he asks, forming his words like he has a mouth full of rocks. "Maybe that's why men in suits look so uptight. They can't breathe, and everything is a very deliberate effort not to choke to death." He laughs out loud.

I smile a little. Ray always had a sense of humor—when he'd let down his guard.

"Give me your keys, Ray," I say and hold out my hand. *Go sleep in the bathtub.*

He doesn't resist.

"I went to the service," he says. "I sat in the back of the church. Me and some guy from Dad's nursing home. He asked me who I was, and I said I was the guy who mowed the family's lawn."

"Mom should fire you," I say, attempting a joke. "The grass looks awful."

He smiles at me. It's a crooked, drunk smile, but I can see Ray underneath the cover of alcohol.

"Where are you going?" he asks me, looking me up and down. "It's after dark."

"Out," I say. "It's getting hard to breathe."

"That's because you got your tie tied too tight," Ray says, tripping over the alliteration.

That may very well be.

Ray struggles to stand up. He wobbles a bit, but manages.

"Going to sleep?" I ask.

"That's a nice way to put it," Ray mumbles and goes off to pass out somewhere.

As a teenager, Ray squealed tires in and out of the driveway, banged in the front door, shot the stink eye at whoever was in his line of sight, then tromped upstairs to his room. He was determined to be angry. Determined to stay agitated and ticked off and if he stepped on your toes on his way across the room, all the better.

I think he hoped we'd kick him out of our lives if he was gruff enough. I saw on the news once where a man had "committed suicide by cop" or some such phrasing. For a time, Mom was sure Ray would do something like that. Pull one of his stunts and get himself killed. But Dad called it. He knew us all so well. He said that Ray wasn't about to get himself killed. Dead, he couldn't go on torturing himself and everyone in his path. Dad didn't say it angry; he didn't mean it as an insult. It was just the truth.

Ray did pull a few stunts that got him handcuffed and locked up for a bit here and there. He'd leave town, then turn back up with a new tattoo but the same angry face. He'd make a half-hearted effort and then disappear. Then he finally got himself put away. Dad said that was what Ray wanted. What better place from which to loath the world and your place in it than prison?

That was right before the stroke.

Now, with Ray safely inside the house, I pull out of the driveway and head into town. I don't want to be alone, but I don't want to talk to anyone either.

There's not much open after nine p.m. on a Thursday except bars and restaurants and both are too lively for someone mourning the dead. So I go into the Book Exchange—a late-night cavernous maze of old books and busts of dead writers with low lighting from antique lamps and soft armchairs to fall into.

I wind my way past a few other patrons who are talking softly to each other over cups of coffee and leaning in to chat about stories other than the ones they are living. This seems the perfect place to hide from the world. I find a spot in the back corners of the room and sink down into a low couch. I lay my head back and close my eyes. I don't find solitude for long.

"Remember me?" a voice says. "Oliver, from Elm Village."

I raise my head and open my eyes. It had only been a few days ago that I had hugged him a good minute longer than was socially acceptable and then kissed him full on the mouth. His hair is the color of soft balsa wood, and even in the low light of the bookstore, his eyes are like the liquid flow and pool of the river's edge, at times both green and blue, murky and translucent.

"May I sit with you?"

I nod, and he sits, shifting around in the seat until he appears much more comfortable than I am.

"Your name's Nina," he says.

"Yes, it is," I reply, trying not to look him in the face again.

"I knew that," he says. "You know—then."

The parking lot.

"I'm glad," I say. "It makes that whole scene slightly less desperate, don't you think?" I reach out to fuss with the magazines on the coffee table in front of us, and the low light of the bookstore catches the gold rings still on my finger.

"Married?" Oliver asks.

I pull my hands back, hiding the rings. My face feels puffy and worn out. "Divorced. Recently." I look away.

"Don't give yourself a hard time. About the kiss, I mean." Oliver dips his head so that he looks me in the eye, stopping my unnecessary straightening of things that were not out of order. "It's part of my job to comfort people."

"Yes, but do most people cling to you and smell your hair? And then kiss you on the mouth like they're not a total stranger?"

He shifts again, looking a little less comfortable, but making no move to leave. The walls seem to close in, and the soft bookstore music becomes more noticeable.

"Did you really smell my hair?" he asks and runs his hand through it almost apologetically.

"I did," I admit. "It smelled nice."

The light is low in the store, but I can still see the pink in his cheeks.

"I get that a lot actually," he says.

"Strange women make passes at you often?" I ask, completely embarrassed.

"You weren't a total stranger. I've seen you around." He smiles at me, and again I feel a sense of comfort wash over me, telling me not to sweat it so much. "And you weren't making a pass," he says. "I know that. And no, I actually don't have a lot of women kissing me. I meant I often run into people who are seeking comfort. It's kind of nice, I have to admit. I wish they weren't sad, but I like being able to help."

"Well, the ladies must eat that up," I say.

"Sometimes," he says with a tilt of his head and a shrug. "It's the scrubs I wear for work. Women go crazy for them in the grocery store. They think I'm a doctor."

"You don't tell them any different?" I say, amused and distracted.

"You kidding?" He leans closer to me as if he's telling me a secret. "Buys me some time. Much better than what I really do."

"What you really do is commendable," I say. "Most people wouldn't be able to face all that every day."

"Maybe I ought to stick with the truth," he says and raises his eyebrows like he's made a joke, but if so, I don't get it. "Different uniform," he says, "same principle."

He leans away from me and fusses with the collar of his shirt.

He meets my gaze and winks at me. I've been out of the dating scene a long time, but I remember a wink being a flirtatious thing. With Oliver, though, I think it's just a wink—what it means, I have no idea.

"It's been awhile since anyone has kissed me," he says. "You caught me off guard."

"Don't worry about it," I say. "I kiss everybody. I just kissed that guy over there."

I point to a patron perusing the ancient history shelves. Oliver laughs out loud.

"It was a nice kiss, I have to confess," he says and looks a little forlorn. "I had forgotten."

He says it like he's much older than he must be. He can't yet be thirty, but he speaks as if he's come back into the world from some faraway place and time. He looks at me, and suddenly there are questions across his face that I think I'm supposed to have an answer to, but I don't quite know what they are. I can only imagine that my face looks much the same.

I should pull away from this, but the feeling of connection is intoxicating. We both seem very aware of an electricity between us. This isn't like me. I don't do things like this. I see other people do it and am envious. I've even "liked" a couple of posts from old high school friends who were in the midst of middle-aged new love.

Seriously, they would write. *I forgot what this feels like. Head over heels.*

I wonder if this is how Jack felt. I can understand how he let himself get carried away by the excitement, the racing heartbeat, the attention. This is how we should have made each other feel, but I suppose it's too late for that now.

"Can I be honest with you about something?" Oliver asks.

"Sure."

"I've been thinking about that kiss," he says very quietly, looking over his shoulder as if someone might hear him. "I've been thinking that I'd like to kiss you again."

He looks different in plain clothes. Older, but not by much. I can almost see forty in my rearview mirror, and if he's twenty-five I'd be amazed.

Oh, my. I am sitting in a dark bookstore with a gorgeous younger man and thinking about doing something really rash.

Do it girlfriend

Send us pictures

How young are we talking?

Like

Like

Like

"I think that would be ok," I say and then shake my head. "Well, that sounded lame. I'm sorry, I'm not used to the dating scene. It's been a while. I didn't expect to be back here again."

"Me either," he says.

Oliver and I sit for a few moments in that uncomfortable sort of silence that's created by wanting to say something but having nothing safe to say. We watch each other watch each other. We laugh at each other's awkwardness a time or two. Whatever this is, the electricity is still sparking and it starts to feel pretty good.

"It was a good funeral," he says, breaking the growing silence and the awkward unanswered offer of kissing and being kissed. "I hope it's all right that I went."

"Of course," I say, impressed that he had been there. "I saw a few faces from Elm Village, but I must not have seen you. Not that I would have had the nerve to speak to you."

He waves his hand to let me know that apologies and regrets are unnecessary.

"I'm glad I had the day off and could attend," he says. "It's weird to come in to work in the morning and be given this laundry list of reports, with part of it being the news that Mrs. So-and-So is in the hospital, and 212A died. I hate when they use the number like that. Nate was more than 212A."

"Thank you for saying that," I say, emotion trekking across my chest.

He smiles and winks at me again. It's completely benign and surprisingly comforting. I feel like I did in the parking lot before I kissed him and made things weird. How he manages to wiggle back and forth between friend and possibility, I'm not sure. Perhaps it's more indecision than anything else. I'm sure he can sense that he's welcome to—but yet, he doesn't.

"So how was the family mourning vigil?" he asks, scooting back from me and hitching his knee up on the couch. "I hate that part. What are you supposed to say to all those people? How many times can you handle someone telling you what a terrible loss it is?" He moves his leg back down and slides back closer to me. "Duh, huh? Thanks for forcing me to talk about it over and over to every unearthed aunt and uncle within a day's drive."

I laugh. An actual laugh, deep and real. One that almost makes me cry, but then pushes into more laughter. It's a different laugh than Lola and I shared in our room reliving old memories and taking about boys.

I need this release from the grief and the weight of missing Dad. I need to get out from under the loss of my marriage and the uncertainty of my future. I need to stop checking my phone every two seconds to see if my teenage daughter still loves me.

I need to find happy again, but I have no idea how to do that.

I've spent the last twenty years of my life being everything to someone else and feeling guilty when I thought of myself. I'm not even sure what I'm guilty of, but it makes me sad. I've been holding onto my guilt like he's an old friend, like I'm showing him around town for the weekend, pointing out all the tourist traps and scenic views. I need to send him home. I need to stop feeling guilty for wanting, dreaming, hoping.

"It was fantastic," I say in answer to Oliver's question.

"Glad to hear it," he says, and the corners of his mouth turn up.

I feel an urge to press my lips to his again. I'm like the last moments of the tulip now. I feel my petals pulling backwards, bending me toward something I don't recognize.

"Want some coffee?" he asks. "Do you have to be home or can you stay?"

"I shouldn't," I say, still thinking about the kiss he offered.

"Drink coffee or stay and talk to me?" he asks, his eyes clearly showing that he hopes I'll stay.

I feel yanked back in time to a place much less burdened with responsibility and the knowledge of life's cruel pranks. I need this escape.

Ok, guilt, I say to my old friend, *you sit over there for a while and read a book. I need a break.*

"Decaf," I say.

He smiles widely, and I can see that I'm in deep trouble.

I'm hooked before my coffee mug is half empty. The longer Oliver and I stay, the closer we get, and by the time the bookstore music loop has repeated itself at least once, we're pressed beside each other on the couch with no more room between us than the space a heartbeat takes.

I look back once at my guilt. He's sitting in on a book club meeting and talking to a lady about *Jane Eyre*.

Just a few more minutes, I signal to him, and he nods.

I turn my focus back to Oliver. This isn't like the parking lot, where I was too caught up in my own crazy grief to notice what being close to Oliver feels like. We sit beside each other, talking about everything and nothing. His knee is against mine, and I touch his arm unnecessarily when I speak. He touches my hand where I have it resting on my own leg just so that it's available. He moves his fingers across the back of my hand, and the softness of his touch electrifies me. As he presses his hand more firmly against mine, I turn my palm over to meet his fingers as they search out mine.

I feel giddy and a little sick to my stomach. We run out of things to say and that offer of another kiss hangs between us, visible and pulsing.

"I don't know if this is the right thing to do," I whisper, my fingers interlaced with his, my face turned to his, my lips inches from his.

His lips press first against my cheek like a test, and I release a breath I didn't know I was holding. Then when he kisses me, I'm aware of nothing but his mouth on mine, warm and unfamiliar. He puts his free hand against my face and then pushes his fingers through my hair until they find the back of my neck. His hands on me feel like I'm coming up out of the water, air hitting wet skin piece by piece. This time, it doesn't feel like the pathetic science movie. This time, it feels like waking up.

I think of Jack and his lopsided smile, and I catch a glimpse of my buddy, guilt, across the room. I close my eyes and ignore both of them.

This divorce isn't what I wanted. Jack did this same thing. I think.

I stop thinking, just in case.

"I think the store is closing," Oliver whispers in my ear, his lips brushing the side of my face when he talks. "Walk with me for a while and talk some more, yes?" He asks like he's seeking permission.

Outside on the sidewalk, Oliver puts his arm around my

waist, and I slide into him. He whispers something in my ear, but his words are breathy and my head is fuzzy so I don't understand him, but I laugh anyway. I turn my face up to his and he kisses my nose. When I look back toward the street, I see Jack across the road.

I blink, and then it's not Jack after all.

We walk past my car in the parking lot and down a few blocks toward a little section of old houses with quirky flower gardens and yard sculptures that catch the moonlight and toss it back out as magic. Oliver stops in front of one of the houses and bounds up the stoop. I remain on the sidewalk, and he looks back at me quizzically.

"Is this your house?" I ask. "Maybe I should go home."

He closes his eyes and turns toward the sky, relief and regret on his face, and I wonder what his story is. Bad breakup? Still in a relationship, perhaps? I realize how much I don't know about him.

He comes back down the steps. I want so much to be that romantic type who throws caution the wind. I imagine said wind, loaded down with the cares of innumerable people caught up in moments too strong for them, too passionate or reckless, desperate and unmanageable. I imagine some French couple at an outdoor café in Paris, sipping their coffee, smoking their cigarettes, being blown right out of their chairs by some rogue, heavy laden wind from the other side of the world. *Crazy American fools,* they would say, righting their chairs, lighting a new cigarette, calling for the garçon to bring new cups of coffee and perhaps a patisserie while he's at it.

"The voice of reason," he says, and reaches for my hand. "Wise and mostly unwelcome by those about to make bad decisions."

I hold his hand and we sit on the stoop. "I'm sorry," I say. "Still recently divorced. Still don't really know what I'm doing."

"Hmm," he says and exhales deeply. "Yeah, I'm coming off a difficult breakup of sorts myself. I have no idea what I'm doing either."

I twist the ring on my finger that, despite the paperwork that's been signed, filed, and finished, I still wear. I know this is impulsive and most likely a bad idea. Yet, I feel like I'm walking backwards, trying to undo something that I really don't want to forget.

"I know what it's like to be caught in between what you know and how you feel," Oliver says. "Let me get you a coat and I'll walk you to your car."

I wrinkle my brow.

"You're shivering," he says. "These spring nights can get chilly."

"I don't think that's why I'm shivering," I say, finding it easy to be honest with him.

I look him in the eye, and he kisses me softly on the lips. The wind blows and I wonder if that poor French couple will forgive me the intrusion on their peaceful day. It's just a light breeze after all, nothing to disrupt them too much. Although it's disrupting me something powerfully.

Oliver leads me up the steps into his house. The interior is clean and sparse. The small living room holds a couch, an old rocker, and a small television. The most dominating thing about the room is a wall of music—songbooks, at least three guitars that I can see, CDs, a stereo system, and an old piano.

"Does anyone still listen to actual CDs anymore?" I ask, running my hand along the line of plastic cases.

"Believe it or not, that's pretty high tech in this house," Oliver says.

"Do you live here alone?" I ask as he closes several large books that were open across each other on the coffee table and tosses them onto the floor beside the couch.

He disappears down the hall and returns with a gray, hooded sweatshirt.

"I do now," he whispers, handing me the hoodie, which I pull over my head and down across my body.

I don't ask for details even though I find myself wanting them. He doesn't offer any more information. This young man's house is far from where I thought I'd be tonight. There's a place in my gut that yells at me for putting Dad aside like this, for pushing Cassie and Jack from my mind. But the option is either this or sleeping in my childhood bed quilted in by the heavy-handed stitching of the way things end up.

"I'll walk you back to your car," he says, and reaches out to adjust the hoodie so it fits properly across my shoulders as best it can.

"Thank you for staying a while," he says after the short and silent walk to my car.

You're welcome seems a strange thing to say so I offer something else even stranger, "Will you kiss me one more time?" I feel foolish now that I've said it out loud.

He looks at me with such focus and concern that I think he's going to say no. He steps closer to me and touches my cheek.

"Nina," he says and pulls me to him in a tight embrace. "I'm glad I found you tonight."

I give in to the hard clinch of muscled arms holding me tight to this semi-stranger who may be the only piece of the world that makes any sense to me right now. I let go of everything that holds me in. Forty years of everything that means anything collects in the palm of my hands, the shallow of my throat, the escape of my breath.

"Me too," I whisper into his hair.

He steps back from the embrace, but his hands are still around my waist. I place my hand on his chest, and he twitches and pulls back just a bit.

"I understand," I say.

"It's not you, Nina," he says. "And, yes, I would like to kiss you again."

Suddenly I feel tears behind my eyes and I couldn't stop them even if I tried, so I don't.

Before I have time to say anything, he presses his lips to my cheeks, my eyes, the tip of my nose. I can't do much but hold on as it all slips out, uncontrolled and unexpected. There is nothing that can be done, but to give way to it.

I have this memory of lying on the ground underneath the dogwood tree in my childhood backyard. I'm seven. Bluish-purple petals float down over me from way above. The sunlight is so sharp I can't see where it's all coming from. I hold my hands up to catch the tiny pieces of blue, satin snow. I turn my head and see Dad's long legs; he's holding a hydrangea bloom like a dandelion puff, wisping it through his hands to let loose the little petals over me.

Oliver kisses my cheek one last time, sighs, and pulls back from me.

"Nina," he says, "I'm sorry. This isn't right. I shouldn't have done this. This isn't what you need now."

"Don't be sorry," I whisper. "I don't know where my mind is right now. I'm just out of sorts."

"Of course you are," he says.

Oliver takes hold of my hand, and the simplicity of the gesture makes me cry again. I rest my head on his shoulder, and we stand quietly in the glow from the streetlamp until I have collected myself.

"I'm ok," I finally say and pull away, searching for my keys and righting myself to leave.

"Take care of yourself," he says.

"I'll try," I say.

Oliver opens the door for me and I get in. He pats the roof once I've closed the door and started the engine. He waves, and as I'm pulling away, my guilt taps on the window. I roll it down a smidge and let him in. He buckles up next to me, and we ride back to Mom's house.

I go upstairs but can't seem to go into my old room where I hope Lola will still be sleeping soundly. I go into the bathroom instead. I don't turn on the light. I just stand there in the dark and breathe. I take a towel off the rack and push open the shower curtain. I make a pillow of the towel and curl up in the tub and fall asleep.

6

Nina."

Someone is calling my name through a thick fog. I hear it again and force my eyes open. Lola is standing over me, and I'm not sure where I am.

"What are you doing in there?" she asks.

"What?" I say, and when I try to move, I find that every inch of my body is sore.

"Why are you sleeping in the bathtub?"

I look up, confused. I'm in Mom's bathroom. The walls are papered with that loud and slightly nauseating big-fat flower motif that makes it feel like you've got your head stuck in a kaleidoscope. It's not helping the headache I developed from sleeping with my neck bent against the side of the tub.

"I woke up and you were gone," she says. "I thought maybe you went home. Maybe to Jack's? I was thinking maybe Cassie called and you went to get her."

"Is Cassie here?" I say, alarmed.

I flounder around, trying to get out of the tub. Lola lends a hand and helps me out.

"Did she call?" I ask.

Lola puts her hands on my shoulders and looks me in the eye. "Oh, my," she says. "You're a wreck. And no, Cassie didn't call, and no, she's not here. Thank goodness. What's the matter with you?"

I sigh and wiggle out from under her touch.

"Have you been in there all night?" she asks, standing behind me so that I can see her over my own shoulder in the bathroom mirror.

"No," I say, wiping my face like I can wipe off the night before. "I went out. I went to the bookstore. I woke up in the bathtub."

"That makes no sense at all." She chuckles.

"I'm a terrible person." I move past her to sit on the rim of the bathtub. "I'm a horrible daughter and a hussy no less."

Lola laughs at the ridiculous word. "Well, that seems a bit much. So you went to Jack's—"

I shake my head.

"You didn't see Jack?"

I shake my head again.

"Oh," she says.

She kneels in front of me and pulls my hands away from where I've covered my face. It feels like we could be teenagers again, talking about Robbie Highsmith and the incident under the football bleachers.

"Nina," she says.

My name alone is a call for me to answer her.

"Remember I told you I kissed some guy in the parking lot of the nursing home when I went to get Dad's things?" I say.

She puts her hands over her mouth in a classic movie moment and sits cross-legged on the plush, mauve bathroom rug.

"Wait a minute," she says, squinching her face. "You went to the nursing home last night? That's really weird, Nina."

"No." I wave off her comment. "I ran into him at the Book Exchange downtown."

"You did it in the bookstore?" she asks, seeming shocked but also impressed.

"No!" I shout. "Of course not."

I put my hands back over my face. She pries them away again and raises her eyebrows for me to continue.

"Nothing like that, but we were talking and flirting on the couch like a couple of teenagers," I say.

"He's a lot closer to that age than you are," she says and nudges my toes with hers.

I sigh a very guilty sigh.

"Did anyone see you?" she asks, and I can't tell what she wants the answer to be.

"I'm pretty sure I heard a few tsk-tsks," I say, mortified.

"Awesome," she says. "You need to take off your Nina costume every once in a while."

I'm not the girl who makes out with strangers. I'm not the girl who does things on a whim. I'm the grown woman who has an IRA and a 401K, a teenage child who barely speaks to me, a failed marriage, and a broken heart because life is unfair. I'm the woman who hasn't been wanted by a man in a long time, not even her own husband, because she was too weighed down in form and purpose and failure to accept pleasure and happiness.

"So how was it?" Lola asks, oblivious to my inner anguish. "Was he a good kisser?"

"That sounds childish," I say and wrinkle my nose.

"Still," Lola says, excited. She moves to sit on the edge of the tub beside me. "I bet it was amazing and you felt ten years younger. No, wait, twenty years younger. Oh my, how old is this guy? I'm not going to have to bail you out of jail when his mother finds out, am I?"

I punch her arm, and we laugh.

"Shut up, Lola," I say, trying to sound serious. "I feel awful.

What could have come over me to hook up with a total stranger on the night of Dad's funeral?"

"He's not a total stranger," Lola says. "He brought you an orange juice that time you spilled your coffee while you were ranting and raving about that nurse who wouldn't listen when Dad first took that bad turn."

"That was him?" I ask. "I forgot about that. How did you remember it?"

"I'm not a sieve," she says. "And there was only one guy working in that department anyway. It has to be him. I can't believe you made out with the orange juice hottie."

"I'm glad I'm making your day." I pretend to scowl at her.

"You always do," she says and holds my hand. "Look, people handle grief the way they handle it."

"I know you're right," I say, "but it's just not me."

"Maybe that's a good thing."

I nod. Lola works her magic over me, telling me not to hate the part of me that has found a way to bear this for a moment.

"Don't torture yourself over this," she says. "There are worse things that you could have done. I'm just joking, you know. I know you aren't the type to go home with some random guy."

"He wasn't that random," I say, finding a smile. "And yes, he was a very good kisser."

I see my guilt hovering by the toilet. I stand up and try to leave the bathroom but Lola stands up with me and holds out her arms to me. I sink into them.

"It's ok," she says.

"I know how Jack feels now," I mumble into her hair.

"That's just the guilt talking," she says.

I look over to the toilet, but my guilt isn't there. I pull my face out of Lola's hair and find him standing right next to me.

"So," Lola says, pulling back, unable to contain herself. "Is he going to ask you to the prom?"

I want to be mad at her, but it's suddenly really funny, and when I laugh, my guilt turns into a thin mist, barely seen.

"Will Dad approve?" she asks, and we stop laughing.

"Of course not," I say. "Dad never liked any of our boyfriends. He was right about every one of them."

"Oh, no," she says. "What do you think he would have said about Chris?"

"He would have ribbed you mercilessly," I say, smoothing down her morning hair. "Then he would have told you to cut the guy some slack."

"You think he would have liked him," she says.

"Not that he would have told you," I say. "But yes. Chris is good to you. And Dad would have approved."

"Do you think you're going to see this guy again?" she asks. "The Orange Juice Hottie?"

I shrug. I'm not really sure what last night was. It didn't feel like a one-night stand—opportunistic and shallow and over before it gets started. This felt like a beginning—not the physical parts, but something deeper.

Lola touches the sleeve of my black dress. "You better change," she says and winks. She runs her hands over my hair, dark, but not as deep and radiant as her own. She tries to sort me out so that I'm presentable. "You're so cliché right now. Last night's dress, hair a mess. This just won't do in our movie, it's way too predictable."

"So what happens next?" I say.

"You change clothes and come to breakfast," she says, hoisting herself up on the counter, thinking. She's telling our story this time. "Mom is none the wiser. You think about Orange Juice Hottie all day. You find out his phone number, call him but hang

93

up when he answers. Then you wander around his block until you accidently bump into him when he's checking his mail."

I wrinkle my nose. "I don't think I'm going to let you write my movie anymore."

"Too cliché?" she asks. "Too 'stalker in the bushes'?"

"Too desperate and sad," I answer and hope that she's not right.

"Anyway," she says and opens the bathroom door. "You've got to see what Mom's been setting up on the dining room table. Clean up and get down there."

Lola leaves me in the bathroom, and I run a shower. I can still feel Oliver's touch, and I'm afraid that the water will wash him away. I was crazy. Impulsive. Totally out of character. But Lola's right—maybe that's a good thing. My character is too sad right now, and I want to be someone else.

This is the part of the movie where the lead shucks off some past heartache and flies to Italy where she will start a new life and find a new man and attempt to be a better version of who she once was, only to find out, of course, that she is who she always was. But now she's just overseas and doesn't understand what anyone is saying. But it's not all bad. Her new man is gorgeous, and she has all the free olives she could ever want.

I towel off and comb through my hair. In the mirror, I see my guilt floating just over my shoulder. For just a second, I see Cassie and Jack in the thick, foggy middle of the guilt. They're talking to each other, and then they notice me and turn away.

Downstairs I see what Lola is talking about. Mom has lost her mind.

"Mom?" I ask, approaching her like she's wearing a vest full of dynamite. "What are you doing?"

"I'm keeping myself busy, Nina," she says, walking around the dining room table, touching a book here and a paper craft there.

"With every hobby known to man?" I ask.

"These are all the things I wanted to try out while your father was at Elm Village," Mom says, admiring the array. "I bought all the supplies. I just never got around to doing them."

The table is "set" with each place setting like a display ad for a different hobby or subject of interest. Lola's childhood place is a "How to Knit Sock Puppets" project, complete with manual, socks, buttons, and yarn. Ray's seat is laid out with tarot cards and a Magic 8-Ball. My place holds a paint-by-numbers set and *Starting Fresh: A Widow's Guide to Second Chances,* while Mom's place at the table is covered in colored tissue paper and sports one pre-made giant tissue paper flower. Dad's is *Mummies for All Occasions: How to Make Your Own Halloween Masks.*

"I'm hoping something will spark my fancy," Mom says and picks up the paper flower to smell it. "Do you think Cassie would want to do one of these with me?"

"Mom," I say. "It's barely daybreak. When did you set this up?"

"Isn't it great?" Lola says, picking up one of Dad's brown dress socks. "Mom, let's do the puppets first."

"I couldn't sleep last night," Mom answers my question. "I didn't want to wake you kids up. Did I?"

Lola and I exchange a quick glance and smile.

Ray comes up from the basement den, rubbing his eyes. I get a flash of Ray as a child, back when he used to meet us in the kitchen for breakfast. Back when there was breakfast. Before Mom was forever at Lola's side and we were left to fend for ourselves. There were also the mornings when Dad made French toast or crepes or something fantastic and elaborate to hold our attention so that we wouldn't ask for mom and he wouldn't have to explain that Mommy was in the bathroom and not feeling well. We knew fancy breakfast meant Mom was hungover.

"Do you miss Mom?" I had asked Ray once after the accident—after Mom flipped a switch.

"She can't help it," Ray had said. "She's in a lose-lose situation."

I didn't really understand what he meant then. But I realize now that Ray was letting her off the hook. He was cutting the apron strings himself. It was brave of him, but, I think in part, it was also his way of taking on all of the blame.

Now, we all stand around looking at him like we've spotted a ghost.

Mom moves her hand like she's going to reach out to him, but she hesitates.

"Good morning, Ray," Lola says and hugs him.

He doesn't put his arms around her, but she doesn't let go. He looks at me over Lola's shoulders, and I nod at him. He wraps his arms around her, but just for a moment. She turns him loose. He picks up a book titled *Contacting the Dead for Dummies.*

"What's going on?" he asks.

"I love you, Mom," Lola says and gives her a hug, too.

"I know," she says. "I know."

Mom is one paper flower away from being committed. She picks up the book from Dad's spot, flips through it, and asks Ray, "Do you want to be a werewolf for Halloween?"

"I'm forty-four years old," he answers.

"Ok, then," Mom says. "A mummy it is."

It's funny and I want to laugh, but I find that I can't give her the satisfaction. I don't like that I'm withholding it from her, even if she doesn't know it.

"I'm going to go into the office," I say and move dramatically—maybe overly so—away from the table of insanity. "I really should get some work done today."

"I thought you took the day off," Mom says. "What about Cassie? When is she coming back from Jack's?"

"I did," I say. "But I'll go crazy just idling around. Too many things to think about. And I don't know that she is coming back from Jack's."

"Oh, don't be melodramatic," Mom says.

"Happy daydreaming," Lola says.

On my way out the door, I hear Ray ask Lola what she's talking about. I don't hear what she tells him. If I've provided a way for them to start talking I won't even be mad.

Reaching for the door handle, I'm reminded of Oliver standing next to me last night, holding me close and kissing the tears off my face. I touch my cheek and think that I can still feel the warmth of his lips against my skin.

At work, I call Cassie and get her voice mail.

"Just call me back," I say, trying not to sound desperate. "You can stay at Dad's if you want to; I just want to talk to you."

I hang up and wait for her to call. I figure she's screening— mostly to avoid me—and try not to be too heartbroken over that. I fail. Her phone is a light blue, glittery extension of her hand. I know she's seen that I have called.

When all else fails, I work. I read over way number sixteen to make lemonade. It involves fresh ginger root. Since the recipes are simple enough, I've decided to actually make them. I'll photograph the ingredients, the process, and finally the finished glass. I'm outside in the "garden," a space the company built for us to go and meditate. Translated: a place to storm off to when the stress is too high. But it is beautiful, and I have this idea to shoot the lemonade as if it were being made in the midst of a lovely, impromptu picnic.

"So, this is what you do all day?" Jack's voice says behind me. "Pour me a glass?"

I turn around to face Jack but all I can see is Oliver. I know I'm blushing, and I have no idea how Jack reads that. I get nervous and drink the glass of ginger lemonade that I'm supposed to photograph. Jack tilts his head at me.

"Let's go inside," I say and hurry Jack out of the garden.

"What about your camera?" he asks as I'm pushing him up the stairs.

I don't really want him to come to my office. I want him to go back out into the street and go away. I feel like I'm going to blurt out what I did and how fantastic it felt—even if I did end up a teary wreck. I need the florescent lights of an office, the whir of the printer, and the low mumble of voices to distract me so I don't spill my guts.

Inside my office, Jack walks around the room. He picks up a knickknack here and there and turns over an award I got last year for a sushi book. Why couldn't they assign me another one of those? There are only so many lemons one person can stand.

"Did I go to this?" he asks, holding out the award to me.

"No," I say. "You were at that conference in Atlanta."

He nods. I don't think he was in Atlanta. I think he was with Ashley. Jack sets the award down and wrinkles his face. I want to hate him. I want to rant about "for better or for worse," but our vows didn't actually say anything about "for sex or for no sex" so I may have to let him off on one of those technicalities. Sure, I had a valid issue with it, as my therapist said, but psychological cause or not, Jack needed physical affirmation from me that he was loved and worthy and I couldn't give it to him. So he got it from his receptionist, Ashley, and his boss's assistant, Sarah, and that so-cute-you-want-to-punch-her hippie chick from the dry cleaners.

Ok, maybe Lola has a point too.

"So, what's Ray been up to?" Jack asks nonchalantly like the answer to that isn't usually "jail time" or "I don't know, no one has heard from him in years."

"What are you doing here, Jack?" I ask. My voice sounds cruel though I don't mean it to. "Where's Cassie?"

He sighs and comes closer to me. He smells nice, and I hate that I notice.

"She's at home," he says. "Your place. I think she just wanted to prove a point by calling me. I don't know what that point was. If you're going to be at your mom's for a while, I can drive her back over there."

"No," I say. "I'll get my stuff after work and go home. I want her to be comfortable. I think she just wants to be where things are familiar."

"I think she'd have to go back in time for that," Jack says, and smirks wistfully. "Look, Nina, can't we try this again? That apartment I rented is crap."

"I thought you were at Bruce's," I say.

"They're coming back soon, and I can't have all my stuff over there getting in their way," he says. "Besides, it's lonely. I miss having someone around."

"Someone," I say. "But not me?"

"I meant you," he says. "Of course you, Nina. You and Cassie. I hate this." He raises and lowers his arms in a frustrated huff.

"Being alone?" I ask. "I hated it, too. I was alone, and you were right there."

"Yeah," he says, his eyes hard and his brow furrowed. "Ditto."

I feel the same old argument coming, and I know the best way to shut him down.

"I'm sort of seeing someone," I say, shocked at myself. It's not true, really, but it could be.

"Yeah, you told me," Jack says, deflating my attempt to stick it to him. "You kissed some kid in the parking lot at the old folks' home. Don't be ridiculous. Is this about the divorce? I gave you everything you wanted."

"Really?" I ask. It's a low blow.

"Nina, I know the whole baby thing has been hard, and I've tried to be supportive, but I'm tired of it all. I just am. I'm sorry."

"Doesn't matter," I say and look away from him. "Like I said, I'm moving on."

I forgot that I told him about kissing Oliver in the parking lot. Jack had called me once I was in the car and I felt so silly and ashamed that I had blurted it out. Like I needed to confess it to him even though we were through.

"Is this about the baby stuff?" he asks. "I didn't mean it."

"Don't," I say, and that's all I can manage on the subject. I know we're both recalling the same conversation. I know he didn't mean what he said.

"I didn't mean it was all for the best," he says anyway. "I said that. But that's not what I meant."

I sit at my desk and focus on memos and paper clips, the phone, my empty coffee cup. Anything.

"We could try again," he says.

"You know there's no need to," I whisper.

"We could adopt." He comes back to me, sits on the edge of the desk. "Cassie would be thrilled, I sure. Or at least, she'd try to be. I can get the money together, and we can get a little Guatemalan baby. You can be like one of those celebrities who adopt a bunch of kids. We'll adopt ten of them. Give those Hollywood types a run for their money."

"I think we'd lose that race," I say and almost smile.

"Are you sure?" Jack asks.

"It's too late for that," I say. "For us."

"Is it? Nina, not having another baby isn't the end of the world. We haven't even tried to be 'us' in forever. We have Cassie, and she's more than enough, isn't she? I really don't know what happened. I don't understand."

"You slept with other women," I say.

He slams his hand down on the desk. "I didn't. I told you that."

I shake my head. "I saw you leaning in against that girl who works at your office, Jack," I say. "I answered the phone a dozen times and someone hung up. Lola showed me the photo of you and the dry cleaner chick on Facebook. I know there were other women."

He shakes his head and sighs. "What does it even matter what I did or didn't do? You've put forth your evidence and convicted me. You're the one who kicked me out."

"Don't blame this on me," I say. I'm doing enough of that on my own.

He stands up, frustrated and irritated. "I see what this is. I get it. I was bad. Now I'm supposed to apologize."

"You don't get it at all," I say. I stand and walk to the door, opening it for him.

"I just apologized," he says, getting angry now.

It's easy to push buttons when you know right where they are. He meets me at the door.

"No, you didn't," I say. "You said you were supposed to apologize. That's not an apology. It's even worse. It's telling me that you know you're supposed to, but you're not going to."

"I don't understand you."

"No," I say. "You don't."

"How many times do I have to say it?" he asks. "I'm sorry about the other woman."

"Women," I correct him.

"I'm sorry we didn't have another baby."

"We did have another baby. I just didn't get to take him

home. You didn't even care that we lost him. You think it was for the best. You said so."

"Don't do that," he says, angry. "Don't you dare make me out to be a monster. I didn't say the miscarriage was for the best. I said not getting pregnant again after that was."

"Isn't that the same thing?" I yell at him so that I don't cry.

"No, it isn't," Jack says. "I know how much losing that pregnancy hurt you. I know how much it made you crazy for another baby. You can't get him back, Nina. But you know what you can get back? Me. I don't want this!"

"Please go," I say.

This is the first time we've talked about the miscarriage since the days after we lost the baby. Nineteen weeks in. Miscarriage is an inadequate word. I had felt him move inside me. We had seen him on the ultrasound. We had named him. Then he was still. Then he was gone.

I couldn't talk to Jack about it. I stopped talking to Jack about anything—except getting pregnant again. He didn't want to talk babies. He didn't really want to try again.

"You're still wearing your rings, Nina," Jack says and reaches out to me, but I pull away. "Think about this. There may still be a way for us to be happy. There may be a way to come back from this."

I'm not sure I want there to be.

7

At home, Cassie meets me at the door in her bathing suit. "I knew you'd forget," she says with her hands on her ever-developing hips. "I don't see why I can't go to the pool by myself. That's what the lifeguard is for, Mother."

Mother. Ouch.

"Is that why you came back from Dad's?" I ask, setting my suitcase down by the couch as I walk through the living room. "The pool thing?"

I don't know what I expect her to say. *No, sweetest Mummy, I came home because I missed you so very much.* British accent and all.

I actually hadn't forgotten. It was the dreaded, weekly Teen Swim. An evening pool party for all the kids in the building. It was supposed to be a way to build community and keep the teenagers out of trouble. I personally didn't see how teenage girls in bikinis were going to keep anyone out of trouble.

"Let me get myself together and we'll go," I say.

Cassie flops down on the couch with a huff.

Thanks ever so much, wonderful Mum, for taking time out of your life to sit in the dank and humid indoor pool whilst I gallivant around with my mates. Bloody good fun.

I hate the pool. It's indoors for crying out loud. I wish I could be one of those mothers who just drops her teenagers off for the day, lets them swim and giggle and flirt. But I can't. Maybe I could have been a mother like that if I'd been able to bring my other baby home from the hospital. If I thought I had any control over anything. But I don't, and that scares me to death. So I end up hanging around places like the indoor pool, growing gills against the thick, moist, chlorine-saturated air.

There's always another mother or two with separation issues of their own, so I'm not alone at least. I think the Teen Swim was supposed to be a chance for the parents to interact as well, but we don't. Mostly, the mothers just keep to themselves, spaced out at socially acceptable distances from each other, talking on the phone to someone more important than the people around them.

I take a book to read, or pretend to. Cassie pretends she's at the pool without me, and I deal with it. I watch her for a bit and then actually read a few pages. We're not there long, when from over the top of my book—pages wilting in the wetness—I catch the frightening sight of my fifteen-year-old daughter talking to a boy. I startle upright in the plastic pool chair and fumble the book into my lap. I know it's a melodramatic reaction, but it just happens that way.

Across the pool, down at the deep end, Cassie is with some teenage boy. Cassie, who has hips and curves and has figured out how to shift her weight from one leg to the other while tossing her perfectly wavy chestnut hair "just so," has an allure that even the swampy air in the indoor, condo pool cannot stifle.

I pick up the book with nervous fingers and place it into my pool bag. The oversized, thick plastic, transparent pool bag with polka dots in a rainbow of colors. It's one of the many shields that a mother tries to wield. That bag of preparedness and protection against any unforeseen event.

Except for this.

I find myself searching through the bag. I have sunscreen—albeit unnecessary indoors—bug repellent, bottled water, an extra towel, a set of dry clothes, Band-Aids, a box of raisins, wet wipes, ChapStick, tampons, a hairbrush, some Tylenol, an empty box of Tic-Tacs, but nothing whatsoever that can do anything about that teenage boy.

Trying to remain calm, I set the bag back on the damp, concrete floor of the pool deck and stand up. I have a choice to make, and I'm pretty sure I will make the wrong one, no matter how it plays out. I should be ok with this. It's totally normal. This is what teenagers do. It's what I did. That's what scares me.

I know calling out to Cassie will be embarrassing for us both, so instead I start waving my arms around wildly in the air in an attempt to get her attention. I roll my eyes at myself, but I don't stop waving my arms around like a fool. It works, to Cassie's obvious annoyance. I point to my wrist in an exaggerated motion to indicate it's time to go—even though we just got there. Across the length of the pool, Cassie twists her mouth and shrugs her shoulders. I repeat the "time to go" mime with bigger and more pronounced movements.

Cassie rolls her eyes at me too and says some words that I can't hear to the boy. I'm being ridiculous. Which is probably what she said to Swimming-Pool Boy. I think of him like that as if it's a superpower, which I guess it is. Cassie stalks over to me; her feet making angry flapping noises on the wet deck.

"What was that about?" Cassie says and repeats the motion I had done—pointing to her own wrist but in a much more petulant way.

"It means it's time to go," I say.

"How does that mean it's time to go?" Cassie asks. "Besides, we just got here."

I realize I haven't actually worn a wristwatch in a decade or more and how the outdated motion doesn't work in the cell phone age. I feel old, and I hear the tick-ticking of a clock in the distance.

"So what do you want, Mother?" Cassie asks.

"Who is that?" I answer with my own question, trying to gesture nonchalantly at the nightmare at the deep end of the pool.

"A guy," Cassie answers with the typical and infuriating teenage combination of stating the obvious while being intentionally vague.

I pick up the pool bag. "Well, he's too old for you."

"He's fifteen," Cassie says, doing that jerky little back-and-forth head bob that they do. "I'm fifteen."

"Well," I stammer, but finish confidently, "he's too tall for you."

I bob my head back and forth too.

"Too tall for me?" Cassie challenges. "What does that mean?"

I turn to look at the kid who is standing and talking to a group of other boys. I clutch the pool bag to my chest with one hand, and with the other, I gesture toward him, moving my hand up and down trying to think of something to say. Words fail, and I just stand there motioning to the boy. The kid has pecs, biceps, and a six-pack, for crying out loud.

"Yeah," Cassie says, a little too swoony. "He's totally hot."

I clutch the pool bag tighter. I'm not ready for this. I'm not ready for this.

"Put some clothes on, kid," I yell across the pool at the boy.

Cassie rolls her eyes and says to me in overly pronounced disgust, "You are so embarrassing."

Cassie stomps away toward the locker room, leaving me feeling strangely satisfied. When Swimming-Pool Boy looks over at me from the other side of the pool, I point at him sharply. He points at himself in return, and although I know I should quit while I'm ahead—if I am—I can't help myself.

"Yeah, you," I yell, like a tough guy, like a thug.

Some of the other parents are looking at me now, and there's nothing left to do but take my useless polka-dotted bag and run for safety—wherever that is.

I feel like I'm gasping for air, and it reminds me of Dad teaching me how to swim.

"What if I drown?" I had asked. I was in water over my head. Dad was holding me up under my belly, my hands and legs sticking straight out like Superman in a wet sky.

"Life is full of what ifs," he said, not really answering me as he moved me through the blue-green water.

Up on the shore, Lola was helping Mom set up a picnic lunch. Ray pitched rocks into the lake. It would still be years before one of them would be broken and the other would be lost to his guilt, but in that moment, such things were impossible.

"It's about time you learned to swim," Dad said.

He moved one hand out from under me. He smiled, and I wasn't sure if he thought I didn't notice the difference or if he was just encouraging me. Either way, I was a little less supported and a little freer to sink or swim. My legs began to lower, and I kicked them out a little harder.

"It's all in the effort," he said.

Again my legs lowered. Again I kicked out. Continuous effort. One attempt does not automatically propel you forward. Sinking is still an option.

Leaving the pool, Cassie tries to get in the elevator without me, but I stick my hand between the closing doors and force them to reopen. She sighs at me and takes a call when her phone rings. I can tell that it's Jack, but I don't ask her about it. Once we're back inside our place, she tosses her things on the living room floor and speaks to me.

"That was Dad," she says. "He wants to know if I can spend

the weekend with him. He wants me to help him pick out furniture for his new place."

I feel like I've stepped into another dimension where my worst nightmares are par for the course.

"I guess that's ok," I say.

"Especially since all you let him take was his recliner," Cassie says. "He doesn't even have a bed."

I want to say that sleeping in someone else's bed isn't a problem for him, but she doesn't know why we split up. Besides, that isn't the whole story anyway, so saying it wouldn't be fair. But not saying anything leaves her to choose sides, to make uninformed decisions, to flail around her own life trying to figure out why things changed.

"So, he really did rent a new place," I say, setting my things on the table by the door and closing it slowly behind me. He said he had, but I figured it was just a ploy.

I thought he wanted us to get back together. Perhaps he took my shutting the office door on him as my answer.

"All I know is he moved out of his friend's house and has a new apartment," she says, going into the kitchen and leaving me in the living room.

I sneak in after her.

"What did he say?" I ask. "Where is it?"

"I don't know." She pulls out a box of Lucky Charms and some milk. "He didn't say anything."

"Will he be living there by himself?" I ask, trying not to sound like I'm asking what I'm asking.

"I'll be there," she says and stuffs her mouth with cereal.

I thought I was worried about some other woman, but this is worse.

"Wait a minute," I say. "You mean for the weekend? Right?"

"I don't know," she says between bites. "We'll see how it goes."

I am so still that I stop breathing.

"You wanted to take time for yourself, right?" she asks. It's her voice, but they're Jack's words. "You should do that. Me and Dad will be fine on our own. If you want to kiss some young guy you don't even know, it's not our place to stop you."

She stares at me while she eats her Lucky Charms. I guess I was wrong about Jack wanting me to reconsider. Jack knows that she will challenge me with his words. He wants me to yell at her and drive her away.

"Sure," I say, infuriated and sick to my stomach. "You can stay with Dad this weekend."

"Great," she says. "I might go ahead and take some things over to his place. Did you let him take enough dishes and things for me too, or should I pack those?"

I'm on a high-wire tightrope being heckled by someone who thinks I like it up here.

"I'm not in charge of your father," I say. "He makes his own decisions. He's the one who decided to leave, Cassie."

She stands up abruptly from the table.

"No, he didn't," she says, her anger suddenly spilling over her cheeks in wet streaks. "I heard you tell him to get out. You did this. You did it. I heard him say he didn't want to go. I heard it, Mother."

She stands there with her hands on her bikini-clad hips, waiting for me to respond. Daring me to.

"Cassie," I say, hating this for her. "You don't know the whole story, sweetie. I don't want things to be like this either, but they are."

"You know what else I heard?" she asks and I'm fearful. "I

heard Dad crying out here that night when he was sleeping on the couch. Did you hear that? Did you even care?"

My foot slips off the tightrope.

"Guilty people cry too, Cassie," I say, knowing I'm about to go too far. "And your father's got a lot of room to talk about kissing other people."

She looks at me and then down at the floor. I know she knows what I mean, and I hate that I'm going back on my agreement with Jack to keep the details private—but I'm not the one who threw the first stone here. I'm just lobbing them back is all.

"I love you, Cassie," I say. "I'm sorry about this. I really am."

"Whatever," she says and pulls out her phone. She taps a message to someone and her phone chirps a reply. "Dad will be right over. I'll get my things and wait for him out front."

She stalks off to her bedroom. In a few minutes she comes back out, dressed, and carrying a duffel bag packed so tight it won't even zip closed.

8

I imagine posting on Facebook: *Today we are burying my father's ashes.*

What?

Aren't you supposed to sprinkle them over the ocean or something?

This was your mother's idea, I take it?

I pick up Cassie from school, promising to take her shopping later if she agrees not to make a fuss. Mostly, I'm just thankful that she came home after the weekend with Jack.

"Which includes not rolling your eyes," I say to her as we park the car in the small lot outside the iron gates. Why do cemeteries have such security measures anyway? Are they trying to keep people out or in?

Cassie exhales purposefully and rolls her eyes.

"Will Uncle Ray be here?" she asks.

"Supposedly," I say and kill the engine. I turn toward her before she can pull the door handle. "Your Uncle Ray is good guy. I don't want you to make assumptions based on what you know about him."

"How could I?" she asks, her face set to challenge whatever I say. "No one talks about him, so I don't know anything at all."

"Well," I say, searching for an excuse, "you were really young when he went to prison."

"He existed before he went to prison, you know," she says.

111

Yeah, he did.

"Ray usually chose to keep a low profile," I say, deciding there's nothing I can explain right now. "He could have come around. He didn't."

"Did you ever stop to wonder why?" she says, as if she knows.

"Always," I answer, not trying to be snotty, but not appreciating the tone I'm getting from my teenage daughter concerning things she doesn't understand.

Cassie reaches for the door. "Well, I think he's cool. I like all the tattoos. I like that he broke free from this family. I wish I could."

"I don't think I'd call what Ray did 'breaking free,'" I say.

"You're not in charge of everyone else's perception," she says.

She gets out of the car and closes the door. I roll my eyes, but only to counteract a very mature observation that frightens me a little.

Mom, Lola, and Ray are already at the gravesite. Mom looks perfectly presentable, apart from the men's tie she's draped around her neck like a scarf and the urn she holds in the crook of her arm like a cradled baby.

"This is weird," Cassie says, loudly enough to be heard. "Do I have to be here?"

"If I have to, you do too, kiddo," Ray says and folds his arms in front of him. He winks at her to let her know he's just joking.

Cassie bites at her lip and steps closer to Ray. She doesn't know him, not really. She hasn't seen him since she was about seven years old. All she knew then was that her uncle had been in jail, and then he'd disappeared and now he was back. She was right—she deserved more of an explanation.

"Hey, Cass," Lola says and pulls Cassie into a side-by-side hug.

"Hey, Aunt Lola." Cassie nuzzles into her side.

The May sky has given way to spring full stop, growing a deeper shade of blue each day as if it's remembering what it once was and could be again.

"Why are we doing this?" I ask, deep in a corner of the cemetery, far from the living sounds of traffic and car radios, deep in the world of the dead and gone away.

"This is your father's burial plot." Mom sweeps one hand around like she's showing off some fabulous gift on a game show. *And what do we have for Nate? That's right; it's a hole in the ground.* In her other hand she holds Dad's ashes in a copper urn.

"Dad was cremated," Ray says matter-of-factly.

"I know that," Mom says, placing her free hand on her hip. "It's just that we have these plots. Mine's over there."

She points to the grass to the side of where we're standing. There's a large tombstone that bears both of their names, each of their birth dates, a dash, and then nothing.

"I don't like that," Lola says. "You don't have one for us out here somewhere do you?"

"Be reasonable," Mom says and sighs.

I look at the burial crew waiting nonchalantly off to the side.

Ray looks uncomfortable—his arms folded in front of him, tattoos washing down his arm like a waterfall that trickles off his fingers. He's shifting his weight back and forth, as if ready to sprint into the distance as soon as no one is looking.

"Anyway," Mom says with a weird permasmile across her face. "I was thinking we should bury the ashes here. That way everyone gets what they want."

Ray shoves his hands deep into his pockets. "Let's get this nightmare started."

Thankfully it's just us at the cemetery—just us and the grave digging crew, of course, and a couple of other folks who must have something to do with this sort of thing. The guy with the shovel jabs it into the grass by his feet, probably eager to get this over with as well.

Dad always loved this time of year. The time when the world decided to start again. He looked forward to turning the earth over and sowing seeds. This was not going to be like that. This is not what Dad would want. He didn't want to be trapped in a body that didn't work, and he wouldn't want to be trapped in a plot in this place of never after.

"Are you taking anything?" I ask Mom, not really sure how to ask such a question in a tactful way and wondering if I should be on something myself.

"Of course not, silly." She bends down to pull a stray weed. "You know how I feel about drugs."

"I didn't mean are you on something," I say and sigh and wonder if her slipups in the days leading to the funeral have not come to an end. "I meant like— Never mind. I don't like the idea of burying the ashes. It seems redundant at best and weird at worst."

"Nina," Mom says, sounding perky, but looking a little off the deep end. "You're too opinionated for your own good. Besides, it's a lot less digging this way."

"Grandma," Cassie says, sounding appalled.

I reach out to comfort her but Ray has already put his arm around her. For a moment, I think about Ray and Lola and the tight little unit they made back then. The unit I wasn't a part of. I try to make myself angry at Ray for trying to steal Cassie, but I can't. She needs something that neither Jack nor I can offer her at the moment. Stability. If she finds it in the thought of Ray, then I suppose that's good for both of them.

"Well, poo," Mom says, still cradling Dad's urn in her arms. "I didn't think about having Reverend Mason out to say a few words."

"I've got a few words I could say," Ray says.

I suspect he might have stopped by the local brewery before meeting us here. I can't fault him.

"Nina," Lola says, innocent and devious at the same time, "why don't you say something?"

"Yeah, Nina," Ray says and winks at Cassie. "Let's hear what you have to say."

I step forward, nodding at the cemetery crew who are both amused and uncomfortable. Ray whispers something into Cassie's ear and she smiles. She looks at me and wipes the emotion off her face.

"Here we are," I say, frustrated. "At Dad's hole in the ground. Ashes to ashes *and* dust to dust. A little redundant, but good and disposed of nonetheless."

"Nina," Mom scolds like I've said a curse word during a Christmas prayer.

Ray laughs, and Lola nudges me in the arm. But I'm irritable. Here Dad is, thrown down a hole at the end of it all.

"Say something nice." Mom dabs at a tear that isn't in her eye.

"Ok." I think for a moment. "Here's to Dad's new resting place. There wasn't enough room for him on the mantel anyway."

"Here, here," Ray says in an imaginary toast.

Cassie giggles. I know she's reacting to Ray, but it was my unintentional joke so perhaps there's a little warmth in her smile for me, too.

"This is good," Lola says, holding her hands out, making a mock frame with her fingers like she's deciding what part of this atrocity to capture on canvas.

"Children," Mom snaps at us. "Take this seriously."

Cassie looks at me, gleeful that I've been scolded.

The cemetery crew shifts around, and the guy with the shovel spades a new spot in the dirt. They look away when my eyes move over to them. Mom nods and hands the urn to someone official-looking.

"Should we say a prayer or something?" Mom asks the cemetery representative.

"I'll do that for you," he says.

The man says some words, and I feel like the hole is widening, not just for Dad, but for all of us. The air around my feet tugs at me like an undertow. It's like standing on the seashore at the edge of the waves where the water is pulling the sand out from under your feet. You look down as the wave recedes and you're standing in two little holes, your toes gripping the wet earth, holding you in place.

After a few minutes, the ceremony is over. Cassie skips back down to the car where she and Lola giggle about something unknown to me. Ray sighs loudly and walks back toward his car parked at the other edge of the cemetery. He gets in the driver's seat but just sits there. I glance at Mom. She looks concerned but not anxious.

"Aren't you afraid he'll leave?" I ask.

"No," she says with certainty. "I have the keys."

"You don't think he can hot-wire that thing if he wants to?" I ask.

"Not all people who have been in prison can hot-wire cars, sweetie," she says, seriously. "Don't make generalizations."

I look over at the car sitting quiet in the parking space.

We're all walking on eggshells around Ray. No one wants to be the one to scare him off. He looks out the car window and catches us looking at him. Mom waves.

"Your brother seems to have something on his mind," Mom says. "Do you think it's just your father's passing? I guess he must feel strange being back after all this time."

"Probably," I lie and try to change the subject from the myriad reasons Ray looks upset.

"I'm sure it will all work out," she says and winks at me.

Mom thanks the crew and then turns away. I watch her sidestep the gravesites as she makes her way to where Ray is sitting behind the wheel. She grows smaller and smaller as the laws of perspective dictate, yet she doesn't seem to be getting any farther away.

"Have you ever done anything like this before?" I ask one of the diggers.

"Honey," he says, "you wouldn't believe what's buried out here. Got a guy who had himself buried with a monkey. Monkey was already in there." He laughs and turns away.

Cassie comes sprinting back to me to ask if she can go to Lola's house for the evening.

"I thought you wanted to go to the mall," I say, hopeful that she'll remember our plans and still want to keep them.

"Aunt Lola can take me," she says. "Or maybe we'll just hang out and watch Netflix. I'll call you later. Tomorrow is Saturday anyway."

"Ok," I say and bob my head up and down like my throat isn't burning and my chest isn't aching.

I miss you. Don't leave me. I want to scream out. *Choose me, choose me.* It's childish, but I can't help it.

I think about Cassie always holed up in her room. She won't let me talk to her about Dad, but I know she's hurting. She's already cut me loose from her life, and I'm not ready for it. I don't know what she's thinking or how she feels about much of anything these days. I didn't even see it coming. She grew up without asking me how I felt about it. She was three and then seven and then twelve and then gone.

I want her to grow up—she must. I knew she would stop

needing me—stop coming to me with every discovery, booboo, and heartache. I knew she would start to form her own opinions and not seek my advice. I knew there would be a time when she'd lead a life I didn't participate in.

I just didn't know it would happen so soon. I didn't know she would leave me while she was still at home.

I'm not ready for this. I miss her, and she's still right here.

My throat gets scratchy, and although I try to bite back the tears, they come anyway.

I sit down in the grass beside Dad's plot—his spot in this new neighborhood. So, this is where we'll come to visit our father, like he has merely moved or gotten a new phone number or a webcam. I envy my mother the optimism that makes her think we can simply open the earth and toss in our sadness.

I don't know how long I sit there at Dad's gravesite. I begin to judge the time by the progression of my crying. Long enough to feel like I might cry, long enough to try not to cry, long enough to give in, begin to sob, stop, then start again. Not long enough, however, to play off the fact that I've been crying.

"Hi." I hear Oliver's voice behind me.

I wipe at my eyes as if I am trying to get out a piece of dust or grit, something that was making my eyes water through no fault of my emotions. I don't know why I feel the need to hide. Crying is an involuntary reaction to a disturbance in the body, like sweating or shivering or even laughing. Although crying is much less socially acceptable.

Oliver walks around and kneels down beside me, giving me time to collect myself.

"I'm beginning to think that you're not real," I finally manage to say.

He laughs, tossing back his head so his face is lost in sunlight. The sound of his laughter glints off the stones, splits the air

118

around us wide open, its bizarre echo ringing in the ears of the dead.

"What does that mean?" He stands up and sticks his hand out to me, helping me up off the ground.

"You only turn up when I'm sad. And you have a weird way of making me feel better about feeling bad."

"So I'm a sort of aptly timed apparition, if you want to keep the graveyard motif going?" Oliver says in his easy way, taking my hand right there in public, as it were. When I stand up, he brushes my hair back from where the breeze had blown it forward.

"Exactly," I answer, very aware of his hand around mine.

Our evening together hangs between us like a book on a shelf that both of us reach for but neither takes down. I'm afraid if I open the pages, I will want to know how it ends.

I wipe the last of the tears from my face. Oliver steps closer to me and I'm drawn in a step as well. He reaches out like he means to touch my face but doesn't.

"Come with me," he says.

He heads deeper into the cemetery. I follow, letting him walk us away from the breathing world.

"I hope you don't mind me finding you here. You weren't at your office," he says as we step over a low hedge and into an older section of the cemetery.

"You went to my work?"

Oliver smiles apologetically. I'm flattered that after only one night he remembered where I said I work. Jack never seemed interested in that part of my life. Truth be told, I'm not sure I was all that interested in his either.

"Who did you tell them you were?" I ask Oliver, watching the ground, avoiding gravesites.

I fear him saying that the receptionist thought he was my son. He's probably only ten years older than Cassie at best.

"I told the girl at the front that I was your priest," Oliver says, looking straight ahead.

"And she bought it?" I ask when he stops walking and turns to me. "You don't look like any of the priests I've ever seen."

"I'll take that as a compliment." He runs his hand through his hair in what I've already come to realize is less of an egocentric mannerism and more a nervous tick.

"What did she say?" I ask, wondering if she said anything about Jack.

"She said your other religious guru was already there so I'd need to make an appointment for some time later in the week."

"She's good cover that way," I say, remembering that she never really liked Jack anyway.

Oliver never tells me what he actually said. As we walk, I let him joke and talk, and his words begin to fade in and out and I lose track of our conversation.

Somewhere near the back of the cemetery, we stop. Standing amid the stones, I feel cold and sad. I shiver like a cloud has crossed the sun suddenly enough to chill the air.

"Nina," Oliver asks. "Are you ok?"

"Yes," I answer.

He pulls me softly towards him and wraps his arms around me in an embrace. I can hear the words that are meant by the gesture, the *I wish you weren't sad,* the *I don't really know what it feels like to lose your father,* the *This is all I know how to do right now to make it better.*

I can't breathe without breathing him in. I step back, but we don't completely separate. For a moment, I think he's going to kiss me, but then he pulls away and lets go.

"What are we doing here?" I ask, taking a long breath to clear my head.

He offers a slight smile. "I wanted to show you this one," he says and kneels in front of an old stone so weathered it is more readable through touch than sight.

I go down on my knees in front of the stone to see what he's looking at. *Oliver and Nina, together in death where it could not be in life—1912.*

"Spooky, huh?" He lies down on the ground beneath his name and pats the spot over the other Nina.

I stand there and look down at the space beside him. He pats the ground again and winks at me. I'm thrown off by him. The wink isn't a come-on, it's a comfort. I stretch out in the grass and weeds beside him and over her. Normally, it would seem like bad luck to walk over a grave, but there's something in the intimacy of this supine position that feels more like connection than irreverence.

"Is this how we end up?" I ask, filling the silence.

"I don't know." He reaches across the scratch of grass between us to take my hand. "The more I figure out, the less I know."

I look over at him and he looks at me. The gravestone with our names protrudes from the ground inches from the tops of our heads.

"Who do you think they were?" I ask.

"People who should have, but didn't," he says, looking up toward the bright spring sky.

"You think this is us?" I ask, worried that this is all some weird fantasy, me with my agenda and he with his—some lady named Nina who fits into his play, some young lover to take my mind off this painful part of my life.

"No." Oliver chuckles. He rolls over onto his side to face me, props his head up with his hand. "I just find it an interesting coincidence. It makes me think about the choices we make and how to know what's right."

"Did you just find this?" I roll to my side, mirroring him.

"No, I took a class in college about genealogy," Oliver says and touches my cheek with his free hand. "Did a paper about life and death and what comes after."

"Cheery stuff."

"Aren't you supposed to be all broody and moody in college?" Oliver brushes his hair away from his eyes. "Anyway, all the writing about death and the afterlife left me thinking, so I came here to tool around and figure things out." He laughs at himself and shakes his head.

"The chicks must have really dug you," I scoff. "We always go for the dark and dangerous."

"Well, we didn't have too many women hanging around the department in my field of study."

"Math geek?" I asked, realizing he'd never said what he went to college for in the first place. I was just glad to hear that he was old enough to have gone already. "One of the Poindexter crowd?"

I picture him in khakis with his shirt tucked in too tight, a pair of thick glasses, and his hair cut too short. No, still too gorgeous to fit that mold.

"No, I'm no good at math," he answers, but doesn't offer an alternative.

We both lay back flat on the ground and rest in silence for a while. I can almost feel this other Nina and Oliver beneath us, all dust and regret—carved only in stone what they should have engraved in the flesh. I feel for a moment like the world is a gaping hole that I must find my way out of. I feel the bone Nina reaching up to take me under with her, while the spirit Oliver sifts up through century-old dirt, easy as smoke, to whisk the living Oliver away.

"What is it that you want?" Oliver asks, a sudden challenge so deep he may not even know what he's asking.

"For things to go as planned," I answer, resting both hands on my stomach.

"And what if that doesn't happen?" he asks, putting his hand behind his head. "Why not choose another path and give that a try?"

"I don't know that I'm that fearless," I say and roll over again to face him. Trying to be brave—to look into his eyes and see a way around my fear.

"You've lost faith, that's all," he says, staring up into the clouds. "It's easy to do."

"Perhaps," I say. "How do I find it again after all this?"

"I'm the wrong person to ask these days," he says. "The meaning of life has eluded me, after all."

"You're pretty deep for a carefree college guy." I nudge him playfully.

"Ex-college guy," he says, looking at me briefly and then glancing back toward the blue above. "Just trying to find myself. Well, maybe I'm trying to find someone else—or find my way back. I don't know." He makes a face and raises his eyebrows at some internal thought. Then he shakes his head like he's wringing something from his mind.

"So what do I do now?" I ask, hoping he has an answer.

I lay back, feeling bone Nina reach out to her Oliver, ever out of her reach, and I know she envies me. I'm sad for her and hope I have enough will to be brave for the both of us. Would she have made a different choice if she had it to do over again, or was the one she made, however hard, the right one?

"You can't turn around and head back down the road you've already traveled," Oliver says as if he can read my thoughts. "All you can do is keep walking forward and hope that you'll come across the path that leads you home."

A couple of years after Lola's accident, Dad took me out on the lake. The dim blue water was lit with thin ripples of sun, white on the tips of the wake. Further out, the sun sparkled like a fistful of glitter cast like a net to drag in something beautiful.

When the two of us dragged in our own cast, a few fish gave way to a net full of crabs. Suddenly they were clicking and sliding along the fiberglass bottom of the boat. I high-stepped it around until I made it up onto the row seat, and Dad laughed as he tossed the crabs one by one back into the water.

"Don't be afraid," he said. "If this was what we were after, we'd be in high cotton."

The claws clip-clapped at him as he reached down. I wanted to be brave enough to toss them out, to not fear the pinch of the claws. One caught Dad on the cuff of his sleeve. I swatted at it, and it fell into the water.

"Good job," Dad said. "Next time we pull this net in, it will be full of fish."

"How do you know that?" I asked. "Can you see what's in the net before you pull it in?"

"If the water is clear," Dad said. "But once you toss it out, you have to pull it in no matter."

"What if it's just crabs again?" I asked.

"Then we toss it out till we get what we came for," he said.

Now, the wind shifts as it sometimes does in spring, and the sky tunes up above us. Hot and cold meet somewhere in the atmosphere, causing a collision so forceful that it draws sound and light out of thin air.

"We should get out of here," Oliver says, sitting up and taking hold of my hand to help me up.

The first warning drops tag my arm, and we both look to the sky. Still holding hands, we run back through the cemetery. The sky is dark and rumbling, but the rain hasn't caught up with it yet.

"Do you have more time?" Oliver asks when we reach my car. "Or do you have to get back to your office?"

"I should," I say, not getting in. "Book deadline."

"Yeah," he says, his eyes lighting up. "I saw some of the cover art in the lobby. Food books. You a good cook?"

"No."

"Well, no worries. I am."

He steps closer to me, and I feel the tiny hairs on my arm stand on end. I could attribute it to the electricity in the air from the storm, but that's not where it's coming from. I shouldn't do this. This isn't something a levelheaded, recently divorced, mother of a teenager should do. My old friend, guilt, sidles up next to me. He's like a chill in the room, and I shiver.

"You're cold," Oliver says as the rain begins to fall. "Follow me."

He takes off, running toward his car, and I'm not sure if I'm supposed to run after him so I just stand there in the rain. He pulls up beside me.

"Get in your car, Nina," he says. "Come with me."

"Are you going to take me to another graveyard?" I say, raising my voice against the wind and blowing rain.

"No," he says and winks at me. "I'm going to make you dinner."

I realize I'm starving and get in my car.

◆　◆　◆

He waits for me outside his house, huddled under the little overhang above his door. He times the opening of the door to match my dash up the stairs and steps aside to let me in.

He drops his keys in a bowl by the door and heads for the kitchen. "Make yourself at home," he calls from the next room. "I'll whip up something quick."

I stand in his living room, confused. I thought dinner meant "dinner," but apparently, it actually means dinner. I feel silly for thinking it might be a ploy to get me alone with him again. In the light of day, I'm a different package than I might seem to be, tucked in the darkened bookshop amid the tales of love and woe. But then there were those kisses and shared looks that I don't think I'm misunderstanding. I listen to the sounds of cooking— the click of the oven coming on, the whoosh of the refrigerator door, the chop of something being diced.

I sit on the couch and wiggle this way and that. *Make myself at home.* I put my feet up on the coffee table, but immediately take them down. I move to the old rocking chair and lean back into its sturdy frame. Outside, the storm catches up with us, turning the sky out his window darker than the day is late.

"Put on some music if you want," he calls out. "I'm assuming you know how to work that old CD player."

I do, but the comment stops me. Do I actually think this young guy has any real interest in me?

Oliver hurries out of the kitchen, holding up a finger to me, gesturing to wait. "On second thought," he says, "how about this?"

He goes right to the shelf of music and slides out a case. He opens the stereo CD drawer and puts in a silver disk. He chooses a track and steps back with his arms open like a conductor waiting to lift his baton. Etta James's low and lingering voice sings through the speakers.

At last, my love has come along . . .

I raise my eyebrows.

"Don't you think is perfect for our doppelgangers?" Oliver

says. "The other Nina and Oliver. Makes you ache on their behalf, doesn't it?"

I feel foolish for thinking the song was about me, but I'm relieved on the other hand. I lift myself out of the rocking chair and meet him on the other side of the room.

"Oliver, what am I doing here?" I ask. "What is this?"

He smiles widely at me and goes back into the kitchen. Moments later, he returns with a tray of flatbread pizzas. He sets it down on the coffee table and does this cute little flourishing bow.

"I saw something like this on the wall at your office," he says. "Ok, it's not really cooking, but it's fast, and, I don't know about you, but I'm starving. I'll do better next time."

I had taken the photo he was talking about. It'd been for the book *Tuscany in a Hurry*.

"Rosemary flatbread focaccia," he says, picking up one and handing it to me. "Pesto, tomato, smoked salmon, and fresh gouda. Little dash of salt. Am I close? Probably mozzarella, but I didn't have that."

"Yes," I say. "Just about perfect."

He nods at me to take a bite. I do and briefly close my eyes in delight.

"This pesto is wonderful," I say.

"Made it myself. Always keep some on hand. Love it. Eat up, eat up."

The food is delicious, and now I'm completely confused. Am I just an extension of my father—is Oliver just taking care of me? *It's time to eat your dinner, Nina. You've got to take your meds and get back into bed soon.*

Etta continues singing and Oliver continues talking about cooking and I continue to feel like the old fool that I might be. We finish eating, and he looks at his watch.

"It's getting late," he says. "Did I make you miss your deadline? Will you be in trouble?"

I shake my head. "Thank you for dinner," I say, getting up from the chair and hesitate as I face the door.

"Sure," Oliver says, seeming hesitant as well. "Anytime."

He follows me to the door, but puts his hand against it when we get there so that I can't open it. He leans closer and looks at me extremely intensely. He seems confused and perhaps a little frustrated. I am too.

"What is this, Oliver?" I ask again.

Oliver takes his hand from the door and runs it through his hair. He smiles shyly. "I apologize for the mixed signals. Seriously, I like you, Nina. Obviously, right?"

I tilt my head, not quite conceding. He steps closer to me and slides his finger down my forearm. The suddenly intimate gesture stops my breath.

"I don't want to rush this. The decisions we make—big or small—they matter, you know? But I'm not even sure which one this is."

I look him hard in the eyes, trying to search out the source of his indecision. My age? Some other relationship?

"I don't get it," I say, settling on the difference in our ages. "What about all the little chickadees you work with? Some of them are really cute. Why in the world do you want an old thing like me?"

He shakes his head, but it explains nothing.

"I want you," he says. "But I want other things too. I don't want to be unfair to you." He steps back from me. "I'm being terribly flaky. I wish I could tell you more, and I probably should . . ."

He opens his mouth like he's about to spill all his secrets, so I step forward and press my finger to his lips.

"You don't owe me anything," I say. "We're not at 'divulge all the secrets' stage yet."

I say it to let him off the hook he's wiggling on, but in truth, I say it to buy myself some more time. If he's about to toss me back into the water, I don't want to go. I'm being awfully selfish, but I need this—him—right now.

He presses his eyes closed as if keeping it in is as hard as letting it out.

"I can't promise you anything," he says. "But I really would like you to stay." He pushes a lock of my hair behind my ears. "If you don't need to leave right away."

"It is pretty messy out there right now," I say, nodding at the door and the storm just outside it.

A good, hard, spring rain blurs the world outside the window, while inside there is the safety of someone moving slowly and intentionally—someone as confused as I am, but someone who desires my company.

"Stay?" he asks softly. "I promise I'll be on my best behavior."

He looks like a lost soul eager to be found. There's a desperate note of urgency to his voice that I can't place and a shadow of distraction to his eyes, as if he's going through some obstacle course no one else can see and he doesn't know the right way to get through it.

"Do you have any lemons?" I ask. "Or cherries?"

"Pardon?" Oliver asks.

"If I stay, I need to work," I say. If I don't I'll get too distracted. "I've got my camera out in the car. I really do have a deadline. Mind if I tool around your kitchen?"

He exhales and smiles.

"Not a bit," he says. "You work. I've got some reading to do. I'll be around."

I have the sudden feeling that I'm in someone else's life, that if I looked in a mirror I'd see someone else's face. I check the clock—seven p.m. I haven't heard from Cassie. I imagine her and Lola curled up on the couch in front of the television.

Oliver helps me bring in my camera equipment from the car. I have a small tabletop setup that allows me to travel shoot. In Oliver's kitchen I find three lemons, a nice blue glass, some basil leaves, and some strawberries. I can work with this. Number twenty-seven is a strawberry and herb-infused concoction.

"I'll give you some space," he says. "Call if you need me. It's nice having you here."

"Thanks," I say, feeling a pleasant wave of relief, a peaceful comfort.

"It's been a while since there was anyone here other than me," Oliver says. "I didn't realize how much I missed the sound of someone else moving around."

He walks out of the kitchen, leaving me with my lemons and too many questions.

I arrange the ingredients and tweak the lighting. I shoot a few shots and then rearrange, take a few more. I don't have to do this now, I could just politely excuse myself, but I want to stay. It seems we are both hiding from something, but for now, that's ok.

I make the recipe as best I can remember it. I taste the lemonade. Not bad. All the while I'm eyeing this angle and setting up for another one, my mind is going back to Oliver. I look around for my old friend, guilt. I wonder if I left him at the cemetery. He's going to be pretty mad when he realizes he has to float home on his own.

I chuckle out loud. *Don't worry, old friend. I'll come get you soon.*

I set up the shoot in a different way and begin again.

"Why are you taking pictures of lemonade?" Oliver asks,

coming back in. "I thought you worked for a cookbook company."

"I do," I say. "This is my job there."

"Lemonade photographer?" he asks. "Cool."

Cool. I'm dating someone who says the word "cool."

I stop short at the word *dating*. Is that what I'm doing? Is that was this is? My heart races at the implication of moving forward like this.

"I'm a food stylist and photographer," I say, talking to stop from thinking. "I'm working on a book called *32 Ways to Make Lemonade*."

"You're kidding," he says and hoists himself up on the far counter. "There are thirty-two ways to make lemonade? I thought it was all lemon juice, water, and sugar."

"Essentially," I say. "I guess the difference is what you do to it then."

"Spice it up, you mean," he says. "You ever tried a Sweet Tart?"

"Like the candy?" I ask and click off another shot.

"Sort of," he says. "It tastes like candy. Before I switched majors, some college friends of mine and I used to drink it all the time. You just take lemonade and add in some Southern Comfort. Voila."

I look up at him, surprised. "You mean to tell me that you and your college dudes were drinking something called a Sweet Tart?"

He winks and smiles. I lift the camera and take a shot of him.

"All right, you got me," he says. "We made it for the ladies. Like I said, it tastes like candy."

"You're the devil," I say, joking.

He chuckles to himself. "I used to be," he says and hops down from the counter. "But I changed my ways and became a new man."

"And now you have it all figured out?" I ask, hopeful that maybe someone does.

"I thought I did. But I took a little tumble along the path, and now I'm not so sure where I'm going."

A wry smile works its way across his face, and I feel the same expression on mine.

"I know what you mean," I say. I take another picture.

I look at my phone—eight thirty p.m.

"Expecting a call?" he asks and kisses me on the head. "Your daughter?"

I look up at him, shocked. "Yes," I say. "She's at my sister's house. She's supposed to call me."

He nods and sips my lemonade.

"You didn't think I knew about her," he says—not a question. "It doesn't bother me. Older women think it makes them less sexy. I'm not after sexy."

"Gee, thanks," I say and toss a lemon at him.

He laughs. "I didn't mean you aren't."

I roll my eyes at him. "Let's not get carried away," I say.

"Her name is Carly?" he asks.

"Cassie," I say.

He was Dad's aide. Of course he had seen us all visiting. Had he seen Jack? I twist my wedding ring around my finger. If Oliver notices me doing it, he doesn't let it show. I gave him a pass on airing his secrets, maybe he's doing the same by not asking why I'm still wearing the rings.

"Teenagers are tough," he says. "Of course, I only know that from being one. I imagine they're more difficult than I know."

"I'm feeling very old," I say. "Perhaps this is why 'older women' don't mention their kids."

"Worry over age is pretty shortsighted," he says and takes

another sip of the lemonade. "Besides, feeling young is over-rated." He winks.

"What does young feel like?" I ask.

"Unburdened," he says, putting down the glass and coming closer to me. "Oblivious. Irresponsible."

"How am I supposed to feel young again?" I ask. "Are you going to make me a Sweet Tart?"

He chuckles. "I enjoy your sense of humor, Nina. You're funnier than you think you are."

"I am?" I ask, a little breathless.

He takes my camera from my hand and sets it carefully on the counter. He pulls me close to him. He's warm and comfortable.

"The other night, out by your car, you asked me if I would kiss you," he says. "I don't think I did."

"That's ok," I say, about to launch into all the reasons why it was wrong of me to ask.

He presses his finger against my lips. "If the offer still stands, I'd like to. I still can't make you any promises. I just know that it feels like I'm falling for you and I'd like to see if I'm right."

He kisses me, softly at first and then more forceful. He pushes us back against the counter and a lemon rolls onto the floor. His lips are soft, and although his hold on me is firm, I feel a measure of restraint on his part. When he lets go of me, I open my eyes and look at him.

"So are you right?" I ask, my heart racing.

"I'm afraid I might be," he says quietly.

Just then, my phone rings. He reaches beside me on the counter and hands me the phone. It's Lola asking if Cassie can stay the night. I say no this time.

"I'll be over to get her in a bit."

I know she won't be happy, but something is happening here

and I think that perhaps I'm the one who's the devil. Best that I go.

"Leaving?" Oliver asks.

"I should."

Oliver nods and rakes his hands through his hair. I think he might want me to stay, but he doesn't stop me from going

"Thank you for dinner and the time to hide out a while," I say as Oliver walks me to the door.

"I understand needing to take a break," he says. "Sometimes you just need to take a step back and figure out what you're doing. Sorry I drank your photo shoot."

I chuckle, and he leans in to kiss me again.

"See you soon?" he asks.

I nod and leave before the devil gets the best of us both.

9

hat's all this craft crap supposed to make anyway?" Ray
says to me when I walk into the room. "What makes
people want to glue felt to a paper plate and then cover it with
glitter?"

"Good morning," I say to Ray.

He's at Mom's dining room table with the Sunday paper
open in front of him, looking at the job listings. He's in his usual
spot, having pushed the hobby supplies to the side to make room
for himself. Why *do* people cut a soda bottle in half and poke
Popsicle sticks through it? It seems a pointless effort to take a
bunch of useless junk and turn it into something someone might
want.

I guess that's why.

"With my record, I'll be lucky if I can get approved for anything other than fry cook," Ray says, crumpling the paper in an
angry attempt to fold it closed. "Good morning, by the way."

Having Ray in Mom's house is still surreal. It almost feels like
one of those reality shows where they toss mismatched people
into the same house and create uncomfortable situations for them
just to see how quickly they'll end up in a fistfight. Or one of the
shows with the disgusting physical challenges like who can eat the
most chicken feet in sixty seconds. I hope that's not the one we're
on. No, Ray would be the surprise guest from the past who has

been flown in to rock the boat just when you thought you had it all figured out. Or was that Oliver? I shake my head to clear away the jumble of thoughts.

"I've got an old friend who might be able to help me out," Ray says as my reality show goes to commercial. "He thinks he might have found me an apartment—crummy, but clean. I'm sure a poor paying job won't be that hard to come by."

"You got a place?" I ask, but he doesn't say anything else about it.

I'm afraid to say anything, not want to break the spell. Ray is looking for a job. Finding something will be difficult and he knows this. Making the effort, however, will have been the hardest part. This is a good step.

Mom breezes through the dining room, but doesn't speak. She's afraid to break the spell, too. Each time she comes in, she gets something else off the table and takes it into the kitchen. Some felt. Googly eyes. Yarn.

I let Ray go on circling ads. I hope he'll take the next step of calling the numbers, speaking nicely over the phone, setting up an interview, dressing appropriately, and actually showing up. There are a lot of steps to take, and there's a good chance he won't make it past the dining room table.

Mom comes back into the room.

"Do those circles mean you're thinking about sticking around?" she asks Ray. She picks up some pipe cleaners from the table and a hot-glue gun.

"I'm thinking about it," Ray answers.

"You can stay here as long as you need to."

"Thanks, Mom," Ray says. "I appreciate it. Really."

He looks at me and shakes his head. He doesn't want me to tell Mom about the apartment. She smiles at him like this little bit of acknowledgment means everything to her, and I think that maybe it does. Ray makes a face like he knows it, too, then another face that means he thinks he's a jerk. All these years, he's thought we were happy to be rid of him. All these years, he's been wrong. His life here has continued on without him, all of us, just waiting for him to reenter stage right and pick up where he left off. Of course, that's easier said than done.

Mom pats Ray's hand. They make eye contact and hold it. It's like a searing pain to watch, and I almost blurt out the secret about Michael in an attempt to make it stop. Like divulging it will lessen the depth of the visual probing. I don't know what either one of them is looking for—sincerity, forgiveness, truth. Then Mom lowers her eyes and smiles to herself. Maybe she wasn't looking for anything from Ray. Maybe she just wanted him to see her.

She disappears into the kitchen again.

Ray manhandles the paper, wrestling it to the table. He gets up and grabs his keys from the key bowl.

"Where you headed?" I ask.

"Into the fire," he says and pulls Michael's picture from his shirt pocket. Ray looks at it and puts it back.

I hear Michael's little voice talking from inside Ray's shirt.

It's a step, Mister. But you better keep stepping.

I go into the kitchen to see what Mom is doing with all the random stuff she kept retrieving from the dining room table. She jumps when I enter the room.

"Oh, Nina!" Mom says, wearing a terribly handmade werewolf mask. "You startled me."

She motions around the room, proud of her work. On little hat stands throughout the kitchen there is a veritable Halloween boutique.

"It's May, Mom," I say.

As usual, I'm unsure of what she expects from me. I tool around the kitchen looking at her handiwork.

"I think your father would have gotten a kick out of this," Mom says through the lopsided mouth hole in the werewolf face.

"Yes," I say in agreement, well aware that today is Dad's birthday. "He really would have."

I finger the masks and think about Michael, Oliver, and mistakes made. I put on the cat face and walk down the hall to Dad's den.

"That glue might still be hot," Mom calls after me.

Dad's den looks as if he might come in at any second, apologize for the disarray on his desk, turn on the radio by the window, and busy himself with the things the man of the house busies himself with. But it's the way the room feels that tells the truth. It's like walking back into your house after you've been gone on a two-week vacation. Nothing has been moved and even the air is undisturbed. The feeling is emptiness.

I sit down at Dad's desk. I know the pipe-cleaner cat whiskers are a pity at this moment, but it helps nonetheless. I touch some of the papers on his desk. I want to speak out loud to him, but I can't. Not at his grave, not in his den. *Not on a train, not in the rain, not in a boat, not with a goat.* Or something like that. I laugh out loud. Typical Dad—making me laugh when my feet are failing beneath me. I see now, how much I had measured myself through him. How I'd used him as my map of the world. My compass pointing due north.

Mom had used a cocktail glass to steady herself. It backfired most of the time, but she had meant well. When Lola woke up after the accident, Mom stopped drinking and poured all her need into caring for Lola. I felt left behind. It had been Dad who scooped me up and set me back on my feet. But Mom seemed to have lost touch with the rest of us.

Lola saw it, though. Lola saw everything.

She knew even then, even when she didn't know more than my name and who I was supposed to be to her, that I was falling through the cracks in the universe, cracks that spread out like spider veins—purple and blotchy, permanent and useless.

Lola was eleven, still using crutches, still in therapy. That part seemed to take a long time. I was fourteen and on the girls' basketball team. Lola made Ray drive her to all my games. Mom had no interest in sports; she was just trying to hold herself together. As much as Dad wanted to see the games, he had taken to working the late shift because the pay was better and there were medical bills left over from the accident and more to come. Lola sat in the bleachers and banged her crutches on the wooden seats when everyone else clapped their hands. Already she had begun to cover the braces with brightly colored leg warmers. Making everything art.

At times, I hated that she was there. She made my legs ache. Sadness rose up in my throat like bright acid. The squawk and stick of sneakers on the gym floor, the rush of the ball through the air, through the net, the crowd thumping in applause was a sick symphony, an ode to the little girl in the neon-green leg warmers who could not run up the court, could not climb the bleachers without help, and could not stop calling my name and waving frantically to me whenever I looked her way. The girl who barely knew who any of us were, but knew we were her world.

Ray didn't watch the games. He'd wait for the two of us in the parking lot, drive home without speaking, drop us off in the driveway, then drive away and not come back until after curfew, long after Mom gave up and went to bed and left Dad awake and worried and me hiding in the hallway making sure that the world didn't come to an end while Lola slept.

The morning after those nights, Mom would ask Lola if she

had a good time at the game. Lola would tell Mom about every basket I scored, every foul shot I made, every time I looked at her and waved.

"Sounds like you had a good time," Mom would say to Lola.

"Make sure your sweaty clothes aren't on the floor," Mom would say to me.

During our last game that year, I broke a school record. I hadn't told anyone how close I had been to it, but Lola must have been keeping track. That night, after the game, she hobbled into our room with celebratory Little Debbie snack cakes and soda, and we stayed up late enough for Ray to come home. He had to walk past our door on the way to his room. Lola waited for him in our doorway.

"Nina has scored more baskets in one season than any player in the history of our school. We're celebrating."

She gave him a cake, and he stood in the doorway to our room and ate it. He nodded at me. He smelled like beer, even from across the room. There was a store in town that would sell to underage kids for an extra ten dollars. Lola waited for him to finish the cake and then hugged him around the waist. He put his arms across her back and turned his face to stone. She let go of him, and for a second, they stood looking at each other. When she gimped back across the room to the bed, he closed his eyes.

He couldn't forgive himself for what he'd done, and he's worked his whole life to get the punishment he thinks he deserves.

On Ray's thirty-ninth birthday he went to jail. Not for the weekend or overnight. Jail.

"I did it," he had said on Lola's voice mail. "I won't get off easy this time. I'll get a year, maybe eighteen months, maybe two years total."

He sounded drunk and happy with himself.

"What am I supposed to do?" Lola said to him through the phone when she and I went to visit Ray in county lockup that preceded his court date and future incarceration.

"Call Dad," I said. "Like Ray should have done. Dad will call a lawyer."

"Don't you dare call Dad," Ray yelled at the protective window, pointing at me where I stood behind Lola. "I'm a grown man. I don't need you calling my daddy."

Lola's face was puffy, and her eyes were fat from crying. I probably just looked put out, like Ray was keeping me from some pressing engagement. That was my way even then, to shut out what was happening—to not deal with it.

"Don't look sad," Ray said to Lola. "I'm happy now."

"Please stop, Ray," Lola said, seeing through him even then, seeing through his stupid attempts to make himself believe that he wanted to hurt.

"I can't stop till I've made it up."

"What is there to make up? It's not your fault."

"But it is," Ray said, looking intensely at her.

Over the years, Lola's memory of certain things had come back to her, but the events just before the accident were still a blur. She knew Ray blamed himself, but she never asked him why and he never told her.

"Don't feel sorry for me," she said into the prison phone. "I like who I am now. I'm this person because of that day."

"I'm this person," Ray said, pointing to himself in jail, "because of that day. You limped around and missed out and got picked on and hurt because of me. You turned out to be someone else. You missed out on who you could have been."

"I'm the one who stepped in front of the car," she said. "You're not the one who hit me."

She had been told she was hit by a car. Whether she actually

remembers the series of events, we don't know. She never said—
and still hasn't.

Ray didn't accept that and after that day, he wouldn't take
visitors. Mom and Dad and I went a few times, but gave up when
he refused to see us. Even though he wouldn't see her, Lola went
every day until the trial was done and Ray was moved to another
facility. Lola went there, too, but he still wouldn't see her.

She picked up Ray when his time was over. He slept on her
couch for a few weeks, but the way she circled jobs for him in the
paper and talked about him getting back on track and pretending
like nothing had happened must have been too much pressure.

I never would have guessed in all that chaos that Nicole was
pregnant and abandoned. I wish that she had told us. Given us
a chance to help her. She's younger than Ray, but more mature
by far. Feisty and determined to make it on her own. I guess you
have to be that way if you love someone like Ray.

I return to the kitchen and sit down on a barstool to watch
the werewolf cook. In a bit, Lola comes through the living room.
We can't seem to stay out of Mom's house now that Dad is gone.
It feels like we're trying to force time backwards. Lola doesn't miss
a beat and chooses a mask before she's even said hello.

"Well, Nina," the gray-skinned goblin says, "Picked any fresh
oranges lately?"

"They're a little harder to peel than I expected," I say and
shrug. "Maybe I'm not cut out for citrus."

"I don't like it when you girls talk like that," the werewolf says
from behind the pantry door. "It makes it sound like you're living
an imaginary, nonsensical life."

Aren't we?

"Oh, that's right, Mother," the goblin says. "You're the one
grounded in reality."

"Very funny," the werewolf says, coming out of the pantry and clawing her dainty hands at the goblin.

The goblin looks at me with her white-blue eyes. She shakes her head and sighs.

Ray comes back into the house through the kitchen door.

"Sorry," he says. "Left my phone. Need to make some calls."

"Who you calling?" the goblin asks.

Ray stops short and looks at the three of us. His face takes on a somber realization.

"Is this for Dad?" he asks.

The air around us is thick with knowledge of the date we have all watched coming on the calendar. The real reason we have all shown up here when there was not an invitation. It's the reason Ray seems ready to jump out of his skin now.

Dad would have been sixty-eight.

Ray slips on a paper devil face with horns. Mom puts her hand on the devil's shoulder, but he brushes it off. The goblin goes to him, and they stand together against the bright white kitchen and its flowered wallpaper and the efforts of the rest of the world to get in. The werewolf and I, a simple house cat, look at each other, and I wonder if one could eat the other whole.

Lola brings the four of us together in an embrace in the center of the kitchen. It's easy to cry to with a mask on. A little hard to dab away the tears though. Ray can't stand it for long and pushes out of the circle.

"Ray," Mom calls to him.

He's already torn off the mask and tossed it on the counter by the kitchen door. I hear his car start up, and Mom nods at me.

"He'll be all right," I say to Lola, both of us taking off our paper shields.

When I get outside, Ray's car hasn't moved. He's just sitting there in the driveway with the engine spinning. I get in the passenger side.

"I'm scaring Lola," he says and looks out the window toward the house like maybe he can see through the bricks and mortar. "I wasn't here," he says. "I'm never here."

"Those choices were yours," I say, and I know I'm not making things better between us.

Ray kills the engine, and we sit for a minute in silence. I reach over and take his hand. The feel of his skin surprises me. Not barbed wire and electricity, but soft and unguarded.

"Go make you calls." I nod at the newspaper on the dashboard. "Don't wear your devil mask when you go to the interviews."

"It's hard to take it off sometimes," he says.

I squeeze his hand.

"Do you think I've messed up too bad to make things right?" he asks.

"There's no use in asking a question like that," I say. "What is there to do but go from here?"

Those were Dad's words. He had been talking about Lola and life and how you can't ever go back and undo the thing that changed the world. You can only deal with things as they are and hope to find a way to change it again.

Ray starts the engine, and I slip out to let him get on with it.

The first family function that occurred once Lola was back home after the accident was Dad's birthday. He thought we should just let it go by. Grown men don't need parties, he had said, and he worried that it was too taxing on Lola's brain to sort out the acceptable words and body language to accompany the birthday of one's forgotten father. She was still trying to remember who we all were and where she fit in with this family of people who seemed to barely know each other themselves.

But Lola read on the calendar that May tenth was Nate's birthday.

"Who's Nate?" she asked, having forgotten her father's name.

"That's Daddy," I said.

She laughed at herself. "Duh. Stupid cheese brain."

The doctor had called what she might deal with "Swiss cheese brain." At the time, Lola didn't know what Swiss cheese was. One of the nurses brought up a slice from the cafeteria to show her.

"I get it," Lola said. "Holes."

As soon as she'd seen the date of Dad's birthday, she had determined that we would have a party. She planned it all out as best she could, and we followed it to the letter. She wrote it all down. What the cake would say. When we would eat it. What to sing. The lyrics to the birthday song.

She was always a good speller. I remember that about her lists. The meaning lost, but the details spelled correctly.

It was a lovely party. Dad had to excuse himself after the song. He told me later that the sight of Lola reading and singing and smiling was too much for a father and he needed a moment in private to put his face back together.

For a while, none of us were sure what memories Lola would get back. Maybe she'd remember the birthday song, but forget Dad altogether. Or remember Aunt Rose but forget how to sing. We celebrated when she made a connection and remembered some lost family vacation. But all the while, we were terrified of the day she would remember the accident. Ray was hanging on by the thinnest of threads and having Lola remember that he was the one who had coaxed her into the street that night would likely cause him to let go.

And if she remembered the accident, then she might remember Mom's drinking. And if she remembered the accident and Mom's drinking, then she might remember the times we walked to school because Mom was in no state to drive us. The stories we practiced on the way so our teachers wouldn't suspect anything. The times we called Dad and told him Mom was sick and could he please go to McDonald's and get dinner. He knew she wasn't sick but he never let on. I figure he must have known we knew that too, but none of us wanted to burst the others' flimsy little bubble.

And if Lola put all these things together, she might figure out that we were all guilty of baiting the hook. Trying to guide her to the memories that were good, and steer her away from the ones that weren't. But the bigger picture was worth protecting. Mom was sober, and Ray would have burst into a million pieces back then if he knew Lola could remember the way it all happened.

It was hard for Dad, though. I think, despite it all, he wanted things to be real. He wanted not to measure what he said or start a sentence that he couldn't finish. He wanted everything back the way it had been, but he knew that was impossible.

"This is a ridiculous game, Cecilia," he had said to Mom once when he didn't know anyone was listening. "I feel like we're in a soap opera and this week the part of the mother is being played by a total stranger, and next week someone will come out of a coma and tell us we've all been brainwashed by the Evil Overlord, and then next month the whole darn thing will be canceled."

"This is a new beginning, Nate," she'd whispered. "I get a chance to start over. I'm taking it."

Mom had stormed off, leaving Dad to sigh in resignation.

"I guess there's nothing to do but go from here," Dad had said.

Ray and I had been listening from the top of the stairs. We thought Lola was asleep in her room. Later that night, I went to check on her, but she wasn't there. I found her on the front porch, sitting on the top step.

"Are Mom and Dad talking about me?" she had asked.

"Of course not," I said.

But my hands began to shake with the fear of what she might be understanding.

"I won't tell," Lola said.

"Tell what?"

I remember she just looked at me and cocked her head, but didn't say anything.

"Go back to bed," I said. "It's cold out here."

"I move into my new place in a couple of weeks," Ray says, bringing me back. "I need you to come with me and see where it is."

"Now?"

"Now."

We don't talk much in the car. Actually, we don't talk at all. There had been a time when Ray and I stood at a fork in the road, one way was family dinners and long chats on the phone, cards at Christmas and photos of the kids on each other's fridge. The other way was where we are now.

He drives us to the park and shuts off the engine.

"Ray," I say, looking around, "this is a park. Are you pitching a tent?"

"Man, you got touchy while I was away. Never mind, you were like that before."

"Away," I repeat. "You make it sound like you were on vacation."

"I really don't want to fight with you right now," he says. "And I'm sorry, by the way. I know you and Jack lost that baby and were trying to have another one."

He looks over at me like he's just figuring something out. Something harsh and hurtful that weighs a ton.

Ray points out the window. I see Nicole, and then there's the boy from the photo. He looks so much like Ray did at that age, though there's something different in the face, maybe the set of the mouth. Looking at Ray's face, I can see how badly he wants the little boy. All of Ray's fight and fury has flown away. I understand now why Ray told me. We're the same. We both want something we think we can't have. Something we think we don't deserve. I imagine there's a lot of fast talking in Heaven being done on Ray's account. I picture Dad up there, going to bat for Ray.

Come on, Big Guy, let him have this one. The kid really needs one good thing. Just one good thing and I bet he'll turn it all around. From one dad to the next, give him another shot.

"This is quite a coincidence," I say, but I know it isn't. "That we stop at this park and there they are."

Ray rolls his eyes at me.

"Tell me why we're here," I say.

Over the dash and through the windshield, we watch people enjoy the lengthening days of warmth. Spring showers have given birth to grass and green and flower.

"Every Wednesday they come to the park," Ray says. "There's some women she hangs around with. I don't recognize any of them. Which means they're probably decent, respectable people."

"Are you going to say hello?"

"No," he says like I've asked the craziest question imaginable. "I don't know how to do that yet."

"So we're just going to stalk them from the car?"

"For now," Ray says.

"Fair enough." I know there's no arguing the point right now.

We watch Michael play. Maybe Ray and I have found a short-cut to that other path—the one with the family dinners and the Christmas cards. It's like we hacked through the briars in just the right place, and with a little stooping down and peering through the weeds, we can see the other path.

Look, one of us says, *you can see it from here. If we can get over this thorny spot, I think we can make it.*

The other one of us agrees. *I think you're right. Looks like you're cooking dinner over there. And Michael is playing in the pool. When did you get a pool?*

Yes, Dad is at bat for all of us, no doubt.

Michael's dark brown hair and freckled cheeks remind me of Ray before he began to blame himself for the faults of circumstance and chance, before he punished himself with alcohol and paid for his grief with time served.

The kid just needs one good thing to turn it all around.

After a few minutes, Ray starts the engine and pulls away from his son. He doesn't speak again until we pull up in front of an apartment building four or five blocks away.

"It's in this one," Ray says, and his voice is rushed and weird. "It's near the school he attends and not far from where Nicole works. They like to eat at that pizza place just over there, and now that I see the park, I know I made the right choice."

I turn my head slowly, sneaking a look at him.

"Ray," I say carefully, speaking to him like he's a child or a mental patient. "Do you miss prison this much?"

"No," he answers, confused.

"Then I suggest you drive back over to the park and say hello."

"What if she doesn't want me to?" He looks at me, not like my scary and tortured older brother, but like a man desperate for answers to the questions he doesn't even know to ask.

"She wouldn't have told you about Michael if she didn't want you to come around."

"Maybe she just wants money," he says and breaks his hand loose from mine.

"Ray, sweetie," I say. "She likely heard about Dad getting sick and had one of those good old-fashioned changes of heart. Now drive back over to the park and say hello."

Ray drives me back home instead.

◆ ◆ ◆

Ray didn't come home from his first year at college until Christmas. He had wanted to join the Marines, but Dad told him to go to school for a year and think about it. Dad was afraid the service might just be a way for Ray to skip town—to go off some place where someone would yell and punish him for all the things they didn't even know he held himself accountable for. Dad was afraid that Ray would get stupid and jump in front of bullet and die with a smile on his face, thinking himself even.

But Ray was eighteen and determined to begin his descent into self-destruction. He came home that winter with a tattoo of the devil on his shoulder, fire shooting from its mouth and running down the length of Ray's arm. Mom cried; Dad asked if it was real and when Ray answered yes, simply shook his head and went back to the newspaper. I asked if it hurt, for lack of knowing what else to say.

"Not enough," Ray had said.

Lola ran her hand across it like she was touching something beautiful and delicate. She kissed the devil on his fire-breathing mouth. Ray looked at her, his face hard and jaw clenched, but for one moment something pained and yet relieved flickered in his eyes. Later, Lola sketched a replica of the tattoo and hung it in her room.

By the time Lola attended the same college Ray had gone too, his arms were covered in ink and his eyes were empty. He dropped out before he finished, got arrested a number of times, and spent more nights in jail than he had spent days in class.

He visited Lola at school a few times. When he did, she would call me, two states over where I was in school. I wanted to see Ray, but I used the distance as an excuse not to. I was afraid to see what he had become.

I remember one of the first times Ray had stormed out of the house, leaving the rest of us to wonder if he'd be back. I remember Dad sitting on the floor outside Ray's room. I watched him through a compact mirror I held out around the corner. I could see him in the little circle of silver. He was whispering, and then he made the sign of the cross. We hadn't been to church in years. I looked at my Hello Kitty clock. It was three in the morning. I heard Ray's car in the driveway and Dad jumped to his feet. Now there were just legs in the mirror. They started back down the hall to my parents' room, and then they returned.

The car door shut. The front door opened. I saw legs turn in a circle of indecision. I tilted the mirror up and saw hands ball into a fist, then relax. I heard the whispering again and tilted the mirror back to his legs so that I wouldn't see his hands cross over his chest again.

I heard Ray walking down the hall. His footsteps were loud and heavy like he could break the house down one step at a time. I saw his legs stop beside Dad's, and I tilted the mirror up, up, trying to find their faces. Dad reached out to Ray, tried to put his hand on Ray's arm. Ray jerked away.

"You're drunk," Dad had said.

"I'm back," Ray nearly spat the words out. "So don't give me a hard time."

"Give me the keys," Dad said, his voice as angry as his fear would allow.

"They're on the kitchen table." Ray reached for the doorknob.

"Apologize to your mother in the morning," Dad said.

"Why? She doesn't even know I was gone." Ray opened the door and disappeared.

I tilted the mirror up again and could see the side of Dad's face. His lips were moving, but there was no sound. He slid out of view. I moved the mirror around, looking for him. Down, to the left, down and over. He was sitting on the floor beside the door to Ray's room with his hands over his face, his shoulders shaking.

10

I reluctantly drop off Cassie at Jack's office. Another weekend
with her dad. I want to say something, but I'm well aware
that the less I say right now the better off we'll all be in the future.
Still, Cassie looks like she's hoping for something when she tells
me good-bye. If I knew the right words, I would say them.

"Have fun."

"Yeah," she says. "This is real fun."

This is what they mean when they say words hurt. She sighs
heavily and slams the car door once she's out. I roll the window
down to call out to her, but she's already walking away without a
glance back.

I drive over to Lola's to take her to the airport to pick up
Chris. He's been racking up the frequent-flier miles between LA
and Lola. While we're waiting, she tells me she had a dream where
she forgot who he was. Not just that he was the guy on TV, but
that when she saw him, she didn't recognize him as Chris. She
said she was searching and searching for him in her dream and
even asked him if he'd seen her boyfriend. To which he'd answered, "Of course, yes, it's me."

"And then there were huge televisions all around and the
commercials were playing on them," she says as we wait in the
baggage claim. "I'm pointing at the screen saying 'There he is,

that's him,' but on television, another actor is playing the part and the real Chris was pleading with me to remember him."

"It was just a dream," I say, smoothing down her thick, dark hair. "As soon as you see his face, you'll fly right to him."

"'Remember me,'" she says, pleading. "That's what he kept saying—'Remember me.'"

"You will," I say.

"Just don't let some stranger come up and kiss me."

"I'd like to promise you that," I say. "But you know how I am about kissing strangers."

"Speaking of the OJH," she says, "how do you feel about Cassie spending so much time at Jack's place?"

"The OJH?"

"Orange Juice Hottie," she says and elbows me gently in the ribs.

"Oh, for heaven's sake. And what does that have to do with Cassie going to Jack's place?"

"Just opening up the door if you want to talk is all," she says.

I start to tell her what's going on, but suddenly she's rereading her flight information and staring at the Arrivals screen.

The baggage claim has always seemed a very anxious place to me. People stake their spot and await their luggage, watching as it circles closer and closer to them. You see them reach out as if to grab it, but it's still too far away so their hand goes back to their side. Then closer and closer until they jerk forward in a panic to pick it up before it passes them by because what if it doesn't come back around and the honor system of "take only the bag you brought" breaks down and their underwear is lost forever.

Occasionally a person who can't bear the strain of it all will weave in and out, looking for their bag, frantic to get it before someone else snatches it up, calling out to no one in particular, "That's mine there, with the red tag, that's mine."

"Oh, look," Lola says, pointing to a screen and holding up her note page. "His flight is in."

It's not long before most of the people standing around us put their cell phones to their ears. All of them, including Lola, getting a call that a loved is now "walking down the hall past the A gates, ok, now I'm passing that panini place I told you about, and I can see the baggage claim sign, ok, now I see you."

Chris comes into view.

"I do remember him," Lola says to me and rushes forward to hug him.

I nod at Chris when he sees me, and the three of us stake our spot at the baggage wheel. Surely between the three of us, we'll be able to retrieve one bag. Lola and Chris are deep in conversation. I know she's telling him about the dream. He shakes his head and smiles at her. People across the way look at Chris and then back to each other and whisper to a third person who looks up quickly and then away just as quickly.

"That's why I should do carry-on," Chris says, having seen them looking.

Lola pokes him in the side, and he smiles. Bags begin to drop out of the hole and people tense up, ready, shifting slightly on their feet like football players at the line of scrimmage.

I picture Oliver slipping down the baggage ramp, sitting cross-legged on the conveyor belt between a big blue Samsonite bag and the hard black case of a tuba. Who plays the tuba? I imagine him riding around toward me. I see him. He sees me. I'm waiting, anxious. He's almost to me, and then some beautiful, young weaver comes along, pushing me aside, yelling, "That one's mine. That one there with the nice hands and soft lips. That one's mine."

I imagine that I'm about to star in Baggage Claim Cage Fight, but then I look at her and her young skin and trim waist, her perfect hair and teeth, and I realize she's right. She grabs Oliver off the conveyor belt and off they go.

Guys—someone grabbed my bag at the airport.

On an adjacent belt from another flight, I picture Jack going around. But he's walking on the belt like it's a people mover. He steps over a paisley roller bag and finds his way off without someone having to reach out their hands for him. I picture him waving to me and leaving the airport by himself, without need of me or being claimed by anyone else.

"There's mine," Chris says, breaking my thoughts.

He lifts his bag off the belt with no detectable anxiety at all, and we head for the door.

I look back at the conveyor belt, trying to see where the imaginary pretty young thing took the imaginary Oliver. I see him, but not her. He's standing beside the belt alone. He starts lifting the bags off the belt and handing them to the people they belong to. I wait for him to look up at me. He does, then winks at me, then goes back to his work.

I realize I'm just standing there, looking at the baggage claim while Lola and Chris move away without me. I hurry to catch up.

"Do you remember where you parked?" Chris asks Lola as casually as anyone would ask that question.

Lola unfolds the pink Post-it Note on which she has written the space number and sticks it to her forehead.

"Very funny," Chris says and takes the note off. "I'm sure Nina would have remembered."

"Nina's in la-la land," Lola says.

"What?" I ask, in that stalling sort of way people do when they know what you said, but they're buying a few more seconds to think about how to reply.

They ignore me.

We get to the car and Chris loads his bag. Lola hands him

her car keys. I ride in the backseat and listen to the rest of their conversation. It takes my mind off people on conveyor belts.

"So, what did you tell you me you did when we met?" Lola asks Chris. "What were you out here for anyway?"

"My cousin's wedding," Chris says, circling through the parking garage, looking for the way out. "I figured I'd never get to see you again. It was amazing talking to someone who didn't know me. Who didn't see me as 'that guy from the commercials.' So I didn't tell you what I did. I was afraid you thought I was being evasive because I kept changing the subject."

"You were acting strangely," Lola says. "Good thing you're so good-looking."

Chris reaches over and touches her face. "I figured I'd get one evening with you and then fly back out and never see you again."

"Seriously?" I feign insult on Lola's behalf. "One date and then you'd get back on a plane to California with an 'I'll call you, babe' as a good-bye?"

"No," he says and looks at Lola. "I knew there was no way I was going to get that lucky. Not with someone who looked like you. Not to mention that you had already been introduced to me as the artist who did the mural at the gallery where the reception was being held."

Chris had been the best man and Lola was a friend of a friend of the bride. Since she had done all the art at the reception location, she was pretty much asked to attend as a name that could be dropped. Local fame has its benefits.

"Why didn't you try to play the Hollywood actor card?" I ask.

"Clearly, you hadn't seen the commercials," he says to Lola. "And that would have been a spin job worthy of D.C."

"They're not that bad," Lola says.

But they sort of are.

"You have to say that because you're dating me," he says.

"Anyway, I just wanted a fresh start. Then you gave me your number and when I called the next morning before I got on the plane, you answered. I was amazed that the number wasn't a fake."

"That could have gone either way," Lola says. "I must have really wanted you to call if I remembered my number without looking."

"You're not that bad," he says.

But she sort of is, sometimes.

"You're just saying that because you're dating me," she says, mirroring his comment.

We stop at a red light. "No, I say that because I love you."

I hear Lola inhale sharply. The light turns green, but Lola and Chris are kissing. Horns blare behind us, and I have to tap Chris's shoulder to get him off Lola and back on the road.

I find myself surprised that Jack crosses my mind when I watch Lola and Chris. We used to be like that. I guess all couples used to be. I feel a pang of confusion that I push aside as fast as thoughts of Oliver will allow.

I realize I need to talk to Oliver and I need to do it quickly. After Lola and Chris are home and I'm set free, I head to Oliver's house. After a few unanswered knocks on the door, I determine he's not home. Taking a chance, I head to the nursing home to see if he's at work.

I tell the front desk attendant that I came to see if all my father's affairs have been settled, all bills paid. Truth is, I'm like a desperate teenager trying to pull the "I can't believe I bumped into you here" game with Oliver.

I linger in the hall longer than necessary, trying to see Oliver without being seen. Nothing seems to have changed since Dad was here. Except that I don't belong. I'm like a character who has wandered into the wrong play. The players look familiar and the set design is the same, but none of my lines match any of the cues.

In a room on the opposite side of the hall from Dad's, a man in his early fifties is talking to an older woman in a wheelchair. He's kneeling in front of her like he's proposing—down on one knee, his hands around hers. He tilts his head at an awkward angle, searching out her eyes buried in wrinkles and unfocused on the present world.

"I just wanted to stop in and see you before we move," he says very loudly, overpronouncing each word. "It was good to say hello, Aunt Millie."

What he's really saying is good-bye. She's being left behind, put on the shelf of memory like one already gone.

"Hello, Nina," Mr. Cole says from the doorframe behind me.

I turn toward my dad's old roommate. He motions me inside and wheels himself back to his corner of the world.

"Hi, Mr. Cole."

"Cricket," he corrects me.

I nod and sit on the edge of his bed. Dad's bed has been stripped, sterilized, and remade with fresh linens. He's been removed so someone new can take his place.

"How have you been?" It's a stupid question to ask someone in a place like this but it's out and I can't reel it back in.

"Still got the place to myself," he says. His speech remains jagged, but I can understand him now that I'm listening. "Almost got me a roomie, but his wife wanted him closer to the nurse's desk. It's not the same without Nate here."

"No, it isn't." I feel my throat tightening.

"Dumb thing to say, I guess," Cricket says.

We sit for a minute in the pseudo silence of the nursing home—things buzzing and announcements being made. *Stand Up is starting in the front room.* Whatever that means.

"It's good to see you again," I say to Cricket, meaning the sentiment wholeheartedly, but aware that my mind is somewhere else.

"Are you ok?" he asks, seeing through me.

My eyes start to water. No. I'm not ok.

"Of course not," he answers for me and puts his hand on my knee like I'm a child.

The gesture comforts me and breaks my heart at the same time. I don't know where to start, what to say, what to leave out. I shake my head and try not to cry, but I fail miserably. He patiently gives me time to collect myself.

"It's just everything," I say lamely. "It's all been so weird. Not just Dad. You know—life." I'm stammering nonsense. "I just wish I knew something. Anything. Why, when. I don't know."

Cricket reaches his hand to mine. The skin on his arm is soft and wrinkled. His knuckles are too big and his veins too blue. Yet, the warm understanding of his palm is, I imagine, the same as it always was.

"No one knows anything, Nina," he says, "Life's a ride. It's a roller coaster, and you can't really see anything but the twist or drop that you're on. And sometimes it's better that way."

I nod. We sit for a minute while he catches his breath and I process his wisdom.

"It won't do you any good to complain," he says. "No good to wish it was different, that it was faster, slower, that you were in the front car, that the people behind you wouldn't scream so loud." Cricket breathes deeply; his talking to me is a labor of love.

A nurse comes in to administer his medicines. She smiles at me, tilting her head like she's trying to remember where she knows me from. So many people come and go that once gone, they're easily forgotten. Cricket swallows all his medicine, and the nurse returns to her cart.

"I just feel out of control," I say.

"Nothing to do but hold on tight when it gets scary," Cricket says and coughs. "You got to take a minute and breathe when you can and enjoy the moment, understand?"

"Thank you, Cricket," I manage to say through the knot in my throat.

He squeezes my hand and smiles at me. "You can come back and see me."

"I will."

"Before this place takes the last of me," he says.

I offer a weak smile, not sure whether to hope that his is a slow decline or a quick one. This place seems like a holding tank, and I don't know if the folks here are looking for the quickest way out or just hoping for another day.

I decide that my eyes are too red and puffy to seek out Oliver, so I head for the exit. I make it as far as the lobby, and just when I think I will escape unnoticed, the Universe delivers him.

"Hi," Oliver says, having seen me first, catching me off guard.

"Hi," I say. My hands go up to fuss around my eyes, trying to hide my emotion.

"What's wrong?" he says in a very endearing rush toward me.

"Nothing," I lie.

"You look sad." He reaches out like he means to touch me, but draws back, looking around nervously. "What happened?"

People in scrubs blur by us, some rushing to the next task, others stopping to talk with the residents trapped in wheelchairs—stuck in a place they never thought they'd be.

"Nothing," I say, fidgeting with my shirt. "I'm fine."

"Then what's wrong with your face?"

"Nothing's wrong with my face," I say defiantly. "This is what my face always looks like."

"No, it isn't," he says and steps closer after all. "What are you doing here? Is everything ok?"

"Trying to accidently run into you," I say, sheepishly. "I think I came here to break up with you."

"Oh." He steps back. The look on his face is somewhere between sad and relieved. "Are you still going to?"

"I don't know."

I want to grab hold of him, kiss him, feel him against me. If I'm picking up the cues of electricity correctly, he wants the same thing, but he doesn't move toward me as usual, and as usual I'm not sure how to read that.

He asks in a whisper, "Want to come over later and we can talk about it? If you still want to end it, I'll understand."

This is the part of the roller coaster that's scary, the part that corkscrews around so I can't see what's coming next

"Do you want me to want to end it?" I ask. "I can't read you at all. I know I'm out of practice with the dating stuff, but you're a closed book."

"I know, Nina," he says and takes my hand. "I don't know how to say no to you."

"Should you?" I ask, concerned.

"It's not about should." He sighs. "Come over tonight. We'll talk."

We step away from each other as the coming and going of the world corkscrews around us.

Later, when he answers the door, I can't help myself, I immediately lean in to kiss him. He pulls us both inside and closes the door with his foot. He kisses me again and slides his hands under the bottom of my shirt, but as soon as his fingers find the skin at the base of my ribs, he jerks his hands away like he's touched an open flame.

I lift my hands up and back like I'm being held up. This is not the response I'm used to.

"I'm so sorry," he says and runs his hands through his hair. "This is embarrassing."

"A little," I say, feeling my cheeks flush with heat.

He shakes his head and takes hold of my hand. "Believe me when I say it's not you, it's me."

"In that case," I say lightly, "I think I'm supposed to say that I think you're a bit of a tease."

He laughs out loud and then exhales roughly. "I'm just a little confused is all. You've got me rattled. This was hard enough without you."

This?

"Should I apologize?" I ask. "Or be flattered?"

"Flattered." He lifts my hand to his lips, kissing it softly. "Forgive me?"

I have no idea what I'm forgiving him for or what he has to be confused about. I want to know, but whatever it is will complicate things—that much I'm sure of. So I let it alone.

"Chinese food?" he asks suddenly and pulls me away from the door and into the living room.

"Sure," I say.

He points to the couch and rushes from the room. I stand in the middle of the living room at a loss. I blow a slow, hard breath through my lips, causing my cheeks to bulge out in confusion of my own.

He returns quickly with two white boxes of leftover Chinese food. Again, feeding me instead.

"I'm sorry," he says as he sits on the arm of the couch. "This is all I have to offer right now."

I sit on the couch beside him, unsure of why what didn't just happen didn't happen. Unsure, but oddly relieved. There is still a band around my finger and a man I once loved who is still sort of in my life and a daughter caught somewhere in the middle. Oliver's uncertainty may be saving me from a huge mistake.

"I'm starving," I say and take a box. "It's perfect."

He slides down the arm of the couch and wiggles in beside me.

We eat, sharing his Kung Pao chicken and my beef and broccoli. He moves in to kiss me and I pull away.

"I have Kung Pao broccoli breath," I say and cover my mouth.

He laughs out loud. Being with him is easy. Confusing, but easy.

"So do I," he says and kisses me anyway.

I see the lines he's drawn—or perhaps the ones he doesn't want to cross. Kissing—yes. More—no. For now at least.

He steals away to the kitchen and comes back with two glasses of lemonade.

"I can't stop drinking it now," he says. "I promise it's not spiked."

We sit on the couch for a long time and I tell him about Ray and Lola—the easy parts at least. I tell him about work and Mom. Cassie. More details about the lemonade book.

"I won't touch your lemons from now on," he says and laughs. "I promise."

"I might be a lemon. You sure you want this?"

"Are you?" Oliver asks, taking my hand. "If you think there's a chance this"—he twists my wedding ring between his fingers—"could work out, if you *want* it to work out, I mean, I won't get in the way."

"What about you?" I ask Oliver, deflecting as usual. "What am I up against? Some pretty young thing from work, no doubt. You seem torn, to put it mildly. Who's my competition?"

He snorts out a little smile, then shakes his head and looks down. He closes his eyes so it looks like he's praying or something equally strange in this moment. Then he gently shakes it off, whatever *it* is, opens his eyes, and looks at me.

"No pretty young thing from work," he says. "Do you have to get home soon? Cassie?"

"She's at her dad's actually. I'm sort of dreading going home to the empty condo, to be honest."

"Then don't. Stay here and take more pictures of lemons. I'll run over to the market and pick some up. I make a mean breakfast. Send you off to work with a smile."

Normally, that implies sex. In this case, I really think he means eggs and bacon.

"You have coffee?"

"Plenty," he says.

◆ ◆ ◆

I stay. Morning sunlight settles in through the window across the room, licking at the foot of the bed like tickling toes. I roll over expecting Oliver but he isn't there. We stayed up late into the night talking. I remember that sweet, sleepy feeling settling over me—eyelids growing heavier and heavier, body sinking deeper and deeper into the couch. The next thing I knew, it was morning. I sit up in Oliver's bed and wonder what in the world I'm doing.

"You're still here," Oliver says, peeking into the room.

"As requested," I say.

He's wearing sweatpants and an old T-shirt and his hair is mussed. He sits on the bed and kisses my forehead. I'm grateful for his passing over my lips and morning breath. He holds up one finger, asking me to wait, and jumps up from the bed. He doesn't return in the amount of time that would seem normal to use the bathroom or brush his teeth or whatever else it may be that he left to do.

"Oliver?" I call out after a while.

"Just a second," he answers from the front of the house.

I hear coffee being ground and made. I slide out of bed and slip down the hall to the bathroom. I take a minute to refresh myself as best I can with no help from products and props.

I remember the toothbrush I keep in my purse for work and am thankful. I use Oliver's comb and my fingers to do the best I can on my hair. Yesterday's work clothes seem a bit too tidy for Saturday morning breakfast, so I return to Oliver's room and rifle around until I find a shirt and pair of sweatpants. I walk through the house, peeking into the living room where I see a pillow and a blanket on the couch.

"I couldn't wait any longer," I say, joining him in the kitchen. I gesture at myself apologetically. "I took some of your clothes."

"They're a bit big, but you look great." He points at the small kitchen table. "I had to make it worth your staying."

The table is set with coffee and juice and blueberry crepes. There's a newspaper on the corner of the table. It was worth my staying even without all this.

"You're a very gracious host."

"Sit," he says and points to a chair. "You can have the paper first."

I oblige, and he joins me at the table, putting too much food on my plate and pouring me a cup of coffee. I open the paper but can't seem to focus on any of the words.

"Sports?" I ask him, sorting through the paper. "Funnies? Current events?"

"Whatever you don't want," he says. "Keep whatever makes you stay. I think I know what I want now."

I don't think we're talking about the newspaper. I wonder if

Jack and I had tried harder to make the good times good if we could have made the bad ones hurt less. I take a sip of coffee and a bite of crepe. Oliver nods at me and begins to eat his breakfast as well.

"So, would this make a good picture in one of your books?" he asks.

"A breakfast book," I say. "You know, I never got to do one of those."

"You should make it your next project," he says. "I can make the breakfast; you can take pictures of it."

"I don't think my house is taking on any new projects," I say. "Makes me anxious actually."

"No need to wait for them," he says. "Do it on your own."

He picks up the paper and starts flipping through it. I feel safe here. I wonder how long I could hide away. How long life would go on without me and leave me here in limbo, this blissful purgatory between world and sky. I look at the rings on my finger. This is not a limbo I can live with.

While Oliver eats and looks at the paper, I hide my hands under the table and toy with the gold on my hand. I slip the rings off, and there is an internal whoosh of letting go. But it's not just Jack and it's not entirely a good whoosh. I feel the rushing away of everything I thought would be. Everything I hoped for. Pulling the rings off is like tossing my map out the window. Facing some unmarked road to who knows where.

What if I had to introduce myself to someone? I would have no qualifiers to attach to my name. *Hi, I'm Nina, I'm Jack's wife, mother of three. We just bought a place out in the country. The kids can't wait to get a dog. We never let them have one in that little city condo, but our family just got so big that we needed more space. You should come out and visit. I'll give you a tour of the garden. You should see it. The previous owners really set us up as far as beautiful landscaping goes.*

None of that was going to happen without those rings on. Maybe none of it was going to happen anyway. But without them, I wasn't sure what to say. *Hi, I'm Nina. I take photos of food for a living. That's pretty much it. Sorry.* You always feel the need to apologize to strangers when your life doesn't work out the way you planned.

"You ok over there?" Oliver asks, the paper on the table, his eyes on me.

"Yeah," I say.

Under the table I put the wedding set on my right-hand pointer finger. It doesn't fit that finger, of course. So when I look down, it looks like a couple of rings that don't belong on my hand. The rings must belong to somebody, just not me. How did I end up with these rings stuck at the knuckle of my right hand? I feel like a person who took a wrong turn a hundred miles back and is just now realizing the mistake, but is so far into the journey that she doesn't want to tell the other passengers they're going the wrong way.

I put the rings on the kitchen table.

"Are you sure about that?" Oliver asks, looking at the rings.

"I'm sure. Although it seems strange for them just to sit there while we eat."

He nods and picks them up. He walks a few steps into the living room and drops the rings into a blue pottery vase sitting on the piano.

"There," he says. "If you change your mind, you know where they are."

He says it like it's an option I'm allowed to take up. I wonder how long it will take those rings to burn a hole in the bottom of that vase.

11

Meeting Oliver for lunch at the café where I first got the news of Dad's was passing is surreal. It's been two months, but it doesn't feel like it's getting any easier yet. The suggestion to meet here was a mix of habit and forgetfulness. My hand on the door brings it all back to me, like meeting myself rushing out, passing at the precipice of hope and knowledge.

Missing Dad is like waking from a good dream only to remember that something sad has happened, but not being able to place right away what that sad thing is. Then remembering.

Oliver greets me with a kiss and slides into the seat across from me. He's casual in his day-off clothes, no scrubs. I wonder if he looks like he could be my little brother, or worse.

"Bad day?" He doesn't open the menu but reaches across the table and touches my hand.

"I was just caught off guard by something," I say and put my other hand over his, like that little childhood game. His hand is strong and warm between mine—solid against the vapor of memory.

"Need to talk?" he asks. "I'm happy to listen."

I shake my head. Although I appreciate his being sensitive to my mood, this isn't the conversation I want to have today, so in true fashion, I change the subject as soon as I get a chance.

"So, tell me, how did you end up working as a nurse's aide?" I ask, having danced around the subject of his past before.

"I dropped out of school," Oliver says. "I just wasn't sure I was on the right path."

"I can understand that," I say, fiddling with my napkin, looking at my bare ring finger. I'm still getting used to it. Thankfully, being with Oliver is comfortable and things are moving pretty slowly.

"Have you ever wondered if you were worthy enough for the thing you want?" His eyes are as serious as I've ever seen them. "Like maybe you're kidding yourself that you'd be good at it, or right for it?"

I think about Ray. Everything he's done since Lola's accident has been a reflection of him thinking that he's not worthy of forgiveness. His hesitation now with his son is not that he doesn't want to be a father, it's that he doesn't think he deserves it, and he surely doesn't think he'll be any good at it.

"I know what you mean," I say, which isn't really an answer, so I return to more solid ground. "Were you close to graduating?"

"Yeah," he says and bites his perfect bottom lip. "Pretty close. Big-time cold feet."

"Sounds like you were headed into a serious field." I push the menu in front of me to the side. "Doctor?"

"Not really," he says, opening his menu—and taking his eyes from mine.

We enter into the accustomed moments of quiet while we each decide on our order. The waitress comes and writes down what we want, leaving us in need of more conversation.

"So, if not a doctor, then how did you end up in a nursing field?" I ask again.

"Fell into it," Oliver says, moving his flatware around and turning his cup up so the waitress could pour coffee for our wait.

"I started looking after my landlord's father. He has Parkinson's disease and his wife had recently died. He needed some help around the house."

We wait for our food, and I listen to Oliver talk about helping his landlord and her father and there's something in his face and voice that moves me. Such a sense of peace in his decision to turn his time over to someone else. Such love and admiration in the carrying out of everyday tasks.

"I started by taking him to doctor's appointments and stuff," he continues. "I took a job in town as well, but then his health went downhill fast, so I started caring for him full-time. I did that for about six months." Oliver pauses, and I see that he's lost in the memory of it. "After a while, he got a lot worse, and his family had to put him in a home."

Dad becomes a white elephant the size of the entire café. I can feel the breath from his trunk and the gentle nudging as he shifts his weight, trying to make room for himself. People come and go, and I wonder how they squeeze by him and whether they feel the need to duck under his belly.

I'm blindsided for a second by the memory of my father and Lola and Ray and me in a Chinese restaurant. Mom was in the hospital recovering from alcohol poisoning, although everyone said it was a bad case of the flu. Dad had balled up little pieces of the paper place settings with the Chinese astrological signs, and we played baseball at the table with the paper wads and chopsticks.

"I wasn't in school anymore," Oliver continues, "so I just applied at a local facility and started working. I had to take a course and pass a test—not much to it, really, when you consider the responsibility you end up with."

The waitress brings our food, and we rearrange again.

"So, you decided to go into that field?" I ask, admiring the conviction. "Just like that?"

"Well, it was more that I couldn't really decide what I wanted to do." Oliver takes a taste of his sandwich and continues after swallowing. "I just like helping people. Sounds like some corny line, but it's true."

"Elm Village is lucky to have you, then," I say. "I guess you found your calling."

Oliver looks up at me and then shifts his gaze somewhere off to the side.

"Sometimes I feel a little like I'm in limbo," Oliver says. "I don't mean to, but I do."

"Yeah," I say and reach across the table to touch his arm.

The rest of our time is easy and passes by too quickly. We linger in the café after we're done eating, but I really do have to work, so we head out onto the street. Outside, summer is coming into its own, and the tourist season has begun. We walk a few blocks and end up in front of my office building to say our good-byes.

"Limbo or not, I like this." Oliver puts his arms around me. "I think I've made the right decision. This is good."

He lingers over the word "think," but I let it go.

I see someone approaching us and realize too late that it's Jack. I pull away quickly, and Oliver seems confused.

"Nina." Jack greets me, but he looks at Oliver.

I know Jack well enough to see his surprise, but he's a good showman.

"Oliver," I say and take hold of his hand, mad at myself for having pulled away. "This is Jack."

Jack shoots his hand out for Oliver to shake, forcing him to release mine. Oliver does so and then puts his arm around me. A bubble seems to form around us, some bizarre snow globe effect of three people on the street, caught in an inescapable moment. I imagine us each miming our hands around the inside of the glass, feeling for a way out.

"Oliver," Jack repeats. "Nina has mentioned you. You'll have to forgive my surprise at being face-to-face with you."

Jack has a way of being honest without seeming worse for the wear—as if it's the other person who should feel awkward.

"Likewise," Oliver says casually, and I love that Jack's desired effect on him falls flat.

"What are you doing here, Jack?" I ask bluntly.

"Nice to see you, too," Jack says with a curt little laugh. "I was just on my way to an appointment. What are you doing here?"

"I work here," I say.

"Still?" He looks around like he's found himself somewhere he didn't mean to be.

"We were just coming back from lunch," I say. "Nice running into you, but we really have to get going."

"Recess over?" Jack says and tries to level Oliver with the jab.

"Good one," Oliver says and gives Jack a playful slap on the arm. Then he pulls me to him and kisses me like Jack wasn't even there. "I'll see you tomorrow, Nina." He turns back to Jack and offers a handshake again. "Nice to meet you, Jack. Take it easy." Oliver winks at me and walks off.

Jack stands his ground, saying nothing until Oliver is out of earshot. Before Oliver disappears into the crowd on the street, I see him glance back at us.

"Are you kidding me, Nina?" Jack says with a condescension he can't seem to control. "He's a child. I hope Cassie isn't with you to see this display."

"You're a jerk," I say and turn to go into the safety of my office building. "And Cassie is at Mom's."

Jack catches me by the arm, stopping me. "I'm sorry," he says. "That whole deal there. I was caught off guard. I actually came this way on purpose. I wanted to see you."

"What about the whole 'Oh, yeah, you work here' bit?" I shake free from him.

"I just didn't expect to see you with someone. I didn't think you were serious when you said you were with some guy."

"Oliver."

"Whoever."

"Oliver," I say again.

The city is busy around us. Tourists, business people, and local hippie types walk the same paths. Smells waft from local eateries and the chime-chime of store doors opening and closing echoes around us.

"Can I take you to lunch?" Jack asks.

"We already ate."

"Coffee?" Jack says, not giving in.

"It's a little too late."

"For coffee? It's early afternoon. Get decaf."

Jack smiles at me, and he's smug and endearing at the same time. It's a quality that piqued my interest when we first met, but became an expression that got on my nerves by the time it all came crashing down. Today it turns something on in my head again.

"It's too late for this," I say, taking my eyes off him. "The divorce is already processed. It's done."

"We're not dead," he says and then looks mock-concerned. "Are we?"

"You're not funny," I say, but really, he is. I miss this side of him. This side that seems to be emerging now that I'm out of the picture. Or perhaps, the side that I'm seeing once again now that I'm looking.

"Come on," Jack says and tilts his head. "You can't be serious about this guy. I get it. You're sad, or mad. At me. The world. Your father passed. I wasn't there for you. You're searching for some new Nina and this kid fits your need for something new right now."

"Don't tell me why I do what I do, or feel what I feel," I say, feeling angry and exposed. "Don't pretend you've had a change of heart. I know you want out, and this is all just a slap to your ego."

"I'm not trying to make you feel guilty," he says. "I'm just stating the truth here. Am I wrong?"

I don't answer, and I know Jack is taking that as proof of his point. He reaches out to me again, and I step back from him. He likes this. This is what he's good at. I know any response will be met with a biting remark, and I'm suddenly much too unhinged to try to win.

"I didn't want out," he says, surprising me. "I wanted things to be different. That's not the same thing."

Jack holds my gaze, and I know he wants me to say something. I touch my bare ring finger and shake my head.

"Think about it," he says. "Think about me. About us."

He turns around and walks away, leaving me alone on the busy sidewalk.

The next evening, while Cassie is still over at Mom's, I hide away at Oliver's and try not to think about Jack. I sit in Oliver's living room listening to music and try not to let Jack's words saturate everything like that annoyingly smooth, movie-trailer voice that makes everything seem much more profound that it actually is. *Just when Nina thought it was safe to love, life suddenly makes no sense, and senseless love may be more dangerous than she expected, and a partridge in a pear tree and isn't the sound of my voice getting on your nerves, Nina?*

I shake my head and wiggle around in my seat.

"Are you all right?" Oliver asks from the chair across the room. "You seem somewhere else tonight."

"Just thinking of Cassie," I say, which isn't at all a lie.

"Nina," Oliver says, his voice laced with concern. "Please don't think you can't tell me no if you'd rather be with your daughter."

"That's the thing," I say, hating what I feel coming out next. "I'm not sure I would rather be with her. Not with the way things are right now. All I seem to do is make things worse between us. I feel like it's better left alone. Jack's taking her this time." I try to snuggle into the couch, but I think I'm really trying to disappear into the cushions.

Oliver closes the thick book he's been reading and puts it face down on the end table beside him. He scoots to the edge of the chair.

"So, that was Jack," Oliver says, and I wonder how long he's been wanting to bring this up.

"Yes," I say, trying to let my lack of elaboration speak to my lack of desire for either Jack or conversation about him.

I look at the pottery vase that still holds my wedding rings.

"He didn't seem to care for me too much," Oliver says.

"I think you had more of an effect on him than he liked," I say. "I think he thought I was lying about you."

"I didn't expect him to be so . . ." Oliver doesn't finish the sentence.

I want to know what Oliver is thinking, but then if I did, I'd probably wish I didn't. I don't pursue the rest of the thought. I should say something to ease Oliver's worry, but I don't know how. I look at the vase again, and I could swear I see smoke spilling out from the top. I look at Oliver and he's following my gaze.

"I'm sorry," I say. "I'm obviously preoccupied, and I don't want you to think I'm thinking about Jack."

"Aren't you?" Oliver asks. "What did the two of you talk about after I left?"

I hesitate and he makes a face.

"I'm sorry," he says. "That's probably none of my business." He slides back into the chair.

"You," I say and try to gauge how he takes this. I can't. "We talked about you."

"Let me guess—he went on about me being younger than you. Made you feel like you were doing something stupid. Am I close at all?"

"You're spot-on." I breathe out heavily.

Now I feel silly for not giving Oliver the credit he deserves.

I want so badly for Jack to be wrong about my relationship with Oliver, but I fear that he's not. Sure, Oliver is younger, but age is just a number, right?

The movie-trailer voice demands my attention. *What was the difference between a boy and a man? Nina couldn't be sure. Was it education? Was it age? Was it the way he looked in a suit? How old was this guy anyway? Did he have to shave every day? Did he wear a clip-on tie?*

"Shut up," I hiss under my breath.

"Excuse me?" Oliver says, and I think at first that he's heard me. "Did you say something?"

"No," I say. "Just clearing my throat."

Oliver seems to know that I'm thinking. He gets up from the chair and goes to sit on the piano bench. "I think Nate would approve of us."

Hearing him refer to Dad as Nate in the present tense reminds me that Dad is gone. It feels like hands slipped suddenly around my heart, squeezing tight like they are trying to keep it from beating.

"What are you afraid of?" Oliver asks, his voice faltering like he's trying for humor, but failing.

Everything. I need to change the subject. My eye falls on the wooden cross hanging above the piano. "I didn't know you were religious," I say.

Oliver turns around on the piano bench. "Would it bother you if I was?"

"No," I say. Now it feels like Oliver is the one who wants to the subject to change, so I ask, "Is your family around here?"

Oliver turns back to the keys and picks out a tune. "They all live in Tennessee."

There's so much about him I still don't know. "What brought you here?"

"School—well, that brought me to North Carolina," he says, his back to me. He repeats the same set of notes, having found the sequence he seemed to be looking for. "I got my bachelors in philosophy back in Tennessee, then I came out to Charlotte to get my master's degree."

"Philosophy," I say, impressed.

"I would have loved to major in music," he says, "but under-grad was just step one of the bigger plan."

I nod even though he can't see. I watch him from the perspective of walking away—his back to me and his thoughts elsewhere. His shoulders and arms move, keeping up with his hands as they slide across the keys. I don't recognize what he plays, but the melancholy of it hurts my throat.

"And you stayed here because of your landlord's father?" I ask, unsure if he can hear me.

"I came here, from there, because of him, yes," Oliver says. "My landlord is out in Charlotte."

"You moved here to take care of her father?" I ask, piecing his earlier story together a bit better. "That's a sacrifice."

"It was an escape, actually," he says, his fingers stopping on top of the keys, hovering, then playing once again.

"How long have you been here?" I ask, trying to piece together his timeline—his rather elusive timeline.

"I've been here a little over a year now."

"How close were you to getting your masters?"

"Had about a year to go. I would have graduated last month."

"But you stayed here," I say, eking the story out of him bit by bit. "You didn't go back to school even after your landlord's father went into a nursing home?"

"Right," he says, then pauses in his playing. He reaches up from the keys and straightens a picture on the piano that I've never taken the time to look at closely.

The Parkinson's patient. I begin to put two and two together.

"You became a nurse's aide so you could still work with him," I say, letting him know that I understand.

"Couldn't bring myself to leave." Oliver plays a few more notes in the melody. "Didn't want to, and I didn't have anywhere else to go anyway."

I look around at the house and it finally strikes me why this place seems so out of the ordinary for a young man in his late-twenties.

"This is his place?" I ask.

Oliver nods, still facing away from me.

"You stay here to take care of the house?" I ask, although there's no question.

"It's a nice arrangement," Oliver says, his voice growing distant. "While it lasts, I guess."

"You miss him."

"Not yet," Oliver says oddly. "But I will."

I get up and go over to the piano. He must feel my approach because he moves over and I sit beside him. He stops playing and looks forward. I follow his line of sight to the photo on the piano. It's a picture of Oliver and Cricket in this living room. It's obvious that the Cricket in this photo is in an earlier stage of his decline than the one in the nursing home. Oliver looks the same, but his hair is shorter.

"Mr. Cole?" I question and answer myself at the same time.

Oliver nods. He pecks out a couple of sad notes and then just lets his hands rest, unmoving, on the keys.

I can't believe that all this time I haven't noticed that photo. It sits right beside that vase with my rings in it and I've never looked at it. I'm always focused on the wrong thing.

"It must be hard to watch him worsen," I say, speaking the words I'm sure Oliver wants to say but can't.

"It's not advisable to get attached."

"It never is," I say. "It's likely to hurt in the end."

Oliver looks over at me and attempts to smile, but his eyes are glazed with tears. "It's worth the risk, though, isn't it?" he says, his fingers resting on whatever notes come next.

"Yes," I say.

He looks back to the keys and resumes playing. I see his mouth tighten and his lips press and release against the emotion they try to conceal. One tear drops suddenly from his eyes onto his hand as it moves along the keys. I lift that hand from the midst of its music and kiss the salty spot on his skin.

"Thank you," he whispers. "I think I'm going to head to bed. Stay?"

"I better go," I say, although I don't want to.

I draw him up from the piano and pull him into an embrace that he lingers in.

"Nina," he says, his breath tangling up in my hair. "There's something else I need to tell you."

"Later," I say. "Get some rest. I'll see you tomorrow." I pull away from him, and he sighs.

"You're welcome to stay," he says. "Finish your book. I'm going to crash—I'm suddenly really exhausted."

He kisses my forehead, says good night, and disappears down the hallway.

I look again at the photo of Oliver and Cricket. I pick up the vase that holds my wedding rings. I shake them around and set the vase back down. I slip outside and pull the door closed behind me.

12

I skip out of work after a meeting that includes the term "restructuring" a few too many times, and I find myself at Lola's front door. I seem determined to avoid all aspects of reality and Lola's house, filled with art and music, is the best place I can think of to hide from Jack, Oliver—everything.

The door, as usual, is open and I let myself in. I hear music from her studio in the sunroom at the end of the hall. Her own artwork and that of other locals whom she admires fills the walls. Vases of fresh flowers—roses and daisies from her yard—brighten the kitchen counter.

She loves flowers. She says that they remind you on their own if they need something so she doesn't have to remember to water or weed. It's evident and that appeals to a person like her.

She's listening to a recording of a soft and somewhat sullen-sounding young man playing the guitar and singing. I don't recognize it, but something about the slow cadence of his voice makes me think of Oliver. I close my eyes and see his hair—the color of wet sand, thick and perpetually mussed up. I see his lashes, long and dark, blinking closed over that indiscernible blue-green of his eyes. I shake him from my vision and search out Lola.

I love to watch her when she doesn't know I'm there. I did it even when we were kids. She has always fascinated me. I envied, and still do, the life she created around herself—the one no one else could see. I used to watch her from the doorway to our room, careful not to breathe too loudly, not to creak the floor and disrupt the magic. She would sit by the window and talk to herself—or to someone else, maybe, I don't know. Sometimes she would play each side of a two-person game, letting the invisible her win most of the time.

What moved me the most was that after the accident, she still played that way. At school, in the neighborhood, she kept quiet so no one would know if she slurred a word or said something that didn't make sense. She tried so hard to hide the braces on her legs, to walk slowly so she wouldn't need to limp, but inside her room, she would take off the leg warmers, sit in the sun, and let the light gleam off the metal casings on her ankles. When she talked, she seemed sometimes to revere the braces as a friend. I wanted to know what it was inside her that made those polar opposites possible.

I stand in her kitchen for a minute and read her day-list on the fridge.

Today is Tuesday
Put out the trash tonight
Use oven mitt—always

I look away from it. I'm used to Lola and the way her mind works now—and the way it doesn't. She has a complex system that allows her to function in the world. She's got it under control—most of the time.

But the list hurts. At the bottom of it, after all the other reminders that I don't let myself read, she's written in one more.

You just drank that tea that you said you wouldn't get again. Stop getting it. You don't like it!

Under a magnet shaped like a tiny spoon is a picture of Chris on a mailer for the insurance company. In what must be his handwriting is a speech bubble drawn over his head. It reads "This is a good guy. You like him. A lot."

I chuckle.

Now, slipping down her hallway, I hear her humming. Today she's coloring. That's what she calls it when the subject is so vague it's all just color and whim. I watch her a while before I let her know I'm there. The room glows like light from beneath the clouds—beams visible and purposeful.

"I like it," I say and slip into view.

"I'm not sure," she says, not startled at all by my voice. I wonder if she's always known I was there all these years. "I'm growing a bit tired of what I usually do. I want to do something else. I'm just not sure what."

I stand beside her and look at the painting. "I know what this is," I say, and she turns to me, excited.

"What is it?" she asks, hopeful about the answer, and I'm struck by the intense black of her hair and blue of her eyes—she outdoes her own work.

"Disney World," I say.

"Yes," Lola says and tilts her head. "It's Ray on Space Mountain."

"The Magic Kingdom," I say. "Is this before or after he puked?"

"Mom told him not to get on," Lola says. "Remember what Dad said when Ray got out of the bushes?"

"'Magic is in the belly of the beholder,'" I say.

Ray was already growing daring, dangerous, and self-destructive. For the first year after Lola's accident he barely spoke, and then when words came back to him they were spiked with metal tips. We scattered from him like he was shotgun blast. Dad tried the hardest, staying in the line of fire, weathering the wounds like he wore a bulletproof vest.

Only in Lola's presence was Ray softer. At first, he couldn't even speak to her; he was a pillar of stone when she came near him. Yet they seemed to share a communication to which no one else was privy. She sat by him on the couch when we watched television. She would put her arm around him or rest her head on his shoulder. His body tensed at her touch, and his breathing became slow and carefully measured. I watched the juxtaposition of their bodies—hers at rest and his tensed to the point of quivering like an arrow drawn.

At first I mistook it for anger, but the more I watched them, the more I saw it for what it was—self-loathing. Ray took responsibility for the accident. Lola couldn't remember the details of it clearly, and none of us ever told her exactly what happened. But Ray knew. He knew what he had done.

Back then, she sought out Ray in the house, forcing him to be near her. He never refused her, but it took years for him to turn from stone to flesh at her touch. She became his calming force, but without her next to him, he was all torment and destruction. When he left at eighteen and couldn't take her with him, I feared he wouldn't survive.

Lola sighs, bringing me away from the past. She points to the painting with her brush. "I can always count on you to make out the meaning."

"That's what I was hoping you would do for me," I say.

She puts down her paintbrush. "What's going on?"

"I'm not sure. Everything feels different."

"Every moment you don't go back in time is different," she says. "That's the way it works."

"I might have started something I shouldn't," I say and walk around her studio, looking at her work like it's my own private gallery showing, searching for something in the brushstrokes that will make the world make sense.

"Like Ray getting on Space Mountain?" she asks.

"It's exactly like Space Mountain."

"I'll make coffee," she says and heads for the kitchen. "The good stuff."

I stand in front of the Space Mountain painting and try to see what else might be in there. I can't find anything so I join Lola in the kitchen.

Chris comes out of the bathroom with a towel around his waist. We catch each other's eye, and I look away.

"Sorry," he says, holding one hand out in front of him. "Didn't know you were here."

"Ditto," I say.

Lola screams, dropping the mug she's holding, and points at Chris. "Who is that? Who are you? What are you doing in here?"

My heart kick-starts in my chest, and I grab hold of her hand.

"Lola," I say, managing a soothing voice that quickly escalates toward panic. "This is Chris. You're dating him. You've just forgotten for a moment. Holes, remember? Holes."

"No," she says, shaking her head and looking at Chris. "I've never seen him before. I wouldn't forget someone I was dating."

Chris clutches the towel around his waist and looks horrified. "You know me," he says and reaches out for her.

"Get away from me." Lola slaps at his hand.

My breath catches in my throat, and I look frantically from Lola to Chris and back again.

"It's me," Chris says and starts singing. "'Your car is broke, and it's no joke. You got a rash . . .'"

Then the both of them start laughing.

I release my breath and my knees get weak. "That was mean," I yell at them, my heart pounding. "You two are just mean."

Chris is laughing so hard he drops his towel, revealing a pair of shorts underneath.

"I'm sorry, sis," Lola says, trying to regain her composure.

"We've been planning that for a while. Just waiting for the perfect opportunity. It was funny, right?" She stands beside Chris, and he puts his arm around her.

"It was her idea," Chris says. "I heard you out here and went for it."

"Just don't pull that on Ray," I say. "Or at least make sure you're dressed again. Getting into a fistfight in the nude is bound to be embarrassing."

"Point taken," Chris says, nodding appreciatively. "I'll leave you girls alone. Unannounced visit from the sister usually means girl talk."

"Thanks, sweetie," Lola says and pecks him on the lips.

I've never seen her joke about her forgetfulness in such an open and carefree way. It makes me like Chris all the more. I still want to pound on both of them for taking a few months off my life, but I like him nonetheless.

"It's a gorgeous day," Lola says to me. "Let's sit outside."

I give Chris the eye, but end up smiling at him. Lola and I finish making our coffee and go out onto her patio.

"I should be ashamed of myself," she says, setting down her coffee on the black iron patio table. "I've been inside all morning painting when it's this beautiful out."

"You can be French and bring your easel outside. That way you can enjoy the fresh air and still get your work done."

"Ever practical," she says to me. "And when it gets dark, I can put candles in my hat like Van Gogh did and work through the night."

"Did he really do that?" I say, picturing it. Picturing Lola.

"Isn't that great?" she says. "Can't you just see him? Explains a lot. Poor guy. I think he was a sweetheart really. Wanted the world to be beautiful and artistic and lovely. But it isn't. Not all the time, anyway. And thinking it will be could drive anyone mad."

"How do you remember all this information about Van Gogh, but you can't remember which tea you like?" I ask in good humor.

"Did you see the note?" She shakes her head. "I don't know how many times I've bought that stupid tea. As Van Gogh would concur—the mind is a terrible thing to lose."

"I agree."

We sip our coffee, and after a bit, Lola waves her hand at me in that "get on with it" motion. She knows I'm here for a reason.

"Oliver," I say, and she just nods. "I think it's turning into something and it shouldn't."

"Are you crazy?" Lola asks like I've just told her I'm thinking of taking a job on an oil rig in Alaska. "He's the Orange Juice Hottie."

"Stop calling him that." I wrinkle my nose at her. "It makes me sound ridiculous. His name is Oliver. And he's a lot different than you'd expect, actually."

"All right," she says. "Then what's the deal? You like him, right?"

"Sure, I like him. But who has the luxury of just liking someone at my age? At his age, you can like and get away with it."

"How old is he anyway?"

"Twenty-eight. But to talk to him, you'd think he was forty-eight."

"Well, to look at him, you wouldn't make that mistake." She winks at me.

I giggle, embarrassed, but happily. We sip our coffees and stare into Lola's yard. The day is bright and easy around us. The flowers in the yard are thick with fragrance and bumblebees. The summer air is sticky-sweet already.

"I ran into Jack on the street," I say. "Oliver was with me."

"You should have run over him on the street," she says, looking me straight in the eye.

"What if I made a mistake?" I say. "I couldn't get Jack out of my head last night. He made me feel so foolish for being with Oliver, but I think underneath it all, I might still want Jack."

"You're just afraid of what comes next," Lola says. "Fear. It's totally natural."

"What does come next?" I ask, thinking she has the answer.

"I don't know." Lola shrugs as if not knowing were totally ok.

"What do you mean you don't know?" I say and mimic her gesture.

"Well, I never know," she says and laughs at her little inside joke. "You should try it sometimes. It's liberating in a weird way."

"You think I should suffer a lasting brain injury?" I tilt my head at her to let her know I'm joking.

"They're less damaging than what you have."

"What's that?" I ask, completely confused.

"A lasting heart injury," she says and puts her hands to her chest.

I sigh.

She reaches across the table and puts her hand over mine. "I'm sorry things didn't work out with you and Jack, but you are forgetting the fact that you two are incapable of seeing each other through the hard times. That his idea of 'working through it' meant cozying up to his receptionist."

"But we could get better at that," I say. "I'm not innocent in all this either. I wasn't that easy to live with. I was so distraught about the miscarriage and infertility issues that I pretty much cut him off."

"Blah blah blah. I've heard all this before. You know you can count on me to listen to a repeat story and not even realize it, but for heaven's sake, Nina, you can't go around and around about this forever. What do you really want?"

"I just think this thing with Oliver is too . . ."

"Exciting, new, wonderful?" she asks, calling me out. "You've just started dating. You don't even know what this relationship is about yet. You haven't even gotten past first base, apparently."

"Is that strange?" I ask, seizing the chance. "We start kissing and then he pulls away. I mean, even now that we've sort of made it official that we're seeing each other, he's still standoffish in that, you know, area," I say, fumbling around saying the actual words.

"He pulls away?" she asks, wrinkling her brow. "Yeah, that's a little strange. Gay?"

"No."

"Married?"

"No."

"Neither are you, anymore," she says. "Just see where it goes. You might be surprised."

"But I'm not sure some good-looking, young guy is where I should be moving on to. Maybe I didn't give me and Jack a fighting chance. What if he wanted intimacy and validation as much as he wanted the sex?"

"Stop watching daytime talk shows this instant," she says and points a finger at me. "Do you hear me?"

"I know." I slump in my chair. "I just don't want to make a mistake."

"Sweetie, that's not possible," she says and reaches over the table to take both of my hands in hers. "Everything could be a mistake. Every time you get out of bed in the morning it might be a mistake. If by mistake, you mean risk."

I envy the way she sees the world.

"Jack invited me out to eat," I say. "Or coffee. I'm not sure where we landed on that one."

"Was that before or after he saw you with Oliver?"

"After."

"Well, there you go," she says as if it's final.

"I know you want to take my side," I say. "I appreciate that. I really do. But I think I'm going to have to break this thing off with Oliver."

"Nina, sweetie," she says. "I love you, but you have a terrible habit of taking a nice glass of lemonade and extracting the water and sugar. You're supposed to turn the lemon into lemonade, not the other way around."

"Do I really do that?"

"Yes," she says pointedly.

"Are we talking about real lemons?"

"Your divorce is the lemon," she says. "Your miscarriage and fertility troubles are a whole bowl of lemons. And now Dad has died, and Cassie is pulling the teenager card for all she's worth. Lemons on top of lemons. Oliver is the sugar and water. Pour a glass, sweetie. Drink it while it's nice and cool."

Perhaps she's right. But what about when the ice melts and it's all watered down? Lemonade seems a drink that's best consumed quickly.

Chris opens the sliding glass door and motions Lola inside. She holds up one finger to me to indicate she'll be right back.

I sit there feeling like a crazy person wearing a hat made out of candles, not even caring that the wax is dripping in my hair.

◆ ◆ ◆

Chris has been called back to LA for a reshoot, so I let him have Lola to himself before he has to fly away.

Still looking for answers, I drop by the nursing home because I know Oliver isn't there. That's not why I'm here today. I slip past the nurses' desk where they have all but forgotten me.

They look at me, and I see that they are trying to place me. Am I the daughter of the lady in room 301? No, I'm the niece of the new Alzheimer's patient. No, am I someone who used to work here? They don't figure it out and give up, nodding and smiling and turning back to their charts so they won't have to pretend to know me.

The door to Cricket's room is already open, and I can see that he's in his wheelchair and dressed for the day, but it seems polite to ask for admission. I knock on the frame, and he looks up at me. I can see in his expression that he expected a nurse or someone else to bother him with some ritual of daily living.

"Hi, there," he says and smiles. "Come on in. I've just had my meds, so pardon me if I say something crazy."

"Hello, Cricket." I lean down to hug him.

"You can sit on that bed," he says. "If those turtles bother you, just put them in the bathtub."

"I like turtles," I say and sit on the edge of the turtle-free bed.

"I know they're not there," Cricket says, "but I still see them. Never mind me—what's got you spending time with an old man today?"

I sigh a bit too deeply, and he guesses the reason for my visit.

"Roller coaster got you down," he says with quick wit and too much memory.

"You got it."

"Well," he says and winks, "it'll do that."

I was hoping for something more. Some sort of advice or special lever to pull to make it all come to a halt.

"I see you have a new roommate." I gesture to the bed by the window. There are new articles on the dresser, new clothes peeking from the small closet. The pictures on the nightstand are of a handsome young man and a pretty, young girl. The man wears an army uniform, and the girl is dressed in a smart, crisp frock that the fading black-and-white image doesn't do justice.

"Oh, good," Cricket says. "I was wondering if he was a hallucination too."

Cricket laughs, and I understand that he's joking.

"So, where you got Nate these days?" he asks a question I don't see coming.

"Six feet under," I say without regard for tact.

"He's probably not happy with that."

"Mom thought it would be a waste of his burial plot not to put him in it," I say.

"That's a darn shame," Cricket says. "She couldn't have just thrown an old jar of pickles in there?"

I can't help but fall in love with his outlook. The television is tuned to a program I figure the nurses' aides like to watch. It's after lunch, and I can tell that Cricket is getting a bit sleepy.

"So, tell me about this ride that's got you in a fuss," he says, not letting his sleepy eyes have their way.

"Oh," I say and shrug my shoulders as if he's asking about something that I didn't drive clear across town just to talk to him about, "you know, just wondering if I got on the right coaster is all."

"Well, now," he says, "there's a question to which there is no answer."

I was afraid of that.

"See, there is no right or wrong to that one. Maybe some bad timing if you just ate a big lunch, but the thing is"—he pauses, taking a few deep breaths, and I'm very aware of how hard every second must be for him—"once that bar comes across you and the ride starts, it doesn't really matter if you shouldn't have gotten on. You're on."

I was afraid of that too.

"I guess you're right," I say. I glance at the daytime program that Cricket didn't choose.

Had I not run into Jack that day on the street, would I even be doubting my feelings about Oliver? And do I really doubt my feelings or just the appropriateness of them, and who's making up the rules of what's appropriate anyway? I'm starting to sound like the voice-over guy.

"He talks about you," Cricket says, startling me.

"Who?"

"The boy," Cricket says and winks at me. "Oliver."

If only there was a way for people to refer to him without the words "boy" or "kid."

"What does he say?" I ask, and my heart beats thick and fast.

"You know the answer to that," Cricket says. "The important parts are between what he says."

I need to know what Oliver says to other people. I want to see his thoughts about this thing through the telescope of someone else's perception. I want to know why he keeps his distance from me.

"I can always tell when he's planning to see you after work," Cricket says. "He's lit up. Makes me remember my younger days. You know, I only knew my wife for a week before we got married. When you know, you know."

"I suppose you do," I say, then I take a risk. "He seems resistant sometimes. Is he coming out of a bad relationship or something?"

I know it's none of my business to ask Cricket these things, but I can't help it.

"The boy's got a lot on his heart," Cricket says. "It makes me happy to see him happy, though. You make him think less. I think he needs that right now."

"Think less?"

"Big decision. Powerful pull that he's struggling with," Cricket says. "Come to think of it, maybe you make him think more. We'll see."

I don't know what that means, but it makes me think too much too. I lean over and kiss Cricket's cheek.

"Don't make the boy jealous now," he says. "Come back around. Seeing you is like having Nate back. This new guy is ok, but he snores."

13

When I get home , I find Cassie packing her suitcase. I notice that she's still using the purple-and-daisy-patterned one she got when we went to Grand Canyon years ago. She was nine.

"What are you doing?" I ask, as if I don't know the terrifying answer already. "I thought you were at Mom's."

"I'm moving in with Dad," she says, not looking up at me. "Uncle Ray drove me here."

"I don't think so." I say it like I'm about to ground her for something. "I don't remember giving you permission to come and go as you please."

I had to work really hard not to finish that sentence with "young lady."

"Well, it's not up to you, now is it?" she says, tossing my own frequent jab back at me.

I don't mean to turn into Monster Mom, but she's brought out by fear and I'm getting really scared.

"It most certainly is," I say, feeling Monster Mom's skin turning green, sensing her getting too big for her britches. "You don't get to just move out."

Cassie tosses a pair of jeans into the case and looks up at me sharply. "Why not? Dad got sick of it here and moved out."

She gestures around her room to indicate "here." I notice new posters on the walls and a picture of the boy from the pool on her mirror. I see that she has turned her bed comforter over so that the blank blue side faces up instead of the hearts and smiley faces that I know are on the other side.

"That's not what happened," I say.

"Isn't it?" she asks, obligatory hand on her hip.

I begin to wonder.

"Don't you need to ask Dad about this first?" I ask, changing the subject.

"I already did," she huffs at me. She rolls her eyes and grabs another pair of jeans from the now half-empty closet.

"Dad said yes?" I ask, hoping for a loophole.

"Of course he did," Cassie says. "Call him if you want to. You know you do."

Now I'm torn between doing the predictable and garnering another eye roll and doing what needs to be done—which unfortunately are the same thing.

"I am going to call your father," I say, seeing Cassie's eyes already starting their circular trip around their sockets. "But not because you baited me to, young lady."

Crap.

"Whatever," she says and folds a shirt into her quickly filling suitcase.

Monster Mom clenches her oversized green fists and stomps out of the room. I call Jack's cell, and he answers already talking.

"Nina," he says. "Just let it happen. She's got a dog in this fight too, you know."

"What fight?" I ask, furious. "I'm not fighting."

"Maybe that's the problem," Jack says. "Look. I tried to get her to stay with you. I'm not the bad guy here. But she needs to throw a couple of punches, and I understand that."

"At me? I'm not the bad guy here either."

"At the world," Jack says, his voice aggravatingly calm. "You're her world. Sorry, but you're going be the one that gets clocked in the face."

"How long?" I ask, stepping out onto the balcony for some air.

"I haven't gotten that far with her," Jack says. "Let her come with me and we'll work this out."

"You want her," I say, trying to breathe, but hyperventilating instead. "Why would I think you're going to work it out for me?"

"Yeah, I do want her," Jack says, his voice getting pointy and jagged. "She's my daughter, and she can stay with me as long as she likes. I'm trying to be accommodating here. I don't know what else to say."

We haven't talked about the details of the divorce much, but we have agreed on joint custody, fifty-fifty, it's up to us how to work it out. That was never a point of contention. It's not about who's getting more time. It's about Cassie not being five years old and us respecting that she has a voice. A voice I'm reluctantly trying to respect at the moment.

"Where are you now?" I look down onto the street as if he might be there.

"Circling town. She's going to text me when she's ready."

Monster Mom's forehead vein is about to pop. I go back inside. "Is this some sort of covert mission that I interrupted? Was I supposed to come home and just find her gone?"

"Of course not," he says. "I told her she had to talk to you, but that I would be available when she was ready. I'm not trying to pull a fast one, Nina."

If you say my name one more time, I'm going to strangle you.

"Fine, Jack," I say and end the call, wishing for old times and a phone receiver to slam into its base.

I pace around the living room, trying, but mostly failing, to get my wits about me. I don't want to make this any worse. I go back into Cassie's room and pretend that I wasn't just acting like a spoiled brat.

"You think I'm just being a petulant teenager, don't you?" she asks, using her annoyingly good vocabulary for a fifteen-year-old. "Do you want to know why I'm really leaving?"

No.

"Yes," I say.

"I'm leaving because you won't know the difference," she says, looking me straight in the eyes.

"What you do mean I won't know the difference?"

"You don't even see me. I'm right here in front of you, and all you can see is the baby you didn't have or the one you still want."

"That's not true. I see you."

"No, you don't," she says softly, petulance gone, sadness in its wake. "You don't even know who I am. You still think I'm some nine-year-old kid. I grew up while you were busy focusing on someone else."

My heart races. Cassie is me, and I am my mother. I feel light-headed. I understand her need to throw the punches. How could I have done this?

"Why wasn't I good enough?" she says, and I hear my own childhood voice in her words.

My heart breaks.

"Of course you're good enough," I say. "People don't want more children because the ones they have aren't good enough."

"I mean *now*," she says, determined to get an answer. "When you lost the baby and couldn't get pregnant again. Why weren't Dad and I good enough for you? Why were you still sad?"

"Oh, honey," I say, unable to explain any of it.

She stands there with the brokenhearted face of the child she still is, expectant and waiting for me to explain the world and all the pieces of it, and I can't. I can't even explain it to myself.

"I'm your kid too," she says. "I can't help what happened. It wasn't my fault."

I move toward her, but she steps back from me. "Cassie," I say. "Please stay."

She looks at the open suitcase, and I think for one crazy moment that she will stay with me, but she closes the top and zips it up. She stalks past me out the bedroom door and through the living room.

"I'm going to wait for Dad in the lobby," she says.

"I love you," I say. I know I'm begging.

She looks away from me and walks out. Monster Mom is long gone and all that's left are a pair of ripped-up pants and a torn shirt. I sit down on the couch and cry.

14

Saturday comes and Cassie is still with Jack. Since I'm "free," I help Ray move into the stalker building. I know he watches Nicole and Michael at the park still. I can't blame him. He wants the little arms and legs and the tiny laugh, the hair puffing up on the wind, the small hand inside his big one.

I wanted it again too. The want of it can drive you crazy. The absence of it feels so much like a weight missing from your body that you look down at yourself to see what's gone. You have arms, legs; your torso is intact. Were you carrying something that you've put down and lost? Were you wearing a coat that you've left at coat check? Did you lose your purse?

I felt like that for a long time after losing the baby. It was such an unidentifiable loss for most people. I wasn't even showing very much at the time. But I had felt the baby move—that small quickening—those first flutters when you know you've got a life inside of you.

"Are you sure this is a good idea?" I ask, holding out my arms for a box.

It's an easy move from Mom's basement to here. Ray doesn't have much. The back of his car is loaded with things that may have been in there for months, maybe years, as he traveled around post-prison from no place to nowhere.

"No, but it's the only idea I have," Ray says and hands me a box marked "stuff from the bathroom."

"Who knows, maybe you'll like your cellmate better this time," I say as I walk up the three flights of stairs to his new place.

"That's very optimistic," Ray says sarcastically from behind me.

"Did you really come to me for optimism?" I note the peeling paint on the steel stairwell.

"Of course not." Ray follows me into his new apartment. "I know better than that."

"Sorry," I say and set the box down amid the few other things we've taken up the stairs already. "This is a big step for you, and I'm not helping at all."

"Of course you are," he says and punches my arm. "You're keeping me from having to make double the trips up and down the stairs."

"Ray," I say, suddenly fearful for him. "Do you really think things are going to work out?"

"I never expect things to work out," he says, defeated already. "That way I'm a lot less disappointed. I just thought I'd try, for once, to do the right thing. Thanks for the support." He puts down a box labeled "crap from the closet."

"I'm sorry."

Ray comes closer and puts his hands on my shoulders. "Sis," he says and sighs. "I know I'm being crazy, and I know you're trying to be helpful, although you're not very good at it. I appreciate the honesty."

He goes back down the stairs before I have a chance to say anything else.

I walk around his place, getting a feel for Ray's new landscape. The furnished apartment is suitable—one bedroom and a fold-out couch, a kitchen designed for takeout, a small living area, the usual necessities. At the window overlooking the street, I see the world that Ray is sneaking through the back door of. I watch people pass on the streets below and feel the helpless desire that draws Ray here. This is Nicole's neighborhood. It's where she walks to the park and where she and Michael go out for ice cream. I imagine Ray standing here at the window for long hours, in wait, in hope, in need of just a glimpse of what he fears might never be.

I get a text from Lola telling me to tell Ray she's glad he found a place and she will see it soon. I had told her about move-in day, but she hadn't responded until now. I hear Ray's feet clanging on the steps. He shoulders open the door and drops a box on the floor.

"I hope that wasn't important," I say.

"None of it is, really." He looks at my phone where my fingers linger over the screen. "Was that Lola?" He runs his hands through his hair. "Is she coming?"

I shake my head at him. "What's up with you two?" I ask, aware that I might just be a stand-in while Ray waits for the star to come back on stage.

"Old ghosts, I guess. I think she's afraid of me."

"Lola's not afraid of anything. Least of all you."

"Something else then," Rays says and shrugs.

It took Ray and Lola a long time after the accident to get comfortable with each other, but once they did, they were inseparable. Almost dependent. This avoidance now is weird. I think back on the times they have been around each other since Dad's funeral, and I can't put my finger on a time where they really connected. Not like they used to.

"I'm not as good as Lola, but I guess I'll have to do for now," I say.

"I don't feel that way about you," he says, shoving aside the slightly dented and now-rattling box.

"What way is that?" I ask.

"That you're just good enough until Lola talks to me again," Ray says. "If I act like that, I'm sorry. It's not the way I feel."

I see the message of truce on his face. I make no snide comment and he relaxes. It's an unspoken decision in that moment, and Ray seems to receive it. I nod at him and he nods in return, and something in the air around us shifts.

"I ordered pizza," he says and drops onto the couch. "Sit and watch some TV with me?"

"You've already got your cable on?"

"After prison, it's the only decent vice I've got left. Of course I've got cable on already."

"Sure," I say. "Maybe we'll see one of Chris's commercials."

"Who's Chris?"

"Lola's boyfriend. You've seen him. He's the guy from those insurance commercials. You know, the ones where he gets in all those crazy jams."

Ray stares at me, his brow furrowed in confusion. "What?" he finally asks, indignant and all big-brother like. "Lola's dating a guy from TV?"

He grabs the remote and flips through channels, presumably searching for Chris.

"Where?" Ray asks, jabbing the remote at the television with each press of the channel button. "What insurance guy? Car insurance?"

I can't help it—I laugh.

"This isn't funny."

"Yes, it is."

Ray makes the round of channels a couple of times and then tosses the remote on the coffee table.

"Have you talked to Nicole?" I ask, trying to change the subject.

"Yeah," he says and gets fidgety. "She was surprised to hear from me. Wanted to know if I got the papers from her lawyer."

"What papers?" I ask, my face furrowed now.

"Just some legal stuff," he says, putting his feet up on the coffee table. "Mostly just letting me know she has representation should she need it."

I nod. Life seems all about the paperwork sometimes. Paper to prove you are who you say you are. Paper to join you together. Paper to tear you apart.

"What does she think I'm going to do?" he asks, sounding insulted but not shocked. "Steal him? How do I even know he's mine? Why would I take some other dude's kid?"

"Did you actually say that?" I ask, incredulous.

"No," he says and wrinkles his face at me.

"Good."

"I thanked her for the picture," Ray says, bobbing his head in challenge. "I told her I wasn't sure what I was supposed to do. And please, Nina, for the love of Pete, don't say 'Be accountable.'"

"I didn't say a word."

He raises one brow at me and waits, but I stay silent.

"She actually apologized for not being honest about him sooner," Ray said. "I told her I didn't blame her. I mean I pretty much vanished into thin air and then reappeared in the pen. Then I popped out of there and into a black hole. Sort of like that guy from *Quantum Leap*, but without the sidekick to help me get home."

"I love that show," I say, smiling at the memory.

"Me too," Ray says, his voice suddenly soft.

We look at each other like the kids we used to be. There's a knock on the door. Ray retrieves the pizza and returns to the couch. We each take a slice and eat. There is silence for a moment. It's comfortable for once.

"So, what happens now?" I reach for a second slice.

"She wants to get together to talk," Ray says.

"How do you feel about that?"

"You know that feeling you get when you almost die in a terrible car accident, but don't?" He takes a big bite of food.

"Yeah."

"That's how I feel," he mumbles.

Me too, lately.

◆ ◆ ◆

Lola was nine when the world stopped spinning. We were like steps down a landing: Ray, weeks away from sixteen; me, twelve; and Lola at the bottom, nine years old. I remember it like the blur of her paintings, only with shots of clarity like thunderclaps and flashes of light that exploded and whizzed down like tiny missiles going nowhere.

We had cotton candy whirled high on a paper stick and no idea that life could change in the tiny moment between one heartbeat and the next. Every year the town closed down a few streets and set up a Fourth of July fair. We were set loose on the night and lost in its magic. Ray led us in and out of the crowd, away from our parents, calling back that just a few streets over we could see where they were launching the fireworks from the park.

Cautious and scared as ever, I didn't want to go past the orange cones and street blockades. Ray huffed at me and turned his attention to our little sister.

Lola will come with me, then.

She looked back at me, and I shook my head.

Come on, Lola, one more street over and you can see how they set them off.

I yelled out for them to come back, but I was no match to big brother.

Lola, don't be a baby. Come with me. Keep up.

Then they were out of sight. I ran after them, passing beyond the orange traffic barriers, catching a glimpse of Lola's hair. The fireworks reflected off its shiny blackness, making it look like a Technicolor halo.

Boom, whiz.

Ray was outrunning her, and in her effort to catch up, she wasn't watching the street around her. I got close enough to reach out and grab her, but I didn't. I just let her run. She wanted so much to be with him—her big brother.

Boom, whiz.

Ray sprinted across the street, and she leaped onto the pavement after him.

Boom, whiz.

Brakes squealed, but not before Lola was clipped at the legs and broken. Ray heard the screeching of the world on its axis and turned back to see what he had done. The part that stands out so clearly to me was Lola's head thudding on the pavement and the blank expression on her little face.

All else is a running together of emergency vehicles and mayhem. Mom stumbling and crying, Dad not being able to save her from the combination of grief and gin, and Ray just being gone.

Dad's voice shouted over the sirens. *Where's Ray? Where's Ray?* He wouldn't leave with the ambulance. He wouldn't leave without Ray. He kept me with him to search while Mom went away with the EMS team. When we found Ray, Dad held his hand behind him in a gesture that meant for me to stop short and I did. There was Ray, his knees folded up against his chest, hiding in the crook of two buildings whose sides didn't quite meet.

I've never seen such a look of terror and torment in a person's eyes as I saw in Ray's that night. Dad kneeled down in front of him, and even though I tried to, I couldn't hear what passed between them in the darkness. Ray shook his head and closed his eyes. Dad put his hand on Ray's arm and helped him stand up. When Ray opened his eyes and stepped forward, he looked to me like a shell of a boy being led by the arm. I imagined that if I spoke loudly into his ear, my voice would echo around in his body, rattle inside his empty chest cavity, and come back out his mouth.

I think Ray is still folded up in that alley, waiting for the shell boy to let himself be forgiven.

15

A few days later, Ray calls saying that he needs me to come over. I was supposed to see Oliver for lunch, but I use Ray's request to buy some time to think. Jack still has me rattled, and when I'm with Oliver, I can't see past those eyes and lips and my mind is too easily clouded by his smile and the easy way he has about him. I'm trying to be practical, and Oliver makes that hard to do.

When I get to Ray's door, I find that I'm afraid to knock. I fear his place will look like the set from a psycho stalker movie—takeout boxes littering the floor, the TV tuned to static, the room drenched in darkness, and Ray with three-day stubble, sitting in a folding chair by the window, face like stone, holding up binoculars fixed out at the park in the distance.

I take a deep breath and knock.

"Ray," I call though the door. "It's Nina."

I hear rustling and shuffling, and I figure he's scooting the chair back from the window and tossing a couple of little paper boxes in the trash. He opens the door.

"Thanks for the warning," he says and smiles. "It gave me enough time to put away the binoculars."

I must look terrified, but he just rolls his eyes and ushers me in.

"That's not what I thought," I lie, though I am relieved to see that his apartment does not, in fact, look like a set from a psycho stalker movie. He's unpacked the boxes, although they are still lying around the apartment. "Did you need something?"

"Can't a brother invite his sister over for a visit?"

I raise my eyebrow at him.

"And, yes, it is what you thought." He goes to the kitchen, I assume, to get a beer from the refrigerator. "Don't look at your watch," he calls to me. "It's after 5:00."

I hate that he knows my suspicions. I hate that I have them. I sit down on the couch, and he sits in the chair beside it. He has two beers with him and hands one to me.

"Come on," he says and opens one. "I got a nice dark one. Have a drink with your brother."

"Thanks." I hesitate to drink and Ray catches it.

"I can drink a beer and not turn into Mom," he says, putting his feet up on the coffee table. "Besides, it's the way I keep in focus."

"Meaning?"

"You know what I mean," he calls me out on it. "You do it too. Maybe not with beer, but you do it." He takes a swig of beer and tilts his head at me.

"Do what?" I ask, but I know. Ray and I have never talked about this. I guess it's about time.

"Tell me what your trick is." He puts his feet back on the floor and inches forward in the chair. "To remember that it's all a game. That you're just playing along."

Ray and I are not so different. I could have guessed all these years that part of what kept him whole was also what tore him apart. I find it hard to answer Ray. Hard to let anyone in.

"Nothing," I say and scoot over on the couch a bit, as if the extra inch or two away from him will save me from this conversation.

"Open a door once in a while, Nina." Ray sits back again, clunking his feet on the table once more.

"What does that mean?"

"Let somebody in. Let yourself out. You pick."

"I tried that," I say. "It didn't work out so well for me."

Ray whips around to look at me, then shakes his head. I think he's annoyed with me, but I'm not the object of his disapproval. He sets his beer down and raises his hands in frustration.

"I'm a jerk," he says. "You're talking about Jack?"

I nod. "It's ok."

"No, it isn't," he says. "Come on, Nina, do your thing. Tell me I'm a jerk because in that moment right there, I forgot about your marriage ending. Here I am, talking about wanting to win my family back, and you're sitting there on the other side of a divorce."

"What do you mean 'do my thing'?" I say, stuck on that part. "I have a thing?"

"And you know what else?" he says. "When I was so eager to tell you about Michael and drag you over to the park to look at him, I forgot that you'd been trying to have to another baby and you can't and here one just falls in my lap and I'm rubbing him in your face."

"You've been away," I say, trying to take the blame off him. "It wasn't part of your world."

"No, it wasn't," he says, and thumps himself on the chest. "Now bless me out about that. I wasn't here. It wasn't part of my world. The only way I even know about any of this is through the family grapevine at Dad's freaking funeral. You weren't part of my world. But you should have been."

"Is that really my thing?" I ask, focusing now on his comment. "To bless people out?"

"Yes," he says, pumping his fist up like I should be glad of it. "That's how you do it. That's how you remember."

"By being a jerk?" I ask disheartened. "Really?"

"By being real," he says, his voice calm and steady. "You don't let anyone get away with anything. You're the voice in my head, you know."

"Don't blame your insanity on me."

"You think it's Lola," he says, looking me in the eye. "You think she's what keeps me straight. She is, in a way. But you—you follow me around like one of those devil and angel things on my shoulder. I hear you all the time. You're all I heard when I was locked up. 'I told you so,' you said. 'You better cut the crap when you get out and do better than this,' you said." He mocks my voice and facial expressions. It's actually sort of funny.

"I would never say 'cut the crap.'"

"Maybe you should." He smiles at me. "You're funnier than you think you are. At least in my head, anyway."

I'm so taken aback by this revelation I could cry. I had no idea Ray felt that way. I knew I was hard on him. I just didn't know that he needed me to be.

"I didn't stay just because of Michael," Ray says and looks toward the window. "I stayed because of you. Because your voice in my head if I had run off from my kid? It would have destroyed me." He looks at me, and his eyes are moist. Mine start to sting, too.

"I don't know him yet," he says. "But now that I'm here and I see what could be, I'm ashamed at not having listened to you all those times before. What else could have been different? Everything."

I can't speak. Forcing sound from my throat right now would cut the threads between us.

He leans forward and brushes a tear off my cheek, like we might survive this after all. I take a couple of sips of my beer to try to wash the lump down my throat.

After a while I'm able to talk.

"Have you heard from Nicole?" I ask.

Ray picks up his beer and leans back in his chair. "We went out to dinner last night," he says. "She hasn't told him yet, though. Who I am, I mean."

"Give it time."

"I will," he says. "I'm used to doing time."

I chuckle and then look at him to check his reaction. He's smiling at me so I know it's ok. I'm giddy with this new closeness to Ray. I feel included in Lola's secret world with him. I'm not going to push buttons today—not about all those years ago, not about his drinking and self-destruction, not even about this reckless attempt to be close to the son he didn't even know he had. Today, I'm going to enjoy what I've missed all these years. My brother. Today I'm going to see what might have been.

"At work, I see how all the other men have framed photos of their family on their desks. I want that. I think I might have a shot at it," Ray says, talking more than I've ever known him to.

"I think you do."

"I don't want to be the screwup," he says. "It's just that I'm good at it, and hey, people like to do what they do well."

"Tell me about dinner," I say.

"I remembered she likes Indian food, so I suggested we meet at Chai Pani," he says.

"I thought you hated spicy food."

"I do. But that was part of the point. She knows I don't like it, so she knew I was there for her."

"What did you guys talk about?"

"I asked her why she told me about Michael," Ray says. "She said he'd started asking about his dad, and she thought she would give me a chance to be the person he's asking about. I told her she might be making a leap of faith there."

"Is there any other kind?" I ask. "Was Michael there?"

"No," Ray says. "But she's going to bring him by."

"That's great, when?"

"In about five minutes," Ray says, sitting up like he's ready to grab me when I try to flee. "Please stay. I need you here."

"Are you kidding me?" I ask.

There's a knock on the door.

"They're early," Ray says, his eyes widening as my mouth gaps open.

Ray opens the door and lets them in, and it's the most awkward hello I can imagine. Nicole nods to me. Ray moves to hug her, but she steps back. She steps forward again to receive the hug, but Ray steps back. They dance around again, and I finally stand up.

"Come in," I say, not sure if I should greet Michael or let Nicole introduce him.

Ray and I move aside to let them in, and they stand in the middle of the living room like people who have found themselves somewhere they didn't mean to be.

"Make yourself comfortable," Ray says because that's what people say, not because he thinks they can.

Nicole and Michael sit on the couch, and I take the chair next to it. Ray just stands there.

"It's nice to see you again, Nicole," I say. "I had just popped over to see Ray, and he said you were stopping by. I can go if you'd like."

"Please stay," Nicole says a little too emphatically.

I look at Michael as he clings to his mother's pants. Ray and Nicole make eye contact, break it, look again. Ray sits down beside them, but not too close. No one seems to know how to start a conversation.

"I like your place," Nicole says. "You didn't tell me you moved to this side of town."

"I was lucky to find anything at all," he says.

I'm sure he's picked up the real meaning of her words—"this side of town" translates to "so close to us." I figure he's trying to chalk it up to the luck of the classifieds, but it comes out sounding more like the truth than he means it to.

"Well," she says.

I know she wants to finish that thought with a much deserved "Whose fault is that?" but she doesn't. Nicole is classy like that.

She stuck out from the group Ray ran with like that much-talked about sore thumb. She was too smart, too motivated, too good for that group. She used to tell Ray that he was too smart to be hanging around with such losers, and he would tell her that she was hanging around them, too. She said hers was a problem of situation and that his was an act of intention.

See, too smart.

Dad had high hopes for Nicole and Ray. He saw her as a life jacket but feared Ray would be too stubborn to grab onto it. I think she loved Ray, but love can only stand so much.

"I got a good job now," Ray says.

"Really," Nicole says. It's not sarcastic. It's like she's checking something off a list. She's got criteria that she's holding Ray up to, and she's pleasantly surprised to see that he's met a goal already.

"It's in the computer department of that graphic design firm down the street," Ray says. "One of the reasons I wanted to be in town here. Easy to get to work."

That's a lie, but if it makes him look a little less desperate and scary, it's one worth telling. Ray would call it luck that he got that job. Dad would have deferred to divine intervention. Given the circumstance, I'd have to agree with Dad. Ray's parole officer had arranged for the interview with a company whose president was someone the parole officer had known back when they were both younger and going to AA. Someone who knew about second chances. Someone who would make sure Ray understood the importance of trying again.

Ray is talking about his job and what he does all day, and I find myself using the opportunity of being forgotten for a moment to steal glances at Michael. I want to look full on at him, to study his features and memorize the way he moves, but I don't want to seem too needy.

"Mommy," Michael says, and it's the first time I've heard his voice. "I'm bored. How long are we staying?"

Nicole gasps in that embarrassed mother sort of way. "Michael," she says. "Don't be rude."

Ray jumps up from the couch. "It's ok," he says, "I'd be bored too. I have some toys you can play with. Come see what I got."

Michael follows Ray down the hall, and Nicole and I are left alone.

"I'm real sorry about your dad," she says. "I always liked him. I wish Michael had gotten to meet him."

"Thanks. I wish he had, too."

Nicole picks at a string that's loose from the couch and looks nervously around the room.

"I'm assuming you know that Ray is Michael's father," she says. "I'm also guessing that you didn't just pop by. Ray asked you to be here when I came over? Yes?"

She meets my eyes, and I smile a small confirmation.

"Evidently," I say. "He's just nervous. I know how crazy this will sound, but give him another chance."

Michael runs back out to Nicole, holding up a pair of Matchbox cars and shouting for her to "Lookit, lookit, these are so cool" before she has a chance to respond to me.

Michael plays over by the window, and Nicole and Ray resume their conversation. I feel like the third wheel that I am, but in this case the cart would fall over without me, so I stay.

"I'm glad to hear about the job, Ray," Nicole says. "Sounds like something you could be good at."

"They've got me working on this computer manual rewrite thing," Ray says. "It's not all that exciting, but I'm learning everything there is to know about what they do and what they're changing. So I'll be the first to know all the new procedures."

Ray talks like he's casting a spell, searching for the right incantation to win over Nicole. She starts asking him questions about his job, giving Ray a chance to say the right words for a change.

"The other day, one of the main systems went out, and the whole place shut down," Ray says, getting animated and excited. "They had one of their senior guys on it, but he couldn't get it back up. I managed to find what was screwing it up and got everybody back online."

Michael comes back over to us and drives the cars over our feet. He looks up at me and wrinkles his brow. Then he looks at Ray.

"Are you two married?" Michael asks Ray.

"No," Ray says. "Why do you ask?"

"Because this place is a mess," Michael says. "You need someone to clean it up."

"Michael," Nicole says to him sharply.

"It's ok, buddy," Ray says and touches the top of Michael's head, then snaps his hand back like he's done something he shouldn't have. "It *is* a mess in here. This lady is my sister."

Your aunt.

"Maybe you could marry Mommy," Michael says.

"Michael," Nicole says again and shakes her head at Ray.

"You always say you need help around the house," Michael says with his little hands on his hips, imitating her. "Maybe you guys can get married and clean each other's houses."

"I'm talking about help from you, little man," Nicole says.

Ray's absence in their life is a neon sign, blinking on and off and sputtering out.

"I don't know if your Mommy would have me," Ray says, glancing quickly at Nicole.

Nicole watches them talk with a wistful look on her face as if there might have been a time when she wanted that too. Her phone rings, and she searches her purse for it.

"I'll just be second," she says. She goes down the hall into the bedroom, and Ray takes the opportunity of being alone with Michael to ask a question.

"Do you know who I am?"

"Ray," I hiss. "What are you doing?"

Ray shoots me the stink eye and then looks back at Michael.

"Somebody Mommy knew a long time ago, before I was born," Michael says.

I wince. It might be a well-deserved sucker punch, but ouch.

"Yes," Ray says quietly. "That's right."

Nicole comes back and apologizes, but doesn't explain. We sit in the living room and stare at the walls. This is awful. Ray looks miserable. He looked less nervous at his sentencing. When Michael moves away from us, Ray speaks again.

"Thanks for coming by," he says. "I know the place is a wreck, but I'm trying."

"I can see that, Ray," she says, but her face says that she doesn't think he's trying hard enough.

"You haven't told him?"

"Not yet."

"I'd like there to be a time when you do."

"I'd like that, too, but I'm not holding my breath."

"Who does he think his father is?"

I find myself looking back and forth between them like I'm at a nerve-racking tennis match.

Ray has the deck stacked against him. I wonder what Nicole has told Michael about his father—what evils Ray will have to come back from. Jail. Worthlessness. The dead. Something even more impossible than that.

"I told him his father was sick and had to go away for help," she says. The explanation stings, but it's got its truth. "That way I can bring you home well. Or I can kill you off. Whatever need be. And that's up to you, Ray."

I imagine being killed off in one's own life—like a soap opera character who suddenly falls down a flight of stairs and breaks his neck because the actor who played him got arrested in real life.

"I'm well, Nicole," Ray pleads and then curses under his breath. "Please tell him his father is well."

I'm shocked by the ferociousness of his feelings. It's endearing and sad at the same time.

"I can't rush it," she says. Her voice isn't mean, just firm.

"I've missed five years," Ray says, watching Michael jump cars off the windowsill.

"And whose fault is that?" she says at last.

"Ok, so spitballing," Ray says, sitting on the coffee table in front of her. "We keep meeting here and there, and you finally tell him who I am. How do you explain that I've been here all this time? That I'm back from whatever imaginary place you sent me to, yet I didn't run right up to him and tell him who I am?"

"I don't know that part yet."

Ray curses again and stands up quickly, knocking back against the table.

"This isn't helping your case," she says in a hushed voice.

"What?"

"That you're cursing at me every other sentence."

"I'm cursing around you, not at you."

"That's not good enough."

"Because why?" he asks. "Because you said so?"

"Because you said you were clean," Nicole says and the words pour out of her. "Because you said you loved me. You said 'I'm going out for a pizza' and you never came back and I'm sitting there waiting for that stupid pizza because I'm starving and pregnant and afraid to tell you because I thought you might ditch me and then you ditched me anyway without any reason at all."

There's not much Ray can say to this. It's true. I think about slipping out—sneaking on tiptoe toward the door. Maybe I could excuse myself to the bathroom. Maybe I could jump out the window.

"I got busted that night," Ray says. "I didn't stop for pizza. I went out to meet up with a guy and got wasted and forgot where I parked so I wired a car but was too jacked up to drive it and I crashed it and landed myself in jail on drug charges, grand theft, DUI, and every other stupid thing I'd ever done."

She takes a deep breath and exhales loudly.

"Did you know the baby was yours?" Nicole asks. "When I came to tell you I was pregnant."

"Yes," Ray says. "You said you didn't want it to be mine."

"I didn't."

Michael looks over at us, and Nicole smiles at him—able to flux between anger and love seamlessly.

"Do you now?" Ray asks.

Nicole looks him full in the face, and both Ray and I brace for the coming tirade. But it doesn't come. She reaches over and takes hold of Ray's hand. He looks at her in shock.

"Ray," she says, "prove yourself wrong for once. This is your chance. I didn't have to call you. I could have let you leave town after your father's funeral and never said a word. Take that for what it's worth and try this time."

I hope so hard that Ray will listen to her.

"You know I'm going to screw up," he says. "Why torture me with a carrot on a string that I can't ever get to?"

"Let's just take it one step at a time," she says. "Hold down that new job you got. Better yet, go all out and do such a good job that you get promoted one day. Clean up your apartment. Meet us at the park Friday, and we'll go from there." She stands up and calls over to Michael.

"Can I keep these?" he asks me, holding up the cars.

Ray opens his mouth to answer, but Nicole speaks first. "Why don't you leave them here—that way you'll have something to play with next time we visit."

Next time. Ray catches it, too, and his head snaps up from where he's hung it low. Nicole gives him a half-smile and nods.

"I'll walk you out," Ray says and leads them through the door.

It's funny how you can see things clearly from the outside. When you have no real stake in an issue, it all makes perfect sense what each party should say and do, but from inside the thicket, it's hard to see a way out that doesn't result in briars and scrapes and a lot of tears.

Ray comes back upstairs and raises his eyebrows at me.

"It went well," I confirm.

"I thought so," he says. "Better than I expected."

I wonder what that was.

"Next time," I say, "try it without me."

"A little weird for you?"

"A smidge third-wheelish."

But really, I'm glad that he asked me to stay. My big brother wants me around. My big, tattooed, ex-con, tortured and somehow still lovable big brother wants me around.

16

At work, there has been more whispering around the water-cooler, as it were, about mergers and shutdowns, and I try to ignore the gossip and keep taking pictures of citrus drinks and condensation on fancy glasses. I think about that bowl of lemons Lola referred to.

Oliver and I have not seen each other since the night he told me about Cricket. I know he says he wants to be with me, but something stands between us, and since I can't see what it is, I don't know how to deal with it. I think about calling him, but I don't. I guess he must need time, too, because he hasn't dialed my number in days either.

When my phone does finally ring, it's Lola doing fish face.

"Can you come help me, Sissy?"

I don't even have to ask if she means now. It's the deep dark of night, and she's breathing too heavy and trying too hard to hold herself together.

When I get to Lola's house, the front door is open. There's a light on in the kitchen, and I walk through the familiar house not expecting to trip over a piece of broken furniture. So when I do, I curse at it. As my eyes become more accustomed to the dark, I see that Lola's house is in shambles. Ransacked.

"Lola," I scream out. "Where are you?"

She steps out from the kitchen into a beam of light. "Here," she says.

I rush to her, stumbling over things that aren't where they should be. I fold her into my arms when I reach her.

"What happened?" I ask.

"A break-in, we're assuming," she says.

While Lola was at the airport picking up Chris someone broke into her house and tore it to shreds. Isn't that the way it goes? As soon as you think you're on the right track, you leap over a burning log and run smack into a monkey with a sledgehammer.

"Where's Chris?" I ask.

"He's on the back porch on the phone with the police," she says.

"Are you ok?" I ask the dumb question.

"The gallery just delivered my remaining unsold paintings yesterday," Lola says after a minute. "Whoever broke in slashed them up pretty bad. Threw paint all over the ones I was working on."

"Lola," I say. It's all I can manage in that sort of desperate shock that makes it possible for you to only utter someone's name and nothing more.

"Well," she says, "the gallery kept a couple for display, so it's not a total loss."

I think about all her work, her art, her effort—gone. "I don't understand why someone would do that. Did they take anything?"

"Not much that we can tell," she says. "The usual—television, laptop—but mostly I think they were just having fun busting things up. Or maybe they were mad that I didn't have more stuff they could pawn. The paintings are the worst loss."

"I guess you could repaint them," I say, searching in vain for something that will make it better.

"That's not showing very much faith in myself, is it?" she says. Her bizarre ability for insight makes me jealous. "To think that the best I can do is what I've already done. No, something different, I think. Something new."

She says it with a wistfulness in her voice that speaks of something to which I'm not privy. As if she's already rising up from some other loss than this. Like this is a clearing out, a preparation for something better. Lola breaks down and then rises back up every time.

The braces she wore on her ankles gave her superpowers. I had always seen them as a cage, a bright and shiny binding to the reality of what life could do to knock you down. I think she saw them like that, too, at first. But she learned how to manipulate them, to trick them. She triumphed over them. Even the memory loss was a gift. Without the recollection of what life was, she was free to make it into anything she wanted. Even now, she uses her memory frailty not as an infirmity but as a many-windowed escape.

Nights like this, I see her the way God must see her—her light and soul. I envy both of them.

"Is Cassie still at Jack's?" she asks me, more concerned with everyone else around her than she is with herself. True Lola fashion.

"Yeah," I say, thinking for a moment that I should try to spin my response so that it seems like a good thing. But it isn't, so I don't. "Everything is awful."

"Sugar and water, Nina," Lola says. "It's not too late."

❖　❖　❖

A few days later, I meet Lola at the landfill. That's what we've taken to calling what's left of her house. The punks had busted out most of the overhead lights so Lola didn't see the whole of the disaster until the light of day. Everything was broken, the walls were covered in graffiti—and not even in an artistic way, Lola had lamented—and nearly every window was broken out.

"I guess this makes a case for having neighbors a bit closer than I do," Lola says while we work to clean up and throw away the remains.

"It's not like you're in the middle of nowhere," I say, pointing up the road. "There's a house right over there."

"Mrs. Grande wouldn't have heard anything if they were in her own house," Lola says. "I'm glad they came here and not there. She would have tried to fight them off, the feisty little thing, and would have probably gotten herself hurt, or worse."

"You are the most gracious person I know."

"How's Ray?" Lola asks. She reaches down to pick up a piece of something. She turns it over and over in her hand, squeezes her eyebrows together, and then tosses it back on the floor.

"He's good," I say. "You should visit. He's got the place set up really nice. Beer in the fridge and everything. Just like he's planning to stay a while."

"I will." She steps away from me and deeper into the broken remains of her house. "If he wants me to."

"Why wouldn't he want you to?"

"I told him," she says and picks up something that looks like part of the washing machine.

"About Chris? I think he knew about that already."

"No," she says. "I told him that I knew what happened."

"What do you mean what happened?" I pick up shards of glass from a broken picture frame and put them carefully into the trash.

"You know what I mean."

I stand there with my mouth agape.

"Close your mouth," she says. "You're letting flies in."

"Lola," I say, frozen to the ground. "I didn't know that you knew."

"Sure you did." She picks up a shard I missed. "But I appreciate the effort. I do. I told Ray as much, but you know how he is."

I do, and now I'm torn between fear and amazement. He knows she knows, and still he stays. This would be the perfect flight opportunity for Ray, but yet, here he remains, nest built and all. Suddenly everything seems fragile.

"You're afraid that he'll leave?" I ask, beginning to understand why she's staying away. "He's not going anywhere. He's here."

She looks at me and kicks at the edge of the knifed-up couch. "Nothing is a given. I don't think I can stand it if he goes away again."

"If you won't even talk to him, what's the difference if he's here or not?"

She looks at me and chuckles. "It's not about me. You guys always made it all about me."

"Babe," Chris says, coming into the room carrying one of Lola's paintings. "Look at this."

It's the Space Mountain painting with the word "Sorry" written in yellow spray paint across the center.

"Well, at least one of them was remorseful," Lola says. "Maybe I'll keep this one. The lettering is pretty well done."

Chris sets down the canvas and retreats back into the depths of the house.

"Why now?" I ask, shifting the question.

"It was time," she says. "Dad is gone. The jig is up. It's ok. Really."

"Is it?" I am brought up short by the memory of everything that ever was.

"Yeah. It would have been ok back then too, but just for me.

It wasn't time for everyone else. Mom needed me to forget, so I played along. Ray needed to forgive himself."

"Do you think he has? Forgiven himself?"

"No," she says. "But he's served enough time. So have I. I understand the desire to create something new from the wreckage. But it was time. I kept my promise as long as I could. It's not about me anymore."

"Your promise?"

Lola shakes her head at me, but smiles. "That night on the porch when we were little," she says. "I'd heard Mom and Dad fighting about me and the way things were before. Bits and pieces had already come back to me, and I was figuring it out pretty fast. I told you I wouldn't tell. And I didn't. But I think it's time we all got on with moving forward, don't you think?"

She says it all so easy and casual. She touches my arm and smiles at me. We pick over the remains of her world, showing each other things and nodding yes or shaking no to indicate their importance. There isn't much that gets a yes.

"You could move in with me until you clean this up," I offer when the conversation drifts that way. "It looks like this is going to take a while."

"Thanks," she says and kicks at a piece of dining room chair with her toe. "But I have somewhere in mind already."

"Ray's?" I ask, stumped.

"Be serious," she says. "Do you think he could look at me every day and not wind up in a puddle under the coffee table?"

"Chris?" I say, excited. "Is he moving here? Don't tell me you're going out there. I couldn't stand it. Don't you dare move to LA. Break up with him," I finish, laughing at my own turnaround in attitude.

"No, I'm not going to LA," she says. "I've been thinking about a new project. I think it's time." She holds out a bag of garbage that used to be her house. "I could become one of those Found Object artists."

"Well, you said you were looking for something new," I say.

"There is something sort of poetic about it. Making art from tragedy—literally."

Her whole life is art from tragedy. I guess I'm not surprised that she knows. I remember that night on the porch. Everything was so fragile, like the world was covered in eggshells. I wanted her to remember, but she was right—it wasn't the time. How gracious of a child to know her place in the world, her hold on the universe. How unselfish to remain quiet when quiet was needed. All this time. It makes Lola seem angelic to me. Capable of love so deep that self is less important.

I watch as Lola looks through the broken contents of her house. She seems happy. Free.

"Lately I feel like there is something else I'm supposed to be doing," she says.

"What do you mean?"

"I feel like I've closed myself inside a little golden birdcage, and I've just been waiting for the door to be left open. Now I think it is. I don't really know if these wings work, but what's the point in having them if I don't give them a try?"

"Is that why you told Ray?" I ask.

"He needs to try, too," she says. "It's time for all of us to fly."

Maybe not today, but one day, I will fly. Lola was six years old when she said that, running as fast as she could across the yard and leaping over the ditch, hoping to catch air and keep going. We were young, and the world had been made just for us.

I've stopped trying to fly. I forgot I had wings.

17

I meet Ray for lunch at the pizza place around the corner from his work. It feels so normal to sit with my brother and share a large spinach-and-Italian-sausage pie. I think about that image of us hacking through the jungle of the path less traveled. I fear rising up from a good dream and thinking that things are right with the world only to have wakefulness dissolve into reality.

I know he knows that Lola knows, but he hasn't said anything and I don't know why. I can't help myself. I blurt it out. "Ray, Lola told me."

"Told you what?" he asks, taking a sip of soda.

I cock my head at him.

"Oh," he says. "Can you believe it? Did you know she knew? You could have told me."

"No, I couldn't have," I say. "But I didn't know."

Not really.

I shrug my shoulders. I think we all wanted so badly for the white picket fence dream to be real, that even as the veil was lifting, we still played along. *Pay no attention the man behind the curtain.* We were all just as guilty as Mom, trying to pretend a better life.

"There were times she said things back then," I say. "You must have had an idea, too."

He shrugs his shoulders back at me. This means yes. But back then, the fear of that knowledge was scary enough to shut Ray up.

"When did she tell you?" I ask.

"At the cemetery. The day Mom buried Dad's ashes."

The waiter comes by and refills our glasses. I was so wrapped up in my own torture, I hadn't even seen Lola talking to Ray. I missed something huge enough to shake the whole world.

"When did she tell you she told me?" Ray asked.

"Yesterday. I went over to her house to help her clean up."

"Was what's-his-name there?"

"Chris," I say. "Yes."

"That's good." Ray nods.

I want to talk more about it, but I know this is already more than Ray can stand. Ray and I finish our lunch, and he calls for the check.

"On me," he says. "No argument."

"I fear the unemployment line is holding a space for me," I say. "So I'll take you up on that."

Ray pays, and we head outside.

"I'm surprised you're still here after she told you," I say. "I would have thought that news would send you into outer space."

"It did," Ray says. He stops right in the middle of the sidewalk, and people part around us like water running past rocks.

"Do you wish you'd known?" I ask. "Back then? Do you think it would have made things better or worse?"

"Do you mean, do I think I'd have messed up my life this bad if I'd known she knew?"

"Yes."

"I think it would have been worse. I don't think I could have handled it back then."

"Now?"

"Now, there's Michael," he says. "And you guys. And Dad is gone, and it's time for old Ray to grow up. If it's not too late."

"I don't think it is," I say. "I don't think it ever is."

Ray starts walking, and I follow. We don't say anything for a while and then he stops again. The people behind us have to short step around us to keep from colliding. Ray grabs hold of my arm.

"I think it might be, though," he says, his voice soft and brittle. "Too late. Nicole is used to living without me. She doesn't need me. And maybe Michael doesn't either. Lola thinks I'll just leave again, and she might be right. I know that's why she won't come around. No one needs me anymore."

"Sure they do," I say. *I do.* "You're hurting my arm, by the way."

Ray turns me loose. "I want to do this the right way, but I don't think I can. I'm not sure she's going to let me in. I can't read her. She keeps me at arm's length, and I'm going to screw it all up. I just know it."

I don't know if he's talking about Lola or Nicole, and I guess it's the same either way.

"Where is this all coming from?" I ask, guessing that Ray must still be in outer space.

"I feel desperate," he says, his eyes darting around. "Like I'm about to do something stupid. I know I shouldn't. But I'll probably do it anyway."

"You're scaring me a little," I say. "A lot. Are you drunk?"

"I'm sorry, Sis." He starts walking away from me so fast that I have to run to keep up.

"Ray," I call after him.

He doesn't slow down even after I catch up with him. He just keeps talking like he knows I'm there.

"I just want it all so bad, but I didn't put in the time—not in the right places, anyway—and it's not mine to have. It's just not mine."

We get to his office, and he leaves without saying good-bye. He opens the glass doors and disappears from view behind them. I stand on the street, shouting his name, but he doesn't come back out.

Later that day at work, I find out that I've joined Ray in his boat called Desperation setting sail on the high seas of Nowhere to Go from Here.

"We've been absorbed," my boss says to me.

"Absorbed?"

"Eaten up," she says. "We're closing. I didn't want you to hear about it with the masses. We've known each other a long time, and I owe you the value of the upper hand going in there."

The staff has been called together, and the watercooler buzz has gone from bad to worse.

"So that's it?" I say. "What about thirty-two stupid ways to make lemonade?"

"We'll wrap up these last few projects, then all the titles will be taken on by another house."

"What about me?" I ask. "Are they taking me on, too?"

"They have their own photographers," she says, her face a squinched-up apology. "Although I'm sure you could give them your resume. I'm sure they freelance. Maybe."

I sigh.

"I really am sorry," she says. "It's still a month off, though."

"Only a month?" I ask incredulously.

"You'll have time to finish the lemonade book. You'll get the photo credits and a nice check. Plus a little bit of a severance and some time to figure out what comes next."

"There's a severance?"

"Not much," she admits. "A couple of months' pay. One of

the perks of being a staff photographer, if you want to look at it that way. You can apply for unemployment. Look for work."

"Have a nervous breakdown." I continue the obvious line of thinking.

"I'm sorry," she says again. "I am. I really am, Nina. You came onboard at my insistence instead of freelancing and consulting, and I had hoped to give you a more steady and secure job. And it didn't pan out."

I'm grateful she doesn't give me the "You'll be ok" pep talk. She looks at her watch and excuses herself. Kids and a husband. Dinner, baths and bedtimes to adhere to.

I go home to my empty condo.

I want Dad. I want to talk to him. Hold-It-In Nina could let it out with him. I want to tell him about Oliver, about running into Jack, losing my job, about giving up. Dad was my flashlight in the dark, my spotlight in success, the sun, the moon, the fluorescents in my office—everything was lit by him. Now the power is out, and I'm stumbling around, banging my knee on the coffee table that I know is there but can't see now that it's dark.

I turn to the only thing of Dad's that I took from Mom's house. His old record player.

I put on his favorite song and pretend I'm not lost at sea.

In the still of the night . . .

I smile and begin to cry. I love this combination of emotion—the way one small thing can make you grieve and recover at the same time, sadness and hope in the same tears.

I held you, held you so tight . . .

. . . in the still of the night.

I sit on the couch and hug a throw pillow.

This is your lemonade year, I can almost hear Dad say to me. *You'll be all right, Sweet Pea. Come on, Big Guy. Give her just one good thing to turn it all around.*

18

I took him," Ray says when I answer the phone. His voice
sounds like he's a recording on an old record.

I'm shooting one of the last lemonade photos over at Mom's
house. It's a tea-infused concoction, which means I can use all of
the unwanted tea Lola has given to Mom.

"Who's that?" Lola asks, perched on the countertop across the
kitchen from me.

"Is that Lola?" Ray asks, having heard her voice. "Pretend I'm
not me."

"Easier said than done," I reply, stepping away from her as if
a few feet will mute the sound of my voice.

"Do not tell her who is on the phone," he says in a hushed,
staccato voice. "Where are you?"

"Mom's."

"Nina," Ray says, "do *not* tell *anyone* who you're talking to."

This is scaring me to death.

"It's Oliver," I lie to Lola in case she can discern a male voice.
"Mom's not home," I say to Ray.

"Oh," Lola says. "Tell the little hottie I said hello."

"Who the heck is Oliver?" Ray asks. "What is Lola talking
about?"

"Never mind," I say and excuse myself from the kitchen so
that Lola can't hear me.

"Are you dating someone from TV too?" Ray says, distracted.

"He's not on TV," I say, hiding behind the dining room table like an idiot. "Tell me what's going on."

"Wait a minute," Ray says. "You're dating someone?"

"I'm not really sure."

"You're not sure?" Ray says, and I can almost see his perplexed expression through the phone line. "What does that mean?"

"I don't know. It's not important right now. What is going on?"

"I took him," he says again. "Michael. I took him from the park."

My brother is an idiot.

We knew that, girl.

Whose isn't?

I always had a crush on Ray.

You guys are no help.

"Don't say anything," Ray says after I've said nothing. "I know it was stupid."

"Understatement," I say, my heart pounding. "Where is Nicole? Does she know you have him?"

"Yes," Ray says, and I sigh loudly. "She's pretty ticked at me about it though."

Lola yells from the kitchen. "I'm going to drink this lemonade if you don't come back in here soon."

I feel like I'm in some twisted play.

"Start from the beginning," I tell Ray. "And don't leave anything out. What did you do?"

I sit down on the floor cross-legged and wait for the story that will likely send my brother back to jail, unless Nicole is more merciful than he deserves.

"I met them at the park," Ray says. "It was great. Nicole was laughing, and Michael was talking to me about this new toy he just got. I swear, Nina, to anyone who didn't know, we looked just like a real family."

"And because things were going well, you decided to sabotage it?"

"No," he says, and then I hear him speaking to Michael in a soft voice, "Finish that up and you can get another one."

"Ray?"

"I asked Nicole if I could take him for a walk—just the two of us," Ray says. "She said yes. He took my hand and went with me. Just like that. He likes me."

I don't say anything. I can't.

"I don't know how to have him to myself any other way," Ray whispers across the phone line. "I'll take him back. I will. I know I will."

"Promise," I say. "And do it fast."

I can't process this.

"I just want it to be like I'm his dad," Ray says with a voice that makes me want to cry. "I want it to be like we're driving to Dairy Queen for ice cream and if he wants to get two scoops I'll let him, even if I think he's just going to drop the whole thing on the seat."

"Ray," I interrupt. "I don't understand this at all."

"When we got back to the playground, Nicole was talking to a friend," Ray says. "I asked Michael if he wanted to go for a drive, and he said yes. So instead of going back to the bench, we got in my car and drove off."

"Without asking Nicole," I say in confirmation.

"She knows I have him. She's left me about six blistering messages telling me to bring him back right away."

"And yet you haven't," I point out.

"He came with me," Ray says from somewhere on the end of the line, somewhere far away. "Just took my hand and smiled at me." Ray sighs. "I'm pretty sure this the last straw, so I might as well make the most of it."

"That's terrible logic."

"I know," he says in a voice so sad my eyes fill with tears.

Lola calls out to me again. "Your lemonade has a funny taste, but I guess it's not all bad."

"I love you," I say to Ray. "I love you so much."

"I know that," he says and ends the call.

Lola's face appears in front of me. "I thought you guys were still trying to see where things were going. I guess they're going well." She grins at me.

"I need to make a call," I say to Lola as I crawl out from behind the table. "I'll be on the porch."

"Sure," she says and tilts her head at me. "Not as good a hiding place, but there's a nice breeze. You're not calling Jack, are you?" she calls to me as I rush to the front door.

Outside, I call an old number I have for Nicole. Turns out the number I have is her mother's. When I give my name, Nicole's mother bursts into tears.

"Please tell me you know where they are," she says. "It was Ray, wasn't it? I told Nicole not to trust him. She won't tell me it's him, but I know it."

I assure her that everything is fine, and after much crying and catching her breath, she gives me Nicole's address.

"Your brother is an idiot," Nicole says when she opens the door and sees that it's me. "He could at least call me back and tell me they're ok. I'm out of my mind here. I mean, I know Ray wouldn't do anything on purpose, but this is Ray we're talking about."

"They're ok," I say, and her shoulders relax into a slump. "They're getting ice cream."

"Ice cream?" she says incredulously and sighs deeply.

She turns away from the door and walks back into her apartment. I'm still standing on the steps outside, unsure if I'm supposed to follow her in or not. After a moment, I step inside and close the door behind me. I find her in the living room, sitting on the couch with her head in her hands.

"Have you called the police?" I sit down beside her.

"The police?" She looks up at me sharply. "No, that's not a scene that I want in Michael's head—being pulled away by an officer while your father is pushed to the ground and handcuffed."

I think about the times Ray has been arrested. I never saw it, and now I have a picture in my mind that hurts my heart.

"Ray is so in love with Michael and so sure he doesn't have a shot at being in his life that he just flipped." I reach out to touch her arm, but draw my hand back. "He would never hurt Michael. He'd never take him from you—not for real. He's just desperate for something he thinks he can't have."

I've never felt so close to Ray as I do in this moment.

"Why didn't he just tell me all that?" Nicole asks. "We were talking. Things were going well. I wanted to be able to let Ray into our lives for real."

"If Ray could do that . . ." I start, but don't finish. "Besides, you knew that. Didn't you?"

"Yes," she says and leans back. "I never thought Ray was a bad guy. I don't think that now, either. I know he means well. He just doesn't know how to *do* well, and I can't spend too much time waiting on him to be different."

"He's on his way back now," I say. "Just give him a little more time."

"He better be back soon," she says, shaking her head.

At home, I pace. I call Ray's phone, but he doesn't answer. I hope he's at Nicole's place, down on his knees, begging her forgiveness.

The phone rings, and I grab for it. It's Oliver. My heart races even more. I want to pick up. I want to tell him what's happened. I want to hear his voice telling me to breathe, but I don't. His voice is too much for me right now. If I talk to him, I'll never be able to think straight again. I let the call go. He doesn't leave a message.

I pull up the lemonade photos on the computer and begin to edit them just to have something to do. I get bleary-eyed after a while, and I must drift off, because I'm startled awake when the phone rings again. It's Ray. I look at the clock. Almost midnight.

"How did it go?" I ask instead of the traditional greeting.

"We're about a block from your apartment," he says.

"We?" I say loudly into the phone. "Please tell me you don't mean you and Michael."

He doesn't answer.

I sigh.

"He knows who I am," Ray says, and there's a little glimmer of happiness in his voice. "I asked him if he knew who I was and he said 'I think you're my daddy.' Did you hear that?" Ray asks. "He knows. Call Nicole and tell her we're coming. I'll give you a couple minutes. And bail me out when she has me arrested."

"She didn't call the police, Ray," I say. "She's wants you to be part of Michael's life. She's giving you a second chance, but you've got to take it the right way."

"I don't know what that is."

"You know it isn't this," I challenge. "What took you so long anyway?"

"I took him back to my place for a while," Ray says. "We spent the afternoon and evening watching cartoons and eating pizza. I just wanted more time. He asked if he could stay until midnight." Ray laughs a little. "He almost made it, but he fell asleep."

"Are you crazy?" I suddenly see a little devil and angel version of myself sitting on either shoulder.

"I watched him sleep for about an hour. Then I scooped him up and put him in the car. I just wanted more time," Ray says again.

I think about the day of Dad's stroke. I said the same thing over and over to myself. *I'm not ready for this. I want more time. I'm not ready. Not ready. More time. I need more time.*

"Yeah," I say. "I know what you mean."

"Will you go with me to drop him off? Not for me—for Nicole. In case she needs someone to watch Michael while she beats the crap out of me."

"You've got it coming," I say, then pause. "Is that really why you want me to go with you?"

"No," Ray says, and his voice is so soft, so broken. "In case it's the last time I get to see him." He pauses, and I hear his emotion in the silence. "I just don't want to be alone."

My throat is tight, and when I breathe in its all snotty.

"Don't cry," he says. "It was worth it. I never would have had a shot at him anyway."

I don't believe that. I think Ray could have been happy, but his fear got the best of him.

"You in?" he says.

"You know I am."

Michael is asleep in the backseat of the car. Ray shrugs at me when I get in. I don't say anything.

"I called Nicole and told her I was on my way," Ray says. "That I was bringing you."

"You think she'll yell any less because I'm there?" I ask, buckling my seat belt.

"No," he says.

Ray starts the engine and then shuts it off again. He turns

in his seat and looks at me. He rubs his hand across his mouth several times the way people do when they're getting ready to say something serious—like they have to warm up their lips and coax the words out.

"Look," he says. "Thanks. For all those years ago when I was being a jerk. Back when we were kids and I didn't know how to cope with what happened to Lola and my part in it all. I should have been there for you, and I wasn't. I know you were coping, too. And then I pulled out of life and got sent away and missed, well, everything. And now I'm doing it again. Screwing everything up. I'll probably disappear again, and I hate that, but it's likely, so I just wanted to say—"

"Stop," I say sternly, actually holding my hand out toward him. "Don't you dare give me a good-bye speech. All we're doing right now is taking Michael home. That's it. Then you're going to go home, go to sleep, get up in the morning, and go to work. Understand?"

He takes hold of my outstretched hand; he is the one to reach out this time.

"I'm really sorry," he says. "I know you're searching for yourself, or something that you think you need. Give yourself a fighting chance. Don't screw up like I did."

"Ray, I mean it. Stop this." Tears are streaming down my face.

Ray squeezes my hand and turns me loose. He starts the car, and we drive in silence to Nicole's apartment building.

She's on the landing with her cell phone in her hand. Ray stops the car, and she walks casually down the steps like she isn't approaching the car of someone who stole her child. Ray gets out and stands next to the open door. She doesn't say anything, just walks up to Ray and slaps him hard in the face.

I look in the backseat where Michael is still asleep.

"What's the matter with you?" she asks Ray. "This is still new.

It's too new for you to sneak off without telling me. What am I talking about—it's *never* all right to sneak off without telling me and then stay out until after midnight without so much as a word, a phone call, a text, nothing. I didn't call the police even though my mother thought I should. I still might."

"Nicole," Ray starts, but she holds up her hand for him to stop.

I can't see their faces, and I'm glad of it. I'm not needed here, which is a good thing, but I feel like I'm spying.

Michael stirs in the backseat. Nicole opens the back door a crack. Michael sees her and smiles.

"This stuff right here is why I didn't tell you, Ray," she says. "Do you know how badly Michael wants you?"

"He does?" Ray asks.

"You're so stupid," she says. "How dare you put me in this position?"

"Nicole," he tries again, but she waves him off.

"We can talk later," Nicole says and opens the back door all the way. Michael hops out and hugs her. "Did you have a good time with Ray?" she asks him like she hasn't been riddled with worry this whole time they've been gone, even if she did know Ray had him.

Mothers can do that—change their voice, their eyes, and their face in a fraction of a second. They can close up the ache in their heart and put a smile on their face and make everything all right for the little three-and-half-foot-tall piece of forever in front of them.

"Mr. Ray is my daddy," Michael says as proudly as anyone has ever said anything.

Nicole looks at Ray, who is looking at Michael with eyes so filled with pain and love that Nicole sighs and confirms it. "Yes, honey. He is."

Ray struggles extremely hard not to cry.

"We got ice cream," Michael says. "I got two scoops. One fell off."

She kneels down in front of him and touches the spot on his shirt. She looks inside the car at me, and we offer pressed-lipped grimaces to each other.

"I see that." Nicole smiles at Michael like she isn't seething inside. "Tell Daddy bye for now and run on inside. It's very late."

I know she's using that term to please Michael, that it's not for Ray's benefit or happiness, and the sound of it makes my stomach ache. It's everything he wanted, and it's further away now than ever.

I crane my neck to see what's happening. I don't care if I'm spying anymore. Michael hugs Ray's legs, and I see Ray tousle Michael's hair, giving him a "See you soon, buddy."

Michael runs inside, and Nicole rounds on Ray.

"I'm sorry," Ray says preemptively. "I just wanted for things to feel normal."

"This is *not* normal," she says. "Did you really not know that? There's a way to do things, and then there's the way *you* do things, and if you can't start doing things the way regular people do them, then I don't think this is going to work."

I inhale sharply.

"What's not going to work?" Ray says, his face out of view, his voice warbling.

"For crying out loud, Ray—you and me and Michael."

She slams the backseat door closed without acknowledging me again. The driver's side door is still ajar.

"What if I don't know how to be normal?" Ray asks.

"You mean, what if you're too afraid to be," Nicole says. "This is all a front, and you know it. All of it. I've set the bar pretty low, and you're failing miserably. I'll tell you what—why

242

don't you think about it, and when you can come up with something normal, call me. I won't be holding my breath."

She goes back into her apartment without another word or glance to either of us. Ray gets back in the car and breaks down into sobs. I put my hand on his shoulder, and he shudders.

◆ ◆ ◆

The next day, Ray calls me from work—which is a relief.

"I need to do something. Will you come with me?"

I don't answer.

"It's nothing illegal or even inherently dumb," he says. "Cut me some slack."

When we get to the cemetery, Ray idles the engine for a while before he shuts it off. He opens the door to get out but then shuts it again. I get out of the passenger side and go around to open his door. He pulls on the handle from the inside so I can't open the door. I yank, and he yanks back.

I lean down to the window so I can see his face. "Get out," I say to him.

"No," he says. "Mistake—get back in."

I know he's still holding the door handle so I deliver a low blow.

"Look at that spider!" I point at some ambiguous spot inside the car.

LOL my scary big brother is afraid of spiders.

"Where?" he shouts, his voice only slightly muffled by the closed door.

He takes his hand off the handle, and I seize the opportunity.

"Get out," I say.

"That was dirty," he says. "I'm impressed."

Ray gets out, and we walk toward Dad's plot. The sky is

overcast today—like it's been special-ordered to fit the scene. Low thunder rumbles over the far left corner of the dead.

The ground is still raised a bit where Dad's urn went in. It looks like a mole hole. Too small for the significance of what's buried there. I don't know why, but I take a picture of it with my phone. Ray looks at me quizzically. I shrug.

The date of Dad's death has been carved in the stone. Now that I see it, I wish it had been left the way it was. It seemed then like something macabre, but in hindsight, it was more like ridiculous hope.

I hear footsteps approaching and turn to see Mom walking toward us with another one of her massive flower creations.

"I just can't catch a break," Ray says.

Mom nods at me and sets the carnation contraption beside Dad's stone.

"How's your father doing?" Mom asks, oblivious.

"Great," I say. "He was just telling me about a fishing trip he's planning with Uncle Paul."

Ray smiles, and Mom purses her lips at me.

"How are things with you, Ray?" she asks like he's her nephew twice removed.

"I think I'm going to be ok," he says, in a peaceful tone of voice. "I hope."

"Did something happen to you?" Mom asks, concerned.

Ray and I look at each other. He wrinkles his brow, and I nod.

"Mom," Ray says, taking her hand. "I need to tell you something."

"Sounds grave," she says and tweaks Ray's nose.

"I've done something stupid," he says. "Again. But I had a really good reason."

Ray seems so childlike to me in this moment. Innocent even.

As if confessing the thing can take it away. Suddenly I fear that one of these gravesites will open up and suck Ray down in it. I imagine the shock on his face when his feet give way beneath him, his eyes catching mine for a second as he drops out of sight—his hand reaches up, but I can't grab it in time and he's gone. The sinister earth closes up over him forever.

"I figured as much," Mom says to Ray and repositions Dad's carnations. "Are you staying for dinner tonight?"

"Don't you want to know what I did? And why?" Ray says.

Mom cocks her head to one side and then the other like she's mulling something over. "Not really. You're not in jail, I didn't see you on the news, and you're not bleeding. I guess whatever this stupid thing is, you have it under control. So, no. I'd rather not know."

"The news, huh," Ray says. "Do people still watch the news?"

"I don't," Mom says. "Too depressing. I feel like a big salad with tons of veggies," she says, presumably about dinner. "What about you?"

"I feel like a chump," Ray says.

"Nina," Mom says, not commenting on Ray's proclamation. "Will you come by, too?"

I nod.

Mom points to the car to indicate that she's ready to leave. As we walk away, I look over my shoulder at Dad's plot. I can imagine him standing there looking at the obnoxious flower arrangement and smiling.

One thing I can say for your mother, when she does something— for the good or the bad—she goes all out. I see him look me straight in the eye and wink at me. *Buck up, kiddo. It's all uphill from here.*

I blow a kiss to Dad and catch up with Ray and Mom's conversation.

"I'm sure it's not as bad as you think," Mom is saying.

"With me, it's usually worse," Ray says.

We get back to the cars and Ray stops Mom from getting in. "Mom," he says. "I get it."

"What's that?" she asks, fishing in her purse for the keys.

"All of it."

Mom's hand freezes in mid-search, and her head pops up. Her eyes lock on Ray. "Thank you," she says.

They could be talking about anything. But they're talking about everything. Everything that doesn't need to be put into words that will never do it justice.

"It might be too late to fix this thing," Ray says, "but I'm going to try to do better."

She takes hold of both his hands and spreads his arms out. She looks at him like she's surveying a wreck.

"Son," she says. "If you touch a lightning bolt, it's going to knock you off your feet. But if the shock doesn't kill you, then you get back up and carry on. Right?"

Ray allows her to hug him.

"Your dad never stopped hoping for you," she says. "Don't you stop either."

◆ ◆ ◆

Before Ray managed to end up in prison for a couple of years, he'd spent more than his fair share of weekends there. He called it his vacation spot. Once, when he'd gotten off on a technicality on an offense that should have sent him away, I pretended I didn't know where he was when Dad asked. Dad didn't believe me and made me drive him to Lola's place in my car, so Ray wouldn't suspect it was him.

Dad flattened himself against the wall beside the front door, the way the police do in the movies—waiting for the bad guy to come outside so they can catch him off guard.

"Ray already saw you and Dad in the parking lot," Lola said, peeping through the door she'd cracked open. All I could see was one eye and the side of her mouth.

"This is ridiculous," I said.

Dad popped out from beside the door, and Lola jumped. "Ray!" he shouted into the house. "Son, I just want to see you."

The sound of Dad's voice made my eyes water. Lola stepped back and let the door swing open. I could see around Dad and over Lola's shoulder and into the hallway. At the end of the hall, Ray stepped into view. His face was fixed and ready, but when his eyes met Dad's, there was a crack in the stone. He stepped out of view again.

"I meant what I said, son," Dad shouted back into the house.

I didn't know what he meant, but words weren't a threat. They were a reminder of that night in the street, when Lola was spirited away in an ambulance and we found Ray huddled in a corner in the alley.

"That will do for now," Dad said to us and walked back to the car.

A father's love is unbreakable.

After that, Ray stuck around, but not for long.

Lola wanted him to come to her very first gallery show. She said he was the special guest. He tried to beg off, saying that he didn't have anything to wear. Lola told him to come anyway— that his arms were art and he'd fit right in. He didn't mean for the tattoos to be art. He meant for them to be a warning. The fire breathing devil down his left arm was matched by more fire and brimstone creeping up his right arm and down the middle of his back. I think, really, they were supposed to be a shield.

Ray said thanks but no thanks and wished her luck. He couldn't stay away though. He had to be near. He tried to skulk along the edges of the gallery and not be seen. But I found him.

"What do you think?" I asked, gesturing at the paintings.

"I didn't know she could do this."

"She's good."

"It's me, isn't it?" he asked. "That one of the devil with the fire-breathing man for arms. I get it."

"You're all she thinks about," I said. "Still."

"I should grant her escape then."

"You want me to believe that you don't need her just as much?" I asked.

"It's all too loud," he said. "The fireworks, the tire squall, the freaking clack-clack of those braces."

"She's upset that you're not here," I said.

"Tell her I saw it," Ray said. "Tell her I see everything. She'll know what that means."

Sometimes Ray seems like a bear coming out of a cave, starving and squinting into the sun, wondering how long he's been out and if there is anything left around him.

19

My last month of work has passed, and to take my mind off my first Monday without a job, I call Carol, my grade-school friend, to meet me for lunch in Oliver's part of town. I aggravate myself by calling it that. Oliver's this, Oliver's that. Delineating sections of the world that belong to another place in my life, places from which I have voluntarily shut myself out.

"You look terrible," Carol says and opens her arms to envelop me.

"That's too generous," I say, falling into the safety of her embrace.

"Sounds like we need a very unhealthy appetizer. Carbs and cheese?"

"You know me too well."

She signals the waiter, and in short time he brings us a plate of breads, oils, and cheeses.

"How's the book coming? What's your next assignment?" Carol's questions make me ashamed of how much I've kept her at a distance these last months.

"Curtain call," I say in a pathetic attempt to catch her up to speed. "The book is done, the house is closed, the unemployment line is in the offing."

"I see," she says, not really needing much more of an explanation.

Good friends are like that.

I don't mention Oliver. She knows all too well the way things unfolded with Jack, having heard about it enough times already. Maybe I feel silly and cliché. Maybe I just want something sacred.

Carol breaks off rosemary focaccia and dips it in some avocado oil. She nibbles on her food, giving me time to continue.

"I'm sorry," I say. "These past months have been a bit more than I'm used to."

"Ok," she says, pushing away the bread and the menu—piecing my life together as best she can with the bits of information I've given her. "The house got bought out and you didn't get bought with it?"

"Bingo." I slide the bread plate closer to me.

"You thought you were in far enough with them to be safely shuttled to the next phase."

"I did," I say, admitting my own arrogance. "Right now, it just seems like another piece of my life that I had wrong. And something else I have to figure out how to fix. It's the least of my problems actually."

"I get the feeling there's more to this than I know," she says.

There's always more to it than anyone knows. I'm tired of compartmentalizing my life and having to keep track of who knows what and who doesn't. It makes everything feel fake. I'm tired of being locked up in the Nina-box. It's cramped and lonely in here.

The waiter comes to check if we are ready to order. We look quickly at the menu and give him our decisions.

"So, you need a job?" Carol asks, knowing when to change the subject.

"You got one?"

"I don't think there's much demand for photos of hospital

cafeteria food," she says. "You're good, sweetie, but I don't think anyone could make that stuff look appetizing."

I fiddle with my silverware and the last of the cheese and try not to breathe in too deeply. I'm afraid the intake of air will be followed by an outpouring of tears.

"What about teaching?" she says. "Isn't that what you wanted to do way back when?"

"Back when we were in school," I say. "And the world was ours."

"It was, wasn't it?" she says, looking fondly into the past.

"I didn't plan to have to reinvent myself at this age," I say, moving the bread plate away as our entrees are set in front of us.

"The whole concept of reinvention is unintentional," she says, arranging her side of the table as well. "No one would need to reinvent anything if they could have seen the right way to do it in the first place."

"You get smarter every time I see you."

"I just know you well enough to know that you can start over and be happy."

"Why don't I know that?"

"Don't you?" she asks in direct challenge.

I look out the window and across the street, prepared to contemplate that notion for a while. But then, there he is.

Oliver, two other young guys, and a girl take seats around an outdoor table at another restaurant across the narrow, downtown street.

It shouldn't surprise me to see him on the side of town he frequents. It shouldn't, but it does. I instinctively slump in my chair. I doubt he could see me, even if he looked. The restaurant we're in is shaded by an awning and masked with tinted windows.

Carol clears her throat, drawing my attention back. "Lost you there for a second," she says, peering down my line of sight. "Do you know those kids?"

Kids.

"What?" I stall. "No, I just thought I saw someone. Sorry."

I take a bite of walnut-crusted salmon and try to appear normal.

"Someone you hoped didn't see you?" she correctly questions, knowing me too well. Our friendship has often paused for periods of time while each of us carries on the lives we've grown into, but it has never disappeared.

I ignore the question, so she continues to talk about other things, things I can't focus on, because across the street I watch the girl nudge one of the guys out of the way and take a seat next to Oliver. Is this what he's been hiding? My heart plummets, but then rebounds when Oliver doesn't seem to pay notice to the girl's continuing advances.

Carol keeps talking about her schedule at the hospital or someone being in the hospital, I'm not sure. I try to look at her as she speaks, but I keep stealing glances out the window whenever she sips her drink or looks at a passerby.

Through the glass, I watch Oliver like he's in a silent play. With no textual cues, I focus on his actions. I study everything about him. Some things I've come to know already, like the way he tugs at his hair while listening to someone else talk. I notice new things, that I haven't seen before, like the way he circles his finger around the top of his glass between sips.

A waitress brings them a basket of chips, and while everyone grabs for a handful, Oliver excuses himself to a bench along the street. He pulls out his phone and places a call.

My phone rings. I thrash around in my bag for the phone. The call screen lights up with a picture of Oliver laughing and biting into a lemon—a silly shot I'd taken weeks ago. I don't answer.

"Not who you were expecting?" Carol asks. I'm sure she noted how quickly I grabbed my phone.

"No," I say, gripping the thin silver case in my hand. "It was just, no one."

Our waiter brings more water and asks if we need anything. I watch Oliver give up on the call and pocket his phone without speaking. Just as he's about to look up and straight into our restaurant, the girl comes over to him. I can't hear what she's saying, but I image it's some seductive attempt to lead him back to their group—to her. But instead he holds up a finger to indicate *one minute*, gets his phone back out, and places another call.

Again, my phone rings.

"Are you sure you shouldn't get it?" Carol asks.

"I shouldn't," I say, and Carol lifts an eyebrow.

I watch Oliver speak into his phone this time. He talks for a couple of minutes, and the anticipation kills me. I watch his face move through a series of expressions that end without resolution. His face is soft and sorrowful. He ends the call and rejoins his friends, his admirer already leaning into him. I press the buttons needed to retrieve my messages. His voice is just as soft and sorrowful as his face was.

"Nina," Oliver says in my ear. "I've been thinking about you. I don't know why you won't talk to me. I don't know what went wrong. I just want you to know"—he pauses—"that I'm sorry it did. I need to talk to you. I need to tell you something."

My heart is racing, and I hold up one finger to Carol to indicate I'll be off the phone in a moment. She waves at me as if to say not to worry. Oliver pauses, and I think the message is over, but then his voice comes across the line again.

"You know what I hear all day? From the people at the

nursing home? I hear what they're stuck in. One lady is afraid her sister is going to call the police and report her for stealing the pink purse that their mother won at the fair. One lady spends all day packing for Denver. She's not going to Denver.

"All day, I hear the insanity in their heads, I hear 'I'm sick, I'm hungry, find my purse, my dog is napping in the oven, I hate you, I love you, what time is it, when the road closes the button gate feels soft,' and it's all just a blaring neon sign saying don't spend your life regretting that you didn't do what you were meant to do. You have to do it while you still know who you are."

There's another pause and then his voice softens.

"I'm completely in love with you, Nina. Maybe I thought I wouldn't fall in love with you. But I did. I really need to see you."

Again, there is a pause, but this time the message stops, and a voice tells me to press one to repeat the message or seven to delete it. I don't want to do either of those things.

I slip the phone back in my bag, apologize to Carol, and then attempt to be friendly and present through the rest of our meal. I'm sure I do a terrible job because I can barely keep my eyes off Oliver as he sits with his friends, eating and talking.

After we pay our checks, Carol and I walk outside. All Oliver would need to do to see me is look up, but he's listening to one of the other guys tell what must be a long and interesting story. I stall, fidget, and then give up.

"You ready?" Carol asks.

"I—" But there is no point in finishing the sentence, and we start to walk away.

I begin to have a panic attack. Maybe not a real one in the true medical sense, but I feel like the air I just inhaled is being ripped back out of my lungs. When I try to breathe again, my air passages are on lockdown. Each step I take away from Oliver shoots fire up my calves, radiating a sense of desperate indecisiveness through my internal navigation system. I want to fling myself into the street for lack of anything better to do.

"Darn," I say with sudden planning. "I don't think the waiter gave me back my debit card."

I stop on the sidewalk and pretend to search my purse. Carol seems to believe me and assumes the proper panic-by-association stance of a good friend.

"You go on ahead," I say to her. "I know you need to get to work. I'll just run back and get the card."

"I can go with you," she says, ever helpful.

"No, no," I say and hope it's not obvious that I'm trying to rid myself of a witness. "I'm sure it's there. I'll call you later."

She hugs me good-bye, and I turn and walk slowly in the other direction. I catch a large group of people crossing the street and duck into their midst. I slip inside the boutique beside the restaurant where Oliver still sits outside with his friends. I stand too long pretending to look at a display of handmade jewelry, and the salesperson comes to ask if she can assist me.

"No, no," I say. "I'm just looking."

Out the window to see which way my sort-of-boyfriend goes so that I can follow him.

Oliver begins to make what looks like good-byes before everyone else has finished, and the lone girl seems reluctant to let him go. He's gracious in his rejection of her, and I remember with a pang the sincerity of his phone message. He drops his share of money on the table and makes his way through the outdoor crowd to the street. I wait for him to walk far enough away to have his back solidly to me and then I exit the shop.

My blood seems to stop in my veins, my hands and feet are cold, and I'm nearly shivering with something like fear but more like hope. I'm no good at the spy thing, and I'm sure I'll be embarrassed in short time. Oliver walks at a slow pace, the pace of someone in no hurry to reach nowhere in particular. He stops on occasion to look at something in a window. He says hello to someone as they pass, and I turn my head in fear that it's a friend who might recognize me, might see me following, and shout out to Oliver that I'm right behind him. That doesn't happen.

We—as if we're in on this together—stop at a local bookshop. It's not the one where we first began whatever this is that we're in. This one is well lit and lively. No cavernous twists and turns in which to hide. Oliver hesitates at the door before going in. I try to read something into that pause, but I don't know what it means.

I know if I go in after him there will be no good place to hide in the intimate interior of the bookstore. I hesitate for a moment myself, letting him move deeper inside the store before I follow. I can still see his back as I open the thick glass door. He is so close that one glance over his shoulder and my acting skills will be tested. He moves to the left toward the small café, and I go around to the right to duck behind the new releases. He goes to the counter, and I think he's going to order a coffee, but then he changes his mind and comes back toward my hiding place. I hurry into the depths of the store, trying to remain unseen, and I lose track of him. It would be smart of me to slip out, but I don't. I ease through the rows, peeking around corners, until I catch sight of him and stop short.

He's in the small Philosophy and Religion section. He's standing very near the shelves, holding a large book not unlike the philosophy tomes I've seen at his house. I want to slip up to him and make a joke or something to break the ice. *Doing a little light reading?* But I stay put. I can see his face in profile, and I watch him turn the pages of the book. He looks surprisingly peaceful.

We're both startled when one of his friends from the restaurant comes around the corner and punches him lightly on the shoulder. Oliver closes the book like he's been caught with something illicit.

"Dude," his friend says, "what was that about?"

"What?" Oliver says, shaking his head.

"I know you're having troubles with that lady friend of yours, but you gotta snap out if it."

At the mention of me, I slink back just enough so that all I can see is the friend's profile and Oliver's feet as he shuffles his weight back and forth.

"Sara throws herself at you, and you just get up and leave."

"Sorry, man," Oliver answers, but his voice doesn't indicate that he is.

"At least you're predictable, and I knew where to find you," his friend huffs. "We're all going over to Flannigan's—you coming?"

"I don't think so, thanks." Oliver's voice sounds young and casual, but also serious and sad.

"I don't get it," his friend says, lifting his hands in disbelief. "Sara is practically a sure thing, and instead I find you reading the Bible or something. What section is this anyway?"

I see his friend look around like he's just discovered he's lost.

"Dude," he continues. "If you're not interested in her, I am."

"Go for it, man," Oliver says from just out of sight.

"Whatever," his friend says and slaps him on the shoulder, bringing the conversation to a close. "I'll see you around."

"See you," Oliver says.

His friend steps out of view and Oliver comes back into it. He opens the book he still has cradled in his hands and resumes reading, oblivious to me or anyone else around him. I watch him for a few minutes. He closes the book and puts it back on the shelf. He picks up another, much smaller book and tucks it under his arm without opening it. He goes up to the counter and pays for the book. I follow him toward the door, but hold back and let him leave me there.

Once I exit, I hurry onto the sidewalk without much regard to being found out. The streets are busy, and I'm lost in the crowd of late-July tourists. I look this way and that, trying to spot him. He's walking more briskly this time, and I duck and weave through the foot traffic to keep up with him. I don't know how to judge where he's going, but when he stops, I understand. We're across the street from my old office building. He doesn't know I don't work there anymore.

Twice, he steps forward to cross the street, but stops both times. He takes out his phone, and I know if he calls me he'll be close enough to hear the ringtone that he assigned himself to my phone. I panic and dart back through the pedestrians, reaching for my phone as I run.

It rings. I don't answer. I hold the phone pressed between my hands and rest it against my lips like it's Oliver himself. When the phone chirps at me, I listen to the message.

"Nina." Oliver's voice is a strange mix of lightness and resignation. "I need to give you something. It can't wait. I need to see you."

Then he leaves me an address, asking if I'll meet him there the next day.

I watch him cross the street toward my building, and I think he's going to go in, but he turns back down the street and I know he's heading home. He's got the little book clutched in his hand.

20

I recognize the street from Oliver's voice mail as being downtown. It's not too far from my old office, but I can't image why he wants to meet at that end of town.

I park at work, my old pass still letting me into the garage for now, and walk along the busy street. I go all the way to the end of the road and arrive at my destination. The Catholic Basilica. I recheck the paper where I have written the address, feeling like a character in a movie who has been given a false clue to lead her off the trail.

I pull open the door and enter the cool darkness of the old building. The noises of traffic and chatter grow dimmer as the door closes behind me, shutting out the bright midday sun. Inside the church, the air is soft and candlelight glows from the votive array—prayers made and vigils begun.

I don't see Oliver. My first thought is to text him, but if he's in here, I don't want the buzz of a phone to disturb the few people sitting in the pews. I move toward the center aisle and look up at the high, domed ceiling. All around me are stained-glass windows with scenes of Jesus and His disciples. It's been awhile since I went to church, but I recognize the story.

I walk down the aisle toward the front, stealing glances at the statues of saints that line the walls and fill the alcoves at the corners of the church. I breathe in warm-smelling incense and imagine I can feel the prayers that have left the lips of the lonely, hurting, and hopeful.

I need to give you something. Oliver's words resound in my mind, and I wonder for just a second if he's going to propose.

At the front of the church, someone steps out of a pew and turns to face me. He's wearing a long black garment that tapers in at the waist. He walks toward me with a familiar gait. It's Oliver. I'm utterly confused. He stops in front of me and offers a small and somewhat apologetic smile.

"Are we going to a costume party?" I ask, trying but failing to make a joke.

He shakes his head and bites on his beautiful bottom lip. I suck in an incense-laden breath of air.

"You're a priest?" I say, more loudly than I mean to, and the sound of the words bangs against the stone walls and comes back to me in an echo.

"Not yet," he says. "But soon. I decided to go back to school."

My mouth falls open, and I look instinctively at the enormous crucifix behind Oliver. All I can think about is Oliver's lips on mine, his hands around my waist, my hands on his chest, me kissing his neck—and then . . . him pulling away. Him. Always.

"Oh, no," I say and quickly put my hand to my mouth as if I can shove the words back in. "I'm so embarrassed."

"Why are you embarrassed?"

"We kissed, and we—" I feel myself blush. I'm stammering, and he's smiling at me. "Well, we *kissed.*"

"I've already talked to the Big Guy about that, believe me." Oliver waves his hand to dismiss my fear. "You don't need to worry over me."

"You?" I ask. "What about me? I'm sure this is frowned upon up there."

"You didn't know," he says apologetically. "So, this is what I've been hiding from you." He gestures to his clothes. "When I said I had dropped out of school, I meant the seminary. When I kept telling you I needed to tell you something—this was it."

"So when you said you were getting your master's degree, you meant Master's in . . ."

"Divinity," he says.

I clap my hands over my mouth again. "I'm going straight to hell," I say, the words mumbled through my fingers.

He suppresses a grin. "Come outside with me." He nods his head for me to follow him.

We exit through the far door of the church and into the sunlight again. Oliver leads me around a shrine of some sort to a small rose garden behind the building, and we sit on a bench at the feet of a large, stone angel.

"I hope you're not angry with me," he says, his voice calm and low. "It's all right if you are."

"This isn't fair, you know," I say, moving my hand up and down to indicate his attire. "They should only let ugly people be priests. You're not nearly ugly enough." The joke is my way of letting him know that I'm not angry. I'm something, but not angry.

"So, I'm sort of ugly," he says, smiling that incredible smile of his at me. "Just not ugly enough."

"No," I say. "You're gorgeous. And that getup does nothing to hide it."

He gestures to the black cassock he's wearing as if to say *this old thing?*

We sit for a moment and just look at each other.

"So you're not mad?" he asks, his brow furrowed.

"I'm confused," I say, but then realize that's not right. "That's not true. This clears up a few things, actually."

"Like why I always pulled back from a relationship?" he says, twisting his mouth in an apology.

I nod, but it's more than that. "You always seemed so sad," I say. "Underneath it all. Was this making you sad? That you had to become a priest?"

Oliver smiles the most gracious and blissful smile I've seen. He chuckles and shakes his head. "Trying to choose the world over God was making me sad. Finding myself in love with you made me sad."

"Excuse me?"

"That came out wrong," he says and takes my hand in his. "I walked away from the seminary before I knew you. I was scared, and I thought that my doubt and everything I'd ever done wrong made me unworthy. So, I left school."

"And came here?"

He nods.

"What about Cricket and working at the nursing home?" I ask, trying to sort out the rest of the story. "What about me?"

"Everything I told you was the truth," he says. "The lie is in what I left out. I was using life like a pair of earplugs so I wouldn't hear Him calling me."

"God?"

Oliver nods again, and there is such a peace about him now that I couldn't stay mad even if I was. I knew he was struggling with something. I just never would have guessed it was this.

"I really hate to be all, so none of that was real," I say, looking back at Oliver's beautiful face lit up from the inside, reflecting the sun back at me, "but was none of that real? Was I some sort of test? Because, if so, you should have given yourself a better shot at it. Why not one of the girls from work or that girl from the restaurant yesterday?"

Oliver tilts his head at me, but he doesn't say anything.

"Did you just pick me out of the blue?" I ask.

"Nina," Oliver says, putting both hands around mine now.

"Why do you think I rushed out to help you put Nate's things in your car back at the nursing home?"

"You're nice?" I offer.

"I'm a helpful guy," he says, "but no. I wasn't ready to see you go. I thought you were the most beautiful thing I'd ever seen. You were so funny and smart. You were passionate about your dad's care. I already felt like I knew you and I already liked you. You were completely oblivious to me, though."

"Not completely."

"It was all real. I didn't seek you out to distract me. If I'd wanted a distraction, I would have gone for some pretty, young thing who just wanted to hook up and hang out at the bar."

"I'll try not to let that comment make me feel as old as I am."

"What I mean is, I was never going to miss the silly games and shallow relationships. Choosing this calling meant sacrificing a real relationship with a woman I respected and loved. I thought I didn't want to make that sacrifice. But it turns out, saying no to what I've always known I wanted was the sacrifice."

I point at the church, and he nods.

"When I fell for you, I thought it meant I was right, that I'd been wrong about this gig." He gestures at his clothes and back at the church. "I just didn't want to listen when God was calling. I thought it would be easier that way—that answering Him would be hard. I didn't want a hard life. I thought that the black robe looked scary, but now, I can't wait to put it on every day. I wanted to open the door, but I knew there would be no going back once I did. Now that it's open, I can't stop myself from wanting to run through it."

I squeeze his hand. "This actually makes me feel better about you turning me down all the time."

"Do you have any idea how hard that was?" he says and smiles a devilish smile. "Letting go of you was a hard decision. Following Him wasn't. I just had to get out of my own way."

"So, once you do this"—I nod at the church behind us—"that's that?"

"You mean dating and women and all that?" He chuckles. "Yep, that's that."

"Ever consider becoming Protestant?" I wink at him.

He laughs out loud, lighting up his beautiful face even more. He is completely at ease, and the difference in his demeanor and mannerisms is noticeable.

"It's going to be totally unfair, you know," I say, glancing around the colorful rose garden, seeing the beauty all around me. "These poor women having to confess to you about being attracted to their priest. Cut a girl some slack."

"You're just flattering me," he says, waving it off, but blushing nonetheless.

"Maybe you can grow a huge beard or let your eyebrows get all wonky," I say.

He laughs again and this time has a hard time getting himself back together. I laugh too.

"I'll miss this part of us the most," he says.

I realize that his hands are still pressed around mine.

"I'll miss you, too," I say and hold tighter to his hand. "So, what now? I guess you're leaving for school?"

"The semester starts in August," he says, "but I've missed registration already. So I'll stay in town until January and go then. I need to get some things settled here anyway and make sure that Mr. Cole is taken care of. His daughter is finally able to move here, so she'll take over the house and be here to look after him. Then I'll head back to Charlotte, finish seminary, and see what God has in store for me. What about you?"

I don't really have any idea. The lemonade book is done. The divorce is final. Cassie is still gone.

"What do you want, Nina?" Oliver asks, his eyes searching mine. "What would make your heart happy?"

"My heart?" I look away. "Aren't you supposed to worry about my soul?"

"Classic Nina deflection," he says and chuckles. "Yes, I'm concerned for your soul, and I'm here for you when you want to talk about that, too."

I wrinkle my brow but stay silent.

Oliver touches my check. "What's broken that needs to be fixed? What were you hiding from while you were at my house taking pictures of lemons? What didn't you want to deal with?"

My marriage, my part in its demise, my teenage daughter growing up, up, and away.

"The easy way out is just a way out," Oliver says. "Then the door shuts behind you, and everything you had is gone. You don't have to let the door close on what you really want."

"This right here is what I'm talking about," I say, and Oliver wrinkles his brow. "How do you expect women to listen to your words of wisdom with that gorgeous face looking at them?"

"It's just the way God made me," he says and winks at me.

"Well done, God," I say and make an exaggerated thumbs-up to the sky. "Well done, indeed."

Oliver blushes and lets go of my hand. I think he's going to stand up and leave, but instead he reaches out and touches my face. He runs a strand of my hair through his fingers and then puts his hands in his lap. This is his good-bye, I can feel it.

He reaches into his pocket and pulls out something. He opens his hand, and I see my wedding rings.

"I think we've both known all along what we really want," he says and nods for me to take the rings. "This is really what you want, isn't it? Your marriage."

I take the rings from his hand and slip them back on my finger.

"You know where to find me," he says and stands up. "I need to get back inside. I have no idea how to say good-bye to you, so I won't. I'm here if you need me."

He bends down and kisses me on the top of the head and walks away.

I slouch back on the bench and look up at the angel above me.

21

"Oliver broke up with me because he's secretly a priest," I say when Lola answers my call.

"I'll be right there," she says, not asking for more details.

She finds me sitting in my car in my usual parking spot. She knocks on the window and holds up a pint of mint chocolate chip ice cream. I get out and she hugs me.

"Cliché, I know," she says. "But who doesn't love ice cream? What are you doing down here? I went up to your place but you weren't there. I almost went back home. You're lucky I remembered you have a parking deck."

"Mrs. Edlerman took Jack's old space," I say. "I guess that makes it official."

"Let's go inside," Lola says. She takes my hand and leads me to the elevator, then down the hall, and inside my condo.

Inside, the condo is dark and lonely. The television is still on. I've never been much of a TV watcher, but the silence in this place is hard to handle and I've taken to turning it on for the sound of voices in the room. I think about turning it off, but don't.

Lola goes to the kitchen to get bowls and spoons.

Outside on my patio at dusk, we sit and look out over the city. Lola heaps us each a bowl of minty escape, and we sit and soak up the night around us. Summer will be over in a few weeks, and Cassie will be back in school. I haven't pressed the custody issue yet, but I'll have to soon. I didn't want to beg for my time with her, but it looks like she's not going to come back on her own.

"You want to tell me what's going on?" Lola asks, raising both eyebrows so high I think they're going to lift right off her head. "Because I would really like to know. It's August. I haven't heard from you since July."

"That was just a couple of weeks ago," I say. "Don't be so melodramatic."

"I can't remember two days passing without talking to you," Lola says. "You haven't called or answered for two weeks. I even checked with Jack to make sure you were ok."

I pick a flower head from the pot of daisies on the table and throw it at her, but it's too light and gets caught in the wind. It lifts up over the railing and sails off into the coming darkness.

"Oliver kept trying to tell me something and I didn't want to hear it," I say.

"Like a confession?" She smiles. "Sorry, that was too easy. Seriously though—what in the world?"

I tell her the whole story, and she tries not to interrupt too often with exclamations of disbelief and surprise.

"I cannot believe Orange Juice Hottie is going to be someone's priest!" She flings herself back against the chair for added drama. "I thought priests had to be old and significantly less attractive."

"That's what I said."

"Sounds like he must have known what he really wanted all along," she says, leaning toward me. "I think you do, too. You're just afraid."

"Afraid of what?"

"All of it. To try and fail. To try and succeed."

"I don't know what you're talking about."

"Yes, you do," she says. "You gave up because things got difficult."

I shrug.

"So, call him," she says.

"I think he's made his choice." I scrape the edges of the empty bowl with my spoon. "And I don't think I can compete with God."

"I didn't mean Oliver," she says.

I look at her and shake my head. She points at the rings that are back on my finger.

"Jack?" I finally ask.

"Yes." She shakes her head at me in exasperation. "Despite it all."

"I thought you hated Jack."

"I hate that you're hurting, but I know you still care about him," she says. "Am I right?"

"Of course I care about him. But I don't know if that's enough of a reason to try again."

"What other reason could there be?" she asks.

She suddenly holds up one finger and I know she's about to change the subject before I can comment further.

"I want to show you something," Lola says in a hushed and hurried voice. "It's a secret. I've been wanting to tell you, but I wasn't sure how you'd react. Chris isn't happy about it, but I just feel like I have to do it."

"I don't think I can handle any more secrets," I say, my head starting to swim. "You're not secretly a nun, are you? Chris and I are going to have to start a support group or something."

"Don't be silly. That's ridiculous."

She reaches for her bag and starts digging around in it. She pushes a flyer across the table at me.

"I've signed up to go to Peru with this missionary group," Lola talks quickly and passionately. "They're rebuilding churches in areas of poverty, and they want me to paint for them. There would be me, this guy who works with wrought iron, and this couple who makes this amazing furniture."

"Peru?" I ask, trying to measure in my head how far away that is, seeing it only as a color splotch on a map in some classroom in my mind. "I thought you said not to be ridiculous."

"Yes, Peru," Lola says, lost in her own excitement. "I picked up this flyer downtown about artists on a mission and they're going to Peru. I signed up."

I look at the flyer: *Artists on a Mission. Ever wonder why you're an artist? Feel like you could be contributing your talent to a bigger cause? You could be. Our next mission starts soon. Reserve your seat on the plane and make a difference.*

"You just picked up a flyer and now you're going to Peru?" I ask, aware that my voice sounds harsh. "It's a good thing you didn't see an ad for basket weaving in the swamps of—well, wherever the heck they have swamps."

I sound ridiculous and lame. I don't care.

"You make it sound so rash," she says.

"Isn't it?" I say. "People don't just pick up and go to Peru. They don't do that."

"Yes, they do," she says. "People get crippled and learn to walk again. They live with holes in their brain. They go through their life being treated like a bird with a broken wing. Then their house gets torn to shreds and they find a flyer and they go to Peru."

"What does Chris say about this?" I ask, deflecting, but I can't help it.

"He thinks I'm crazy. I think he's just scared for me."

"I think he doesn't want to lose you."

"I'm not going to be lost," she says. "To any of you."

"Does Ray know about this?"

She ignores the question. "The job doesn't pay anything," she says. "Just, you know, food and a place to stay, art supplies and such. What do you think?"

"I think it's crazy," I say, all my other emotions falling away until my voice is small with fear.

"Jump, and the net will appear, Nina."

Lola thinks that I am the one who shores her up, who gives her a pattern of flight. I see now that I'm the one clutching tight, her feathers held firm in my fingers.

"What will I do without you?" I say.

"You'll live," she says. "How well, though, is totally up to you."

"What about Chris?"

"I don't know. I hope he'll be here when I get back. This ice cream is making me thirsty."

She gets up from the table and goes back into the condo. She's in there about three minutes when she shouts in surprise. "Ray's on TV!"

My heart sinks. My legs are jelly, and I can hardly get them moving toward the living room and the television set and the confirmation that Nicole pressed charges after all and Ray is going back to prison. I expect to see an old mug shot of Ray while someone talks to Nicole's neighbor about how she's always been too nice for her own good.

Lola is pointing at the television with her mouth agape. She jabs her finger at the set as I approach. The newscaster is standing in front of the local public park downtown.

"A crowd has formed around this man and his demonstration of apology," the newswoman says in her news voice. "It's a grand gesture that I, for one, hope does not go unnoticed."

The camera pans over, and there's Ray.

"There he is," Lola says, jabbing her finger at the set. "There he is."

His name pops up at the bottom of the screen—"Ray"—in quotes as if they're not sure he is who he says he is. He's wearing a sandwich board on which he has painted an apology to Nicole. *Stupid Man Seeks Forgiveness from Wonderful Mother of His Child.* Ray turns around, and the camera focuses on the back of the sign: *Nicole and Michael—I may never be able to do things the "normal" way, but I love you and I need you in my life. Please forgive me.*

"So, tell us, Ray," the newswoman says. "What's this all about?" She holds out the mic to him.

Lola sucks in a breath and reaches out to me. She doesn't know about any of this.

"It's ok," I whisper to Lola, my heart racing.

Ray looks nervous but determined.

"Well, Kate," he says to the newswoman. "I'm a stupid man who did a stupid thing—many stupid things, actually—and I'm sorry. I'm desperate and sorry."

"Is this the act of a desperate man?" Kate seems to ask of no one in particular. "We'll see."

I wonder, all of a sudden, if Ray has some stunt planned. Perhaps he's going to fling off the sandwich board and scale the side of a building.

My brother is on the news! Panic!

What channel?

That crazy Ray!

Sorry about your dad, by the way.

"I just want her to see me," Ray says. "I'm making a promise in front of everyone in the city and everyone watching from your living rooms—I will be a decent man."

Ray takes the mic from Kate, and she looks nervous.

"I'm sorry, Nicole," he says, and the camera zooms in on his face. "I'm always going to be stupid ol' Ray. But I mean well. I'm not a bad guy. I used to think I was. But I'm hoping I'm not. And I promise to be a good man and a good father."

Kate reaches out for the mic, but Ray steps away from her.

"I'm going to walk the city wearing this board and telling people how sorry I am and how wonderful you are until I tell everyone," he says. "Until you forgive me."

"That's quite an undertaking," Kate says. "How long do you think this will take?" She reaches out again for the microphone, but Ray won't give it up.

"I don't care," he says. "I'm starting now."

He takes off with the mic, and the cameraman follows after him. People on the streets start applauding. Ray starts shaking hands with people.

"Hi," he says to a guy passing by. "I'm Ray, and I'm hoping to win my family back. I'm not drunk. This is me, totally sober."

He holds the mic over to the gentleman.

"Good luck to you, man," the guy says into the mic and smiles at the camera.

"Let's go," Ray says, looking into the camera and motioning us all forward with him.

"What are you doing, Jim?" Kate says off camera.

"This dude's a riot," Jim's voice replies.

There's about ten more seconds of Ray heading into the crowd and then it cuts back to the newsroom where the evening news crew is laughing.

"Did you know about this?" Lola looks at me, knowing already that I knew. "Ray has a kid? Why didn't anyone tell me? I'm sick of secrets. I hate this."

She storms off into Cassie's bedroom, leaving me and the news report alone in the living room.

22

Two months come and go while I putter around my empty house. I haven't seen Oliver again. Lola won't speak to me—or anyone else for that matter. Cassie won't come home, and Jack won't make her. My severance is almost up and something's got to give.

I'm hoping the spirits of Halloween will settle around us and work that kind of magic you believe in as a child when imagination can make you something other than what you are.

Lola is set on Peru now, and not even Chris can talk her out of it. She's mad at Ray for keeping Michael a secret and seems to be keeping her new mission a mystery out of spite. I want to tell Ray about Peru, but it's not my place. I want to talk to Lola about Michael, but that isn't mine either. All this not talking is making my head spin, and I decide that too much silence is enough.

Mom is over at her sister's house for the night, so I have lured Lola over with the promise of dinner and neutral ground. She doesn't know I've invited Ray, and he doesn't know she's here. I wish Mom hadn't gotten rid of the Halloween masks she made. The devil would be perfect for me tonight.

There's a knock on the door, and Lola glances at me suspiciously. She looks like she's about to make a break for it, and I hold my hand out in a stop motion. I slip into the foyer and open the door.

"You don't have to knock," I say to Ray when I open the door.

"Is that Lola's car?" Ray points over his shoulder to the driveway. "Did you do this? Is she still mad at me?"

"I never said I played fair," I answer. "Get in here. Enough already. We're not kids anymore. Just talk to her."

"Is she mad I didn't tell her about Michael?" Ray asks.

"She's hurt."

"That's worse." He steps back like my words have hit him in the gut.

I yank on his tattooed arm and pull him inside. Lola is standing by the coffee table, surveying the living room like she's looking for an escape.

"Knock it off," I say to them, and I swear I can hear fireworks in my head.

I'm standing between the two of them like I'm about to hold off a fistfight. I feel like we're back in time—back before Ray and Lola learned to cling to each other for safety, back before they were each other's breath, back to the day Lola came home from the hospital and any terrible new arrangement of life was possible. I look back and forth between them for a signal on what to do next. Ray makes the first move.

"I'm not going to leave," he says. "I'm not going anywhere."

Well played. I wish Lola would say the same thing. I step out of the way, and Ray moves closer to Lola. He reaches out to her. She doesn't step back, but she doesn't go to him either. He sighs and runs his hand through his hair.

"I didn't know how to tell you," he says. "I didn't know if I'd be able to do the right thing."

She doesn't say anything. She just lets him fill the space between them with words.

"Don't turn me away," he says. "I couldn't bear it. Be angry, but don't shut me out. I act like I want to be left alone, but I don't."

"I didn't turn you away before," she says. "Even after I remembered. You know me better than that. Act like it."

"Yeah." Ray's eyes get glassy. "I know."

"Don't make us come banging on the door again," Lola says, shaking her head at him. "Just open it. We wouldn't be banging on it if we didn't want you to come out."

Ray drops his head and nods at his shoes. Lola steps forward and takes hold of his hand.

It's a tentative truce, and it's enough for the moment. We sit around Mom's dining room table for dinner. We've never sat here, just the three of us without either parent.

"It's like we're little kids at the grown-up table at Thanksgiving," Ray says.

"And all the grown-ups are at a card table in the kitchen," Lola finishes his line of thinking.

We all laugh—better that than the thought of one day being parentless together.

Throughout dinner, I toss softball questions to Lola and Ray, easy leads into the things they need to say to each other. But neither one takes a swing.

Eventually, we move to the living room couch, our feet on the coffee table. I'm probably pressing too hard and should be happy with the progress they've made. But being satisfied with what I have isn't something I'm good at. I'm about to give up when I get an idea. I jump up from the couch and run out of the room. When I moved all of Mom's hobby projects from the table so that we could sit together, I remember that she had a few games in the mix.

"Look at these," I say, returning to the living room with a deck of tarot cards.

"Where did you get those?" Lola says, jumping back from the cards.

"Mom's hobby stash," I say. "What do you think? Should we play?"

"Absolutely not," Lola says. "Get those devil cards away from me."

"It's just a game," Ray scoots down to the floor to be closer to the deck.

"Why not?" I ask Lola. "It's Halloween. The night when the truth comes out."

"Halloween is when the spooks come out," Ray says. "Not the truth. What truth anyway—haven't we spilled all the beans?"

Almost.

"I don't want to find spooks *or* the truth," Lola says. "Those cards freak me out."

"Ok," I sigh and leave the room again, returning this time with a Magic 8-Ball.

Both Lola and Ray laugh and reach for the ball.

"Now we're talking," Lola says.

"What do we do now?" Ray says and looks at me.

"We ask it something," I say.

"Do you think it will really be able to answer us?" Ray asks, looking much more serious about this game than he should.

"Of course not," Lola says, but inches down beside us on the floor.

We look at each other, waiting for someone to start. In the dim light from the lamp and the moon outside, we could be kids again. The kids we were before the world shifted course. The kids we could have been. But who would those kids be now? I think that obsessing over the way it all might have been has kept me from seeing the wonder of what is. I think about my ruined marriage and my ruined relationship with Cassie. Hindsight is a ghost floating just over my shoulder. I send him outside with my old friend, guilt. Maybe they can go trick-or-treating and bring me back a chocolate bar.

Ray takes the ball and holds it in his hands. He closes his eyes and just when I think he might ask a serious question, he puts on a canned séance-style voice and says, "Will Nina ever learn to mind her own business?"

"Don't be ridiculous," I say.

"What does it say, Ray?" Lola asks.

"Hey, this thing really works," Ray says, looking at the answer window. "It says 'Don't count on it.'"

They laugh out loud at my expense, and I couldn't be happier.

I watch the two of them giggle and carry on. Lola hasn't asked Ray yet for details about Michael, nor has she told him about Peru. Maybe it's not my place to force their secrets out of them. I think they're just enjoying each other for the moment.

This night is like a pit stop. Like stopping at a hotel in the middle of a long trip. Limbo. Once the car is moving again with the destination in sight, you have no choice but to head full steam into whatever is waiting for you when you get there.

"Let me ask it something," I say and reach out for the ball.

Ray holds it tight to his chest and shakes his head. Children's voices pitch through the night; countless kids are somewhere out on the sidewalk making plans, collecting candy.

"No way," he says. "This thing is mine. Magic 8-Ball, did Mom buy any candy for the trick-or-treaters?" He turns it to face us. "'My sources say no.'"

"Looks like neighbor kids are going to T.P. her house," Lola says and laughs.

Ray looks very sternly at the 8-ball.

"What about her mints?" I say. "We could pass those out."

"Her mints!" Ray shouts. "I forgot all about those."

Our whole childhood smelled like those pastel mints at the register of the Chinese restaurant.

"Where do you think she keeps them?" I ask. "In case the bell rings and we're on the spot."

"Let's ask Dad." Ray shakes the ball. "This thing says it has sources—maybe Dad is one."

"Don't you dare," Lola says. "If that thing starts answering like Dad, you'll see a Lola-sized hole in the front door."

"Is that actually what you'd want to ask Dad?" I say, realizing Ray is serious. "If you could really tune him in on this silly thing."

"Like a transistor radio?" Ray smirks.

"Dad, does Mom keep the mints in the pantry?" Lola asks the ball and looks at me sheepishly. "Shake it, Ray."

Ray looks up to the ceiling, suddenly anxious and breathy. He shakes the Magic 8-Ball. "'Most likely,'" he whispers.

"I don't want to do this anymore." I stand up quickly, retreating to the other side of the room. "Maybe this was a bad idea."

Ray squints his eyes at the ball like he's trying to see inside it, like he believes that it's really Dad.

"Do you still mean what you said?" Ray asks.

I think he's talking to me, but I soon understand that he isn't.

"Stop," Lola whispers. "It's over. Let it go."

"It's not over for me," Ray says, shaking the ball.

"This is a bad idea," I say. "Let's play truth or dare or something else childish. Ray, you start."

Ray shakes the ball and asks again, "Do you still mean what you said?"

Lola runs out of the room, and Ray sets the ball down and goes out the front door. I pick up the ball and look in the little plastic window.

Without a doubt.

279

◆ ◆ ◆

After a few minutes, I go outside looking for Ray. Late October is something akin to heaven, I think—golden and easy. The hardened leaves that still clinging to the trees rustle together in what must be the sound of perseverance. I find Ray sitting on the steps of the front porch.

"What a weird night," he says. "I guess Lola saw me on the news."

"Before it went viral on YouTube." I sit down beside him. "Or so I hear. I don't know how Mom doesn't know."

"Momland," Ray says. "You remember that?"

"I do," I say. "I feel like we're all on the edge of a cliff. Does it seem that way to you?"

"Always."

"I need to tell you something," I say. "I wanted Lola to tell you herself, but maybe it's better that you have a heads-up."

"Don't say things like that," Ray says. "I think the prelude to the bad news is worse than the news."

"Lola is going to Peru on a mission trip. Some artist thing. But what scares me is that I'm not sure she plans to come back."

"Ok, the prelude is not worse than the news," Ray says, putting his hands over his ears like if he can shut out the sound of my voice none of it will be true. "Peru? That's far away," he says when he finally takes his hands down.

"Yeah."

Kids run across the front lawn unaware that we can see them. Darkness and costumes are a cloak of invisibility.

"I'm supposed to be the one who leaves," Ray says, shaking his head. "That's going to sting. What about this commercial character she's dating?"

"Chris. He's not going to replace you if that's what you're worried about."

He chuckles. Pegged.

"Why don't you think she'll come back?" Ray looks at me pointedly, his green eyes electric with fear. "Of course she'll come back. Right?"

"She seems to be cleaning house and taking stock, and it scares me."

"Better than kicking butt and taking names," he says. "No, actually the way you say it is worse." He pats my knee and sighs. "She'll come back. If I came back, she'll come back. This is home. Like it or not."

I suppose so.

"What about you?" he says. "I've been pretty self-absorbed lately. How's your world?"

"Falling apart," I say, but offering no details. "And it's just human nature—being self-absorbed. Don't sweat it."

We sit and stare into the darkness of our childhood street. A ghost, a princess, and a Batman run by, and I think of the three of us in easier times when we could throw on a costume and satiate ourselves with sugar and chocolate and make the world a better place. Funny, I think we still do that—albeit the costumes and consumables have changed over the years.

"What fell apart?" Ray asks, not letting me off the hook.

"My illusions," I say, realizing the truth. "That life would be easy. That marriage would an unbreakable bond. That I'd have tons of kids and none of them would ever want to leave me."

"Where did you get that illusion?" He smiles understandably at me. "She'll come back."

I think he's talking about Lola, but he corrects me.

"Cassie," he says. "She's just lashing out. She thinks she's making you pay for some injustice. She doesn't know that life has no rules and reason is mostly unsound. The punishment almost never fits the crime—thank heavens for that."

281

"How do you know that's what Cassie is doing?"

"I did the same thing. Spent way too much time trying to exact revenge—mostly on myself. She'll figure it out. Especially once she has kids of her own."

I roll my eyes. "Do I have to wait until then?"

"What else?" Ray asks, sensing that isn't everything.

"I started dating a priest," I say, leaving out the "almost" part because I know it will amuse Ray. "It didn't work out."

This brings a huge smile to Ray's face and he laughs. It sounds good—not the raspy, jagged knife sound that he made just months ago.

"I don't know if you're joking or not," he says, "but I think that means you're not ready to give up on your marriage. People get back together sometimes, you know."

He reaches his hand out across the small space between us, and I take hold of it. "Life is weird," he says. "Most of the time I feel like I'm playing one game while everybody at the table is playing something else."

"What did Dad say to you that night?" I ask, feeling both brave and desperate.

Ray looks at me, and I know he knows which night I'm talking about.

"Did he blame you?" I ask.

The darkness makes a safety net around us.

"He knew it was my fault," Ray says, nodding. "That was easy enough to figure. Hiding from the world when I messed up didn't start with that night, you know. I've always been good at that."

"It was an accident, Ray," I say. "You know that, right?"

"It was still my fault."

"Is that what he said?" It seems a logical thing to assume. "That he knew it was you?"

"When Dad found me that night," Ray says, squeezing my hand against the memory, "I knew Lola was hurt. I was afraid of hearing 'Your sister is dead, and it's all your fault' or some version of that. It would have left me to rot in that alley forever. I guess I rotted there anyway, even though that's not what Dad said."

"You looked like he'd said the most unimaginable thing to you. What did he say?"

"I knew Lola was hurt bad," Ray says again. "I knew all our lives had just been yanked out from under us. I knew it was my fault. There was no way to know that Lola was going to make it. Dad knew I was already spinning out of control."

I squeeze Ray's hand; I can't stand it.

"He said, 'I love you, no matter what.' Simple as that. I was floored. That he took the time to find me. That he didn't go off with the ambulance and just leave me. There's no way someone can love you like that, is there? How did he know me so well? I barely even knew myself. I spent every day after that trying my hardest to prove there was something I could do to make him not love me. I became the most unlovable version of myself that I could. I had to prove to him that I was the bad guy, because that's how I felt."

"That's a risky test to conduct."

"I ticked him off from time to time," Ray says. "I got that part right. Man, he could get mad at me. He told me all the time that I wasn't measuring up to what I could be, that I was making one bad decision on top of the next. Which was true."

I rest my head on Ray's shoulder. The fire-breathing devil just under the surface of his sleeve breathes out a puff of smoke.

"Dad sure didn't mind telling you when you'd made a bad decision," I say. "But he always loved us."

"I couldn't do it." Ray sighs. "I couldn't make him stop loving me. I wanted him to. I wanted Lola to. I wanted all of you to."

"Sometimes we don't get what we want."

"I know," Ray says. "Thankfully."

We sit for a good while. Trick-or-treaters are long home and high on sugar. A couple of neighborhood teenagers slip around the side of the house across the street. I imagine in the morning it will be wrapped in white paper and the magic of tonight's mischief will be someone else's mess to clean up.

I imagine a lot of things will be different in the morning.

"I never said it back to him," Ray says, barely getting the words out. "I never said it back."

"Say it now," I tell Ray. "You don't need a Magic 8-Ball for him to hear you."

Ray starts to cry instead.

23

My phone buzzes and, like always, I grab it, hoping it's Cassie wanting to come home. It's not.

"What's up, Mom?" I ask.

"Can you meet me at the cemetery?"

"Why?"

"Don't play twenty questions, Nina, just meet me there."

"It was just the one question."

Silence on her end.

"Ok."

When I get there, Mom is setting up one of the flower arrangements beside Dad's redundant grave. I can hear her talking to him. I hang back, but I listen anyway.

"I've arranged flowers," Mom says. "I've made masks. I took out the tarot cards but that just seemed silly. I'm running out of things to do, Nate. Your part of my life is over, and I'm at a loss for how to fill my time."

I feel like an eavesdropper on everyone else's life these days.

"I know things weren't always easy between us," Mom continues, unaware that I'm right behind her. "But they're harder now than ever. I know you put on a face for me that wasn't real. I know you pretended I didn't spend years breaking your heart. I know all that. I hope you know I appreciated it."

I clear my throat. I shouldn't let her go on so personally and privately with an audience.

"Oh, Nina," she says, her cheeks turning slightly pink. "Can you go back to the car and get the rose arrangement out of the trunk?"

"Sure, Mom."

She starts talking again, and I know she's talking to Dad and not me. She talks likes he's sitting right there, but in that way you would talk to someone who was in a coma. The way you would talk when you felt at liberty to say everything you ever wanted to say, just the way you wanted to say it.

A memory of Lola in the hospital rushes up on me, and my legs get wobbly. This was the way Mom had talked to Lola when she was unconscious after the accident and no one really knew whether or not she would come back to us. It was good-bye talk. And it scared me sick.

It was the way I had talked to Dad in the nursing home when I'd pop by to see him and he was so drugged out that all he did was sleep. I sat by the bed and told him all the things that were happening with Jack and our efforts and failures to get pregnant and then about losing the baby.

I told him about Cassie and my job and how I knew even then both of those things were slipping away from me. At the time, I glossed over Cassie. I know now it was because the loss of her was the worst of it all. I could feel her pulling away, and I wasn't doing anything to grab hold of her.

I told him I loved him and missed him. I said all the things I wanted to say when he was alive but never did, desperately hoping that he could hear me and that somehow, I could reach through the darkness and pull him back.

I open Mom's trunk; it stinks of flowers. *Stop and be overpowered by the roses.* The arrangement is actually sort of pretty, and I wonder if maybe Mom has stumbled upon some hidden talent. I lift it out carefully and walk back to her. I set the arrangement on the other side of the headstone.

"So, imagine this—Ray is staying in town," Mom says, and I almost think she's talking to me. "He's got a job and an apartment. I suspect something's up, but I don't know what that something is. I don't care though. He's here. He wanted to tell me about something he's done, and one of my friends said they saw him on that internet, but I'm not going to look. It doesn't make any difference to me what he's done. He's here. He's back."

Mom looks at me, suspecting that I know what the something is.

"No matter," she says to Dad. "Ray feels awful that he didn't get to say good-bye."

"Mom," I interrupt. "Did you need me?"

"Just a second, sweetie," she says. "I'm catching Dad up on the news."

I turn away, looking into the distance at the old section of the cemetery, out where Oliver had shown me our doppelganger graves. I half-expect Oliver to turn up again, but he doesn't.

"Lola is doing well," Mom is saying to Dad. "Keeping the gaps closed for the most part. It was worth it, wasn't it? Oh, you will never guess who she's dating—that guy from the insurance commercials. The ones with that ridiculous jingle and all the crazy stunts. Do you remember those? Or did they start airing after the stroke? I forget. He came to the funeral. Nina says he's good to Lola. That's all that matters."

The cemetery is quiet, the way they somehow always are. Even nature seems reverent—or fearful, the difference is hard to negotiate sometimes.

"Speaking of Nina," I hear Mom say, and I turn to face her.

"Nate," she says, but she's looking right at me. "Your eldest daughter is struggling."

So here it is. This is the way that Mom can talk to me. I shouldn't be surprised. Dad had often relayed messages and sentiments. *Your mother wants you to know that she loves you. She didn't mean to forget your ball game. It's just with all the stress from Lola and everything, she gets overwhelmed. She's human. We all are.*

I look at Mom and raise an eyebrow.

This conversation is a long time coming, but now that it's here, I'm not sure I'm ready for it.

"She and Jack finally went through with the divorce," Mom tells Dad. "Cassie has been living with Jack. Nina lost her job and started dating that young guy you liked so much at the nursing home. You know the one I mean, that nice one who was always talking to your roommate, Mr. Cole. Sweet boy. She hasn't brought him around though."

"Mom?" I interrupt. "Really."

"She would have told you all about it herself, Nate," Mom says, still looking at me. "She always told you everything. But she can't talk to me. I think she needs to get some things off her chest, though. I think it's time. Maybe with you here for support she'll be able to."

Ready or not, the words pour out of me, like all the things I wanted to say have been right on the end of my tongue all these years and now that I have permission, they're all tumbling out.

"Did you know Dad bought me my first training bra?" I ask, hands on my hips just like Cassie does. "Not Grandma, like he told you."

I tilt my head like I've delivered a good hard blow.

"I knew that." Mom nods. "Your father always tried to spare my feelings. Your grandmother would have rather taped your breasts down and pretended the whole thing wasn't happening. The older you got, the closer to death she got—according to her."

That sounds like Grandma. I want to laugh, but I'm not going to let Mom lighten this moment. She asked for it, and she's going to get it.

"Do you know when I started my period?" I ask, sounding like a petulant child.

"You were about fifteen," Mom says, squinting her eyes into the past. "I remember because it seemed a bit late to start."

Ha, I think. I've got her.

"No." I shake my head at her, and she winces. "I was thirteen. Right on time. Textbook. I told Dad because you were still wearing your Lola-goggles at the time."

"That's not fair." She turns to Dad's headstone. "Nate, you can vouch for me."

"Dad's dead," I shout at her point-blank. "Talk to me. Take off the blinders, Mom, and see me. That's all I ever wanted, and you still can't do it."

We stand there, staring at each other in the cemetery. The grass is too green and the trees are too perfectly spaced and the whole place seems like a picture of somewhere you'd want to have a picnic—were it not for all the gravestones.

"I saw you," she says, her eyes filling with hurt and anger—at me or herself, I'm not sure.

"No, you didn't," I say. "You saw Lola, and you saw Ray, and I think you noticed Dad from time to time, but I could have been gone a week and you wouldn't have noticed the difference."

"That's not fair," Mom says. "You know how much physical therapy Lola needed. I was busy, is all. It's not like she could take herself to her appointments and back." She stops talking and looks at me as if this settles it. I look back at her and raise an eyebrow.

"Is that all you have? You were busy with Lola—that's it?"

I click my teeth at her rudely. I want to play fair, really, but if she thinks she's going to get off easy, she's wrong.

No, that's a lie. I don't want to play fair at all.

Mom shifts her weight around and looks back and forth between me and Dad's rock.

"Well," she continues, "I was busy, too, with the meetings and, you know."

"It's all in the end of that sentence," I say, my eyes burning a challenge. "Isn't it?"

"That's water under the bridge," she says, tossing the cliché at me like it's supposed to close the subject. But it's more like she's the troll under the bridge and we're the three billy goats gruff. "But I know you need to say it. I understand. That's why I asked you here."

"It's not water under the bridge, Mom. It's a raging flood, and I'm clinging to the railing trying not to get washed away. Do you really not know that? Do you really not know how much your drinking hurt us? We were just kids. How did you think we were supposed to take care of ourselves without you? We needed you."

Mom looks at me, and I see that she wants to throw out another platitude, but I also see that she knows it's more complicated than that.

"I asked for this," she says and touches my arm gently. "Go ahead and tell me."

I could scream, I'm so mad at her for thinking that all I need is to get a few thoughts off my chest.

"Ray and I still mattered," I say, my rage audible beneath the wavering of my voice.

"Resentment is a useless emotion," she says and smiles at me. "There is never a way to go back."

"Why weren't we important enough to change for? How did

you think I could forget about all those years I spent not being as important as the bottom of a vodka bottle?"

"You're not pulling any punches are you, Nina?"

"No," I say, firmly. "I intend to land every one of them."

"Nina," she says and then offers up the truth of it. "I'm just a person. Being a mother doesn't stop me from doing things wrong. It doesn't give me superpowers. The most disheartening thing you realize as a parent is that no matter how hard you try, you're still just a regular human being. No cape or magic rope or invisible airplane can help you. You will screw up your kids. It's just a matter of how badly. You see it happening right in front of you, yet you're powerless to stop it. Life spins out of control, and you are who you are. I guess the best superpower is having the courage to admit you have none."

"Is that some sort of apology?" I ask. "What are you apologizing for, exactly? Before the accident or after? Because you were just as bad after as you were before—just different. It wasn't better. None of it was good. None of it was fair."

For some reason, the memory of our last vacation before the accident comes to me. Mom sat under a huge umbrella stuck deep in the sand. It was late in the day for her to be as sober as she was. Dad and Ray were out in the ocean, out where the water caught the sunlight and sparked it back toward the beach. Lola and I made castles at the edge of the water, laughing at how fast we could build something before the ocean came and erased it away. We looked back at Mom from time to time, like she was a beacon from the shore and we were mapping our place according to her. She didn't realize she was leaving us to drift aimlessly farther and farther out into the black waters of the open sea.

"Nina," Mom says, bringing me back. "If there was a way to undo everything I've done wrong, don't you think I would?"

"Would you? I don't know. You're being all pithy and tossing out quotes and it's ticking me off. The truth is that you forgot us. You let Ray drown in his own guilt, and you didn't do anything to help him. I think you actually wanted him to suffer."

"I did not!" Anger finally boils over in her as well. "You have a child of your own. You tell me that if Cassie did something stupid—accident or not—that you would want her to suffer for it. Would you?"

"Of course not," I scream back at her, like she didn't just prove her point.

"I prayed for Ray every night," she says, pointing her finger at me. "Just as hard as I prayed for Lola. I couldn't do anything but stand by and watch what happened to both of them."

I see a chance to bring her down, and I take it.

"You prayed for Ray. You prayed for Lola," I say, bobbing my head, revving up. "Did you ever pray for me?"

She sucks in a breath of air, and I think she's going to spit something out at me, but she just stands there, looking at me. Beaten.

"No," she says, and the honesty of it hits me in the stomach. "I don't know that I did. I didn't think you needed it. I thought you were strong enough to handle things on your own. You always seem so strong."

"I wasn't."

Anger is quickly losing ground to devastation. I'm one small word away from losing my backbone and crumpling into a heap.

"I don't think you understand what you've done," I say. "I needed you to love me too."

"Of course I loved you. I *do* love you," Mom says, still sounding angry. "You have no idea how much I love the three of you. Yes, I made a huge mess of things. But not for lack of trying."

"You call what you did trying?" It's a mean thing to say and I know it. I feel bad right away. I don't know that I'm doing any better with Cassie. Honestly, I think I'm doing worse. Everything I'm saying to my mother, I know that Cassie could say to me. In her own way, she already has.

"Now you stop right there," Mom says, talking to me like I'm still a teenager. Maybe this is a conversation we should have had when I was. "Don't you dare doubt my love for you. I know I have hurt you, and you have every right to tell me about it, but don't for one second think that anything I did was out of any other motivation than to love you and care for you. Even the drinking—and yes, I know that sounds crazy. I drank to take the edge off, so I wouldn't snap at you kids because I'd had a stressful day. Sure, it was a bad road to start down, and I went down it a lot farther than most people. I got lost, and when I tried to find my way back, I went the wrong direction."

"What does any of that mean? What am I supposed to do about that now?"

"I'm hoping there is a way to salvage our relationship, Nina. Some way to turn this back to what it could have been."

"I don't want to salvage our relationship," I say, and her face falls. "It wasn't worth saving."

I don't mean it like she thinks I do, but she starts talking before I can explain myself.

"Nina, look," she says and puts her hand on mine. "I know what I put you and Ray and your father through. Saying I'm sorry can't smooth this over, I know that."

"I don't think you understand," I say. "You tossed us into this other life and expected that we'd know how to make our way."

"But wasn't it better?" she asks, her face a ball of confusion and expectation. "Without me drinking?"

I pause in my anger, and my field of vision clears slightly. "It was different. I don't know that *better* is the right word."

"I see."

"It was fragile," I say, having found the phrase to fit it. "It was brought on by things that had nothing to do with us and dependent on things that we couldn't control. That's tough for a kid."

Life before Lola's accident had been a glass bottle that we could see and touch. We could gauge our world by the measure of liquid inside. Not that we wanted Mom to keep drinking—no one wanted that—but life after Lola's accident was like fog drifting around our feet, vaporous but still able to trip us up. We didn't know how to navigate that life.

"There are things you don't understand either," she says. "It was a chance for me to be what a mother was supposed to be. That was more intoxicating than any drink had ever been."

"You were my mother too," I say, the anger welling again. "I was just as broken as Lola and Ray. Just because I was better at hiding it didn't mean I was whole."

In the eyes of a child, a mother is infallible. Truth is what she says it is. She's Wonder Mom, superhero.

"Will it be good enough if I say it?" she asks.

"I don't know," I say. "I don't know."

"I am," she says and puts her hand back on mine. "I am sorry."

"I know," I say and let her fingers rest on top of mine.

This is why Lola played along.

"Is there not some way to save us?" she asks. "I needed help, but I didn't ask. All I had to do was ask. Even though I failed, I wanted to be a good mother. I wanted it so badly."

I'm stopped in my petulant tracks. For all my talk about her not seeing me when I needed her, I realize that I did see her when she needed me, but I looked away.

"I think you did ask," I say. I'm humbled and sad and my voice breaks when I speak again. "We just didn't understand you."

"I didn't ask in a way that you could have," she says. "You were children. It wasn't your fault. But I am asking now."

"For help?" I ask, tears welling in my eyes. "Do you still need help?"

"I need forgiveness."

I look away. Help is easy. Forgiveness is hard.

"I don't understand why you drank, Mom. I don't understand how you could forget that I still needed a mother. I don't understand any of it."

"Understanding why someone did something doesn't change anything," she says. "Forgiving does, and that doesn't require understanding. We have to start with forgiveness or else there's no point in trying to move forward."

"But how does forgiving you change the past?" I ask, my throat tightening.

"It doesn't. It changes the future. That's all we can do."

I open my mouth to speak, but nothing comes out.

"Nate," Mom says, turning back to Dad. "If you would, put in a good word for her up there. She's giving up, and I don't want her to. She needs you right now, Nate, and I know I'm a poor substitute."

I shake my head and fight back tears. My throat has jagged rocks in it, and they hurt when I swallow.

"You're not a poor substitute," I eke out, tears spilling over again.

Mom presses something into the palm of my hand. I know right away what it is. The round, stone beads are still hot with prayer—from this morning, yesterday, years ago.

"You try too hard to figure things out on your own," she says to me. "Sometimes you have to give up control. Because if you want to know the truth, control wasn't yours to begin with. You're scraping and clawing to hold the reins of a horse that you can't lead. Turn them loose, baby."

"I don't know how."

"Well," she says, "I guess I have something to pray for you about now. You start on your end, and I'll start on mine. You'll get there."

I burst into hot tears, thick heavy sobs, and for the first time in a terribly long time, Mom puts her arms around me and doesn't let go.

I finally see that Mom just wanted to be Wonder Woman, but her cape was constantly stuck in the door of the invisible airplane and she couldn't see where the door handle was to release it.

She holds on tight, and I let her.

"So, did you reach him?" Mom asks after the lull.

"Reach who?" I ask, pulling out of her embrace so I can look at her

"Your father," she says, holding my hand. "On that Magic-8 Ball."

"No," I say. "Well, probably not. How did you know?"

"You left the game out," she says and pats her other hand over our interlaced fingers. "And you ate all my chips."

"I'm sorry."

"Let's get out of here," she says. "I'll talk to you later, Nate."

Mom heads back to her car, and I stand there looking at Dad's headstone.

Cut your mother some slack, I feel him say. *Cut yourself some too.*

"See you later, Dad." I hurry to catch up with Mom.

"What did Dad tell you on the Magic-8 Ball?" Mom asks.

"We asked him where you keep the mints. In case we got a trick-or-treater."

"He doesn't know."

"That's pretty much what he said."

I stop at her car and wait for her to open the door.

"Go make up with your sister," she says before she closes the door.

I don't ask her how she knows things are askew. Mothers just know.

◆ ◆ ◆

"You want to recast me, don't you?" I say when Lola opens our bedroom door.

"I thought about it," she says with a small smile. "But you really are perfect for the part. I have to think about the greater good of the film."

"I'm sorry," I say, sitting down on one of the twin beds.

"Me too," she says, sliding down to the floor at my feet. "I'm sorry I didn't come back out to talk to you and Ray last night. I just wanted to be alone. I thought we all needed a little space to process."

"Come up here," I say, and she wiggles up beside me on the bed.

"You were right last night," she says. "I am tired of all the secrets. I should have told everyone when I started to remember things."

"To what end? There was never going to be a good time to reveal that. Is that what's got you upset?"

"I guess." She grabs the pillow from the head of the bed and hugs it close to her chest. "Is that why Ray didn't tell me the truth. Habit?"

"No," I say. "Fear. Sometimes saying something out loud makes it too real."

"But he told you. All this time, you thought you and Ray didn't have a bond. But you do. You always did."

"I guess you're right."

"Can I ask you something?" she asks but doesn't wait for permission. "Sometimes I worry about what's real. Were all the things we shared as kids real? All the things we laughed about and all the stories we told each other? Was the lying just about what happened before the accident, or was my whole life after that make-believe?"

I angle toward her so we sit cross-legged in front of each other with our knees touching. This has always been our signal of truce, of confidence, of sacred space.

I take her hands in mine. "This is real. Everything I've ever said to you is real. Ray is real." I squeeze her hands tighter. "You are real. Everything you feel, and the way you see the world, and the things you paint—it's all real."

She grips my hands and I grip hers. We hold on for dear life.

"I miss you already," I say, and the thought of her leaving feels much more real than anything.

She pulls me toward her, and we lay down with our arms around each other. Holding on—blood thicker than anger, than fear, than time.

"We shouldn't tell Mom that I know," she says. "Ray will have to tell her about Michael. And I guess I'll have to tell her about Peru. Otherwise she's going to wonder where the heck I am. I guess we all have a part to play in things."

"Life is a stage, and all the men and women in it are merely players. Or something like that," I say.

I want to ask Lola if Peru is forever, but I can't. She says it's just a mission trip, and right now she probably thinks it is. But what about when she gets there and learns how to fly? What if she just keeps going?

Maybe not today, but one day, I will fly.

"Do you think we make things harder than they need to be?" she asks.

"Most of the time."

I know I do. Maybe I've made everything harder than it needs to be. I decide to make a call in the morning and try again.

24

Come home I said, and they did.

I open the door and there stands Cassie with her purple-and-daisy-patterned suitcase and Jack with his arms folded across his chest. No suitcase.

I step back to let them in. I want to reach out to Cassie, but I need to let her call the shots. She chooses to slip past me and disappears into her bedroom.

"Am I too late?" I ask Jack.

"I don't know," he says. "I really don't."

He closes the door behind him and stands in the entryway to the living room. His eyes fix on my face like he's sizing me up.

"I told Cassie she could go to Teen Swim this evening," Jack says. "You and I should talk."

I've said that sentence a time or two and it's never been pleasant.

"I thought you wanted to try again," I say, jumping to conclusions.

"I do, Nina," Jack says. "I just don't know if I can. Those aren't the same thing."

Cassie comes out of her room wearing her swimsuit and carrying a bag of clothes. She looks at me in challenge and puts her hand on her bathing suit-clad hip. "Aren't you going to tell me I can't go?"

"We can go."

"No," she says and actually stomps her foot. "Dad says I can go alone. Zach's dad is going to be there anyway."

"Who's Zach?" I ask, looking at Jack.

"My boyfriend," Cassie says and clicks her tongue at me. Like mother, like daughter.

I open my mouth, but I hear Jack's voice.

"I've already worked it out, Nina," he says. "Zach's dad will take them back to their place after the swim, and we can pick up Cassie after dinner."

Cassie stands so firmly in place that her feet grow roots down into the carpet. Her stare stings my skin, and I sigh out an agreement.

"I don't like this," I say once she's gone. "I feel like I've been out of the loop for years, not months."

"You have," Jack says.

"Tell me this isn't better than pizza and a movie," Jack says across the candlelit table of a local restaurant.

"Is that what you think it's like with Oliver?" I ask.

Jack doesn't know how things ended with Oliver, and I find that I don't want to tell him that it's over. Jack picks up his water, and the gold on his ring finger clicks against the glass.

"Ok," Jack concedes. "So, what, he's the coffeehouse-and-book-reading type? Does he quote you lines from some dead poet?"

Jack smirks to himself and cuts into his steak.

I can't talk about Oliver with Jack. I can't talk about him at all. My phone registers a text message, and I fumble frantically, thinking it might be from Cassie. It's a note from Carol.

Saw you go into Limones with Jack. What's up?

I don't answer. I don't know what's up.

"Is that him?" Jack asks, taking a sip of water. "Are you going to tell him where you are?"

"Is this night about you and me? Or you and Oliver? What if it was Cassie? What if she needs me and I'm sitting in some restaurant eating seared scallops and stone-ground grits?"

"She's fine," Jack says. "And that's new by the way. I knew you'd order that."

"Is this your spot?" I ask, bold. "Is this where you took them? Did you come here so often you know the menu by heart?"

"Took who?"

I roll my eyes like a teenager, and Jack lets out a chortle.

"You think I brought other women here. I'm not that suave, I promise you. Who do you think I am, anyway?"

I'm not sure that I know.

"So you went straight to the motel, then?" I'm angry, and maybe a little jealous.

He sighs. "What do you want me to say? Because I've told you in these exact words a number of times—I did not have an affair, multiple affairs, or any other loophole of syntax that you're trying to catch me in."

"Whatever, Jack. I don't expect you to own up to it. Let's just eat."

"What do you want, Nina?" Jack waves his hand in resignation, yet doesn't answer any of my questions. "Do you want to adopt? Do you want me to apologize for ruining your life? What?"

"You didn't ruin my life. I don't know what I want."

"That's the problem," Jack says and pushes his half-eaten dinner aside. "You're always looking ahead for something that might never come. You're never happy with where you are, what you have, who you have."

I look up sharply at this comment. The truth of it is a perfectly round floodlight in a high school play, illuminating the two of us at the table.

In the play, the "me" character gets up and steps into the darkness. It's like walking behind a wall the contrast is so sharp. In the play, she will emerge on the other side of the darkness and step into another ball of light where she will deliver an emotional and weighty monologue that changes the course of the rest of the play. But instead of surfacing on the other side like I should do, I just keep stumbling around the stage in the dark, getting caught in the curtain and falling down.

"You're right," I say. "I don't know what to do about that."

"I don't know either." Jack takes hold of my left hand across the table, rubbing his finger across the rings I'm wearing. "I don't know if it's too late or not. I don't know if we can get past the things that haunt us. I don't know if you can let go."

He's talking about the nursery—the secret shrine in the third bedroom. He'll want to box it up and put it in the storage unit in the basement of the building and all my hope will be in the dark and damp of that forgotten nowhere where people dump old grills and camping equipment and bicycles with flat tires and boxes of things from their childhood that they can't throw away but don't really need and when the baby finally gets here, I'll have to explain to people that the nursery is in the basement.

How will you hear him crying way down there? they will ask.

"I don't know if I can either," I say. "I don't know how."

"Do you want us back?" Jack asks.

"I want Cassie back," I say, honestly.

"Is this about Elliot?" Jack says.

"Oliver," I correct him. "And no, it isn't. He and I aren't together. I don't know that we ever were, really. Not like that. I know I'm not going to have another baby. I know I neglected Cassie, and I ran you off. I know all the things are my fault. I just don't know that I can forgive you. I don't know that you can forgive me."

"Maybe not," Jack says and lowers his head.

"I have to go," I say. "Good-bye, Jack."

Desperate to get out of the restaurant, I hurry past the people waiting in the foyer and fling myself out into crisp night air. The heat from the restaurant gives way to the chill of early November.

I remember Lola and me as teenagers in the grocery store, staring at the ice cream. Lola couldn't remember what any of it tasted like.

What does mint taste like with chocolate? What is fudge? Black cherry? Toffee?

She opened up the cooler and cold air fell out as she reached in and picked a pint.

You don't like cherries.

I put it back and handed her a different pint.

This is your favorite one—cookie dough. She took the container and looked at it, then back at me, as if waiting for instructions. *You always save two little balls of dough for the very end. You pick around them and save them for last.*

She had no idea if what I said was true. This wasn't forgetting Aunt Rose's name or the words to the birthday song. It wasn't about remembering the past. It was about living in the present and knowing what mint chocolate chip ice cream tasted like.

I remember Mom found us by the ice cream coolers.

Everything ok?

She picked cookie dough. Just like always.

Lola looked scared.

Everything's fine, I said to her. *Everything is fine.*

Are you sure? the genie I had hoped for says to me, straightening out his cummerbund and righting his hat.

I don't know.

"Nina," I hear Jack calling me, and I turn around to meet his frightened eyes. He's out of breath like he's been running, even though we're just outside the restaurant door. "Cassie. She's hurt."

◆ ◆ ◆

A doctor relays all the details of the accident as told to him by the father of Cassie's "boyfriend."

"A simple case of running around the pool," he says as if our daughter isn't lying there with all manner of tubes and wires protruding from her, with monitors timing the rhythm of her heart, her breath.

I try to piece together the story. Apparently, Cassie was running around at the edge of the pool playing tag with this boy, Zach, and she slipped. Her feet came out from under her, and she fell directly onto the back of her head. She slipped off the pool deck and under the water. It took a few moments for Zach to drag her out.

I hear it, but it doesn't seem real. I feel like I'm underneath the water, drowning.

"All her organs are functioning," the doctor is saying, still talking at a fast clip as if he thinks there is any way I could be keeping up with this. "Watching for brain swelling . . ."

I'm sinking, sinking down to the bottom of the pool with Cassie.

". . . will be critical. We'll have to see if there is any lasting damage."

I look up from beneath the water and see fireworks.

Not again. Please, not again.

Jack puts his arm around me, and I don't shrug it off. I'm too stunned to cling to him, to fall to my knees, to cry out, or any other dramatic thing I've seen in the movies. I just stand there, tears burning silent trails down my face, looking at Cassie lying still and quiet except for the beeping of the monitors which are all I have that tells me she's still in there somewhere.

Jack has my phone and calls Mom and Lola and Ray. He asks me if I want to talk to them, but I shake my head. So long as I don't have to speak about it, this might not actually be happening.

While Jack stands by the window talking on the phone, nurses and doctors and people whose purpose I'm unsure of come and go on an invisible tide. I sit, holding Cassie's hand, and say nothing to anyone. I'm reminded of watching the waves at the beach. Seeing them roll up in sets. Sudden and furious, one on top of the other and then nothing—while another set builds in the far-off distance, waiting its turn to reach the shore.

There's a frenzy when the waves wash in, all bustle and white water and chatter like the noise of seagulls. Then silence for long stretches of time as the next sets builds.

"Your mother and Lola are on their way," Jack says from somewhere behind me on the dunes. "I left Ray a message. I'm sure he'll come too."

Neither of us has compared this to Lola's accident, but Jack's eyes tells me what he fears. He comes around to the other side of the bed to hold Cassie's needle-punctured hand.

"You don't have to be here when they arrive." He knows that I can't handle someone else's initial shock, that I can't relay the story without breaking apart against it. "I can let them know what's going on. Why don't you take a break?"

I nod and let go of Cassie's hand, still feeling the cool of her skin against the heat of mine. Jack hands me my phone and says he will call when it's ok to come back or if something changes.

I leave the ICU and wander the halls of the hospital until I see a sign directing me to the chapel. I take out my phone and make a call.

I hear the whoosh of the chapel door opening behind me. I don't need to turn around to know that it's Oliver. An aura of peace surrounds him like the sweet incense from the censers in the basilica. I stand up and step into the aisle. He doesn't stop when he reaches me; he just folds me into a hug. I rest in his arms for a moment and then pull myself free.

"Thank you for wearing jeans," I say in greeting.

"I don't often go out in public without pants," Oliver says. "Sometimes, but not often."

He smiles at me, and I know he knows what I mean.

He motions to the pew, and we sit down. It's nice to be close to him again. I thought it would be awkward, but it's just easy.

"Tell me what's happening," he says, his voice soft and soothing. He holds my hand between both of his. He doesn't speak; he just listens.

"I let Cassie go to the Teen Swim without me, and she slipped on the pool deck and hit her head. She fell into the water and took fluid into her lungs." I try to say it very clinically so that emotion doesn't find me. "They're worried about the fluid, but they're more worried about the head trauma. She hit really hard."

Oliver nods at me and squeezes my hand. *Go on,* he says with his eyes.

"I wasn't there," I say, emotion finding me anyway. My heart is beating so hard it chokes my breath, making my words come out like strangled whispers. "I wasn't there. I let her go on her own, and I went into town to have dinner with Jack. We were talking about patching things up, maybe. I don't know—I think we were just fighting again."

"About what?" Oliver asks, coaxing the confession out of me.

"About everything that went wrong." I sigh heavily as the

truth makes its way to the surface. "A while ago, I lost a baby in a late-term miscarriage. Nineteen weeks. A boy. I never got over it. I forgot the family I already had and set out to have another baby like some crazy person on a mission. I drove Jack away, and I made Cassie feel like she wasn't the sun around which I orbited. She was, they were—both of them—but I got lost in space, I guess."

I chuckle at my bad analogy to keep from crying, but my voice is shaking so I stop talking.

Oliver presses his hands tighter around mine. "I know telling you that this accident isn't your fault doesn't help you in this moment, that your being there would not have stopped it, but guilt and worry are evil cousins. For now, we focus on Cassie getting better."

"Ok," I say, nodding my head pitifully.

"Do you want to do something you and I have never done together?"

I look up at him and see a peace in his eyes that stills me. "What's that?" I ask, apprehensively.

"Pray," he says.

Yes, please. My throat tightens, and I want to answer him, but I can't speak. He doesn't need my words though. He leans over and runs his thumb over my cheek where tears have slipped from my eyes.

He prays. His voice falls across his lips in a low timbre so soothing it slows my heart and breath, and I am calm.

When he is finished, he pats my hand, and I look up at him.

"Can I confess something to you?" I ask.

"I'm not technically able to receive confession," Oliver says and winks. "But we are always able to confess ourselves to each other."

"Ray, Lola, and I tried to contact my father with a Magic 8-Ball on Halloween," I say quickly and sigh out the guilt of it.

Oliver chuckles and then covers his mouth. "I'm going to have to work on my reactions, aren't I? Did you get ahold of him?"

I shake my head.

"You know what you need?" Oliver pulls something from his back pocket. "It's not as spectral as a Magic 8-Ball, but it's a whole lot more effective. And it fits into your pocket."

In his hands, he holds a small, black Bible. It looks like the little book I saw him buy at the bookstore. Already it's worn from reading.

"It's just the New Testament," he says and cocks his head a bit. "Well, not 'just,'" he clarifies. "You should read the rest of it, too, but it's not so bad to start this particular book further in."

He hands it to me. I look at him, suspiciously, as if he's handing me a snake—but I guess that's the other guy.

Oliver nods at me to go ahead and take it. "You called me, after all. I don't believe in coincidences, but I do believe in divine intervention. There's a reason we met, Nina. Perhaps many. And God knows what He's doing."

"But this looks like yours," I say. "I don't want to take your Bible."

"I'll get another one. And with any luck, I'll give that one away too. I'm sort of like an encyclopedia salesman, but I've just got the one book and it's free."

"Good thing you don't work on commission."

"There she is," he says and winks at me again.

I smile—it hurts, but it's real underneath the strain.

"Is Jack here?" Oliver asks, and I nod. "You should sit with him. He needs you."

I know Oliver is right. Jack is a wreck even though he's putting on a brave face for me. This is our chance to come together for each other like we should have after we lost the baby. This is my chance to accept the comfort and support from Jack that I couldn't let myself accept before.

"Thank you," I say.

"Always," Oliver says. "Keep me posted. Please."

"I will. I'm going to rest here a minute."

"Would you like me to stay?"

"I could use a moment alone," I say, and when he raises his eyebrow I add, "Yeah, I know, I'm not alone in here."

We stand up, and I start to hug him and then hesitate, unsure if I'm allowed to touch him really. He laughs that amazing and magical laugh of his and opens his arms to me. We embrace tightly, and he whispers into my ear words of peace and love. I don't know that I hear them all, my mind as addled as it is, but I feel them and that's all that matters.

A few minutes later, I round the corner from the chapel and run into Jack.

"What's happened?" I say frantically.

"Was that him?" he says, pointing down the hallway—jabbing his finger angrily.

"Who?"

"Oliver," Jack spits out. "Did you call that guy to come here?"

"As a matter of fact, I did," I say and try to push past Jack. I get around him, but he grabs my wrist and pulls me back around to face him.

"Why? I'm right here, Nina. I'm right here at the hospital, going through all this with you, talking to the doctors and your family and being just as scared as you are and you go and call your boyfriend. I don't get it."

"He's not my boyfriend." I yank free. "He's a priest."

Jack's mouth is open to fling some comeback at me, but my words smack his cheek and he falls silent.

"What?" he asks.

"Never mind. Can we just go back to the room? Are Mom and Lola there? Did Ray get your message?"

We argue all the way down the hallway, but in the limbo of the elevator, we're silent.

"Why weren't Cassie and I enough for you?" Jack asks suddenly, pointedly, as the doors open onto the fifth floor. This is where we take another elevator to the ICU. It's a secret transport that only goes to that floor, a portal into the waiting room of devastation.

"I can't do this with you right now, Jack. It's not a good time."

I try to walk toward the second elevator, but he stops me again. Pulling me closer to him than I've been in a long time.

"It's never a good time for me."

"What do you mean?"

"You know what I mean."

And I do. I know exactly what he means. I just didn't know he felt that way. I didn't feel that way, but that's not the point when you're faced with the evidence of the message you sent. I know this is what he had wanted to ask earlier in the restaurant when steak and rosemary fingerling potatoes still made sense. I know this is what he wanted to ask every day for years.

"I just wanted more children," I finally say. "Is that so awful?"

"Did you ever think the reason I didn't want to try again after we lost him was that I didn't want to get my heart broken?" Jack asks, holding us in place in front of the elevators—people coming and going around us. "Did you ever think I desperately needed to feel wanted for just a moment?"

I duck away from him and hurry through the hall to the other elevator, as if getting there first will accomplish anything. He catches up to me and steps between me and the silver door of doom.

"Don't even try it," I say, letting my fear bubble out as anger. "You wanted something easier than what we had. You wanted someone you didn't feel obligated to when things got dark."

"I wanted someone I didn't care about," Jack says, circling his hands tight on my wrists.

"That's awful," I say and yank free of him.

"You don't understand. I didn't want to care about her, and I didn't want her to care about me. I didn't want to get my heart broken. I didn't want to fall in love. It wasn't about that. It was about—"

"Sex."

Jack lets go of my wrists and rubs his hands down the sides of his temples like he's trying to explain a complicated concept to a toddler.

"No," he says. "I wanted warmth and kissing and touching and connection. I wanted *you*—but you didn't want me."

The secret door opens, and we enter. It takes us up half a flight and into the waiting room.

"That's not a reason to sleep with someone else," I whisper harshly as we pass by all the people waiting for the next round of visiting hours.

"It is for a lot of people," Jack says. "But—"

I push him aside and tell the attendant at the door who we are and why we're there. She calls someone on the other side of the ICU entrance door, and we're buzzed through. The automated doors slowly start to open.

"But not me. I didn't—"

"Didn't what?" I say, scooting through as soon as there's an opening big enough for me to pass through.

"I didn't sleep with anyone else," he says, clipping my heel, he's so close behind me. "Just because I said I wanted someone else doesn't mean there *was* someone else."

"I saw you." I stop in the hallway, rounding on him. "With that girl from your work. She was hanging all over you."

"Yeah, she was," Jack says, glancing at the nurses behind the desk, but continuing to talk. "We kissed; it was nice. I'm not going to lie to you. The affection and attention were pretty intoxicating if you want the ugly truth, and I almost let myself give into it. But I didn't. I never did."

Everything in me stops. My feet. My breath. My heart. I'm surrounded by glass doors and windows of the ICU, but I feel like I've run into a brick wall.

Jack stops too, perhaps assuming there's something I want to say. There is, but I'm not sure where to start.

"I didn't want the attention from her," Jack says quietly. "I wanted it from you. I still do. I didn't sleep with her or anyone else. I just wanted to be wanted. You just thought I did more, and I didn't tell you different. I let you think what you wanted to think."

This is not the first time Jack has said these words to me, but it is the first time they make me think of Oliver. We kissed, and it was nice. It was nice to be wanted. His affection and attention had been tempting, and I could have let myself give into it. But I didn't. And even if Oliver had wanted to, I know that I wouldn't have.

I finally believe the words Jack has told me over and over.

I move away from him and continue down the hall, turning corners that I know will lead me to Cassie. I stop outside the last door.

"Why?" I ask, but the heat is gone from my voice.

"Because it was easy," he says quietly. "At least at the time. I was tired, and it was easy to let you be mad at me and me not have to do anything. I just couldn't deal with it anymore."

"Well, that's stupid," I say, pushing through the door.

"This whole thing is stupid," Jack says, following me past the glass walls and through the curtain.

Then Cassie comes into view, and we both stop short. Mom, Lola, and Ray are all standing outside her door. Jack reaches out for my hand and I reach out for his.

25

I t was a roller coaster the likes of which Cricket warned me about—except there was no enjoying the ride, only immense relief when it was done. We dipped into a drop of unknown hours waiting for Cassie's body to do what it could while the doctors and medicines and, most importantly, God did the rest. We had moments where we thought it was over, only to corkscrew back into dangerous fevers and blood-pressure plummets. Then suddenly—she opened her eyes and spoke to me and the ride slowed. The cart stopped and the lap bar lifted. We got off the coaster and left the hospital, and she was fine.

She is fine.

Now, I'm in the grocery store with Mom on Thanksgiving Day buying an apple pie and a box of macaroni and cheese.

Lola is looking after Cassie where she's resting before dinner at Mom's house. Lola was the strongest of us all. Her hope made all the difference. Cassie has been out of the hospital for a week, and we're still taking cautious steps, although she's ready to get back into the pool.

She's already upset that she missed two Teen Swim events. I met Zach, who turns out not to be the tall boy with six-pack abs. He's sweet and concerned about Cassie, and although I'm not ready for my little girl to be interested in boys, Zach isn't all bad. Life goes on like it should.

This Thanksgiving, I had hoped for something a little less traditional and more laid back, but Mom's house is about to fill up with aunts and uncles and well-wishers on this first holiday without Dad. His absence looms large in the wake of Cassie's accident and the coming of a holiday and the end of a year. Time will go on, and I'm not sure how to measure it.

"Do you think Cassie will be able to eat this?" Mom says, holding up the Kraft box.

"Mom, Cassie had a head injury, not a root canal," I say, trying to be reassuring, but likely coming off as sarcastic.

Mom puts the macaroni in the cart. "Someone might want it," she says and shrugs cheerfully.

My phone rings in my purse, and I thrash around to find it—afraid that it's Cassie, afraid there's something wrong.

"Hey, there," Jack says across the phone line.

"Hi," I say, finding myself happy to hear his voice, my heartbeat slowing at the sound of his words.

"Just checking in," he says. "Happy Thanksgiving. How's Cass today?"

Jack and I did well in the hospital, when it was about Cassie. As parents, we were in sync. As "us," I don't know. The thought of it hangs overhead like a book on a tall shelf—just out of reach. I want to grab it, but I need some help. After the fight in the hallway, we agreed that the hospital would be neutral ground. Cassie came first, and we would deal with the rest of it later.

It's later.

"Are you sure you can't come?" I say, re-inviting him to dinner. "Cassie would really love to see you."

"I'll just be in the way. It's about Cassie and your dad this time. Maybe when things shake out I'll come around again. If that's ok?"

Suddenly, it's like I can see the door closing on what could be, and I feel an overwhelming need to push it back open. I know that things don't "shake out." We make them fall into the place they fall into—whether by action or inaction, but still, it's in our hands. I don't want to wait for it all to fall into place. I've been in the place where things fall, and I'm not interested in staying there.

"Where are you?" I ask.

"Home. Well, my apartment."

"I'm coming over. Wait there."

I take the cart from Mom and wheel around to the next aisle. I grab something off the shelf and head for the checkout. Mom calls to me from somewhere inside the store. I hear her voice getting closer until she finds me on my way out the door.

"Were you just going to leave me here?" she asks, walking briskly to keep up with me.

"I knew you'd catch up," I say, sliding into the driver's seat.

I drop her off at her house—making sure to hand her the bag with the pie and the noodles.

"Where are you going?" she asks.

"I have to pick up a few things."

"We were just at the store," she says, hesitating to get out of the car.

I wave her out and reach over to close the door behind her. She jumps out of the way so as not to get clipped in the rump. She stands in her driveway looking at me indignantly and then winks.

"Come with me," I say to Jack when he opens the door.

There's one injustice that still needs to be undone in order to have a proper Thanksgiving Day. I take Jack by the arm, pulling him through the door and out to my car. I slide in and start the engine. Jack opens the passenger door and gets inside even as I'm pulling the car away from the curb. He doesn't ask where we're going. He doesn't say anything at all. Out of the corner of my eye, I can see him looking at me. We drive in silence. Finally, we pull off the road and pass through the predictable iron gates of the cemetery.

"What are we doing here?" Jack utters the words so slowly they don't seem to go together in the same sentence.

I kill the engine and get out. I open the trunk like we're in some bad movie and pull out a shovel. I'm manic with the idea of this shovel, which I'd stuck in the trunk last winter, before Dad passed, after spending the day planting bulbs in mom's yard—those pink and white tulips that seemed so out of place in front of the house the day of the funeral. Turns out you don't need a shovel this big to plant bulbs.

I walk into the graveyard like a woman possessed, unnecessary shovel in hand, and mind determined to undo what never should have been done. Jack catches up to me when I stop at my dad's headstone. He takes the shovel from me and spades the edge into the ground.

"What are we doing here?" he asks again, more firmly this time.

I've finally figured out what has been pecking at my ribs all this time. I know now what will begin to make this better.

"We're digging up my father's ashes," I say.

"Oh, Nina, no."

"It's cathartic," I say, and grab the spade from the earth. "Besides, isn't this the sort of wild and crazy thing that people do when they're grieving the loss of their dad and rejoicing because their child almost died but didn't?"

"No, this isn't the sort of wild and crazy thing that people do," he says, calmly. "This is what lunatics do. This is what psychos in the movies do." He grabs the shovel away from me.

"Just start digging." I point to the gray stone marker that bears my father's name.

"Look, Nina, if you're trying to take the heat off Ray by being the crazy one at dinner," Jack says, looking from me to the head-stone, "I think you can let him fend for himself."

I grab the shovel back from him. "Give me some credit, please."

"That's really hard to do when you drag me out to a cemetery on Thanksgiving Day and ask me to help you dig up your father's ashes," he says, talking to me like I'm four years old.

We both stand there looking at each other, at the shovel, at the name—Nathaniel Baker. Beloved Father. Cherished Husband.

I take out my phone and find the picture of the grave. I hold it out to the real thing and compare the image. I point to the spot where the urn is buried. I look around to see if anyone is watching, spending the holiday with a dead loved one.

"Why did you guys bury the ashes?" Jack speaks softly, breaking the stillness around us. "Aren't you supposed to put them somewhere important?"

I look at him and burst into tears.

"Oh," he says.

He takes the shovel from me and starts digging. That's when I start to think there might be hope for us yet.

When we hear the clink of shovel against metal, we both get down on our hands and knees. Like kids digging in the sand at the beach, we swipe at the dirt, brushing it away until we've reached our goal. Dad's urn.

Jack pulls Dad from the earth and hands him to me. We sit there looking at each other and then Jack voices what I'm think-ing.

"Run," he says, and we do.

By the time we reach the car, we're laughing and panting. I hold Dad close with one hand and reach in my pocket for the keys with the other. Jack takes the urn from me and sets it on top of the car. I make a move to reach for it, and Jack takes my hand.

"Your father is fine," he says and steps in close, pressing me up against the side of the car.

Jack runs his finger over my wedding rings and then brushes a strand of hair from my face. His body is warm against me. He leans in close, brushing his lips across the edge of my ear.

"We forgot the shovel," he says, his words brushing against my skin.

"Never mind it," I say, my heart racing.

"It looked like a good shovel," Jack says and kisses my neck.

I can't breathe. I pull in little ragged tufts of air.

"It's yours," I whisper, breathlessly.

"I know."

"You want to go get it?" I press my body harder against his.

"No," he says. "I want to kiss you."

"Ok," I say into the warmth of his neck. "Kiss me."

Jack pulls back from me and looks me in the eye. I think for one moment that this is some twisted trick of my imagination, but then Jack puts his arm around my waist and pulls me to him hard. He touches my lips with his finger for just a second as if he's checking to see if they're real. Then he presses his lips to mine and kisses me slow and deep. His hands move into my hair, gripping tight like he's hanging on for life. I hope he is. I am.

Guys—I just dug up my father's ashes and made out with my ex-husband. Oh, and Happy Thanksgiving.

The kiss ends, and I take a moment to catch my breath.

"There's something else I need to do," I say.

Jack looks at me quizzically.

"It's not anything weird."

"Comparatively?" He touches my hair again.

"Everything's relative."

We get back into the car, and I drive to our condo building.

"Did you need to get a change of clothes?" he asks.

"No. I need to show you something."

We ride the elevator up in silence. Jack is holding Dad's urn. I turn on the light in the entry hall, and Jack looks around like he's never seen the place. I go inside, but he hesitates at the door.

"Come in," I say. "You don't need an invitation."

Jack holds onto Dad and steps inside. I motion Jack toward the nursery door.

"I need to show you this," I say.

"Nina." Jack's voice is suddenly breathy with fear and trepidation. "I've seen the room. I've seen it too much. I can't go back to this."

I open the door and turn on the light. The room is empty. I stand in the middle of the space.

Jack steps in. He sets Dad on the floor.

"I created a shrine to something that wasn't going to happen," I say. "I polished it and decorated it. Meanwhile, everything else was getting covered in dust. Forgotten."

I take his hand and pull him from that room to Cassie's room. I open her door and turn on the light. This room is alive with teenage girl—pictures on the mirror, clothes on the bed, posters on the wall, fingernail polish and hair accessories flung across the dresser.

"I was looking for a miracle across the hall," I say. "When there was one right here." I move closer to Jack and put my hand over his heart. "And another one right here."

He puts his hand over mine, and I know there is hope for sure.

"The woman from your office?" I ask, and he raises his eyebrows at my change of subject. "Did she want something more?"

"Yes."

"Is she still there?"

"No." He takes hold of both of my hands. "She left. Her replacement is terrible. He's not nearly as cute."

I give him a look, and he nods concession. "Ok, so we're not making jokes yet. Maybe we never will. That's ok. I have absolutely no desire to break up our family. I don't want to live in a terribly sad apartment on the opposite side of town from you and Cassie. I also have no delusions that fixing this will be easy. I'm ok with that. I'm ok with a period of difficulty so long as it's putting us back together again. I'm not ready to give up." Jack looks directly into my eyes. "Are you?"

I can't speak around the lump in my throat, so I shake my head.

"Good," he says. "Now, I don't want to keep running into you with that guy—even if he is a priest." Jack winks at me, turning his command into a request.

"Technically he's not a priest yet," I say. "But he will be."

"Is that the guy you kissed in the parking lot at the nursing home?"

"And a few times after that, too," I confess.

Jack turns one of my hands loose and motions for me to stop. "I don't want to know about that. I don't care. Wait—how close to being a priest is this guy? Did you two, you know . . ."

"No, we didn't," I say. "He was pretty saintly actually."

Jack nods. "Good," he says. He steps across the hall and picks up Dad's urn again. "A priest," he says and chuckles. He thumbs his finger toward the front door. "I think we should get this show on the road."

26

"Do you want us to wait in the car?" Jack asks when I pull up in front of Nicole's apartment building. I love that he says "us."

"You're neck deep already," I say, shutting off the engine and unbuckling my seat belt. "No sense sitting it out now."

I ring Nicole's bell and wait. Jack stands with Dad in the crook of his arm. We stare at the door.

"I really appreciate this, by the way," I say, not looking at him.

"I'm not sure appreciation is the right sentiment for this." Jack shifts Dad to the other arm. "It seems a little lackluster."

I look at him, thinking he's serious, but he's smiling instead.

"I'll try to do better later," I say.

"I missed you, you know," Jack says. "That's the whole story. Beginning, middle, and end."

I can't keep a smile from dividing the clouds on my face. I hear noise behind the door, and then it opens. Nicole looks perplexed. Not surprised—perplexed. She doesn't say hello.

"Come to Thanksgiving dinner with us," I say. "With me and Jack and Dad."

"What?" she asks, looking at Jack and then at the urn.

"I'm sorry," I say, something occurring to me. "I'm assuming you don't already have plans."

"Actually," Nicole says, still looking at the urn, "Ray invited me. But I'm not sure I'm over it yet. I know he was trying to make it better with that news stunt, but I'm just not sure."

"That was Ray?" Jack asks. "The guys at work were talking about that video, but I didn't see it. What's he done now?"

"He left me while I was pregnant and then he got sent to prison," Nicole says. "Then he kidnapped our son."

Jack's mouth opens and he looks at me. "Ray has a kid? How did I not know this?"

"It wasn't kidnapping. He brought him back," I say, looking at Nicole. "You're leaving out parts."

Nicole cocks her head at me, and I return the gesture.

"Please, Nicole," I say. "I just dug up my father's ashes from the cemetery."

"Well, actually," Jack chimes in, "I dug them up."

"I suppose you did do most of the work," I say, looking at the cemetery dirt rubbed into his pant legs.

While we stand there discussing the details of Dad's extraction from the ground, Michael walks up beside Nicole and wraps his arms around her leg.

"What's that?" he asks, pointing to the urn.

"It's your granddad." Jack kneels down so he and Dad are eye to eye to urn with Michael. "I'm your uncle."

Nicole puts her hand on top of Michael's head and tries to push him behind her. He doesn't budge.

"This isn't a good idea," Nicole says. "I'm not even sure I'm willing to give Ray another shot, so the whole family holiday thing is more than I can do. I'm sorry."

"Please, Nicole," I say.

She sighs and closes the door on us.

Jack stands up and shrugs at me.

There is more noise behind the door and, after a moment,

Nicole and Michael emerge with coats and hats. The five of us walk in silence to my car.

"Are we going to Pizza Hut?" Michael asks once we're on the road.

"No, sweetie," Nicole says. "We're going to dinner with some crazy people."

"And your grandfather," Jack says, looking into the backseat and holding up the urn.

"Let's take him to Pizza Hut," Michael says.

When I ring the bell at Mom's, Lola answers the door.

"You're late," Lola says. "Everyone is already sitting down to dinner. Why did you ring the bell?"

"I don't know," I say exchanging the pizza box I'm holding for the urn in Jack's hands.

"Oh, no," Lola exclaims. "Is that Dad?"

She looks at the urn and then at me—and then at Jack and Nicole and Michael.

"Who is that?" Lola asks, nodding to Michael, who is clinging to Nicole's leg. "Is that him?"

Awkward silence.

"Happy Thanksgiving," Jack says overly enthusiastically, holding out the pizza box. "Bet you didn't expect to see me again, huh? Yep, I'm back."

"This is going to end badly," Nicole says. "Michael, say hello to your Aunt Lola."

Lola gasps. An audible and beautiful gasp.

Lola steps aside to let us pass. She grabs my hand and mouths "What are you doing?" to me. I can't answer. I just walk past her. At the dinner table, surrounded by aunts, uncles, and cousins—all the usual suspects—I put Dad down in his spot, which had been left empty as I suspected it would be.

"Nina, what is that?" Mom scoots her chair back from the

table, standing up as she speaks. "Where did you get that? Have you lost your mind?"

"We've all lost our minds," I say. "But I think it might still be reversible."

"Jack?" Mom nods to him. "Nice to see you. Ray, will you please bring in another chair?"

"Thanks for having me over," Jack says, sounding like it's our first date. He sets the pizza box down on the table in front of Dad. "Hey, sweetie," he says to Cassie, whose face is lit with nervous excitement. "You look lovely."

"Dad?" she asks like he's a figment of her imagination.

He winks, and her eyes well up with tears.

Ray stands up to get a chair and sees Nicole and Michael standing behind us. Ray freezes, mid-motion like an actor in a high school play doing a freeze-frame so the audience will focus elsewhere. But they don't. The aunts and uncles swivel their heads back and forth like they're at a tennis match.

I nudge Ray into motion, and he slips past Nicole and Michael, touching her quickly on the arm. Everyone scoots their chairs and plates and glasses around to make room for three new guests. There is much tinkling of china and glass and silverware. Someone knocks over the bowl of dinner rolls, and one falls to the floor. Jack picks it up.

"Here you go, Rose," he says and hands her the roll.

Everyone looks expectantly at me.

"Nina," Mom whispers, "get your father off the dining room table. This is very uncouth."

"Uncouth?" I wedge my seat between Mom and Jack. "Is that what's bothering you? It isn't proper? Dad doesn't fit the table décor, maybe. Should I open him up and stick some daisies in there?"

"That's gross," Cassie says. "Can I sit by Dad?"

"Of course," Jack says and waves Uncle Paul over a seat.

Ray comes back with two folding chairs from the garage. He opens the chairs and brushes them off. He frowns at their condition and makes Aunt Rose and an uncle we don't see very often get up and switch seats.

"This is just like you to try to bring your father back from the dead," Mom says and then sees Nicole and Michael for the first time now that they have sat down. "Nicole, I didn't see you there."

"I brought him back from the *grave*," I clarify. "There's a difference. Can I have the sweet potatoes, Uncle Paul?"

Uncle Paul puts down the glass of tea he's been holding and reaches quickly for potatoes.

"Can I have a piece of pizza?" Michael speaks up.

Ray jumps up and presses himself past the other people at the table to get to the pizza box. He knocks over Uncle Paul's glass of tea. I see Nicole smile just a bit.

"Me too," Cassie says. "After all that hospital food and Grandma's mush diet, I want some real food."

Nicole looks at Cassie, and her eyes widen just a moment before she looks at me, and I know she's transforming her abstract understanding that Michael has a cousin into the real fact that she and Michael have a family.

The doorbell rings, and everyone looks in that direction.

"I'll get it," I shout and jump up from the table.

I know who it will be. He's already told me he was coming.

"Hey, babe," Chris says to Lola when I've shown him to the table.

Lola stands up but doesn't move away from the table. Heads start swiveling again.

"I thought you were in LA. Thinking," Lola says.

Chris walks over to her, excusing himself to get past the people in his way.

"Turns out there wasn't that much to think about," he says. "Not when it came right down to it. Not when the choices were you or no you."

Lola looks at me and all the years between then and now collect in the corners of her eyes and roll gently down her cheek. Chris takes Uncle Paul's napkin and hands it to Lola.

"Lola," Chris says, his voice low but still audible. "Do you know how annoying it is to have people singing that stupid jingle at me all day? I go to the grocery store and the clerk sings it, the guy at the movie theater sings it, the mailman sings it. I hide in the house and wait for him to drive away before I can get the mail. I have moved four times in the same city because each new neighbor thinks they're the first to sing it to me and they get such a kick out of it I can hear it through the stinking walls. But you— you didn't know."

Chris holds Lola's hand, twisting her fingers in his like he's trying to tie the two of them together so she won't slip away.

"It was so liberating," he says. "And then I figured out why you didn't know. And I felt like a jerk. But I couldn't tell you. Then you found out, but you didn't seem to care. You took me for me, not the character that people think I am. You're the only person I can be me with. I'd be crazy to let you get on that plane and fly away to Peru or Timbuktu or wherever the heck you're going without me."

Chris gets down on one knee and pulls out a little box.

Lola pulls in a sharp breath, and I see her wings unfurling—feathery and shimmering. She's going to take off, against all odds—just like that owl from underneath my car—suddenly and surely as if there was never any doubt she was going to be ok.

I want Ray to see the wings, too, to know he had a hand in helping them spread open.

Chris takes out the ring and holds it up to Lola.

"If you don't love it, we'll get a different one," Chris saying. "I got it from the airport. I don't even know if it's real. You're the only thing that's real. Stay with me, and please don't let them put that jingle on my tombstone. I will stay with you and make sure you don't buy that tea that you can't remember you don't like. And I won't let you order the number thirteen special at Chai Pani because it has ginger and you're allergic. I promise to turn the channel when the scary previews come on because I know they give you nightmares. And if you want to go to Peru, I will go there with you. What do you say?"

"That's so romantic," Cassie says, her hands pressed over her heart.

"That's the weirdest proposal I think I've ever heard," Lola says. "But yes, you can keep me from eating ginger and drinking terrible tea and I will stay with you and make sure they don't put that jingle on your tombstone."

"So it's a yes?" he says.

"Yes," Lola says.

"Peru?" Mom says from across the table.

"That's who you are," Nicole says, delighted, pointing at Chris. "You're that guy."

I look at Chris and expect to see a grimace on his face.

"Yes," he says and winks at Lola. "I'm that guy."

Michael jumps up from his chair and says, "I like the one where you ride the bathtub down the mudslide."

"That's my favorite one, too," Chris says with a smile.

Mom looks at Michael and her eyes widen. "Ray?" she asks.

"Oh, come on, Mom," I say. "Do you even have to question it?"

The tennis match restarts, and everyone looks in synchro-
nized swivels from Mom to Ray to Michael and back to Ray. No
one speaks. Finally, Jack breaks the tension and serves himself
dinner.

"This looks great," he says. "Cassie, pass me the potatoes."

He scoops a helping onto his plate and begins a conversation
with no one in particular as if there is nothing strange about this
at all. "So I took a promotion at work. It's not really more money,
but the office is bigger and it's closer to the break room. Anybody
want some potatoes?" he asks, holding out the dish.

"I love you," I whisper to him.

"I know," he says and smiles. "It's nice to hear you admit it."

Cassie draws in a breath of air and sighs out too deep a worry
for a teenage girl. I look at her, and our eyes meet in a way neither
of us has allowed in a long time. I see her and she sees me. We see
the future.

Nicole reaches out and takes the dish from Jack.

"This is Michael," Ray says to Mom and serves him another
slice of pizza. "And yes, there's a reason he looks just like me."

Everyone stares at Michael as he eats his slice of pizza. Cassie
looks positively elated. Mom looks like she's going to cry or dance
or burst into a million points of light.

Ray points at Dad's jar. "Did you just dig that up?" he asks
me.

"There's still dirt on it," Lola says. "Nice to see you again,
Jack. Back in the saddle, so to speak?"

Jack chokes a bit on Mom's lumpy mashed potatoes.
"Hopefully," he says.

"Dad," Cassie says, embarrassment on her cheeks, happiness
in her eyes.

"Uncle Paul," I say, "will you pass me some turkey?"

He does, and I take a bite, not looking up at the urn.

"Mom," I say, "this is really tender, the best yet."

"Thank you, sweetheart," Mom says. "I was wondering why you were late, but, well, I wouldn't have guessed this." She points at Dad. "Or that." She points at Nicole and Michael. "Or you either," she says to Jack. "But I'm glad."

I smile and take a sip of tea. "And don't worry, Mom, we took care of the plot at the cemetery."

"You left it empty?" she says, slightly aghast at the thought of the waste of a good plot of dirt.

"No," I say. "We replaced Dad with a jar of pickles."

Everyone's fork stops in mid-air. We didn't really; I left them in the car. Suddenly the ridiculousness of it sets in, and we all break into uncontrollable laughter. For a moment, laughter does one of its jobs. It smooths its hand over heartache, just long enough for you to see through to the other side. Maybe not long enough to get there, but knowing it exists gives you the ability to press forward.

Thanksgiving dinner goes on with Dad at the head of the table and the requisite clinking of forks on china, laughter, and all the little nothings that make something out of all the chaos.

During coffee and pie, Ray speaks up. "Where do you think Dad wanted to go?"

"He wanted to be right here," I say.

"You're right," Lola says. "Dad was always happiest at home. That was one of the great things about him. He loved being here with us. Even I remember that."

"Brush the dirt off at least," Mom says.

She can't keep her eyes off Michael. She talks to him about his friends and his school and all the things that she and he will do now that they're acquainted.

I steal a look every now and then at Dad, there at the head of the table. I can't help but see him as he was before the stroke, before the nursing home, before the shortest passing of a year that I can recall. So much has changed, but looking around the table, I see how much has remained the same—all the truly important things.

I steal even more glances at Jack and catch him looking at me most of the time.

Finally, after the usual sighs of contentment and happiness, folks begin to gather themselves to say good-bye.

"I think we're going to go, Cecilia," Aunt Rose says to my mother. "This has been . . . memorable."

Mom sees them out, and everyone excuses themselves from the table to mill about the good-byes at the door. Michael seems drawn to Jack and Cassie and pulls them into the living room where the three of them sit on the floor playing a made-up game. For a minute, Dad and I are alone in the kitchen.

"I'm glad you could be here," I say, speaking out loud to him at last. "It wouldn't have seemed right without you. Sorry about the jar of pickles joke. Cricket came up with it."

The front door closes, and Chris and Lola, Ray and Nicole come back into the dining room. Nicole and Ray navigate each other's space, awkwardly but purposefully. It will take some time to sort things out between them. Little moments are easy; the span of time is tougher to predict.

Lola is gazing at her left ring finger with a faraway look on her face. She and Chris whisper to each other, and the distance between here and Peru seems greater every second, but I will let her fly and be happy for her.

I spy on Jack and Michael for a moment.

Mom slips up beside me. "Ok," she says, "burying the ashes was stupid."

"Not as stupid as digging them up," I say, and we laugh, our signal that there will eventually be a truce, that our attempt at a new and better relationship has passed its first test.

"I can't believe I have another grandchild," Mom says, and the look in her eyes tells me that just his being here makes the world a new place for her. She looks at me. "So, you and Jack?"

"I'm optimistic."

"At last." Mom puts her arm around my waist and gives me a squeeze.

"Jack," she calls over to him. "Could I have some time with my grandchildren?"

Jack stands up, and Michael takes hold of Cassie's hand as they walk toward the kitchen.

"I think we should eat more pie," Cassie says.

"More pie," Michael shouts.

"You should talk to him," Mom nods at Jack but speaks quietly so he won't hear. "So that you don't run off and leave me in the grocery store again."

Jack gives Michael and Cassie over to Mom, and as she passes the kitchen table, she kisses her fingertips and touches them to Dad's urn.

"Mom," I call after her, and she turns back. "You didn't mess up. You made everything interesting. You still do. All the things that you want me to know—I know them."

Mom dips her head and takes a deep breath. She looks up, nods, and walks away with Michael and Cassie. Nothing will be easy, but it will possible. Perhaps the difference in those two things is not as staggering after all.

"Will you wait for me for a minute?" I ask Jack. "I need to do something."

"I'm neck deep already," Jack says and touches my face. "Just the way I want it to be."

I take Dad onto the front porch. It's nearly dark, and the stars are popping on. Ray comes outside.

"I'm going to drive them home," he says. "If I can get Michael away from Mom, that is. Do you think it went well?"

"Ray," I say and set Dad on the porch railing, "I don't think given the circumstances, we could have hoped for any better."

Ray nods in agreement and puts his arm around my shoulder. He turns me around and pulls me into a hug.

"Thanks, Sis," he says quietly into my hair.

"You're welcome."

"I guess now the rest is up to me. Let's hope I don't screw it up."

There's a very real chance of that, and I sense Ray knows it.

"You know I'd do anything for you," I say. "Don't you?"

"Yeah," he says. "I do."

Michael and Nicole come out onto the porch. Nicole gives me a hug.

"It will be good to have you around again," I say to her. "We missed you."

"Thanks for the dinner invitation," she says. "It was weird. But I'm glad we came." She looks at Ray and the corners of her mouth turn up. It's a start.

"I'll pull my car around," he says.

Nicole picks up Michael in her arms, and he's face to face with me.

"I didn't really introduce myself," I say. "I'm your Aunt Nina. I'm glad you came for dinner."

"Me too," says Michael. "Will I see Uncle Jack again? He's fun."

"I'm sure you will," I say, thinking of divorce papers and wedding rings and new beginnings.

Nicole meets Ray at the back door of the car, and they situate their son in the car seat I made Ray buy. Ray takes Nicole's hand. She steps back from him and then steps forward. It's a hard dance to watch.

"Do you think they'll make it?" Lola says from behind me.

"I hope so," I say.

Lola and I sit in the rocking chairs on the porch and watch Ray and his family drive away.

"So," Lola says with a smile on her face. "Jack, huh?"

"Yeah. What do you think about that?"

"Too much lemonade and orange juice will give you a belly-ache anyway." She kicks her foot playfully against mine. "Jack is a good guy."

"He is."

"I'm going to miss you."

"You can tell me all about it when you get back. Before you set off again on your next adventure."

"You think I will?" she asks, and I can tell this is something she's been thinking about.

"Come back?" I ask, my heart thudding. "I hope so."

"No," she says. "Of course I'll come back. I mean, do you think there will be other adventures?"

Maybe not today, but one day, I will fly.

"Yes," I say. "I think you're ready to go."

"Where?"

She looks at me, and we're little one last time. I see us on this porch—me and her on the steps, young, watching Ray in the yard. Dad is washing the car and Mom is in the kitchen making dinner and everything that ever will be is still out there, some-where in front of us.

"Everywhere," I say to her now, the two of us in the rocking chairs, Ray with his family, Dad on the porch rail, Mom eating pie with Cassie, and my Jack and her Chris waiting to see what is waiting for them.

"I always felt like you were my fortress," she says. "The wall keeping out everything that could hurt me. What will I do without it?"

"What I should have let you do all along."

"Fend for myself," she says, joking.

"No," I say, less of a joke. "Let you face the world."

"What if there's an army of angry villagers out there?"

"Then you call in Ray," I say. "You know he orbits you like you're the sun."

She nods. I know she will miss him more than she misses me in many ways. I'm ok with that.

"And besides," I say. "What if it's your handsome prince outside the wall, lost in the woods and tired of fending off insurance questions?"

"We've really got to learn to face life without our internal movie cameras on," Lola says.

"That would take all the fun out."

"You did always make it fun."

"Promise me something."

"What?"

"That you won't film the wedding scene without us."

"Wouldn't dare," she says and then winks at me. "I'm going to take Dad in before he falls off the porch. Should I send Jack out?"

"You requested my presence?" Jack says.

I stand up and he takes my hand.

"Come with me," I say and lead us down the porch steps.

"This isn't going to involve another shovel, is it?" Jack asks, although he doesn't hesitate.

"No," I say. "I want to show you something."

I lead us out into the backyard. The feel of his hand around mine is pressure and release at the same time. Way back in the corner of the yard, by the hydrangea that is not in bloom now, is a dogwood tree—bare and patient. Hanging midway up is a metal mobile.

"What's that?" Jack asks when I point it out.

"Something I forgot about. Something I made a long time ago."

The cold evening breeze blows a chill through the metal memory and it *clink-clanks, clink-clanks* all around us. Jack looks up into the branches, but I look at him.

"What?" He smiles when he looks back down and meets my eyes.

"I made something out of what wasn't supposed to have been." I look at the pieces of Lola's leg braces held together with wire. "I took the pieces and strung them together."

"Whose shoes are those?" Jack points to the smallish blue Converse sneakers wired amidst the metal.

"Ray's," I say, remembering the night I stole them from his room. "I took them not long after the accident. Years before the braces came off. I hid them in my closet."

I hadn't known why I needed to take the shoes. But I put them in a box and let them wait until the time was right.

"That's the way life goes," I say. "You take the bits and pieces, and one day it makes something you didn't expect."

"Is this one of those things?" Jack puts his arms around me, pulling me to him.

"I believe it is."

"Good," Jack says. "I'm not letting go this time."

Jack closes his eyes and releases a breath so hard it seems he must have been holding it since we parted. He kisses me, soft and somewhat hesitant at first, but then his arms tighten around me and his lips press sure and sweet over my own. Jack's body is warm and right against mine, and his arms hold me together in all the places I was afraid had fallen apart.

◆ ◆ ◆

Later, when Jack and I go back inside to collect Cassie and say good-bye to Mom, I find Dad back on the kitchen table. The house is warm and still smells of spice pie and turkey. Tomorrow, as tradition, we'll search for a Christmas tree, then come home to hot cocoa and tree trimming and tales of Christmases past.

I hope Lola will bring Chris and share some time with us before they head off to Peru and whatever adventure comes after that. I hope Nicole and Michael will come, making an old tradition new. I hope Ray will let loose his devils. I hope I will too. I hope.

I leave Jack and Cassie in the kitchen with Mom. I pick up Dad and take him to the living room. I set the urn on the mantel and step back to evaluate the placement.

"I think we're going to be ok, Dad," I say. "And don't worry, I promise I won't strap you in the front seat tomorrow and take you to the Christmas tree lot."

Pick out a big one, Sweet Pea. Don't worry if there are a few too many wonky branches. It's better that way.

It's amazing, how life is laid out. The way we have to ride through the laughter and the tears. How hope is a release into the space around everything that hurts, giving all our pain somewhere to go, so that peace can find its way home.

Acknowledgments

What a blessing it is to have an opportunity to thank people for helping me reach this part of my publishing journey. First, I thank and praise God for all the undeserved but so greatly appreciated blessings in my life, one of which is this book and the chance to see it in print.

I thank my husband, R.J. Burle, for his unfailing support and encouragement. People always ask me how I find the time to write amid raising four children, teaching, and keeping the day-to-day world of my family spinning. God gave me a partner in life and love who has my back at every turn, and as far as writing goes, that means graciously taking over household and kid duty while I head to a nearby bookstore to write.

I also thank my children, who don't begrudge their mother the time to write and work toward a goal. I hope they will see it as an example of how important it is to pursue their own dreams, whatever they may be.

I thank my mother and father and well as my brother and sister—about whom this book is not. Except for the love—that part is true. Family is a delicate thing. If we're lucky (and I was), we come out with an understanding of unconditional love and unflappable dedication. Family is our first knowledge of self and where we fit into this world. All my love and devotion to you, my first loves, always.

Acknowledgments

Thank you to the myriad writers who have helped me along the way, including Luke Whisnant, my first writing teacher at East Carolina University. Long had I held the secret desire to be a writer, but not until that first class did I believe it a real possibility. Thank you to my very first writer's group: Luke, Heather Burt, Chip and the late Ann Sullivan, and some others who came and went along the way. Thank you to Judi Hill and all the writers at Wildacres Writer's Workshop. Thank you to the Missouri writing groups who showed me the importance of having a trusted writing community as well as the value of having friends who write. Thank you, Samantha Redstreake Geary, my current writing partner in crime—I mean, fiction—for keeping my creative soul alive and well fed.

Thank you to my amazing agent, Julie Gwinn. I knew as soon as I saw your listing that you were the agent God had selected for me, and although I'm not right about much, I had that one pegged. I couldn't be happier.

Thank you to Lisa Mangum, my editor, for falling in love with these characters and working on their behalf in a way that humbles and delights me, thus making this book everything I meant for it to be. Thank you to everyone at Shadow Mountain Publishing for make this dream come true, especially Heidi Taylor Gordon.

Thank you Malaprop's Bookstore in Asheville, North Carolina, for letting me take up a seat in the café for hours at a time writing, plotting, planning, and dreaming. (I'm sitting here with a cup of coffee even now as I write these acknowledgments.)

And finally, although I already thanked Him (once is never enough), I give my undying gratitude to God for every breath I take. It's all your design, and I am happy to be a part of it.

Discussion Questions

1. Mother and daughter relationships are central in this novel. What are some opportunities that Nina has either missed or taken in order to have a better relationship with her daughter as well as with her own mother? Where did Nina and her mother fail or succeed in their relationship?

2. The theme of fatherhood also runs throughout this story. Discuss the fathers in this novel and the roles they play. Discuss the roles that men play in a family as a whole and how their absence and/or presence is felt.

3. Family is the tie that binds, but those bonds can sometimes feel like restraints. Discuss the ways in which family ties are used in this story. To what degree are those constraints true or the product of misunderstandings?

4. In this novel, Nina wants desperately to achieve a goal that is out of her control. What role does Nina's own desperation play in the demise of her marriage? Have you ever let your own desires for something negatively affect a relationship? Were you able to see it in time to save that connection? If so, how did you change the course of your thoughts and actions? If not, what would you do in hindsight to have kept the relationship intact?

5. Hindsight is 20/20. Characters often misunderstand each other throughout this story. What are some of the major

misunderstandings or misconceptions that affected the lives of these characters?

6. Both Nina and Oliver are looking for the right path for their lives. Each has a hesitation that is brought on by fear. What fears are keeping them from their true paths? Have you ever hesitated to follow your true path because of fear? What was that path and the fear that kept you from seeking it? What did you ultimately do, and would you do anything differently if you had a chance?

7. The unique connection between siblings is a powerful part of this story. Despite the tensions within the family, Nina, Lola, and Ray have a bond that, although tested, seems unbreakable. Discuss the importance of this familial bond and the role it plays in shaping our ideas of love as well as the length to which we go for others in our lives.

8. Nina is experiencing a lemonade year. Everything that can go wrong seems to be going that way. Some of these things are considerable losses. Discuss her ability or inability to reach out for help and to recover from loss. How does that affect her decisions throughout the novel? Are there losses from which you have not recovered? What avenues for help have you sought or rejected that might make a difference to you?

9. There is a family secret at the heart of the hard feelings and dysfunction within Nina's childhood family. Do you think Ray, Nina, and Nate were asked to go too far in keeping that secret? What role does truth play in the outcome of this family's life? Nina asks if things would have been better had they all been truthful. When there may be no clear cut path to follow, how do you decide what to do?

10. When Nina notices a cross hanging on the wall of Oliver's house, she asks him if he's religious. He answers with the question "Would it bother you if I was?" Is there something about yourself or a loved one that you have hidden or avoided

because you thought you would be judged because of it? Discuss the outcome.

11. Reconciliation and forgiveness are important themes in this novel. Discuss the scenarios in which the characters have an opportunity to both give and receive forgiveness (Nina with her mother, daughter, and/or ex-husband) and the incidents in which a character may not be able to (Ray with his deceased father). Discuss the characters' ability or inability to forgive themselves. Have you ever given or withheld these gifts, or had them given or withheld from you? How has that affected the story of your own life?

12. The book ends with hope and the possibility to begin again. Discuss the ways in which Nina, Ray, Lola, Jack, and Oliver have a chance to begin again. Based on what you know of these characters, what are your predictions for their futures?

Interview with the Author

Q *What inspired you to write* The Lemonade Year?

The voices in my head—and one from the backseat of my car. I typically start by hearing a character speaking like I'm over-hearing a conversation in a café. Not out loud—don't have me committed yet—it's more like I hear it in the part of my brain that won't stop making up stories no matter how much laundry there is to do.

Nina came to me, telling me the story of a childhood trip to Disney World in which her father took care of her at a time when her mother couldn't. It was a nice memory, but then I realized that her father had just died and she was brokenhearted. She didn't tell me outright at first, but her marriage was also in trouble and her sister was suffering from some sort of strange illness, and I felt so sad for Nina. Everything that could go wrong seemed to be going that way.

Her story was originally a short story, entitled "The Conspicuous Absence of Knowing," mostly because Nina wasn't all that eager to share her thoughts with me (typical Nina) and it took a while for her to open up.

Once I started writing her story as a novel, I was thinking about a title and my youngest daughter, Delia, was singing a made-up song in the backseat of the car. She sang the line, "When life gives you lemons, make lemonade." Bam, there it was. Life had given Nina all kinds of lemons. This was her lemonade year.

Q *What was the hardest part of writing this book? What were some of the obstacles you had to overcome?*

For me, the hardest part of writing any book is that I don't typically write chronologically. And I'm not a big "pre-plotter," which makes figuring out what's going on difficult sometimes. Usually I hear a voice or see an image and then I start writing so I can uncover what it's all about. Along the way, I take some wrong turns and spend time off in the weeds. But sooner or later, one of my characters will get me back on track by doing or saying something that I hadn't expected.

Even though my method results in a huge chunks of "highlight and delete," I actually love when that happens, because it sets me back on course. I love the revising and editing stages of writing, but one of the things that is hard for me to accept is when I know that something I've been trying to make work just isn't right for the book.

This book has taught me a great deal about letting the true story unfold. I'm glad I did. I couldn't be happier.

Q *Nina's relationship with her family is at the heart of this book. Tell us a little about your own family, both growing up and now.*

My family is my heart. No one's family is perfect, and mine wasn't (isn't) either, but one of the greatest lessons that I learned— and one that continues to be reinforced for me—is that no matter the issue, there is no giving up on anyone. I can't think of anything I could do that would cause my family to shut the door to me and vice versa.

While *The Lemonade Year* is not the story of my childhood, I do have a brother and a sister, for whom I would stop the universe if need be. My parents are not Nina's parents, but they are the sun and moon to my little world.

God has blessed me with four kids and a patient and loving husband, and my family is everything to me. We're learning and growing together. I probably mess up as often as I get it right, but then again, there is no right, only love.

Q *Nina learns to find peace and hope in her life and her relationships. What would you say to a reader who might be struggling to find that same peace and hope?*

There's a place in the book where Nina's mother tells her to "let go." Pardon my getting very personal, but for me, the ability to let go and find peace is found in my relationship with Jesus. I turn to Him for everything from lost keys to surviving personal devastation. Things don't always turn out the way I want them to, but I am able to be at peace because He's with me.

I find hope in knowing that it's not my job to control the turnings of the world. Someone with a better understanding than I have is running the show. My hope is found in Jesus and in the knowledge of His love. I would tell readers to reach out for help when you need it. You are not alone. God is with you.

Q *You've written both short fiction and novels. How do you decide which format to use for your stories? Do you find one length easier to write than the other?*

I joke that I have two word counts—either 1,000 words or 100,000. I don't decide on the length, the characters do. I always aim to tell the whole story when I start out, and sometimes as that 1,000-word mark approaches, I know that I've told all those characters needed me to tell. But sometimes I know I haven't, and in those cases, I take a breath and stare off into space for a moment while the reality sinks in, and then I say to them, "Ok, guys, here we go," and I start a new novel.

Q *Fast Five Favorites!*

Favorite book: Could I get an easier question, like "What is the meaning of life?" I've been in love with so many books, I couldn't narrow it down to just one, and the answer would change in a month anyway. I will say that the book I've read the most number of times is *Hula* by Lisa Shea. It's the first book I fell in love with as a grown-up reader.

Favorite movie: Too many to name! My husband can attest that I will watch the same movie over and over until I can practically recite it. I love stories no matter what form they are in. I'm a sucker for a romantic dramedy, especially if it's heavy on character and relationships. But no jump scares, please, my startle reflex is too strong and I don't want to knock over my snacks.

Favorite food: Sushi. (Wow, I answered that in one word!)

Favorite place to vacation: Pioneer Park, Lake Michigan. I grew up in Kure Beach, North Carolina, and now live in Asheville, North Carolina, so I've been blessed to live every day in vacation spots. Lake Michigan is beautiful, but it's my favorite because it's a week-long campout with family. Each year, relatives that I don't see often enough meet there for a reunion. Campfires, cookouts, gorgeous sunsets and all day to relax with family—my favorite.

Favorite thing to do besides write: Cook. No, eat. No, definitely cook—that way I can share. I really want to learn how to make sushi, and when I do, I'm inviting you all over for dinner!

About the Author

Photo by Delia Burle

AMY WILLOUGHBY-BURLE is a writer and teacher living in Asheville, North Carolina, with her husband and four children. She writes about the mystery and wonder of everyday life. Her contemporary fiction focuses on the themes of second chances, redemption, and finding the beauty in the world around us. She is the author of a collection of short stories entitled *Out across the Nowhere* and a contributor to the anthology *Of Mist and Magic*. Visit her at amywilloughbyburle.com.